MW00618981

EVERNIGHT PUBLISHING ®

www.evernightpublishing.com

Copyright© 2017

12 Author Anthology

Editor: Audrey Bobak

Proofreader: CA Clauson

Cover Artist: Jay Aheer

ISBN: 978-1-77339-256-1

ALL RIGHTS RESERVED

OWNED BY THE ALPHA

12 Author Dark Paranormal Anthology

The Alpha lives for the hunt...

Driven by instinct, an Alpha shifter recognizes his fated mate from one scent, one touch. He'll pursue his woman, regardless of the cost, and anyone else would be smart to get out of his way. He won't stop until he takes possession of his prize.

Although the hunter doesn't need convincing, his mate certainly does. The Alpha will have to prove himself as a lover and convince his woman that he plays for keeps.

Table of Contents

SCENT OF DESTINY

Rose Wulf

Copyright © 2017

Chapter One

"You'd have better luck picking up a pig in a barn!"

Willa Thompson took a deep breath and pushed the asshole's jeering voice down in her memory. She refused to acknowledge the echo of his laughter as it rang through her mind. That infuriating, horrifying incident had been almost a week ago. She hadn't spoken to him since. Though she had to admit she didn't know how long she'd be able to keep it that way. The ass did work two cubicles over from her.

I wasn't even talking to him.

No, she'd been on her cell in the breakroom, talking with her best friend. Stupidly thinking it was safe to quietly talk about a good-looking man she'd seen a few times in a nearby café. Asshole had picked up on a few key words in their conversation, had begun laughing, and loudly called out to her.

Willa ground her teeth and wiped her sweaty palms on her favorite jeans. *This is ridiculous. What will this even prove?*

She looked up at the flickering neon sign over the building before her. It was taunting her. Daring her to step inside, step into a world she'd only read about in novels. She'd never even set foot on this *street* before, and now she was about to enter an actual biker bar.

The rumbling roar of a motorcycle engine startled Willa, pulling her gaze away from the sign and over to the parking lot she'd just crossed through. She watched as a large man in an actual leather vest parked his fiery-themed motorcycle just a few feet away. He popped a cigarette in his mouth before he even got off the bike, and she looked away. *Please let there be someone more my type in this place!*

Then again, Willa thought to herself as she took her first step inside, was that even possible?

Her brown eyes went wide as the combined scents of tobacco smoke, strong alcohol, and sweat assaulted her nose. There were bodies squeezing together everywhere. Women wearing more makeup than fabric were grinding into men, and other women, on what Willa presumed was the dance floor. All three pool tables were occupied by mostly large, leather-clad men with too many tattoos or piercings. A few had skinny females curled around them while they played.

In fact, all the women Willa could see were significantly thinner and more culturally attractive than she herself. She swallowed, choking on an intake of breath. *I knew that would happen.* She hadn't come to this bar to blend in. She'd come to prove a point. To prove to herself, if no one else, that she *could*, in fact, still pick up a man when she tried. Never mind the kind of man she usually sought never seemed to look twice at her anymore.

It's not impossible for a man to be interested in me. I'm not hideous.

Sure, she was overweight. And she didn't often feel particularly pretty. She wasn't disgusting, either. She hoped.

Willa did her best to disguise her nerves and walked straight up to the bar. Most of the tables she could see were occupied, and since she was there alone—and *wanting* to be noticed—she figured sitting at the bar better suited her needs. She only hoped no one saw her fumble in her attempt to situate herself on the classically round barstool.

The scent of alcohol was, of course, stronger at the bar. But the stools on either side of her were vacant, just as she'd been counting on, and quick glances to either side assured her the people nearest her hadn't paid her any attention. Yet. That was fine. She needed a drink before she was ready to begin her self-assigned mission, anyway. On her third attempt, she successfully waved the bartender over and ordered a rum and Coke.

Figuring that putting her back to the majority of the people in the bar would be counterproductive to her goal, Willa took a gulp of her drink and swiveled around. Nearly slamming into a broad-shouldered mountain of a man in the process.

"Oh!" Willa exclaimed, jumping in her seat. "I'm so sorry!" She barely noticed the chill of the drink as a few droplets sloshed over the side and onto her hand.

The man she'd just about kneed in the groin had straightened to an impressive height and was blatantly raking his piercing emerald gaze over her. Her mouth went dry. This guy was *built*. Muscles bulged from beneath his black t-shirt, curving down his bare arms and disappearing beneath the belt over his black cargo pants. All that muscle and black clothing was like something out of a military movie. Combined with his thick head of shaggy black hair, Willa was absolutely *not* sorry to have earned this man's attention. Not even for a moment.

Those emerald eyes were focused on hers when a

corner of his lips twitched in a brief grin. His nostrils flared with a visible breath and he said, "You're forgiven."

Goosebumps raced up Willa's arms as a delightful chill shot down her back. That grin. That voice. *This* was the man she wanted. This was the man who could convince her she was still a desirable female. *Get real, Willa. Men like him don't even try to remember women like you.*

"Didn't mean to make you spill your drink," the gorgeous stranger said, apparently oblivious to her distracted thoughts. She was working on corralling her tongue when he reached out, gently pried the glass from her hand, and set it on the bar behind her. The action brought him several inches closer. She could smell him now. His scent was surprisingly fresh for being found in a biker bar. She had to resist the urge to press her nose to his neck for a better whiff.

The next thing she knew, he'd grasped her wrist and was using a napkin to gently wipe the spilled alcohol off her hand. Willa could feel the contained strength in the fingers loosely holding her hand in place, yet it felt as though he were barely touching her. The contrast was appealing and the contact had her heart beating faster.

"Y-you really don't have to—"

He lifted his stare back to her eyes and words failed her. "I insist." Had his voice really come out in a sort of deep, vibrating purr, or was her imagination kicking into overdrive?

Willa swallowed heavily and prayed she wouldn't stutter when she next opened her mouth. "I'm Willa, by the way."

Those lips lifted in another grin, this one lingering several seconds, and he deposited the napkin back onto the bar. He refrained from releasing her wrist. "Ryker," he said.

Ryker. It was different, but not off-the-wall kind of different. It was sexy.

Her belly did a clumsy summersault at about the same time as she let her lips lift in a smile of her own. "Do you … come here often?"

Oh my God, Willa. You came here to pick up a guy, yes, but you don't have to be so cliché *about it!*

Ryker's smile returned, lasting this time. It lightened his already breathtaking eyes and eased the intensity of his features without taking away any of his heaping sex appeal. Willa doubted she'd ever even *spoken* to a man this mouthwatering before. And she likely never would again, either.

"Not often enough," he said, a trace of amusement in his deep, rumbling voice. He gave a tug of her wrist and added, "Come sit with me. The bar's no place for a beautiful woman."

Willa was sure her expression gave away her shock. Had he just asked her to sit with him? Had he just said she was *beautiful*? Surely this was some sort of joke. Did he have a hidden camera on him? Or maybe he had some friends egging him on, daring him to flirt with the lonely woman at the bar until she figured him out?

"I … would love to," she said, despite her fear. She didn't really see how this was anything more than a drunken bet or a prank, but she had to test it. Just in case. There was always the chance that he'd been drawn in by her deliberately paired siren-red nails and lips. A choice she was extra glad she'd made now, as the red so deliciously complemented the green of his eyes.

He grinned and helped her off the stool, releasing her wrist only in favor of resting his palm at the small of her back. The heat from his touch seared through her as if she were naked. Willa gulped and clung to her glass, her purse slung over her opposite shoulder. It would not do at all to be daydreaming about getting naked with a man this godly when she suspected she was being pranked.

Ryker led her to a table near the back, just behind a rowdy group of twenty-somethings. He guided her to the farther bench, slid in, and tugged her down beside him.

Her heartbeat doubled.

Chapter Two

Ryker knew the stories. He'd heard similar tales often in his childhood, passed down from previous generations. His mother had always told him that one day he would meet a woman he couldn't walk away from. When he'd asked how she could know such a thing, how *he* would know if it ever happened, she'd merely said that he'd *know*.

Damned if his mother hadn't been right.

All he'd wanted was a drink when he'd made his way up to the bar. The scent of the attractive, respectfully-dressed woman sitting front and center had barely reached his nose over the usual stench that accumulated in a biker bar at night. But the moment it did, the moment he processed that amazingly alluring smell, he'd froze. Right up until she'd turned around and damned near kneed his suddenly straining erection.

At first Ryker told himself it'd just been too long since he'd bedded a woman. Especially a woman with real curves. He tried convincing himself he simply needed a good lay and he'd forget all about this luscious female he was practically fucking drooling over. But by the time he'd escorted her to the table he usually claimed when he drank here, there was no denying it. Never in his long life had he wanted a woman so powerfully.

All he really knew about her, aside from her destiny, was her first name. He needed to take the time to learn more.

It was hard to focus, though, when his instincts begged him to pull her into his lap and bury his aching cock inside her. Public, clothes, and decency be damned.

Doing his best to keep his focus *away* from that temptation, Ryker refrained from draping his arm around

Willa's shoulders and leaned into the wall for easier conversation. "You don't strike me as the kind of woman who spends a lot of time in dives like this."

Willa wrapped both hands around her glass, the siren-red nail polish reflecting off the fluorescent lighting overhead. He could hear her heart racing and he watched her chest rise with a deep breath. "To be honest," she said, her voice wavering for the first few syllables, "this is my first time here."

Ryker smirked. *Lucky me.* "What inspired you?"

She turned a sweet smile to him and his breath caught in his chest. "Thought I'd try something new."

His eyes narrowed the moment she looked away again. *She's lying.* But he had to let that go. For the time being, at least. She didn't know she was his. Curling his fingers into the vinyl of the booth behind her to keep his arm in place, Ryker asked, "Any reason?"

Willa pulled her lip between her teeth for a long second, one finger drawing patterns in the sweat on the side of her glass. "Ah, I just realized I needed to live a little more, you know? Expand my horizons."

Oh, that was absolutely not her real answer. So much for hoping she'd spill with a little prodding. But he could tell from her scent that she was *trying* to mean what she'd said, and that perplexed him more.

Ryker took a breath, attempting to find a reasonable response that wouldn't send his apparently-innocent human running in terror. "Expand your horizons?" he repeated slowly. "That could mean a lot of things."

Her smile returned, teasing now, and he sensed a wave of determination wafting from her. "I suppose it could," she agreed. Her gaze flicked away for a moment, toward the crowd in front of the bar, and she asked, "Do you dance?"

Knowing perfectly well that his meaning showed in his eyes, Ryker lowered his voice a bit and said, "Not in public."

Her sparkling brown eyes went wide and he could make out a tinge of pink on her cheeks before she dropped her gaze to her drink. She chewed her lip as if contemplating something and proceeded to knock back the rest of her rum and Coke.

Ryker leaned forward until his lips were *barely* not brushing her ear and whispered, "Relax, Willa. I only dance with a willing partner." The desire in her scent spiked in tandem with her heart rate. It was all he could do not to let his tongue slip out and taste her skin.

Her response was not what he anticipated.

She turned to face him before he'd pulled back, and he was suddenly staring into her eyes. He curled his fingers harder into the vinyl and locked his muscles in place. Her full lips, coated in a shade of red that matched her nails, parted and he couldn't stop his stare from falling to watch as they formed words.

"Be honest with me," she said firmly. "Is this some kind of prank?"

Ryker's gaze snapped back up to hers. He said nothing for a long moment as he tried to form a coherent enough thought to understand her question. *Prank?*

Willa released a breath and her shoulders slouched ever-so-slightly. "Someone put you up to this, didn't they? Dared you to flirt with me or something?"

Was that the treatment she was used to? He didn't know. But he did know she'd never be asking that question again. "No," he said, his own eyes narrowed with intensity.

She blinked up at him for a second, sighed, and said, "It's okay. I understand. But I think I'm going to go now."

Releasing a growl on a harsh exhale, Ryker released his death-grip on the vinyl, buried his hand beneath her wavy, deep-red hair and hauled her lips up to his. He kept his free hand fisted on the table top to minimize temptation and stroked her lips with his tongue. A soft, whimpered sound bubbled up her throat, and her lips parted. He wasted no time sweeping his tongue inside, letting the taste of her wash over him. It was hard not to growl into the kiss. Harder still not to pull her body flush against his. But he kept his lips to hers, kept one hand in her hair and the other off her entirely. He was making a point, not just seeking satisfaction.

Her hands had landed on his chest, just beneath his shoulders, as soon as he'd kissed her. By the time his tongue was mapping out her sweet mouth, her fingers were curled in his shirt. Holding on.

He released her from his kiss with foreign reluctance and eased back just enough to give her room to breathe. The hand in her hair slid down to the nape of her neck. "Willa," he said, his voice rough. "Make no mistake. I want you. No one's put me up to this. No one had to."

She was still taking heaving breaths as the shock settled on her face. The disbelief was obvious in her eyes when she quietly asked, "You … want me?"

Ryker grinned and brushed the side of her throat with his thumb. "Badly." He suspected if he were too honest too soon, she'd flee, so he opted to leave it at that.

Willa broke from his stare and looked him over as if for the first time. He held still, letting her absorb his words. Confusion and desire vied for dominance in her scent. He really wanted to ask why—why she would possibly be so shocked to be wanted. But he held himself in check, just this once.

Her tongue darted out, trailing slowly over her

smeared lipstick as she lifted her gaze back to his. "Can we ditch this place?"

Chapter Three

Willa could barely catch her breath as Ryker kissed her. Never, in all her thirty-two years, had she been kissed like this.

Her back was pressed against a wall just inside wherever it was Ryker had taken her, and his tongue was stroking hers sensuously. She curled her arms around his shoulders as he leaned down and slipped both hands beneath her ass. With not nearly enough effort, he lifted her and pressed her properly on the wall. She let her legs wind around his hips and gasped at the pressure of a hardened cock against her inner thigh.

He really *did* want her.

Later, maybe, she'd wonder how she'd managed to capture the attention of a man like him. For now, though, she was all too eager to reciprocate his affections. It'd been so long since she'd even kissed a man, she worried she'd forgotten how the rest of it worked. But if anyone could scrape off her rust, it was surely Ryker.

Why had she worn *jeans* tonight?

One of Ryker's large, scalding, powerful hands lifted from her butt and slipped beneath her blouse. Her skin immediately burned in the best possible way and Willa arched, breaking the kiss on a gasp. Over a *touch*.

Ryker rumbled what she hoped was an appreciative sound and began trailing hot, wet kisses along her jaw and down her throat. Licking. Sucking. Nipping. Kissing. In no particular order, over and over again. His hand curved around her abdomen, shooting electricity through her body until it was cupping her nearest breast through her bra.

Willa knew she'd never felt like this. Some part of her registered how outrageous this whole thing was, but she shoved that idiotic voice back. No *way* was she going to overthink this moment. Instead, she buried one set of recently painted nails in his surprisingly soft hair and slipped the other hand beneath the collar of his shirt, pressing her palm directly over his shoulder blades. His skin was warm and taut and she swore he growled at the contact.

Suddenly his breath was rushing along her throat and his lips were teasing her ear. "Willa," he said, his voice strained, "I can't promise to be gentle tonight."

Her eyes nearly rolled back in her head just from the tone of his voice and the *idea* of what he was saying. "No promises," she managed between gasps. "Just … make me feel beautiful."

Ryker rumbled, the sound vibrating like a purr, and nuzzled the skin beneath her ear. "You should *always* feel beautiful," he said.

Her heart stumbled. "You don't have to sweet talk me at this point."

He caught her earlobe with his teeth, tugging lightly, and released her breast in favor of stepping away from the wall. His other arm looped beneath her butt, keeping her in place around his hips, and he lifted a smoldering emerald gaze to her. "Then let me convince you."

Willa could only stare at him, still catching her breath, as they moved down a dark hall. Her arms were still around his neck, her legs still locked around his waist. By the time it occurred to her to ask where they even were, light flooded the room and her back had hit a large mattress.

Ryker kneeled over her, one hand braced on the bed to support his weight, and Willa drew a long breath. There was no mistaking the fire in his eyes. No confusing the erection pressing into her covered center. She was going to have sex with, hands-down, the sexiest man she had ever seen. Probably, she should've felt at least a twinge of guilt. She didn't.

Instead, she let her arms fall back, over her head, and watched him look her over. With interest. *Desire*, even. It left her speechless.

Something flickered in his eyes that she couldn't name. No sooner had she decided she liked whatever it was than he released an audible growl, sat up straighter, and grabbed fistfuls of her shirt. The next thing she knew, he'd given a sharp jerk of his wrists and her buttons snapped. All of them. Like something out of a movie.

How—?

She ceased to care the moment his lips descended on her collar bone. All she knew then was the slick, tingling trail of his talented tongue as it lowered to her chest. He shifted his weight, lifting a hand to guide one breast from her bra cup, and her nipple disappeared into his hot, moist mouth.

Ryker sucked, swirled his tongue around her hardened nipple, and grazed his teeth over the sensitive flesh. With his available hand, he reached into the other side of her bra and began fingering her neglected breast. Flicking, molding, squeezing. Sucking, licking, grazing.

Just when she didn't think she could take another moment of his divine torture, he pulled back, releasing her chest entirely. But instead of returning to her mouth, he bent lower and resumed his course down her torso. Over her stomach, teasing her navel, until he leaned back and ran his fingertips along the edge of her waistband.

His piercing gaze was suddenly pinning her to the pillows beneath her head and, voice thick with desire, he said, "I'm going to taste your orgasm before I take you. And once I'm inside you, I'm not going to stop until neither of us can move."

Her chest heaved with the effort it took to breathe properly. "God, I hope you keep that promise."

Ryker flashed her a smoldering grin, popped the button on her jeans free, and she let her legs slide to the mattress. He wouldn't be able to fulfill his promise, after all, if she didn't first let him remove her clothing.

Instead of tearing her pants off in a feverish frenzy like the one that had destroyed her blouse, Ryker slid back and tugged her jeans off carefully. Her skin was still tingling when her heels, jeans, and panties were lost somewhere on the floor behind him. Her lower half was entirely bared to his burning stare and a flicker of self-consciousness flared to life.

Would he turn away?

His large hands curved around her thighs, touch heavy, but tender, and as she watched, he bowed his head and inhaled. Long and deep. Another of those purr-like rumbles vibrated up from him and he said, "You smell so fucking good. I have to have you."

Willa swallowed, but failed to find her voice when he proceeded to run his tongue up the length of her folds. Her eyes rolled back in her head and she moaned thoughtlessly. She offered no resistance when he eased her legs farther apart, slipped a hand beneath her ass, and lifted her from the mattress. With one hand. The next thing she knew, his tongue was surging inside her and he'd found her clit with his thumb.

All thought scattered as her hips began rocking in time to the swipes of his hungry, swirling tongue. He licked and pinched. She felt a graze of teeth and her body exploded. Everything went white and she was only slightly aware of her hips grinding against his face.

Deep, husky chuckling drew her back to reality. "I'd recommend you stay awake for the next part."

Willa drew a deep breath and blinked her eyes

open, finding Ryker stretched out at her side. Devoid of a single piece of clothing. Her mouth watered all over again at the sight of his exposed body. It was more impressive than she'd expected.

Ryker's lips found her cheek and trailed to her jaw as he murmured, "Keep staring like that and it'll be over before it begins."

"Did I pass out?"

He chuckled again and slipped a hand beneath her back, quickly finding the clasp on her bra. "No, baby. I was just in a hurry."

"Oh." She was a bit disappointed to have missed the show, but he was kissing her again and she forgot to care.

Her bra loosened and he pulled back, leaning over her now. "I don't want anything between us," he declared as he guided her arms out of the loops. She realized, belatedly, that he'd also pulled off the sleeves of her destroyed shirt.

By the time he returned his gaze to her, she could feel her body warming up again. "Ryker," Willa whispered, reaching to touch his spectacularly sculpted chest. "Don't hold back."

He grinned, the expression devilish and sexy at the same time. "I don't think I could, baby." Ryker leaned forward as he settled between her legs. With his lips teasing the shell of her ear he added, "Hold on to me."

Willa wasted no time wrapping her arms around his torso, digging her fingertips into his sturdy muscles. He covered her lips with his in a powerful kiss, both arms braced at her shoulders, and then he filled her more completely than she'd ever known possible. She lifted her legs without thought and wrapped them back around his hips. He was buried so deeply inside her she felt him with each ragged breath.

Then he clamped a strong hand on her hip, growled against her lips, and let loose.

Ryker moved against her powerfully, surging rapidly into her body, holding her hips so tightly she was sure she'd bruise. He tore from her lips and attached himself to her throat as he pumped into her repeatedly. Filling her as he sucked on her throat and squeezing her hip as his pelvis ground against hers.

Willa gasped, arching and digging her nails into his skin. She'd never had sex like this before. Never been the recipient of such intense, fiery passion. Her entire body was on fire. Spots were already popping up behind her eyes. She thought she might have heard her voice in the air, but she wasn't aware enough to know what she may have said.

He rumbled a growl against her, slammed into her body one more time, and everything exploded.

Ryker nuzzled her neck, still somewhat braced above her and still nestled between her legs, as Willa slowly floated back to proper consciousness. The pleasant, faintly ticklish, soothing sensation of his lips and nose brushing her throat finally broke through the euphoric haze surrounding her mind.

Wow....

"Don't fall asleep yet, baby," Ryker murmured against her skin. "I'm just getting started."

Willa drew in a breath as her heart—and parts south—fluttered. "I might … need a few minutes." At least. Except certain parts of her body didn't seem so opposed to jumping right back in.

She swore she could feel his grin. "I can help you with that."

Stretching and stroking her fingers over his skin, Willa licked her lips as Ryker kissed the underside of her jaw. She found herself wondering what position they'd try next, or if Ryker would just continue to pin her to his bed with his thick cock, and the images those thoughts generated in her mind sparked renewed heat in her belly. "Mmm."

Ryker's deep, vibrating chuckle rolled up her chest and tickled the edges of her lips as he leaned directly over her. "I'm going to insist you tell me about that thought."

"What thou—"

Her question, and their moment, was ruined by an unexpected male voice.

"I hope you haven't claimed her yet. Be a shame to kill a female with so many curves."

Chapter Four

Ryker spun around, tucking Willa behind him and entirely out of view as he narrowed a glare on his unwelcome guest.

Nash.

Of all the fucking times for Nash to catch his scent.

Knowing full well the growl would be audible when he spoke, Ryker curled his fingers into the bunched up comforter beneath him, willing his claws to stay hidden. "Got a death wish, asshole?"

Nash, who had been leaning against the open doorframe as though they were having a casual conversation, rolled his eyes. "You're the moron who dropped his guard, Ryker. Frankly, you're lucky I gave you a warning."

Ryker could feel his blood boiling. It'd been nearly two years since their last fight. Always before he'd held back out of love for the brotherhood they'd once shared. But this was different. He'd found his mate. Nash was threatening not only his chances at convincing her to accept him, but her very *life*.

It took him a moment to register the sensation of Willa scrambling behind him, and not until he felt a slight tug on the comforter did he realize she was trying to cover herself up. The confusion she'd initially felt at Nash's interruption had waned and fear wafted off her like a cloying perfume. "What the hell is going on?"

Ryker slid forward until his feet were on the floor, keeping himself between Nash and Willa. "Just stay there, baby," he said without removing his glare from Nash. "I'm going to have to deal with this first."

Nash smirked, his dark-blue eyes flashing with

the promise of danger. "Yes, *baby*, please stay there. I'll want to celebrate after I rip out your lover's intestines."

The fear in her scent kicked up several more notches. Ryker heard her scoot back on the bed until the headboard was pressed against the wall.

Ryker curled his hands into fists, the tips of his claws breaking the skin over his nails in response to his anger. "Don't even fucking *think* about it." He needed to hold on to his temper. This was absolutely not the way to reveal his secret to Willa. But he also needed to tear his former friend's head off.

Nash straightened and popped his neck. "Oh, it's too late for that. But I have to admit I've never seen you so … territorial. I definitely have to taste her once I'm through with you."

It was too much. *No one* had the right to talk about Willa that way. And for as long as he continued to breathe, he'd make *damn* sure no one ever did again.

Ryker let out a furious roar and lunged forward, spreading his fingers wide as his claws finally tore free. He could feel the fur of his shifted form prickling at his skin, begging him to let the tiger completely out of its cage. But for the moment, he resisted. He wanted to see Nash's face when he ripped the ungrateful, over-confident bastard to shreds. He went for the obvious swipe first, knowing full well Nash would dodge, and tackled his enemy to the floor.

Willa let loose a shrill, panicked shriek when the fight began.

Nash grunted and attempted to roll free of Ryker's grip. When that failed, Nash shifted his weight and brought a clawed foot up sharply into Ryker's thigh. As soon as Ryker released him, Nash did a backflip and landed on his hands and feet. Crouched. Ready. "Tonight we'll finish this, *brother*."

Ryker settled on one knee, hands braced on the ground, ready to spring. "It's your funeral." He was done taking it easy on Nash. Done waiting for his old friend to resurface. No, ever since their elder had passed the mantle of leader to him instead of Nash, Nash had become violent. Unstable.

"Phone," Willa said even as Ryker noted the first ripple dance across Nash's skin. "Do you have a phone in your pants pocket? Toss it to me, I can call the police!" She was obviously attempting to gather herself. Her fear was still thick enough to choke on, but she was trying valiantly to push past it. He had to admire her for that. Even if her should-be-rational solution was a poor one.

"Trust me," Ryker said as Nash's body arched. "The police would just make things worse."

"Oh ... my ... God..." Willa mumbled, shock, confusion, and a whole new kind of terror leaping to the front of her scent. He didn't need to look to know her gaze was locked on Nash.

Ryker watched with the patience and focus of the predator he was as Nash's skin sprouted thick orange fur with wide black stripes. Feline ears formed atop his head, whiskers grew on his transformed face, and a violently swishing tail swung out from his rear. Nash had bulked up a little since their last encounter. That was smart. It was just unfortunate for him that Ryker had the edge in motivation.

He barely heard Willa's breathless gasp over Nash's threatening roar.

Nash burst forward with all the speed and strength of his shifted tiger form. He was counting on Ryker's need to protect Willa to keep Ryker in position.

But Ryker didn't like playing defense.

Locking his jaw in place, Ryker ducked at the last second and threw his body weight and considerable strength into Nash's chest. Claws sank into his back moments after the impact as Nash's jaw made an involuntary snapping sound.

Willa screamed again.

Ryker tackled Nash to the floor, rolling his enemy away from the bed and doing his best to keep Nash from tearing a chunk out of his side. When they were properly in the hall again, Ryker kneed Nash hard in the gut, used the extra couple of inches Nash put between them to get his feet under Nash, and shoved with all his strength. Nash cried out and skidded several feet down the hall, into the living room.

Wishing there was time to explain some of this, Ryker cast a glance at Willa to be sure she was still in place on his bed. She was, but he hoped he would never have to see the look of disbelieving terror on her face again.

Focus.

Nash wouldn't wait for him to gather himself.

Ryker growled low and finally unlocked the cage. His body burned, his skin stretched, and his bones snapped. Power and anger surged to the surface in equal waves, bursting forth in the form of orange and black fur, sharp claws, and pointed ears. He heard his own tail swish from side to side as he flexed his paws over the carpet in the hall. Now Nash would pay.

"R-Ryker…?" The hesitant, frightened question was Willa's, of course.

But he couldn't answer her in this form. At least, not until they were truly mated. So he cast another glance at her, hoping she would see enough of him in his eyes— the only things that stayed the same outwardly—to trust he was still there.

Her eyes went wide and she looked past him just as his ears registered movement on the carpet.

Ryker whipped his attention back around a moment too late. Nash had taken advantage of his distraction. They toppled to the floor, roaring and swiping with their massive paws. Sharp, stinging pain seared through one of Ryker's front legs. He sank his fangs into the nearest fur-covered flesh he could find that wasn't his own. Nash's pained outcry sang in his ears. Nash pulled back quickly, growling and snapping his tail back and forth in the hall.

His back to the doorway of the bedroom, Ryker lowered his head and growled the only warning he was willing to offer. His left front leg was still bleeding, but not as badly as Nash's shoulder.

The flash of fury in Nash's eyes was answer enough. He wouldn't be backing down, not this time. There would be no last-minute retreat, no surrender. No, tonight, their feud would end in blood.

Heart heavy, Ryker sprinted forward, determined to force Nash as far away from Willa as possible. He may not have had a choice in revealing his true nature, but he would do his best to keep her from having to witness the battle ahead.

Nash didn't back down, didn't turn to run away. He found his feet and let loose an impressive roar as their upper bodies locked in combat.

Ryker held him in place, but failed to force him back to the ground. Instead, they wrestled, awkwardly swiping at each other. Nash missed completely on his next swing and Ryker dove for the exposed flesh beneath his outstretched leg. He sank his fangs in as firmly as possible, making sure to shake his head in order to tear the wound. Nash reared back, smacking the side of Ryker's face, but drawing little blood. He managed to free his leg from Ryker's jaw and moved back, keeping weight on his remaining three paws.

Nash bared his fangs at Ryker in an obvious stalling tactic.

Ryker leaped forward, faking a dive at Nash's unharmed front leg. Nash fell for it and threw his weight sloppily to the other side, exposing his hind legs and flank. Ryker wasted no time bringing down the full might of his claws on another chunk of Nash's body.

The scent of blood filled the air as Nash hit the floor, moaning in pain.

This was usually the part where Ryker shifted back and walked away, knowing the battle was won for the day. He had no doubt that was what Nash expected again.

Instead, Ryker planted a strong paw on Nash's exposed throat and glared into Nash's eyes. *"Surrender."*

Nash lifted a lip in a curling sneer. *"That's what I'm gonna tell your bitch when I—"*

Rage filled Ryker's vision, and with a mighty roar, he tore his claws through the vulnerable flesh below them.

Chapter Five

Willa could barely breathe, her gaze glued to the hallway where she'd lost sight of the brawling *tigers*. One of whom she'd let take her to bed not even thirty minutes prior. Her stomach rolled threateningly and she clenched tighter to the comforter in front of her chin. She barely even felt the prickling sting of tears of terror as they rolled past her eyelids.

What am I supposed to do?

Did she stay as she was, naked beneath someone else's comforter, and pray she survived this night somehow? *What if Ryker loses?* She'd be dead by dawn for sure if Ryker lost.

Wait ... why ... am I rooting for Ryker?

Yes, he was the one she'd met—briefly—before the tiger-shifting madness began. And sure, he hadn't done anything to her she hadn't pretty much begged for. It hadn't occurred to her to be afraid of him until ... whatever that was happened. But that didn't change the fact some veritable stranger had taken her to a place she was unfamiliar with, fucked her, and promptly become a freaking *tiger*. Fighting another man-tiger. Was this some sort of game? Was it an act?

A strangled, feline cry of pain echoed down the hall and Willa jumped in place.

Whether or not she could really trust Ryker remained to be seen. She *knew* she couldn't trust the other one—whoever he was.

She had to do *something*.

Willa drew a deep breath and tore her stare away from the hall, trying valiantly to ignore the sounds drifting into the room. If she really wanted to survive, this was her best chance. Her gaze landed on her discarded jeans. She licked her lips as her body tensed and threw herself toward the foot of the bed. She went straight for the pants, opting to go commando in favor of saving a few precious seconds. But she drew up short when she looked down at herself. She certainly couldn't run through town without some kind of top. Ryker had destroyed hers, a memory that still sent a shiver of delight down her spine.

This is a terrible time to be turned on, Willa.

Then she saw the large, men's shirt rumpled on the floor. The very shirt he'd been wearing earlier. It would do. Without taking the time to second-guess herself, Willa moved and snatched it up. His intoxicating male scent washed over her as the shirt fell past her sides. Despite herself, she paused and lifted the collar to her nose for another sniff. In all the chaos, she'd forgotten how delicious he smelled.

Maybe she could trust him? Maybe she didn't need to run?

And maybe the other guy will win.

It wasn't worth the risk, no matter how amazing the sex had been. The next problem, though, had her coming up short. She could only see one way out of the room. Through the doorway the tigers had previously rolled through. No way would she be able to sneak past.

Willa pulled her stare away from the hall, hoping to find a window she could squeeze through, but her gaze lingered over a couple of dark crimson spots on the floor and her heart froze.

Blood... She'd nearly forgotten. Ryker, before he'd turned into a tiger, he'd been bleeding. He was hurt. And for whatever reason, the very idea of that made her want to cry. It made no sense.

A bone-shaking roar pierced through her emotional confusion as it filled the building, echoing off the walls. The sound was full of agony. Grief.

Lump in her throat, Willa moved back until the mattress prevented her from taking another step. She was trapped.

After a long, terrible second, a tall, broad, sculpted male stepped into view. He stopped barely a foot into the room, his naked body taking up most of the entrance. It was Ryker.

Sadness dulled his emerald eyes as he dropped his gaze.

The wound in his leg, the one that had bled on the carpet, looked like a recent scar now, emphasizing how little of this situation she really understood.

"I'm sorry," Ryker said, jerking her back to the moment. He met her gaze again. "That wasn't how I wanted you to learn my secret."

Willa's mouth dropped open, but she couldn't remember how to form words. Did that mean he'd *intended* to tell her? *Why…?* And why did her heart beat a little faster at the notion?

"I understand if you're scared," Ryker said, obviously choosing his words carefully. "I won't hurt you."

Pulling in a breath through her nose and releasing it deliberately through her mouth, Willa hesitantly asked, "What … what happened? What *is* this? Why would you *want* to tell me something so … significant?" And why did she immediately believe him when he swore not to hurt her? Had she really lost her mind?

Ryker released his own breath, harsh and frustrated. "You've heard of werewolves?"

Willa felt her eyes widen. "Yes." She didn't live under a rock. Hollywood loved werewolves.

His Adam's apple bobbed with a heavy swallow and he locked his stare onto her. "I'm a were*tiger*. One of

33

the few remaining."

Her head spun and she quickly braced herself on the mattress behind her knees. "I'm sorry," she said slowly. "You're a … *what*? You expect me to believe that?" But hadn't she seen it with her own eyes? Hadn't she watched, helpless and frightened, as the stranger and Ryker both transformed from human to tiger?

"I know it's a lot," Ryker assured her, his deep, rumbling voice massaging her nerves from halfway across the room.

All at once she remembered, distantly, having compared a timbre in his voice to some kind of purr. As if that explained everything.

"Why … why tell me?" Willa finally asked. She forced her gaze to linger on Ryker's this time, suspecting he'd just saved her life regardless of the details. She owed him that much.

His jaw tensed for a moment, but he didn't look away. "Because you're my mate."

Willa hit her butt, nearly sliding off the edge of the bed. "I'm your *what*?" Had he taken a hard swipe to the head in that hallway? She shook her head before he could respond. "I'm your *nothing*. We haven't even *known* each other for *twelve hours*. You couldn't possibly believe we're … soulmates, or whatever. That's impossible."

One of his lips twitched in that sexy, confident grin he'd seduced her with and he asked, "When you walked into that bar, did you believe in weretigers?"

He had her there. Of course. She scrunched her lips, refusing to admit defeat. "I still don't buy it. Even if you were right—how could you know so fast?" Why the hell was that the question she was going with? This man was nuts!

Or maybe I am? Maybe the bartender spiked my

drink with something other than rum? Could she be hallucinating the entire night?

Memories—images, sensations—from her time in Ryker's arms flooded her mind's eye and she swallowed heavily. She really didn't want that to be a hallucination. She wanted to believe that somehow, someway, a soft-spoken, overweight woman like her sparked such a powerful, burning desire in a man like him. Though it did sound outrageous when she thought of it that way.

A warm, gentle, calloused thumb brushed the line of her jaw and startled her back to the moment. She found herself drowning in molten emerald.

"I just *know*," Ryker said, his tone hushed and patient. "You're *mine*, Willa. We were made for each other."

Her mouth ran dry as more tears stung the backs of her eyes.

How could a man so sinfully sexy, so powerful and dangerous, want her? *No.* That wasn't what he was saying. He wasn't saying he wanted to be with her. He was saying they were *destined* to be together. That was heavier.

"I ... I don't know," she whispered. "I've never really believed in that kind of thing." She swallowed, flicking a glance to the hallway. "Where's the other guy, anyway? Is this even a good time to be having this conversation?"

Ryker released a breath and straightened, letting his touch fall away. "Unfortunately, this is the *only* time. Nash is in the hallway. And we don't want to be here when someone finds him."

Vomit bubbled up in her throat. Willa choked it back and turned an undoubtedly mortified expression back to Ryker. "You mean he's *dead*?"

Emerald gaze darkening, Ryker replied, "He'd

have killed you if I held back. Maybe not today, maybe not this decade, but he would have. I couldn't let that happen."

Willa clamped a hand over her mouth as tears fell down her cheeks. He'd killed that other tiger guy for *her*? How was she supposed to live with that?

The bed dipped beside her, blocking her view of the hall, and a strong, warm arm curled around her waist. Another hand settled on her shoulder, tucking her into a muscular chest. "This isn't your fault, baby," he said softly. "Nash has been coming after me for a long time. I shouldn't have let it get this bad."

It was too much. She'd been emotionally unstable when she'd walked into that bar. Now there was a dead guy in the hallway and a weretiger talking about destiny with his arms around her. Her life had never been this remarkable. She didn't know how to handle it. So she let the tears fall, not allowing herself to question the sense of security she found in Ryker's embrace. If she expected to function properly in any sense of the term, she first needed to release some of the stress and confusion.

After a short stretch of time, Willa realized Ryker had bowed his head into her hair. He was nuzzling her neck and ear with his nose, reminiscent of what he'd done before Nash had interrupted them. The tender way he'd held her. Never, before tonight, had she ever been held like this.

Like she was a treasure. A precious, priceless, beloved object.

She'd always wanted to be held like this.

The thought helped to slow her tears and she curled her fingertips into his bare chest. "How do we … avoid being arrested for murder?"

Ryker took a slow, deep breath and eased back to meet her gaze. "We run."

Chapter Six

"Tell me again how it works," Willa requested unexpectedly.

Ryker glanced over at her, finding she hadn't moved from the window seat of their beachside rental house. Her eyes were still pointed out the window, toward the rolling waves of the Pacific, but he doubted she saw the ocean.

It'd been a couple of weeks since he'd had to rip out Nash's throat.

A couple of weeks since he'd had to awkwardly explain to his destined mate that he was a weretiger and she was supposed to be his. But in the end she'd been right, it hadn't been the time to finish that conversation. She'd let him drag her out of town with surprisingly minimal resistance to the idea of abandoning the life she'd been leading.

Even so, nearly a week had gone by before she'd awkwardly brought the subject up again. She hadn't yet let him share her bed. But he understood she needed time to process everything. It was a lot to handle even without having had it all thrown in her face at once.

Willa finally turned enough to look in his direction. "Mating," she clarified. As if he'd misunderstood.

Ryker held his seat on the large sofa, not wanting to crowd her and scare her off. "We lock ourselves away for a couple of days. Make love literally until we pass out. Legend goes we'll wake with the next sunrise, the female—you—will climb on top and focus solely on bringing herself to orgasm. The male—me—isn't allowed to touch, or kiss, or otherwise actively participate. Your orgasm should trigger mine automatically. Somehow this synchronizes our bodies, binds our life forces, and allows us to communicate even when I'm shifted."

Willa arched a brow, her reaction much more contained than the first time he'd explained this process, and said, "But conveniently, we won't have confirmation of this destiny thing until *after* the endless hours of mind-blowing sex?"

He couldn't stop the grin this time. "And that's only if I can control my need to taste you in the morning."

Her cheeks flushed adorably and she looked away. "Ryker," she said, voice soft. "This whole destiny thing is overwhelming. But … I've never felt the way I feel around you. I'm not usually the kind of woman who trusts a stranger enough to share a *table* with them, let alone all this."

"Baby, if you're not ready—"

"That's just it," she interrupted, drawing a breath and gifting him with another small smile. "I'm scared, and uncertain, when I think about it. But it's all I can dream about now. I feel like my body is physically *itching* for you. When you go out, to get groceries or walk the beach or whatever, I *miss* you. I worry as soon as the door's shut. It's crazy."

Ryker stood and stepped up to her, letting the tips of his fingers brush her jaw as he tilted her head up to meet his gaze again. "None of that's crazy. Not to me. When I leave you alone for *anything*, I can't help but worry something's going wrong." He took a breath and lowered his lips to hers for a slow, wet kiss. "You are everything to me, Willa."

She was smiling again when he pulled back enough to see her expression. Tears clouded her eyes, but he smelled no sadness or fear. Only mild hesitation and excitement. "Can we … have dinner first?"

****

The first thing Willa registered as the fog of sleep faded from her mind was warmth. An all-encompassing, comforting, yet tantalizing warmth. She knew without a doubt it was because of the magnificent man wrapped around her. Ryker's arms were locked tight around her waist, his nose pressed against her throat. Their bodies were flush, her breasts pleasantly crushed against his chest while a delicious hardness poked her hip.

Though how in the world his body could have recovered from the night they'd shared was beyond her. It was a mix of erotic images and tingling, explosive pleasure in her memory. He'd kissed her and touched her *everywhere*. Of course, she'd done the same things to him in return.

Her body warmed with the thought.

She'd run her fingers and her tongue and her lips over every single muscle she could reach. The taste of his skin was branded on her tongue. It made her want to taste him again. To see if he tasted differently in the morning.

Willa blinked her eyes properly open, squinting briefly into the bright morning sunlight. The air in the room was cool, telling her that despite the light filtering in, it was probably still early. And now she understood how he could be ready to go again, because reflecting on the way he'd made her feel the night before had woken her up, too.

"Ryker," she whispered, knowing with his enhanced feline hearing there was no way he would sleep through her voice.

The arms around her tensed for a moment before loosening and Ryker lifted his head. "Mmm, good morning." His deep, enticing voice danced a sensual rhythm down her spine. She let him pull her in for a slow kiss, enjoying each stroke of his tongue along hers. But just for a minute.

Willa planted her palms against his chest and pushed lightly. She clucked her tongue, looked into his beautiful eyes, and said, "Lie back."

Ryker released his hold on her with a heavy, lingering touch and adjusted himself until he was properly on his back. With one hand on his stomach, the other still warming her skin, he arched a brow at her and asked, "Like this?"

"Exactly like that," she assured him. She gently moved the forearm he'd rested across his abdomen as she climbed over and straddled him. Her tangled hair fell to either side of her head as if creating a curtain around them. "I know you said I'm supposed to focus on my own pleasure, but I promise you, we're both going to enjoy this."

His eyes darkened with desire and he smirked. "That is the general idea, yeah." He deliberately raised his arms up and shoved his hands beneath the pillow supporting his head. "I'm all yours, baby."

Willa smiled and teased his cheek with a light kiss before straightening over him. She licked her lips, the rampant, burning lust in her veins barely even cooled by the brief flash of nerves rolling through her stomach. But they faded before she could give them any thought, so she trailed the tips of her fingers down his perfectly sculpted chest. Down, until she had wrapped both hands around his cock. She adjusted her weight, rolled her hips, and impaled herself thoroughly.

Ryker groaned, his head falling back to the pillow again, as Willa smoothed her hands once more over his abdomen. The sensations of his enjoyment were as thrilling to her as the feeling of having his rigid cock buried in her core.

And all at once she *had* to move.

Body burning with need more powerfully than she'd ever imagined, Willa gave in to her instincts and threw her head back as she began a bouncing, rocking rhythm. She curled her nails into his skin, occasionally adjusting her angle or her pace, and focused on the glorious feeling of *him*.

She wished he could touch her. Wished she could feel his calloused hands around her breasts or his skilled lips at her throat. Instead she lifted her hands from his skin and cupped her breasts herself. It wasn't quite the same, but she imagined her hands were his and followed the pattern he'd developed the night before. Rolling, pinching, rocking, grinding. She moved over him, her eyes closed, and lost herself in bliss.

He was groaning and half growling beneath her, his body tense in restraint.

When she opened her eyes again to look at him, he was watching her intensely. His gaze burned up and down her body. As she studied his expression, he swallowed heavily and his jaw tightened. He wanted her. He wanted to touch her, to take control. She could see it clearly.

He was right.

It hit her like light flooding a darkened room, dawning over her heart like the barely finished sunrise outside. She understood now. They were destined to be together.

The realization overwhelmed her and Willa released her nipples in favor of anchoring herself on his chest. She kicked up the pace, grinding harder into his hips, and finally, *finally*, her release burst inside her. She barely even heard herself scream out his name.

When her senses settled again several minutes later, Willa was on her back, covered head to toe with Ryker's body. He was dropping kisses along her face.

Just light, sweet, chaste kisses.

Her heart melted.

"Ryker," she murmured, reaching up and curling her fingers into his sides. She teased one of his calves with her toes.

"That was so fucking beautiful," he whispered, his voice rough and thick, as his lips grazed her ear.

Willa opened her mouth to ask the all-important question. But just before the first word could fall from her lips, she realized she didn't need to. She already knew. Tears stung her eyes as a smile lifted her lips and she wound her arms around him as best she could. "I love you."

Six Months Later

Willa paused as she stepped out of the cell phone store, intending to use her brand-new phone to let Ryker know that she was on her way home, when her brain finally processed the brightly colored sign of the store across the way. It was an art supply store. As she took in the different sized easels and blank, rectangular canvases in the left window, an old memory returned.

Once upon a time, when she was young, Willa had loved painting. She'd painted everything she could imagine. Block shapes, nature scenes, amateur profiles of all her friends. Landscapes had been her favorite. Then, early in her Freshman year of high school, she'd been sketching out an idea and an upper classman had come by, loudly declaring that her art was as ugly as she was.

Willa pursed her lips at the offensive memory. She'd cried so hard the school had sent her home early. She'd thrown out all her unused supplies and destroyed nearly every piece of "ugly" art she'd created. *Come to think of it, that was how it started.* She didn't know the kind of woman she might have grown into if that rude boy hadn't come by. And as recently as a year ago, she would have looked back on that memory with anger. He'd inadvertently set her down a hard, self-loathing path.

Now, though, she was glad for it. Because she loved the life she'd found with Ryker.

Still, a woman needs her hobbies.

Returning her purse to her shoulder and adjusting her grip of the bag in her other hand, Willa made her way to the art store. She didn't know precisely what she was looking for, as it had been nearly two decades since she'd allowed herself to consider painting or even sketching, but she was ready to try again. An image of Ryker, shifted and lazing under the shade of the tree in their new backyard, danced across her mind's eye. She was going to have to try her hand at animals, because all of a sudden they *needed* a painting of a majestic tiger on their living room wall.

The End

TAKEN MATE

Sam Crescent

Copyright © 2017

Chapter One

Hayley Ford paused near her apartment and glanced around the street. There were many people going about their business. No one seemed interested in her, and yet she couldn't shake the feeling that someone was watching.

Putting her key in the lock, she gave it a turn, and entered the main floor of the apartment building. After going to her postal box, she opened it up, taking out the letters before heading upstairs.

It's okay, Hayley. You're just losing your mind.

She walked up the three floors until she got to her room. There was a lot of unlocking of doors, but she was all alone in the big city. No family to speak of, and she had learned long ago not to get too attached to anyone.

Just get inside.

Opening the door, she slammed it closed and rested her head against the door. She didn't understand why her heart was pounding. Nothing made any sense.

Earlier in the day when she went to lunch she had felt like someone was watching her. She hated that feeling, and it never failed to make her sick.

"You can turn around now."

She gasped and spun around. There was not a single figure she could make out in the darkness. Reaching out, she flicked the light on and stared at a man she hadn't given much thought to in a long time. "Micah?"

He sat down in a chair, staring at her. The guy she had met three weeks ago when she went on vacation to an out-of-the-world resort near a large forest and lake, Forest Palm. She had just been leaving after a week's stay when she bumped into the man who right now sat in a chair in her living room.

She didn't get it. They had met for like five minutes as she was packing her car up. Other than admiring his action hero style of muscles, and learning his name, there was no way he should be at her home, let alone inside it.

"It took me a while to find you," he said.

After glancing at her door, she turned toward him. "I really don't understand. Did I get drunk or something?" She couldn't recall sharing anything with him.

He stood up and stepped toward her. The shirt he wore was tight across his chest, and her mouth went dry.

Hayley had never had a man like him in her home. In fact, she had never brought any of the men she dated back here. This was her safe haven, and no one was allowed at her home.

With each step he took, he moved closer to her, and her heart began to race. Again, there was that feeling of being watched, which made no sense. The only person who was here was Micah.

"Have you been watching me?" she asked.

"You made it hard for me to find you. Do you know how difficult it was for me to scent you?" Micah asked. "Cars, pollution—it doesn't help to filter the air—

along with the millions of people here." He pressed his hand against the door, which visibly shook underneath his grip.

"Wait? What?" Micah invaded her space, and she frowned as he inhaled the air around her. His dark-brown eyes flashed, and she gasped. "You're a wolf!" It wasn't a question. She had heard of the multiple clans of wolves around the world. Not many people knew about them, but she had searched for them when she was older.

No pack wanted a human near them, and so she had no choice but to back away. Their wolf status wasn't well known. Only a select group of humans knew about them. All wolves that she had known tended to stick to small towns near open forest and lots of space to roam, kind of like Forest Palm.

Wolf packs were very secretive as well. Outsiders and outcasts were not allowed.

"So you know what I am," he said, leaning in close and sniffing her neck. "Fuck me, you smell so good."

This man could tear out her throat with ease. *You need to get him away from your throat.*

Reaching out, she gripped his shoulders and tried to give him a little push. It didn't work. He stayed right where he was.

"I feel how nervous you are, baby. You don't need to be nervous. I would never hurt you. I fucking need you."

He growled each word against her neck, and it didn't help, not one bit.

"Look, I don't know who you are. I thought you were a gentleman, and clearly that was my mistake. You've broken into my apartment, and now you're sniffing me."

He chuckled.

How dare he!

"Micah, I mean it, back the fuck off!" She rarely cursed, but this man was starting to piss her off. Wolves never searched for a human, let alone a human female. They considered humans weaker, feeble, and pathetic. She had been told it enough times. In fact, there had even been a wolf in a bar about three years ago who had told her that even with a body like hers, they wouldn't find it attractive.

She wasn't slim, far from it. At a size eighteen, she had been called out for being fat, a pig, a cow. Pretty much every single mean name one could think of, she had been called it. Over the years since she was a kid, the names had started to hurt less. The numbness was a lot easier to go with.

"You're mine," he said.

His eyes flashed amber and had her heart racing.

"Excuse me?"

"You're mine, Hayley. My mate, my soul, my very life, and I've come for you."

She still held onto his arms, and it took her a few moments to figure out what the hell he was talking about. This had to be a prank. She burst out laughing. "Yeah, nice one. I know you can't take a human for a mate. Good joke, man, now leave so that I can get on with my night."

The hands at her waist didn't let her go.

Micah held her and invaded her space once again. "I'm not joking!"

Well, shit.

****

It took every ounce of control not to take her right then and there. For now, Micah was just happy to scent her. She smelled amazing. He'd been dreaming of this woman, desperate to finally be near her once again.

Hayley Ford was one of a kind. She was one of the rare human women who had been mated to an alpha shifter, and he was alpha. The bitches in his pack would try to fight her, but he would kill everyone and anyone who tried to take her place, or who tried to take her away from him.

His wolf had calmed for the first time in weeks. Just by being near her he was able to focus, and to actually breathe normally.

Peace settled over him, and he was inches away from kissing her when she slapped her hand across his lips.

"What the hell are you doing?"

"You're my mate, Hayley. I'm going to kiss you, and then I'm going to take you back to my place where we're going to be mated and have lots of wolf pups."

She burst out laughing and then stopped. "Oh, my God. You really think that is going to happen." She laughed even harder. "You are crazy."

He wasn't impressed. This was the first time a female had ever laughed at him, and he wasn't enjoying the experience. "I am not joking." He annunciated each word so she wouldn't mistake what he was saying.

"I don't care if you're joking or not. There is no way I'm going with you."

"You're my mate."

"I met you as I was loading up my car. I don't know you."

"You know of wolves."

"So? A lot of human people know about wolves. The difference is, none of us will ever admit it."

It was a good job as well. Many humans who had claimed to have met a werewolf often ended up dead or in some kind of special facility. It helped that the wolf packs had a special agreement with the government. They kept quiet and didn't hunt or experiment on them, and in return, they didn't kill them. To a lot of wolves, it was a fair trade, and if the government ever asked them for help, they agreed.

A charming relationship that kept the wolves and the humans safe. If anything ever started happening to packs, there would be no telling what fellow wolves would do.

"How do you know about wolves?" he asked.

She paused and bit her lip. "I don't want to tell you."

"Just tell me. I am one. I've just spent the past couple of weeks hunting for you."

"Fine. There was a friend I had in foster care. She was dumped there one day by her parents. We got close, and she confided to me what she was. Her parents discovered the truth and they put her in care, not wanting anything to do with her. During the full moon, I would cover for her, and it would help tame the wolf. Being in the city, it helped anyway, but at times it drove her crazy."

"This girl is not living with you now?"

"No. She was at the care home a year before someone took her. I got a single letter telling me she had finally found her real family, and I didn't see the point in forcing her friendship. I know wolves don't really like humans. You deal with us, you don't make friends."

Micah stared at her. She was a beautiful woman. Long blonde hair that landed at her ass in curls. Blue eyes that sparkled fire at him. Her figure was mouthwatering and he couldn't wait to get his hands on her and drive his cock deep inside her. The need to claim her was so strong, and he wanted all of his scent around her so no other male could have her. His cock was already hard, and he knew there was a bed just across from the living room. He'd been waiting for her for over an hour, so of course he explored her home. It was small, and his home in the forest with the rest of the pack was huge.

He already had clothes being sent for her, not that she would need them. The large forests would offer them privacy that meant they could run around naked. He had so many plans for the two of them and couldn't wait to get started.

"I'm more than happy to be your friend." He stroked her cheek, and she frowned, swatting at his hand.

"Please leave. I don't want to be a wolf's mate, and there's no way I'm leaving."

She ducked underneath his arm and removed her coat, revealing a crisp white shirt and a figure-hugging black skirt. She was a receptionist in a corporate building. He had seen her before heading toward her apartment.

He hated the city.

"Babe, you think I'm giving you a choice."

"You will give me a choice. You're no mate of me."

She turned her back on him. Micah had hoped she would be willing, but he had prepared in case she wasn't. He removed his shirt, covered it in the special sleeping liquid, and pressed the cloth against her mouth. She grabbed his arms, and he kissed her head. "I'm sorry, sweet, but I wasn't asking."

Seconds passed and the fight inside her died. When her whole body collapsed against him, Micah cradled her in his arms. Finally, after so many years of searching, he had found his mate, and there was no way he was ever going to let her go.

"I love you, Hayley. One day soon you will love me also."

He left her apartment without a glance back. There was no way he was going to fail.

Chapter Two

Hayley groaned and began to stretch her arms above her head. The bed was so good, and she loved how soft it felt. She must have found a man last night on the way home, because her bed was not this comfortable.

During her stretch, she paused as last night's events rushed over her.

"Oh, good, you're awake."

She sat up in bed and gasped. The room she was in wasn't her apartment, nor was it any kind that would be in the city. She was back at the motel she had stayed at for her vacation.

Glancing around, she saw it wasn't the motel. There were logs all around the cabin, and there was also a large window.

"Where the hell am I?" she asked.

"This is my home." Micah took a seat on the bed, and she frowned. She wasn't afraid of him, and yet he had kidnapped her.

"What is going on?"

"I brought you to my home."

"But I didn't want to be here. I want my own life at home!"

He snorted. "Your home? That place is so small and it was so scheduled. You deserve better, babe, and I'm the one to give it."

Glancing down at the bedding, she saw she was also naked, and quickly lifted the covers over her body. "Why aren't I afraid of you?" she asked.

"You don't need to be. I would never hurt you."

"You drugged me!"

"No, I didn't."

"I'm here and I don't know how the hell I got here!" She was yelling and she was so angry. *I love it here. It's so pretty.* "Ugh!" She shouted and slammed her hands on the blanket.

"I may have used some chloroform."

Hayley stared at him, really stared. He was a handsome man, sexy as well. She had noticed him even before he had seen her. Packing up her car, she had looked toward the café, smelling the coffee all the way across the street. She had wanted a cup, and right before she decided against it, Micah had walked out. His shirt had been stretched over his impressive muscular chest. He was tall, over six feet, and for the first time in her life, a guy made her feel small and delicate. Short brown hair, and brown eyes she had seen spark with amber.

Damn it.

Her pussy was already getting wet, and she didn't like it. She didn't want to desire him, or have anything to do with him.

"You know this is really creepy, and last time I checked, kidnapping is against the law."

"The law doesn't count here or with mates."

"I am not your mate."

"You are. You just keep fighting it."

"You're annoying!" She climbed out of the bed, pulling the blanket along with her, and wrapping it around her body.

"Will you stop?" he asked. "Just lie down. Let me get you some food."

She shook her head.

"I can smell the fact you want to fuck me."

Spinning around, she glared at him. "I don't know you. I don't want to know you. You're not making me want to even like you. Where is the bathroom? Unlike some people, humans need to use the bathroom."

He pointed toward a door on the left.

"Thank you." She found it next to impossible to

be rude. Politeness was part of who she was, even with a man who had kidnapped her and claimed they were mates.

"I will go and make some food."

She slammed the door closed and finally released the blanket, stepping out of it. Moving toward the mirror, she checked that she hadn't been bit or showed any mark that he may have bit her.

Some of the stuff she knew from friends, other information she learned from books and the Internet.

"You will not fall for this." A mate was something for life, and she wasn't interested in living with a man who would kidnap her.

Mates were supposed to be something deep and meaningful, and it lasted forever. There would be no one else but Micah.

There was a knock at the door. "Leave me alone, Micah." *You don't want him and yet you remembered his name.*

She hadn't been able to forget him, not once. If she also told the truth, she would have to admit she had also been dreaming about him a lot.

"It's not Micah. I'm Darla. Micah asked me to come and see how you're doing."

Picking up the blanket, she opened the door and saw a tall woman with long brown hair and sparkling eyes.

"Micah is my brother."

"Oh."

"Yeah, no worries. I'm mated to his best friend, and I have to say I'm so excited about you right now. My brother has finally found his mate, and believe me, it's so fun to watch him eat his own words."

"Eat his own words?"

"Yep. He's always joking around with the mated

males. Telling them how we've got them held by the balls. Please tell me you intend to hold Micah by the balls? Don't make it easy for him."

"I'm here because he kidnapped me." She folded her arms, which was hard to do as the blanket was so thick.

"Holy shit, you're not joking? He couldn't even wait?"

"He came to my apartment, told me how he'd been hunting me, and then he drugged me with chloroform, and I woke up here."

"That asshole." Darla bent over and burst out laughing. "This is going to be so much fun watching you guys. Micah likes to say how no woman would ever make him fall in love with them. I can't wait to see what you've got planned."

"Can you get me back home?" Hayley asked. Darla seemed nice, but this wasn't her home, nor even close.

"I can't. Pack law states that we can't interfere with mates. You may not feel your connection, but it is there."

Hayley growled.

Great.

She was stuck here.

****

Right. Pancakes were good. Bacon was even better, and scrambled eggs. What about dinner rolls? Micah emptied out most of the food from the fridge, and was whipping up pancakes with as many sides as he could think of. He even had some maple syrup to warm up.

"Wow, who are you feeding? A tiger?" David asked.

David was a fellow wolf shifter, his best friend,

and mated to his sister.

"I'm making some food for my mate. She's going to need her strength."

David sniffed the air. "You've not mated her yet."

"I will."

He couldn't look at his friend. When he had seen that David had mated to Darla, Micah recalled all of the jokes and ribbing he gave his friend.

"You will?"

"Well, first I've got to get her to agree to stay. I kind of … kidnapped her."

David burst out laughing.

"It's fine. She just doesn't know what we're like."

"This is just too good. You always said that your mate would be so easy and she would know how important it was for you two to be mated together. Now you're telling me your woman doesn't even want you?"

"It's not that she doesn't want me. She doesn't get how important it is for us to be together. No problem."

"I've got to meet this woman. She's after my own heart."

Micah growled. He couldn't help it. The thought of any man touching what belonged to him made him want to tear out his throat.

"Whoa, you do know I'm mated, right? There's no chance in hell of me ever wanting anyone else but my own woman."

"I don't care. You stay away from Hayley."

"Hayley? Wait, why do I recognize that name." David frowned and rubbed his chin.

Micah gritted his teeth.

"Holy shit, this woman is the one who stayed over at the motel. She loved to take walks in the forest."

"I wasn't around while she was here. I left, remember?"

"Yeah, you went mate searching and all the time, your mate came home."

Micah didn't need to relive his own mistake. He had heard many times that mates would find a way to be together. It was some kind of gravitational pull. Two souls that were meant to be together no matter what. He never believed in it thinking it was an old wives' tale, or something like that.

If only he had some faith, he would have been able to date Hayley and not kidnap her.

"I like her," Darla said, entering the kitchen.

"Where is she?" Micah asked, dolloping mounds of pancake batter into a skillet.

"She's heading down."

He heard her walking downstairs. Seconds later, she appeared in the doorway, and his heart squeezed. She wore one of his old shirts, and a pair of boxer briefs. He was bigger than her in everything. Her blonde hair was also down and all around her shoulders. She looked so beautiful.

"Morning," he said.

She glared at him, but still muttered a 'morning'.

"Here, Hayley. This is my mate, David."

"Hey, David," Hayley said, taking a seat beside Darla. The sound of her stomach growling filled the entire kitchen.

In a flash, Micah placed a bowl of diced fruit in front of her. "Please, eat something."

She stared at the fruit and then at his hand before looking back at the fruit. He handed her a fork, and she took it. "Thank you."

"No problem." He watched as she speared a mango slice, taking a bite.

Satisfied that she was eating, he went back to flipping pancakes.

His mate was in his home.
He was feeding her.

The wolf inside him was dancing and so damn happy right now. Micah couldn't help but smile. This was the first time in his entire life that he had felt truly content.

"So, Hayley, how are you finding Forest Palm?" David asked.

"I loved it the last time I was here. I didn't expect to be back so soon."

Micah looked up to see that she was looking at him.

"She's here against her will," Micah said. "She doesn't believe that we're mates, and she doesn't care how important that means to me."

"How dare you? You expect me to give up my whole life because you say so? You ... pig."

"First, I'm a wolf, babe. Remember that. Second, what life? You lived alone, and from the smell of the apartment, you hadn't been with a man in a long time. I'd have smelled him." And he would have killed him. There was no way his wolf would have been able to handle that kind of intimate touch between his mate and another man.

"You ... ugh, I don't like you. How come this is the first time I've met you?" she asked. "Do you even live here, or is this someone else's house?"

"I live here, babe. This is my place."

"So why didn't I see you before? I was here for like two weeks, and you're telling me that not once during that time you didn't venture out to town?"

David laughed. "Micah was out ... hunting, weren't you, mate?"

Micah glared.

"Hunting? Like rabbit and deer or stuff?" Hayley asked, eating a piece of strawberry now.

"No. I was actually out hunting for my mate."
This was not going well for him, not well at all.

She stopped eating and stared at him. "Oh, wait a second. You're telling me that you could have been here when I was here, but you were determined to find a mate, and you went looking elsewhere?"

"Yes."

Hayley started laughing. "I really shouldn't laugh, but it is so funny."

He was screwed, royally screwed.

Finishing the pancakes, he handed them out to Hayley first, and then his sister and brother-in-law. During breakfast, he watched Hayley talk with Darla and David. She seemed happy talking to them, and he was pleased he didn't send them away so he could be alone with Hayley. She wasn't ready for that, not yet anyway.

Her body wanted him. He smelled her arousal, but her mind was nowhere near where her body wanted to be.

Chapter Three

Darla and David, the double Ds, didn't stay for long. Hayley stared out the window, watching the car drive away. The house had gone really quiet, and she didn't know if she even wanted to be left alone with Micah.

Her body was betraying her.

Every second she spent with him, the more aroused she became. Her clit was so swollen, begging to be touched. She knew it had to do with being close to Micah.

"Is this normal?" she asked.

She knew he was in the room even before he made a sound.

"Yes. You want me, and your body wants me."

"I'm not a wolf."

"You feel me, and your body senses me. We don't know how humans are able to get the same cravings, only that they do." He moved up behind her, and she closed her eyes as he gripped her shoulders. "It will get worse."

She couldn't even think of it getting worse right now. All of her life, she had never felt the desire to screw anyone, and yet, she wanted to jump on his dick and ride it. This was not like her, not even close.

"I don't do stuff like this. Not with complete strangers."

"I'm not a stranger, and there is only one of me. I can take care of you. I won't let anyone else touch you. You belong to me."

"That's what bothers me." She spun around to face him. He held onto her arms, and she didn't like how they seemed to burn. Not in a bad way either. No, she wanted him so much it made her ache for him in ways she didn't like. "I don't know you, and I don't want to have sex with you."

"We're mates. It's going to happen." He ran his hand down her arm. She didn't like how the burn eased under his touch and became pleasurable. "You feel that. You need me, Hayley."

"I don't want to need anyone."

"Whatever happened to that girl from foster care?" he asked, causing her to frown.

"I told you. She got adopted and after a letter, I never heard from her again."

"Did it bother you?" he asked.

"Not really. I was happy that she had finally found a home. When you're in care, you don't really think about anything else. She got a home, and I moved on. Last I heard she was happy, why dwell?"

"Your curiosity about the wolves, it never faded."

"Not for a second, but I can't go around begging people for answers."

"Babe, I've told you we're destined to be mates. From the moment I smelled you across the street as you were packing up your car, I knew."

She frowned. "You never said anything. You *demanded* my name."

"I was reeling. Especially as I'd been in the café and several of the pack were talking about you. You liked to take long treks alone in the forest."

"I love the forest," she said.

"Why live in a city?" he asked.

She didn't know why, and told him so. "It doesn't matter now. It's over."

"It's never over. Do you believe in fate?"

"No."

"Well, I do. I believe we were bound to meet and bound to be together. It's what drove you here, and it also helped that you were intrigued by our kind." He took hold of her hand and pressed it against his chest.

She didn't like how the need faded out, and she was able to focus. There was no way she was going to be hanging off his every word just to stop the arousal.

"You're not my prisoner here. I can give you a life you've always wanted."

"What's the catch?" she asked. She didn't like how tempted she was.

"Give me a chance. Give the two of us a chance to mean something to each other."

"Micah, I don't know. This thing between us, it scares me. I'm not used to not having control."

He pushed some of her hair off her face. "You think I don't feel that? Never have I felt this overwhelmed before in my life. I adore you and yet you flinch away from my touch, even though I know I make you feel amazing."

She understood his frustration. Taking hold of his hand, she couldn't resist tracing a finger down his palm. "Fine. I'll do it." She had nothing left to lose and everything to gain.

"It requires you spending time with me."

"I get it. I'm at your mercy and I'm to give you as much of myself as possible."

Micah cupped the back of her head and leaned in close. His breath fanned across her face, and he was so close that she was sure he was going to kiss her. Suddenly, he pulled away. "You won't regret it. I promise."

She was going to regret it. She loved his touch too much to be able to resist for long. This was going to be the hardest time of her life.

****

"What did you think of Forest Palm?" Micah asked.

They walked side by side as they made their way down the long stretch of town. Hayley's arms were folded, and she was wearing one of his red checkered shirts. It was one of his favorites, and especially now as she was inside it. The scent of her was keeping his wolf at bay. So long as his wolf didn't want to come out and play, he would be fine. He would never hurt his mate, nor would his wolf. The biggest problem was if he felt there was a threat. His wolf wasn't exactly known for drawing the women to him, not human women anyway. The only woman he wanted was right beside him.

The urge to touch her was so strong that he was having to fist his hands to keep from reaching out.

Men, women, and kids were looking toward them.

"Everyone is staring," she said.

He chuckled. "They all know who you are."

"They do?" She stepped closer to him, and he had no choice but to wrap his arm around her shoulders.

"Yeah. I told them straight that the next woman I'd be walking around town with would be my mate."

"They look like they want to kill me."

"I'll protect you. I've told you that." He closed his eyes as he breathed in her scent. Never had he met a more stubborn woman.

"So weird."

"What is?" he asked.

"All of my life I've been curious about wolves, and what it would be like to finally meet one, yet here I am, and I'm so confused."

"Ask me anything. If you remember that girl's name, I can try to find her."

Hayley stopped and looked at him. "You can?"

"If she's part of a pack, I can certainly call around. That's what packs do. We connect, we help each other, and we band together."

"Kind of like a family?"

"Kind of. I'm not saying it's all peaceful. There have been a few problems between packs. It happens when one pack gets too big and starts encroaching on another's land."

"Are you big? This is a pretty big place."

"Nope. There's not another pack for miles around. We're safe here, and everyone here just wants to live their lives in peace. What more can a guy or woman ask for?"

He loved it when she smiled, and right now she was doing exactly that.

"I do love it here. I found … I don't know. Like you said, it was peaceful, and I didn't have to worry about banging into anyone or causing any trouble. It was nice."

"Why did you live in the city if you hate it so much?" he asked. He loathed going to the city. The smells from such a heavily crowded place always interfered with his sense of smell. It had been next to impossible to find her, and he hadn't liked that. If she had been anywhere else, he'd have found her in a matter of hours.

"I'm hungry," she said.

It had been nearly four hours since breakfast. After taking her on a tour of the house, he had also taken her for a long walk around his cabin and surrounding woodland before walking out to town. She did enjoy long walks.

"There's a diner just up ahead." He held her hand, running his thumb across the back of her hand.

No one interrupted them as they made their way inside the diner and toward a booth. The scents of burgers, fried chicken, and pasta were heavy in the air. The thing about being a wolf, it meant he had an appetite and was always hungry.

Hayley took a seat opposite him and tucked some hair behind her ear. "I loved coming here."

"I can't believe I picked the week you visited to go mate hunting."

"Why did you decide to go mate hunting?" she asked.

Micah chuckled. "If I told you that I'm sixty years old, what would you think?"

Her gaze was on him. "There's no way you're sixty. I wouldn't put you a day over thirty."

"I'm sixty-one in November."

"Wow!"

"It's a wolf thing. We age slower than everyone else. You'll have a long life."

"Wait, how? I'm not even a wolf."

"When we complete the mating, you and I, we'll be connected. You'll age slower."

"What happened to your parents? Do they know you've mated with a human?" she asked, glancing around the diner.

"My parents are dead."

"Oh, sorry." He saw her frown. "How?"

"You're a curious person."

"Wouldn't you rather me be curious than, I don't know, screaming and scared?"

"You're right. I wouldn't want you screaming away from me." He reached across the table, taking hold of her hands.

"Is this another part of it?" she asked. "Holding hands, touching me."

"Yeah, it really is. You have no idea how calming it is to me just to hold you."

The smile was back on her face.

"Her name was Lettie. Lettie Sandsman. I would

appreciate it if you could at least tell me if she's happy. I'd like to know that," she said.

"I'll start making calls. You didn't know anything else about her or where she went?" Micah asked.

"I don't. I only know it was a pack, and that she was loving it there. I just want to make sure. A lot of bad shit can happen and I'm hoping it didn't happen to her."

"You cared about her?"

"A lot. She was my family for a while. We relied on each other."

"Now you can rely on me, babe." He stroked over her pulse, feeling as it raced beneath his touch. She felt it, too, but he wasn't going to argue or force her to be with him more, not until she was ready.

Chapter Four

Later that night, Hayley groaned as another wave of heat washed over her. Pressing her thighs together, she rolled over in bed, trying to relieve the ache inside her. Her pussy was on fire, and she needed him so badly. She had gone to bed early, leaving Micah alone in his library.

The day with Micah had been so amazing. She hadn't wanted it to end, but how could she have given in to him so soon? He took her against her will. *You want him.*

She released a whimper, cupping her pussy. The contact didn't ease, not even when she slid a finger between her slit.

There was a knock on the door. "Hayley, baby, you need me."

She cried out, tears running down her cheeks. She wanted him so much.

"Micah, please."

He entered the room without another word, and he was on the bed.

"Why is this doing this?" she asked.

"Because we're close. A full moon is going to happen soon, and even if your heart doesn't know it, your body, it wants me."

"I'm not a wolf."

"But you're still controlled by hormones and stuff. Look, no one really knows why shit happens, but it does, and it's killing me seeing you like this. Please, I can relieve you."

"I don't want to have sex. And why aren't you in any kind of pain?"

"I'm a wolf. I know how to control it, but it doesn't mean that I'm not feeling this as well. I know you need me, Hayley. Let me help you."

"I don't have sex with strangers. I have to be in a commitment."

"I'm going to love you for the rest of our lives, baby. I'm committed to you and only you. I'll never hurt you, never cheat, and you will have my undivided attention. I will love and provide for you."

Tears sprang to her eyes. She felt so bad because she was such a horrible person. This man was prepared to devote the rest of his life to her, and she couldn't even bring herself to tell him that she trusted him. She didn't have any wolf senses and didn't know if there would be a difference in her feelings toward him.

He touched her wrist and that single caress felt so good.

"Please, I won't do anything else that you don't agree to."

She closed her eyes. *Let him. You want him. Give in.*

"Yes. Please, Micah, make it stop."

He moved over her, slamming his lips down on hers. She didn't put up a fight. The moment he was above her, she felt the tension within her start to ease. Releasing a breath, she ran her hands up and down his arms, marveling at his strength.

"If you want me to stop, I will."

"I don't." She stopped thinking and allowed her body to take over. Not that she had much of a choice. The choice had been taken from her right now, but she was giving herself over to Micah willingly.

Micah moved between her thighs, and she closed her eyes, basking in his touch. In the back of her mind, she knew she should be embarrassed, but she wouldn't let it take over, and instead she opened her legs wide, wanting him.

Her pussy was so slick, and her clit aching. Even

as she touched herself, there was no way for her ease that pain.

"You're so beautiful, and you smell so good." He pressed kisses to her neck, sucking over her pulse before moving down her body.

The sheer negligee she was wearing, he tore off her body with one easy tug. She didn't care. The sound of the tearing fabric turned her on even more.

Arching up, she screamed his name as he sucked one nipple into his mouth, followed by the other. He trailed a pathway between her breasts before moving down, dipping into her belly button, and finally he was at her pussy.

He opened the lips of her pussy and stroked his tongue down her slit. In one swift thrust, he pushed his tongue inside her, making her moan and call his name.

"Micah, please." It had been so long and she knew without a doubt she wouldn't last long at all. He moved his tongue back up to her slit and began to stroke over her clit, each flick driving her even wilder to the point of no return.

He flung her into orgasm, startling her with how hard and pleasurable it was. She'd had orgasms before, but nothing like this.

She arched up, and he held her down, prolonging her orgasm.

Only when she begged him to stop, did he.

Collapsing to the bed, Hayley panted, basking in the afterglow bliss of her orgasm.

"You're much better now," he said.

She turned to find him lying beside her, smiling. "Would you like me to take care of you?" she asked.

He shook his head. "Already done. Your orgasm helped me."

"What?"

"Yep. I have no shame."

"But, both of your hands were on me. How?"

"I don't know. I'm going to put it down to that awesome wolf gene that I possess. Mates can make each other do the craziest things."

"Like bring each other to orgasm?" she asked.

"Does it embarrass you?" he asked.

She thought about it for a second. "I don't think it's embarrassing. Kind of cool." She rolled over so that she was completely facing him.

"Would you like me to leave?"

"No. I'd like your company."

She reached out, touching his hand. When she wasn't happy with just touching, she held his hand, locking their fingers together.

"Thank you," she said.

"You're my mate. I'd do anything for you."

"I don't know if I like that. It's almost as if someone has taken my freewill, and I don't like that," she said. "You should be able to mate with whoever you want, and not be held by what your body thinks."

He smiled. "I don't consider my freewill taken. Far from it. I'm free to come and go as I please."

"But you have no choice in this. Tell me you wouldn't want someone amazing and hot."

"You are amazing and hot," he said, cupping her face. "I think you're awesome."

She smiled. "Are you sure?"

"I don't know how the whole mating thing works, to be honest. What my parents always told me was that fate or the universe was able to detect mates who were more suitable and compatible to each other."

She giggled. "Compatible? That is so romantic."

This time he chuckled. "Think about it. It kind of is. In a world full of people, you and I, we're meant to be together. There is no one out there but you. I don't want anyone else but you." He rolled over like she had. "There's no one else for me but you."

****

The following day, Micah walked with Hayley as they made their way toward the lake. It was really hot outside, and the only way to cool down was to go swimming in the lake. When he had asked her to go naked, she had given him that look that told him "not a chance."

Thinking about it, there were going to be other pack members, and he had no interest in any of them seeing his woman. The more she covered up, the better. So, instead of getting her a bikini, which he would have loved to have seen her in, he got her a one piece that was still going to show off way too much flesh, but it was a compromise. He wanted to keep all of his man parts.

Last night had been a step in the right direction. When he had offered to leave her in peace, she had asked him to stay. That morning when he woke up, it was to find her in his arms, snuggled against him. Now he only prayed for winter so that he could turn the heating off, and have her snuggled in his arms more often.

"What are you thinking?" she asked.

"You really don't want to know."

She chuckled. "Are you having sexy thoughts?"

"Definitely. Does that surprise you?"

She paused, stopping to reach up toward a leaf hanging from a branch. "Hmm, I don't think so. Are wolves, you know, more sexually primed?"

He saw her cheeks heat, and he found her embarrassment so cute. "Yes, we are."

"You're not even going to pretend to be modest?"

"Why would I do that?" he asked.

"In all seriousness?" She moved away from the

tree, and headed straight ahead along the dirt path.

"We are, and it's not me ego boosting either. We're bigger, stronger, meaner, and we brood more. Our appetites are equal to us, as well. Sex, food, the rush of the chase. You name it, we've got that need multiplied."

"Last night was the first time that I had ever ..."

"Got licked by what you call a stranger."

"You're one of the hardest men I've been around."

You've not felt my dick yet, baby. When you feel that, you'll know.

She slapped a hand to her head. "Ugh, that sounded so dirty, didn't it?"

"Just a little bit." They made it out of the clearing, and he saw several of the pack were at the lake already. None of them had turned. He'd asked them not to, at least not until he'd mated Hayley to him. He hoped she was ready by the next full moon.

Micah knew he would never hurt her, but he didn't want to have to curb his wolf for fear of how she felt around him.

"This is so beautiful."

The trees offered a lot of shade, so it was cooler than being out in the sun. It was beautiful as rays of sunshine came through.

"Hey, Micah."

He nodded toward the greeting, taking Hayley toward a rocky area.

"Who was that?" she asked, leaning against him.

"One of my pack."

"Will David and Darla be here?" she asked.

"Yes. I figured you would be more comfortable with my sister here."

"How long ago did you lose your parents?"

"Twenty years ago. They were quite old," he said.

Her curiosity always got the better of her. "How old?"

"They were nearing two hundred."

"Wow."

"Yes, wow. They had us at a very late age."

"Did you love them?" she asked.

"Very much. They were amazing parents, and my father was an alpha."

"Was it tough to take his place?"

"Every single day. There are times I feel like I don't match up to him. So many people rely on me. I don't want to screw it up."

She patted his chest. "I really don't think that is possible." She smiled. "I can see how everyone loves you. They have a great respect for you. That is only the kind that is earned."

He pulled his shirt over his head at the same time that she did. She revealed the plain black swimsuit that he'd bought her. To him it was still too revealing, the fabric molding to every single curve, and showing off her generous tits.

His cock started to get hard and he took a seat, doing his best to hide it.

"It's so hot." She didn't sit with him. She rushed toward the water, jumped in, and sighed. "Bliss." She ducked under and then broke the water. "Are you coming in?"

Unable to resist his mate, he got to his feet, not hiding his arousal.

"Oh my," she said.

Diving into the water, he headed toward her. She backed away, giggling. "What are you doing?" she asked.

Trapping her between a rock and his body, he rested his hands on either side of her head. "That is what you do to me." He pressed his cock against her body. She melted instantly. "You want me, too."

"I do," she said, wrapping her arms around his neck. "I want it to mean something, Micah. I want to know that we'll be good for each other."

"We will. I won't let anything happen to you. I'll protect you, and when we have kids, I'll be a good father."

She pressed her head against his and groaned. "I wish you had come to me five years ago. Everything would have been different now."

He gripped the back of her head. "We've got the rest of our lives. I can wait, and I will wait. I'll prove to you every second you're with me that we're meant to be." He pressed a kiss to her lips and pulled away. "Hello, Darla," he said.

"You're keeping her all to yourself and you know I don't like that."

Micah pulled away, reluctantly. There would be a time where he'd get to growl and keep his mate to himself. That time was not now.

Chapter Five

"My brother loves you," Darla said.

Hayley looked toward the barbeque the guys had set up. She couldn't believe how fast food had arrived when all she said was that she was hungry. Micah had acted instantly, and had announced he was heading into town to get a bunch of food. All the other guys had to do was to get a pit ready for him to cook on.

"I, erm, this is really hard for me."

"With the whole kidnapping thing?"

"Yeah. It's not something we humans handle easily. In fact, it's against the law from where I come from."

"When it comes to pack law, taking a human is not against the law, especially if that human is a mate. Micah, in his weird alpha way, thought he was acting ... romantically," Darla said.

Hayley chuckled. "Is it wrong that I can see that? He believes that everything he does is romantic?"

"Not everything. Just this, honey. He loves you, and when you're near your mate, that means something, more than anything."

Hayley watched as Micah and David were laughing and joking. It had only been a couple of days, and yet, she sensed how much he cared about her. Everything he did was for her, and it was next to impossible to ignore that. Every woman would love for a man to be devoted to them, and she had it right now.

"Do you feel similar with David?" she asked. "Your mating call?"

"Yeah, it does. The moment I saw him, I knew, and it was so hard to try and put perspective on everything. I wanted to trust the mating call, you know. Out of every single man in the world, I was mated to my brother's best friend. It is hard, and as wolves, we do fight it. There's always that niggling doubt. Some of us just bask in finding our mate, but we're not all the same."

Hayley looked away. "So you're not upset with me for having doubts?"

"Not at all. I'd be more upset if you just gave in to it. It's not how love works, is it?"

"Love?"

"If you allow Micah to mate with you, you're going to be alive for a really long time, Hayley. Make sure it's the right decision," Darla said.

"What are you two ladies talking about?" David asked, moving in beside his woman.

"Love," they both said at the same time, and then chuckled.

"Here, you ask and I bring," Micah said, holding out a large burger.

"Wow, that was fast." She took the burger, and the little serviette he'd given her. Taking a bite, she closed her eyes with a moan. "That's so good." A nice spicy burger, cheese, onions, everything she loved in food in one big burger. "Did you make this?"

"I got the burgers from the diner. I know I can trust their food, and I saw how you reacted to it the other day."

She laughed. "I'm not even going to say anything about that. It really was so good."

"Really, really good." He had his own burger as well.

Glancing toward the barbeque pit, she saw people just putting on new food, and taking the cooked food off.

She finished her burger, while David, Darla, and Micah ate another four burgers each. She decided to have a spicy chicken leg, and watched as the little group they had formed ate even more. It was refreshing being around people who ate more than her.

Later that night, as she was getting ready for bed, she sensed Micah in the room. She wore a pair of shorts and a crop shirt. "You weren't lying about eating a lot, were you?"

"We were all hungry, and it was a great day to have a barbeque. I heard what you and Darla were talking about. She's right. You need to know this is what you want for the rest of your life."

She sat down on the bed, crossing her legs, and staring at him. He was leaning against the doorframe, staring at her. "What do you mean?"

"Once you accept me as your mate, there won't be any going back to the city. I can't be there. This is my home, and I'm hoping you'll see this as your home as well. The point is, there will only be me. There won't be any chance of you finding anyone else."

"You sound so sure of that."

"I know I am. I won't be able to live with another man touching you. I'm an animal, Hayley. To the core, that is what I am. I will kill them."

"What about me?" she asked.

"I'd never hurt you. It's not in my nature." He turned to leave.

"Wait," she said. "You don't have to leave."

"I think I do. I want this. I want you here as my mate. I want to fuck, make love, have babies, build a life with you. I kidnapped you for that very purpose. Hearing my sister, she put things into perspective for me without even realizing it. This is not a life you walk away from. We mate, and we're together forever. I need you to make that choice without me trying to make it for you."

With that, he walked away.

Hayley missed him, and something hollow settled in her heart. She didn't want him to walk away.

****

"Why are you not at home cooking breakfast?" Darla asked, taking a seat opposite him. Micah glanced around looking for her mate, but saw no David. "He's not here. I told him I was going to come alone."

"Right, because he listens to you."

"He does. Unlike you." She reached across the table, taking one of his uneaten pancakes. "Are you starving yourself now?"

"I'm not hungry."

"Your first week with a mate, and already you're by yourself, moody, and you're not eating. What did you do?"

He sighed, pushing the plate of pancakes toward her. For the past five days he had been leaving Hayley to her own devices. Trying to give her the space that he should have in the beginning.

"You were right."

"About?"

"Waiting. I should have waited and courted with Hayley. Done things completely different."

"Doing things my way isn't exactly in your nature, Micah."

She was right again. It was next to impossible for him to be patient. When he wanted something, he had to have it. Even though he was trying to give Hayley space, it didn't always work. He found himself following her, just to make sure she was okay, or just to be near her. "I can't lose her, Darla. I've already screwed up and done things the wrong way. I don't know how I'm going to make it right with her."

Darla stopped in her chewing, and stared at him. "Why are you moping?"

"Hello, I've got problems."

"No. You've got a curious and confused mate,

that is not the same thing as having problems. You went to Hayley. Everyone you asked advice for, we told you the same thing, to do what normal humans do. They spend time, they date, and they fall in love before springing up the wolf talk," Darla said. "You, you were determined to do this your own way, and for the past five days, you've left her alone." She started chewing on a pancake. "Makes you a lame ass mate if you ask me."

"What do you expect me to do? I heard your advice to her. How am I supposed to work with that?" he asked.

"Simple. Show her what being a mate really is like. Don't give her space, and make her think that you're bored, regardless of if you got to the sexy time yet. Stop being a selfish ass, and think about someone who is not you for a change." Darla finished off his pile of pancakes. "Delicious. She's down by the lake again, and she's sad."

Micah got up, and without saying another word, headed out of the diner and toward the lake.

Once he got to the forest, he ran toward the lake and found her within minutes. Her jeans were rolled up, and one strap of the crop top she was wearing had slid down her arm. Her hair was still down, around her like beautiful blonde waves. She was walking through the lake, looking so gorgeous.

"Hey," he said.

She looked up and frowned at him. "Do I need to go somewhere else now?" she asked.

"Huh?"

"Every time I've come near you, you walk away. You're here now. Do you want me to leave?" She folded her arms and looked incredibly pissed off at him. "Are we even mates or is this some ridiculous charade?"

"We're mates."

"We are? You see, that's strange to me," she said.

"Why?"

"If we're mates, tell me why you've suddenly gone and started to do your own thing. Why leave me alone? Can I go back to my life? The one you took me from?"

Tears had filled her eyes.

"I'm sorry."

"You're sorry?"

"Yeah, I fucked up." He entered the lake and walked right up to her. "I heard what Darla said to you, and I thought about everything that I had done. I'd not gotten you flowers, gotten to know you, or even taken you on dates, or anything. I just took you, and decided that nothing else mattered. I had found my mate, only there is a problem. I shouldn't have taken you. I made a big mistake."

"You think I'm a big mistake?"

"No. I think by doing this the way that I had, I made a mistake. I love you, Hayley. Really, I do, and I don't know any other way of showing you how I feel. I'm used to just clicking my fingers and getting what I want. You're not like that, and I want to be better. I want to be the man you deserve, more than anything else." He reached out, cupping her face. "I want to give you the world, baby, and I want you to be happy here, to love it here." Then, he couldn't resist another moment. He slammed his lips down on hers, taking the kiss he'd been so desperate for.

Chapter Six

"So who is this?" Hayley asked, pointing at another black and white photograph.

"That is actually my mom and dad."

"Really?" She looked closer. The photo was taken nearly a hundred years ago. "This is really weird. I can't believe your parents were that old." Her cheeks heated. "You know what I mean."

"I do know what you mean, and you're right. My parents were really, really old. They were around for so many events in the world. War, peace, war again, color television."

She chuckled. "You were around for color television?"

"Yep, I was."

Again, she laughed. "This is amazing. You have so much history. So much you must have witnessed firsthand."

"There was a lot of it, I know."

She turned a page and saw a picture of Darla and David. It was their wedding photo. "They look so happy."

"They are. They're trying for a baby right now."

"Wolves can still have kids?" she asked.

"Of course. The more kids the better."

"There's only you and your sister, though?"

"Yes, there's only me and my sister. My parents didn't want any more kids after the two of us. Dad was helping the whole pack, and we all work together. You've seen us. It's one big family, and we all take care of each other."

"It must be nice."

"Foster homes for you, right?" he asked.

"Yeah. I was the girl who was always overlooked. I was never wanted."

"You are wanted."

"Now I am. Back then, I wasn't. There were a few times I nearly got a family, but they always wanted someone … different. I didn't talk a lot when I was younger. I was always a little withdrawn. Didn't trust easily either."

He reached out, tucking a strand of hair behind her ear. "Lettie?"

"She was the first person I trusted. Her secret was always safe with me."

Hayley looked up and saw he held out a piece of paper. "What is this?" she asked.

"I had to call in a couple of favors, but I found her. She lives in England with her very wealthy mate, and she didn't forget about you either. I've invited her to come and visit us, and she would really like to see you."

She took the piece of paper. "What is this?"

"Contact details. They'll be arriving before the next full moon, but if you wanted to get in touch with her before then, her details are there."

"She's happy?"

"She is very happy, and very married, and very mated." He laughed. "The moment I said your name, she asked how you were, and that she tried to get her family to take you. It's against pack law to take in a human female. They don't think it's healthy for you to grow up with people you'll never share that connection with."

"I get it, I do. I always wondered about her. I didn't even know where to start looking. It's so good to know she's happy." She placed the photo album to one side, and kneeled in front of him. "Thank you." Wrapping her arms around his neck, she held on tight, giving him a squeeze. It had been three days since she argued with him at the lake. Since then, he hadn't gone hiding. He had stayed with her, and they had been playing some games to help get to know each other.

They went to the lake often. She had found that she loved spending time with him.

Suddenly, he pulled away. "I'm just going to head to the shower."

She watched him leave, bereft at the empty feeling he had left behind. They had known each other a matter of days. Since that first night, she had been craving his touch even more. The pain had lessened, but the need was still there, and she was desperate for him. She wanted him so much.

Getting up from the bed, she made her way toward the bathroom door. Was it wrong that she craved him? That night they had spent together, holding each other, it made her crave so much more with him.

Watching Darla and David together made her yearn for something like what they shared. *You could have that.*

Before she could talk herself out of what she was about to do, she quickly removed her clothes, and entered the bathroom. Her heart pounded. She opened the shower door and stepped inside.

Micah was waiting for her.

"You knew I was coming?" she asked.

"I heard your heartbeat. It's racing. I don't want you to do anything you don't want to do."

She closed the door and faced him. "I want this, Micah. I need to be with you, more than anything else." She took a step closer and reached behind him for the soap, her nipples grazing his chest as she did. "Would you like me to go?"

"Hell no."

She smiled. "Then I'm here to stay." As she spoke those words, she knew it meant a lot more than just sex. She wanted to be his mate, and to be part of him, and to share this life with him.

Why deny something that they both wanted?

Soaping her hands, she handed him the bar and then began to wash his body. He was so hard, so big, and he belonged to her.

****

The moment Hayley's hands touched him, Micah's heart soared. He had been feeling their connection getting stronger, and he didn't want to lose that. Finding Lettie hadn't been easy. She had started with a pack in the states, and during a visit from a pack in England, her mate had been there.

"Touch me, Micah."

They were the words he loved to hear. Gripping her hips, he pulled her closer, and pressed his lips against her head.

"Don't you want to wash me as well?" she asked, teasing him.

He chuckled, grabbing the soap, which he had dropped. He soaped his hands, and had them on her body within a matter of seconds. He loved her curves. Her heavy tits, the roundness of her stomach, and the fullness of her hips. He loved every part of her.

Running his hands over her body, he felt the weight of her tits and glided down over her hips until he finally kneeled before her.

"Micah?"

"I've got to clean all of you." He lifted her foot to his shoulder, and started to run his hands up and down her thigh, teasing her close to her pussy, but never actually touching her. With her leg up, the lips of her sex were open, and he saw how aroused she was.

Placing her leg down, he did the same with the other. When he was done, he washed the soap off and then stood. He heard her moan, and her legs pressed together.

He held her chin, tilting her head back, and stared in her blue eyes. "You're so beautiful." He had thought that the first time he saw her, and his feelings had only gotten deeper.

With his other hand, he stroked down her body, finally cupping her between her thighs. She gasped his name, opening her thighs, giving him better access. Stroking her clit, he watched the arousal in her eyes.

"You're mine, Hayley."

"Yes."

She didn't fight him. Sliding his finger down to her core, he filled her pussy, marveling at how tight she was. He was going to have to bring her to orgasm, and prepare her. His cock was big, and if he didn't prepare her, he would probably hurt her.

Adding a second finger inside her, he pressed his thumb against her clit, teasing her.

"I want you, Micah. I want to be yours and belong to you."

"What changed your mind?" he asked, dropping a kiss to her neck.

"Because, I want to give this a try. I love being with you, and I believe you, Micah. Don't you feel how close we are?"

He did. He didn't know she was starting to feel the same. "I kidnapped you."

She chuckled. "I didn't say it was going to be easy, did I?"

He laughed along with her.

"I want you to make love to me tonight, Micah. Just make love, no mating, not yet. I want to talk about that."

"Okay, baby." He could make love to her. He was more than happy to make love to her all night long.

Spinning her around so that her back was pressed against his front, he teased her pussy at the same time he cupped her tit. Pinching the nipple, he stroked over her clit. Moving between her thighs, he alternated from stroking her nub, to filling her pussy. He wished it was his cock, but it would be soon.

She reached between them, and cupped him in her hand. "I'm not a virgin, Micah. You don't need to be gentle with me."

He nibbled her neck, sucking on her pulse. "I'm not going to be gentle with you. You feel how big I am. I'm going to make you come, and then I'm going to fuck you."

Pulling his fingers from her pussy, he stroked over her clit. Her orgasm began to build, and he kissed her neck, kissing along the back, and teasing her.

"I'm not going to last, Micah." She spoke his name on a scream as she came. He listened to the sound, relishing the scent in the room.

Before she had even finished, he picked her up in his arms, and carried her toward their bedroom. Dropping her down on the bed, he stared at her. His woman, his mate, slick with the water from the shower, and tempting him in ways he had never felt.

His cock was leaking pre-cum. "Do you want me to wear a condom? I'm clean. I don't carry disease, and you're not fertile."

"No. I don't want anything between us. I want to feel you inside me."

Gripping his cock, he placed the tip at her entrance, and slowly, inch by inch, sank inside her.

Filling his mate, he wrapped his arms around her, staring into her eyes as he thrust the final inches inside her.

"I love you, Hayley. I love you more every single

day."

She cupped his cheek. "I think I'm falling in love with you, too. It's crazy. Love is supposed to take years, but I don't know what it is." She chuckled. "Maybe it was you kidnapping me? Kind of romantic."

He pulled out of her pussy until only the tip of him was inside. He watched her, making sure that he didn't hurt her.

"You feel amazing," he said as he began to slowly rock inside her.

Her hands moved to his back, her nails sinking into his flesh as she held onto him. "Please, Micah. Oh, my."

His slow thrusts turned up a notch until he was driving inside her with so much force that the bed was hitting the wall.

"I love you, Hayley. Fuck, baby," he said, groaning as, with a final thrust, he came, filling her up.

The pleasure consumed both of them, and the spilling of his seed set Hayley off on a second orgasm. He held her tightly to him, never wanting to let go.

Chapter Seven

Three days later

Hayley moaned as she lowered herself onto Micah's hard cock. They were sat in his living room. The television played in the background.

"How does the mating work?" she asked.

"I have to bite you."

"Bite? I thought that was vampire." She groaned as he gripped her hips and slammed her down onto his cock. The past three days had been spent in a sexual bliss of fucking. They hadn't done much in the way of mating talk, and most nights Hayley dreamed about it. Her dreams were spent thinking about belonging to Micah, of being his mate, of having his children, and a life together.

She had gotten over their initial meeting. He wasn't a bad man, and even though he shouldn't have kidnapped her, she kind of understood why he did it. Micah was acting on instinct. He needed his mate, and she had been difficult with him. There was no way she would have ever gone with him without being forced. She knew that, and deep down, so did Micah.

"No, vampires need to kill first, drain you, and then feed you their blood."

"How does it work with a mate then?" she asked.

"I bind you to me with sex and a bite. You have to be willing to become mine, baby, and it has to be at the full moon."

"Why the full moon?"

"It has power all on its own. Each mated couple has to wait for the full moon."

"Does it have to be this full moon, or can it be when you're ready?" she said.

He slid a finger between her slit and began to

stroke her clit. "It can be any full moon. Mates can wait months, or even years if they want. I've never heard of mates doing that though. It's always done as soon as possible."

She didn't stop thrusting up and down on his cock as he teased her clit. Seating him to the hilt inside her, she screamed his name, needing him deeper even still.

"I don't want to wait either," she said. Holding onto his thick shoulders, she fucked him harder, knowing in her heart she was making the right decision. "I want us to mate at the full moon, Micah. No more waiting."

He stopped, and she groaned, wriggling on his lap. "Please, don't stop."

"You don't want to go back to your old life?" he asked.

"No. I want this life with you."

He stroked her clit to orgasm, and only when her cream soaked his cock, did he take her to the sofa, and start to fuck her hard. She loved it when he took charge. Sex with Micah was completely out of this world. He stared into her eyes and looked deep inside her. There was always something between them. Was it their mating? They belonged together, and whenever she was with him, the world fell away. They shared a passion she wasn't used to, but she relished every second with him, and she loved him. She had tried to fight it, but she did love him. How could she not?

She cried his name like she always did when he came inside her, his cum filling her up once again as he collapsed over her. He always moved a little so he wouldn't hurt her.

"You won't regret giving yourself to me."

She smiled. "I know I won't. I don't regret anything. Not one second of it." She locked their fingers together. "The pain inside me, it's lessening. Why?"

"You're accepting me now. Before, you were fighting what our souls needed."

"Souls are not real."

"I think they are. We're joined, Hayley. Together, and there is no getting away from that. We belong to each other."

The pain inside her had lessened, and she had found the arousal easier to deal with. She had stopped fighting. She didn't know exactly when, but it had happened.

"I never thought something like this would happen to me," she said. "Do you think that was why I was always interested in wolves? On a deeper level, I was mated to one, or at least, destined to be mated to one."

"It could have been. I don't know much about human and wolf matings. I know they're rare, but that doesn't mean they're any less special."

She smiled. "I'm special to you?"

"You wouldn't see me calling in a bunch of favors for just anyone, babe, and I certainly wouldn't have risked getting on the wrong side of the law if I didn't want you."

She touched his face, stroking over the hard bristles of his day-old stubble. "Thank you."

"For what?" he asked.

"For not being normal, and for coming to take me. I know we've had a few problems, but I love being here. I loved being here for my vacation, and I knew I was going to return."

"How did you end up in Forest Palm?" he asked.

"I closed my eyes and dropped my finger to a map. I think fate had something to do with this."

He groaned. "What am I going to do with you?"

"Love me for the rest of our lives?"

"Love you, that's exactly what I'm going to do."

****

"I've not seen Lettie so excited about anything. When she got your call, she was like a different person," William said. "How long have you been together?"

"A couple of weeks. You know she doesn't wear a mating mark," Micah said. "We're mating at the next full moon in a couple of days."

He watched Lettie and Hayley in the backyard of his cabin. They were sat on the steps, and he saw they were both talking at the same time. Every now and again, they would stop and hug. They were clearly close, and he was happy to see that. Okay, he was a little jealous as someone had known Hayley for longer, but there was nothing he could do about that now. Nothing at all.

"You're handling this okay," William said.

"Did Lettie talk about her?"

"Her human friend? Yes, she did. She wanted to find her, and I was worried that her search would lead to nothing. Still, I asked for her pack to look into what happened to Hayley Ford. I was going to reach out and see if she wanted to meet Lettie."

"Why were you worried?"

"People change. I didn't know if Lettie's memories were the same, or if Hayley would want anything to do with the girl who abandoned her. Lettie felt that was what she did, abandoned her. Humans are strange creatures. Lettie adored her, and I love my mate. I'll do anything for her."

"Me, too."

There was another hug, and he saw both women were crying together. It was next to impossible not to listen in on their conversation, so he did.

"You're so beautiful, Hayley. You always were."

"You've always been sweet."

"And you're a mate. I should have known you

were. You were always so trusting. Most people would have screamed when they saw parts of me changing. Not you. You were always there, keeping an eye on me." Lettie reached out, touching a curl. "I missed you."

"I missed you, too. I didn't know who had taken you, and I'm not a rich woman, far from it. I wanted to search for you every single day. Just to know you were happy. Even if you didn't want to see me, you know?"

"I know, and now you're about to be mated. I mean, I can't believe it. We're not losing touch again."

They hugged.

"How is your rich English man? He looks a bit … stern," Hayley said.

At his side, William tensed. "He's not stern. He's lovely. You just need to get to know him."

"You're stern," Micah said. "I was a kidnapper a few weeks ago. Don't worry about it."

"I'm not. I'm used to being called many things. I've got a stick up my ass, straitlaced, and all other kinds of things. Stern is quite mild."

"You're welcome to stay as long as you want," Micah said. "Our women are going to visit."

"I already figured that. We'll talk more in the future. I'm just happy to see my woman exactly that: happy."

Micah could relate.

Later that night, Hayley leaned against the doorframe, rubbing moisturizer on her hands, as she smiled at him. Micah sat on the bed, pretending to do a crossword puzzle. "That look doesn't suit you," she said.

"It doesn't?"

"Nope. We need to be married for twenty years before you start doing the crossword in bed."

He put the paper down, along with the pen, and eased the blankets back, revealing his rock hard cock.

"What about this? Does this seem more me?"

She nodded and walked toward him. "Thank you for inviting Lettie here. It was wonderful being with her. The years faded away, and it didn't feel like we were alone anymore."

He picked her up and positioned her to straddle his hips. "I will do whatever you need. All you ever have to do is ask."

"Lettie approves of you."

"She does?" he asked, already knowing Lettie did. They had talked on the phone before her visit. She had asked him a hundred and one questions, making sure he was the right guy for her friend.

"You know she does. She told me that you talked a lot."

"I didn't want you getting hurt."

"I love you, Micah. Really, I do. I thought you were an ass with the whole kidnapping thing. You love so much, and you act in ways that make no sense, but in a weird kind of way, they do."

He touched her cheek. "I only knew that I wanted you, and I had to have you."

"Romantic," she said, chuckling.

"No regrets?" he asked.

"Ask me in twenty years if I have any regrets."

Epilogue

Mating moon

Micah stood behind his mate as she stared at the mark he had given her. He had taken her to the lake, ordering the rest of the pack away. Lettie and William had also given them their privacy.

"This means I belong to you?" she asked.

"Don't you feel me?" He wrapped his arm around her waist, pressing his body against hers. Their bond was sealed, and their fates now entwined together. He sensed the love she felt for him, and he allowed her to feel his own love for her.

She closed her eyes. "Micah?"

"It's how you make me feel. I'm totally, utterly devoted to you. There are no words that are worthy of the love I feel for you." He kissed her neck.

"I can feel it." She rested against him. "I love you, too, Micah. So much."

"Any regrets?" he asked again. He couldn't help it.

She chuckled. "I told you to ask me that in twenty years. I don't have any regrets, and I know I'm never going to have them. The way you make me feel, not many have that, Micah. I love you, and I know my feelings for you are only going to get better."

He turned her in his arms.

The moment the full moon had been high in the sky, he had led her down to the lake, knowing she loved that part of the forest. They had torn each other's clothes off, and he had brought her to orgasm with his mouth on her pussy twice. Only when she was ready had he filled her with his cock, and then marked her flesh. When he came, he'd filled her with his cum, sealing their mating together.

Hayley had been open to him, and he'd felt her love for him pour into him with each thrust of his cock. He hoped he would make her happy, that he would give her everything as she had given him. Against all of the odds, she had fallen in love with him.

"Ask me again in twenty years if I have any regrets. I know what I'm going to say."

He smiled, and twenty years later, he asked, and she told him to come back in another twenty. Ten kids together, dogs, cats, and a pack to look after, he knew there was no chance of her ever having regrets. He loved her more than any man ever could, and in return, she gave him her heart.

The End

FINDERS KEEPERS

Stacey Espino

Copyright © 2017

Chapter One

"I'm sure it was just a misunderstanding. He could have missed his flight. Maybe—"

"Stop," said Hailey. "Just stop."

Her asshole of a fiancé had skipped out of their official engagement dinner, but that was the least of her worries. Their entire relationship was a joke. After eight months together, two of them secretly engaged, she knew he'd cheated on her at least twice. George's wingman always defended him, insisting men had "needs". Just because Hailey wanted to save her virginity for the right time didn't make his other women okay. She never should have forgiven him the first time. He'd crushed her already fragile self-esteem, and now she felt fractured beyond repair.

"I'll try his cell again," said Karl.

"Forget it. Cancel the dinner, cancel everything. I'm done." Hailey adjusted her purse over her shoulder and marched out of the hotel lobby with as much dignity as possible—which wasn't much at this point. She felt small and stupid, like a Grade-A idiot for believing she could build a future with a spoiled playboy like George.

"Hailey, wait…"

She ignored Karl, and George's other friends, as

she walked back to her car. They'd never liked her anyway—she wasn't high society or a size zero. She'd only met George because she worked at the coffee shop near his office. He'd been fun and flirty at first, but he soon lost interest, turning his attention to new conquests.

Once in the safety of her car, she locked the door, gripped the steering wheel, and stared blankly at the windshield. She felt numb, lost, and before long, a deep sadness settled in. Why was she so unlovable? Hailey was thirty-two, not twenty-two, so her hope of finding Prince Charming dwindled with each passing year. Without warning, her eyes welled up with tears. She felt like a child, the same one who'd been shipped from one foster home to another—never wanted, never belonging. Her vision blurred, all her emotions rushing to the surface, a volatile mixture of anger and despair. She would have sat in the parked car feeling sorry for herself indefinitely, but George's horde of friends slowly gravitated to the parking lot, so she decided to get the hell out of Dodge.

According to the whispers in the lobby, George was spending the weekend with his new flavor of the month. The coward could have at least had the decency to cancel the fucking engagement dinner.

It had been a five-hour drive to the new mountain-side hotel surrounded by hundreds of acres of nature. Hailey was in no shape to make the long trek home. Not yet. She drove a few miles from the hotel, turned down a narrow roadway, and parked when she hit a dead end. She stepped out of the car and took a deep, cleansing breath. The air smelled of pine and earth, nothing like she was used to, living in the city. The only sounds were the multitude of birds, insects, and the soft crunch of leaves beneath her flats. It was like another world in the old growth forest, and she definitely needed an escape.

Maybe she'd stay here forever, avoiding reality and the never-ending heartbreak that was her life. Hailey had no destination or plan, she just kept hiking deeper and deeper, her mind scattered in a hundred different directions.

After traversing the forest for well over an hour, she could hardly move another muscle. Exhaustion from the physical and mental stress pulled at her, so she settled on a bed of matted leaves, too tired to care about creepy crawlies. She thought about George and wondered if he ever really cared about her. She wondered if she could handle seeing him at the coffee shop again. God, how would she ever be able to face her life again?

****

Darius did his third patrol of the new resort. It was difficult convincing his wolf to accept the monstrosity. Nine months had passed since the ribbon-cutting, so he expected to be more at peace with himself.

"Reports about wolf sightings won't go over well. Just sayin'."

Darius wanted to ignore Thorn. His beta was all for progress, blending their wolf and human worlds into some seamless paradise. It wasn't natural, and Darius only reluctantly accepted the change. If it were up to him, he'd keep their ancient forests as pristine as they were centuries earlier. His wolf was not tolerant of humans on their land, and even now it took all his resolve not to make a scene.

"Trust me, I don't look forward to these patrols."

"Then why bother?" asked Thorn.

Patrols might have been common pack duties, not something fit for the alpha, but Darius felt the need to keep tabs on the resort. At the first signs of what he considered an inevitable disaster, he wanted to deal with it personally. He refused to blindly look the other way in the name of progress.

"I think you're going soft in your old age. Are you sure you're not more human than wolf?" Darius asked.

"Without change comes extinction. Don't forget that."

He didn't have to argue with his beta, because within seconds his presence was gone. The thoughts in his head cleared, leaving only the peaceful lull of the forest. These days, Darius wasn't so sure if it was peaceful or lonely. He had his pack, but lately he felt like a lone wolf. In over five generations of alpha shifters, at forty-five, he was now the oldest on record to still be unmated. Thorn thought Darius was a stone-cold bastard with no room for a female in his life. Maybe he was right.

Before he let his thoughts destroy him, he began to run—away from the resort, away from the silence, away from his growing bitterness. He used to be satisfied with his place as alpha of the Northern Summit Pack, and it seriously pissed him off that the darkness inside him was throwing his life off its axis. It was easy to blame the new resort, giving him an outlet to vent his frustration, but it was so much more.

Darius didn't slow down the punishing pace, darting around trees, leaping over exposed roots, and running until his muscles burned. His black wolf savored the freedom, the shelter of the woodland, and the physical exertion. He knew this forest better than he knew himself, every tree and rocky outcropping. There was comfort in the familiarity.

He had no destination, only focusing on the wind caressing his fur—until an unusual scent halted his course. He stopped dead, his hackles instinctively rising, his lips pulling up over lethal fangs. Darius did not tolerate intruders. If one of those drunken tourists were lost in his woods again, he'd give them a nightmare to remember. If a rival wolf dared to cross Northern Summit territory lines, he'd pay with his life.

Darius moved with focus and stealth, barely disturbing a leaf. He kept low, using all his senses as he moved in on the potential threat. His packmates weren't nearby, probably drooling over the modern marvel with its human luxuries.

When he found a body on the ground, he began to circle. The sleeping female was far from the resort or any other human establishment. She wasn't dressed for the woods, wearing shoes that were too delicate for the terrain and clothes that wouldn't protect her from the rough elements. She was curled up on her side, her lush curves not easy to hide under her layer of clothing. Mascara stained her cheek, a sign she'd been crying. He growled involuntarily.

Thorn would nag him for not keeping his distance, but he couldn't keep away. Why was he so fascinated? He moved in closer, breathing in deeply at her neckline. When he exhaled, her brown waves of hair briefly fluttered. Her scent was sweet and decadent. He closed his eyes and relished the sensation of every cell in his body coming to life. For a brief moment, Darius truly believed she'd been sent by the gods. Then he thought better. Nothing had ever been handed to him. He'd worked for every rank and dollar, and it seemed too good to be true that his mate would be delivered on his proverbial doorstep. When she began to stir, he moved to the shelter of the brushwood, not wanting to startle her. And terrorizing humans was usually his favorite pastime.

She pushed herself up into a sit, tucking hair behind an ear. Her eyes were glassy and confused as she took in her surroundings. "Where am I?" she whispered to herself. "Shit!"

The human muttered as she struggled to stand,

complaining about her aches and the setting sun. All Darius could see was fucking perfection—thick curves and natural beauty like he'd never seen in his lifetime. A deep-seated possessiveness flooded his veins, something new and all-encompassing.

He wanted to fuck her. To own her.

Darius stepped back, scarcely able to keep his wolf in check. Could this little human be his woman, his mate? He'd either lost his mind or fate had a sick sense of humor. Why would he feel such a connection to a human? And he had no doubt she was human. He expected to find a she-wolf, like all the alphas before him, if he found a mate at all.

She stumbled along the unbeaten paths, using low tree branches and saplings for leverage. Within the next twenty minutes, the sun would completely set, all the northern forest predators coming to life. Nothing in the darkness inspired fear in Darius, but this human female would be an easy target. His need to protect her overwhelmed him.

"I'm such an idiot!" she shouted. Too loud. The last thing she needed was attention drawn to her. These woods were rife with wolves, bears, coyotes, and wild cats.

She unceremoniously trudged in the direction of the roadway, so he slipped ahead to investigate. When he finally reached a dirt road, he found her car. It was a beige two-door with rust along the lower frame. Was that duct tape holding the side mirror on the car? When he leaped up against the glass and saw her purse on the passenger seat, he was tempted to shift into his skin so he could find out more about this mysterious woman. But before he could shed his fur, he heard her scream.

Chapter Two

How had she slept so long? She didn't even know what time it was, but it was dark. Darker than she'd known possible. Every little noise made her adrenaline spike. She might have entered the forest for an escape, but now all she wanted to see was her piece of shit car. Hailey wasn't even sure if she was moving in the right direction, but she progressed quickly, eager to reach the edge of the woods and some sort of civilization. When she heard the yipping of dogs, she knew she was in trouble.

Stay calm, Hailey. She'd never felt so alone, and she'd thought she hit rock bottom in the parking lot of the resort. This was so much worse. Her feet were wet, her body chilled to the core, and she couldn't even count the number of cuts and scratches she had from wandering blindly through the thick underbrush. George was probably fucking his new plaything while Hailey was about to die a grizzly death. She would have screamed for help again, but knew it would only attract unwanted attention.

More animals moved in, the eerie sounds coming from all around her. Hailey's mind was a whirlwind of thoughts as she tried to remember every nature show she'd ever watched. The growling and barking echoed in all directions. It was complete chaos, a horror show she wanted no part of. She fell to her knees every few steps, exhausted and nearly hopeless. Hailey almost laughed aloud as she imagined what a great meal she'd make compared to one of George's stick-thin girlfriends. She was only a breath away from losing it.

"Don't be afraid." The male voice was deep and surreal. Was she hearing God in her last minutes? When very real hands hoisted her easily to her feet, she gasped, reality rushing back to her clouded mind.

"Who's there?"

He didn't answer her question, but took one of her hands and pressed it against a large tree to balance her. "Stay here. Don't move until I come back."

Who was she to argue? At this point, the stranger was her only hope.

****

Darius had crossed too many lines to fathom. Luckily, the sun had set, so the human couldn't see he was naked and oddly aroused. The animals closing in on her weren't shifters. They were just wild coyotes and it wouldn't take much for him to scare them off once he shifted back into his alpha wolf. He was more concerned with the fact his own pack was coming to investigate. They'd all wonder why he was protecting the human female. He didn't know how he'd explain what was happening. Darius wasn't so sure himself.

The little bastards lunged at him. Even in his human skin, he had his wolven night vision. He smirked as he began to shift, looking forward to dealing with the pests. His bones elongated, his teeth and claws sharpening. Within seconds, he was larger than any natural wolf. He was the alpha of these woods, and the hungry coyotes surrounding his woman quickly realized the fact. They backed off after scenting his dominant wolf. If he wanted to, he could take on the seven of them without breaking a sweat. With his packmates now minutes away, it would be a bloodbath. But Darius had no desire for carnage tonight. He only wanted to keep the human safe. He chased them clear of the area, putting the fear of the devil in them.

Once the evening hush settling back in, Darius shifted. He needed to know everything he could about this human besides the fact she made his cock harder than oak.

"What's your name, little one?" he asked.

She hadn't moved. The scent of fear tainted the air. "*Hailey.*"

"What are you doing way out here? Don't you know the forest is a dangerous place at night? You could have been killed."

"I thought it was a good idea before the sun set," she said. "But now you're here."

"Yes. I am." Where was his usual distain for humans? There wasn't anywhere in the world he'd rather be than by her side.

"Were those wolves?"

"If they were wolves, you wouldn't have heard them coming. They were coyotes."

"Still sounds bad. Are they gone?"

"There's nothing to worry about. I won't let anything hurt you."

His pack surrounded them. He could see Thorn's wolf in the near distance. "Let's get you back to your car."

He didn't want to be disturbed. Darius pressed a hand to the small of her back and led her through the forest. She reached for him when she couldn't keep her balance, but he reluctantly kept his distance. Darius had never been more confused, and as alpha, he prided himself on always knowing his next move. He wasn't even sure what he'd do once they got to her car. His wolf demanded he keep her, and although he agreed, part of him felt he was betraying his heritage by not keeping tradition.

"What were you doing out here anyway?" she asked, her breath labored as she plodded along.

"I live nearby."

"In the forest?"

"Nearby."

Her fear had completely subsided, and it pleased him that his presence made her feel safe. There was nothing he couldn't protect her from. They'd almost reached her car. The longer he walked with her, the more her scent permeated every facet of his being. He was becoming addicted.

"I'm not used to any of this. I live in the city."

"You're far from home," he said.

"I was at the new resort for my engagement dinner. But I guess I was dumped, jilted, whatever you want to call it." She sighed. "It was probably a blessing in disguise."

He bristled, not liking the sound of another man in the picture. "Then he's a fool. And you deserve much better."

She chuckled. "Sure. When you see me in the light of day, you might not feel the same."

How could any man choose to walk away from her? Human men were fickle and weak. All he could think about was claiming her, sinking his fangs into her tender skin as a warning to other males to stay away. Darius had fucked enough human women, but not a single one had this effect on him.

Hailey was different, special, *his*.

He'd be a fool to ignore the mating call, and that was exactly what it was. How was he supposed to convince her that she was his mate? It would be so simple with a she-wolf, instinct taking the place of courting. Hailey might be his biggest challenge yet.

He stopped, tilting her chin up to make his point clear. "I promise, I like everything I see. I've never wanted another woman more."

She gasped, her lips parting. The scent of her

desire wasn't lost on him. "You don't even know me. I don't know you…"

"Then we need to change that." He ran the backs of his fingers along the side of her face. Gods, she was beautiful. Her eyes were a vivid shade of blue, a contrast to her dark hair. A spattering of freckles across her nose and minimal make-up gave her an air of innocence.

"That's easier said than done," she said.

"Are you worried you won't be attracted to *me*?"

"No… I'm just scared to trust again. Everyone I've ever cared about has let me down. I'm not sure I'm up for more disappointment."

"Then I'll have to show you," he said.

"Show me what?"

"How a real man treats a woman."

****

Holy shit. Hailey's body was lighting up like a Christmas tree. Was she that desperate for love that she'd fall for the sweet words of a complete stranger? One she couldn't even see? But his voice … it was so deep and gravelly, making her knees weak. For all she knew, he could be a crazy axe-murderer. Yes, she was definitely desperate. She was too emotionally damaged from the whole George ordeal to think clearly.

And even though she was in no position to judge, he could be some toothless hillbilly. Maybe he was if he lived in the bush. She just needed to forget the whole weekend and get back to the city. Falling for a stranger's sweet words was a very bad idea.

"I really need to go…"

"Your car's just ahead," he said. "You'll be able to find your way from here."

She expected him to argue and push for a date. It was kind of disappointing when he didn't. She still remembered the way he touched her, his skin so warm and rough, making her dream up all kinds of fantasies. But happily ever afters weren't in the cards for Hailey. She fiddled with the keys in her pocket and got the headlights to snap on when she unlocked the doors. Her body nearly melted into the ground with relief. It was so good to have her sight back. As soon as she got her bearings, she turned to the side to get the first glimpse of her rescuer.

He was gone.

Hailey whirled around, a full three-sixty, and still nothing. How could he have disappeared so quickly? It didn't make sense. Had she insulted him? She didn't even know his name. After her initial shock wore off, she rushed to get into the safety of her car. It was time to make the long drive home. Hailey needed to erase this day from memory, but forgetting her mystery hero might not be so easy.

****

"What was that about?" asked Thorn.

Darius stood motionless as the cones of light from Hailey's car disappeared from view. It had taken all his resolve not to stop her from leaving. He clenched his fists at his sides as his wolf thrashed within him. Darius could scarcely control his volatile energy.

"Boss?"

"That car doesn't leave Northern Summit territory," Darius said. "I don't care how, but that female will be staying at the resort tonight. *Unharmed.*"

Normally his beta would argue or ask for clarification, but not now. All three of his packmates shifted seamlessly together, rushing off as ordered. Even though most his pack was currently off territory, he had complete faith in his men to get the job done. If only he had as much conviction in his ability to court a human. His alpha aura would have been enough for a she-wolf.

Hailey was new terrain. The mating call still hummed within him, instinct demanding he claim what was rightfully his. His previously scattered emotions had been solidified. Nothing would stop him from making Hailey his.

Chapter Three

She never wanted to set foot in this lobby again. Just being back at the resort brought back the menagerie of negative feelings that had nearly destroyed her earlier.

"Can I help you?" asked the man at the front desk.

"I had a room reserved for the weekend under Hailey Robinson."

The cops at the road block insisted her only option for the night was the resort. So, she was back where she started, the last place she wanted to be. She already began mentally calculating how much the room charge was going to set her back this month. Hailey was going to have to live off Ramen Noodles for a few weeks.

After unpacking her small bag and preparing for bed, she turned off all the lights and wrapped a blanket over her shoulders. She slid open the patio door and stepped out onto the shadowed balcony. There was a sharp chill in the air, only the vague outline of the forest in the distance. She took a deep breath, closing her eyes as she leaned against the wall. A few stars still shone through despite the unnatural lighting created by the resort. She wanted to make a wish, but she knew it wouldn't come true. How many times had she asked for a family, a good job, a perfect body, or a man to love her? She'd given up on her dream for love, but still believed it was better than settling for George.

Hailey had a deep-seated need to belong, and a craving for a love so unconditional it probably didn't exist. She could blame her insecurities on her dysfunctional life as a foster kid, but she was a grown woman now and could only fault herself.

What she couldn't get off her mind was her mystery man. Just his voice had made her swoon. He sounded so confident in his ability to be everything she could ever want in a man. And she desperately wanted to believe him. Only he was gone, like everyone else who'd walked out of her life.

A wolf bayed in the distance, then another. It gave her the chills. She was safe on the fourth floor, but decided to get inside for the night.

****

"Are you going to tell me what the fuck's going on?" asked Thorn.

His beta and packmates did as he'd ordered, getting Hailey safely to the resort for the night. Now he had time to breathe, time to think.

"She was lost in the forest. I was just making sure she got home all right."

Thorn scoffed. "Don't try to bullshit a bullshitter, Darius."

He exhaled, knowing he couldn't hide the truth forever, especially since he'd never shown kindness to a human before. "Fine. I want her," he admitted.

"Then why didn't you take her?"

"She's a human."

"We've both fucked humans before. What's the difference now?" asked Thorn.

Darius stood up and paced around the campfire they'd started earlier. The sparks and embers danced up towards the blackened sky. "I don't want to fuck her. I want to keep her." At this point, he wasn't interested in twisting the facts. Darius was alpha and his word was law. "She's my mate."

Thorn bolted to his feet, and Jacob and Brass couldn't hide the shock on their faces. "Your mate? That's impossible!"

"How do you know?" asked Brass.

He shrugged. "I can't explain it. I don't *need* to

explain it. My problem is figuring out how to convince that girl she belongs here. With me."

"With a werewolf," Thorn corrected.

"Yeah, a werewolf. You're not helping." Darius had no one to advise him because he'd never heard of a shifter and human mating. And he knew Hailey wasn't just any human, but a fucking virgin. His wolf sensed it almost immediately.

"You want us to bring her to you?" asked Jacob.

Darius shook his head. "I have to do things right. Kidnapping her definitely won't earn me any points."

"This can't go well. Humans and shifters don't mix, Darius," said Brass. "You're the one who taught us to stay away from them."

"It's fucking unnatural," said Thorn.

Darius cracked his neck to each side, his skin flushing hot. "This isn't a debate. That female is mine, and I fully plan on claiming her."

"Well, this should be entertaining," said Thorn, settling back on the downed log.

"It will, because you'll all be helping me. Get ready to play human."

Tomorrow would be pivotal in his courting of Hailey. He was excited that fate gave him a mate, but also cautious. She seemed too good to be true—beautiful, sexy, sweet, and innocent to men. Darius wanted to promise her the world. And an alpha always kept his word.

****

Before Hailey opened her eyes, she'd almost believed the George fiasco was a nightmare. And her forest hero was a dream. It took her a few minutes to remember where she was and what had transpired the day before, and then reality came crashing down. *You sure know how to pick 'em, Hailey.*

Although not giving George sex could have been one of the factors to push him away, she was glad she hadn't given a cheater like him her virginity. She might have been thirty-two, but her innocence wasn't a hindrance as most would suspect. It was her only possession of value. She'd had too many chances to lose it, and sometimes had to fight to keep it, even as a child, but she had. It was hers, and it gave her a small sense of control in an otherwise powerless life.

She reached for the invoice under the door, but it was actually an invitation. Hailey had to read it twice because it said she was invited to a ball. She laughed out loud as she imagined a pumpkin coach and fairy godmother.

"A ball? Really?" she said. "Yeah, I think I'll pass." She tossed the invitation on the bed before preparing for the day. It was time to get back to reality and put the past behind her.

As she made her way down the stairs to check-out, she heard familiar voices in the lobby. She stopped to listen before opening the final door in the hallway. It was Karl and … George. *You've got to be kidding me!*

There was no way she could face him, not now or ever. Hailey decided George couldn't stay in the lobby indefinitely, and she had another few hours until she had to turn her key-cards in, so she escaped out the back door to waste some time exploring the well-manicured grounds.

Why had George bothered to show up? Had he tired of his new fling already? Had he made another mistake and wanted to beg for her forgiveness again? She had none left to give.

The sky was a brilliant blue, the air sweet and crisp. A delicate layer of dew still carpeted the grass, darkening the edges of her running shoes. She didn't care. Hailey wanted to savor the sights, to enjoy this brief escape. As she cut across the lawns, she admired the lavish flower gardens—purples, reds, and pinks. Back home in the city, the only beauty she could have found were the hanging flower baskets along the downtown strip.

Forget George, forget everything, she reminded herself. She inhaled some of that fresh country air and kept walking toward the woods. It was morning, so that foreboding element was no longer present. Instead, the wall of massive oaks represented a hideaway, a refuge she desperately needed for a short while.

She found an old tree stump a few yards into the forest and sat down, closing her eyes as she tried to absorb the multitude of sounds from insects and birds, to the squirrels scampering in the branches above. She was so content that she couldn't help but smile. When she opened her eyes again, there was a large gray wolf standing directly in front of her. She hadn't even heard a leaf being disturbed. Hailey froze, unsure what she should do. The wolf stared intently, its upper lip quivering. It looked intense, its ears back and hackle forming. Should she play dead? What would it feel like to be eaten alive?

She swallowed hard.

Hailey was in shock, not daring to move a muscle. They were at a stalemate when a massive wolf leaped out from behind her. The new beast knocked the other away with its sheer size and strength. They rolled briefly, the ground shuddering, until standing off, head to head. A fresh rush of adrenaline coursed through her body, making her light-headed. This wolf was much larger, pitch black, and looked ready to kill. It challenged the gray wolf with two-inch long fangs and enough bravado to make a Grizzly submit.

She held her breath, hoping for a miracle, and scolding herself for entering a forest again. When the gray wolf slowly backed away in defeat, she knew she was the next victim.

****

"Don't get that close to her again," Darius warned. He took a few breaths to calm his beast. His territorial nature was off the fucking charts. Catching Brass up close and personal with his woman made him see red.

"I was just looking out for her, like you wanted," said Brass, as he lowered his head in submission and slowly retreated.

Darius knew his wolf would only get worse until he marked Hailey as his mate. *"Keep your distance."*

Once he'd gathered his wits, he remembered the human. The scent of her fear was sharp in the air, and he was the reason. He had planned to find her in his human form, not like this. He'd deal with Brass for putting him in this position. He'd broken their law—wolves and humans didn't mix. But then again, a human was Darius's mate. *Un-fucking-believable.*

He turned to face Hailey. She hadn't moved, her body paralyzed like a deer in his sights. How could he fix this? Darius would have to earn her trust. She'd have to get used to his wolf form eventually.

He lowered to the ground, and settled in front of her, trying to appear peaceful and gentle. She stared, only her eyes moving. Gods, she was immeasurably more beautiful in the light of day. He wanted to talk to her, convince her that they were meant for each other, but he had to wait.

Every passing minute made him more anxious. She hadn't moved, her fear still ripe. He had to make first contact.

Darius sniffed her shoe and then rose to his feet and nudged her knee. He licked her hand, the only exposed skin he could find. She gasped and pulled back so fast it startled his wolf. He nuzzled his head in her lap, desperate to feel her affection. It took a lot of coaxing before she dared to touch him. The moment he felt her fingers comb into his fur, he wanted to purr like a fucking cat.

She cautiously stroked his head, so he stayed as still as he could. The last thing he wanted to do was spook her again. When her fear subsided, he looked up into her eyes, hoping to spark some sort of connection. Would she sense he was more than a common wolf? Did humans feel the mating bond? Her blue eyes were stunning, and she held eye contact with him as he'd hoped. When he stole a quick lick of her cheek, she actually giggled, stealing his heart completely.

"Am I in the Twilight Zone?" she asked. "Or maybe I'm dreaming…"

He couldn't answer, only able to savor the physical connection while it lasted. Darius imagined it would take a lot more effort to get this close as a human man. But as much as he wanted to be near Hailey, he needed to keep to his plan. He reluctantly backed away.

"It's okay. I won't hurt you," she said. She beckoned for him, reaching out a hand. It took all his resolve to deny her and retreat into the forest.

Chapter Four

Hailey finally made it to the check-out in the lobby, now clear of anyone familiar. She was still in a daze after her crazy run-in with the wild wolves. Either the resort fed and tamed them, or she'd had a once-in-a-lifetime experience. She'd felt a connection with the massive beast, and she wished he hadn't rushed away so quickly.

"I'd like to check out from room 405." She set the key-cards on the counter and waited, occasionally stealing peripheral glances around the lobby.

"I have a notice on file for you, ma'am. The roads to the city are closed. You've been given a complimentary room." He gave her a new set of keys. "We hope to see you at the luncheon this afternoon. It's included with your package."

She stood slack-jawed for a moment too long. "I don't understand. The roads can't be closed. I've seen new people arriving." Hailey wasn't going to specifically mention George's name.

"The sheriff was just in with the notice. I apologize for the inconvenience."

Hailey shook her head. She couldn't stay here indefinitely. Not to mention she had to be at work on Monday morning. "I'd like to speak with him, if possible."

"Of course." He picked up the phone, turned his head slightly to mask the brief conversation, and then faced her again. "The sheriff should be in conference room two, just down the hall to the right."

"Thank you." She took the new key-cards, just in case, and made her way down the hall. It was about time she got some real answers. Being trapped in the same hotel as George and his entourage was a living nightmare.

The door in question was partially open. She gave it a slight push. The focal point of the conference room was the massive oval table with a black mirror-finish. To her left was a full bar and floor-to-ceiling whiteboard. This was no Holiday Inn. Everything screamed money. By the far window stood two men in uniform. They were huge and muscular, definitely not the donut-eaters who frequented her coffee shop.

"Hailey Robinson?"

"Yes. Are you the sheriff?"

"No, I'm Officer Jacob. This is Officer Brass. The sheriff isn't on site. I was told you have questions about the road closure?"

She snapped back to the present, briefly taken aback by their larger-than-life presence. Hailey vaguely remembered them from last night at the road block. "Why is there a closure? I haven't heard about any bad weather. I really need to get home today."

"That's not possible."

Hailey frowned. "Why not?"

The men glanced at each other before Officer Jacob finally returned his attention to her. "It's dangerous. And top secret."

Really? "Was there a murder or something?"

"Something like that."

Heat began to creep up her collar as frustration settled in. She was going to demand to speak with the sheriff. "Surely they can allow cars to pass through. What about one lane? They can't just trap people here with no answers."

"Be a good girl and accept the free room," said Officer Brass.

Hailey crossed her arms over her chest. The nerve of these assholes. These backwoods cops were too much, way too much. They could at least pretend to be politically correct.

"And if I don't accept?"

"You can sleep in the lobby."

"Whatever." She turned to leave the room, her teeth grating so hard her jaw ached. There was no point in arguing with the cops, so she'd wait until she could get answers from the actual sheriff. As she stormed out the room, she crashed into a man walking down the hallway.

"I'm so sorry," she repeated as the stranger righted her with a hand to each shoulder, saving her from falling on her ass. He wore expensive Armani. She'd seen enough suits a week working downtown to know quality when she saw it. The businessman even smelled amazing—rich and musky.

"Why the rush?" he asked, his voice smooth and controlled. When she looked *up, up, up,* he had the cutest smirk on his face.

"I'm just a bit upset about the road closure."

He nodded thoughtfully. "It's a necessary inconvenience, but I'm a firm believer of making the best out of any given situation … like this one."

Her previous irritation fizzled away. This new guy stole all her focus. He was exactly what she envisioned a real man should be—five o'clock shadow, mature lines at the corners of his eyes, and a body built like a brick shithouse. His lips were full and the way he moved them was distracting.

"Will you be attending the luncheon?"

Hailey opened her mouth to speak, but no words came out. She felt like a lovesick school girl. The man's dark, narrowed eyes were sexy as sin. And the way he watched her every move made her squirmy in a very distracting way.

"Were you not invited?"

"Yes, I'll be going," she said, easily making up her mind.

He ran a hand through his tousled black hair. "I'd love to meet you there, *Hailey*."

The way he pronounced her name sent tingles to all the right places. *Wait, how does he know my name?* Maybe he was one of George's friends. She held her breath, uncertainty clouding her thoughts.

"Are you feeling okay?" He brushed the backs of his fingers along her cheek. She closed her eyes, savouring the familiar touch.

"It's you!" she blurted, taking a step back. She didn't even have to ask, she just knew this was her mysterious stranger, the one starring in all her recent fantasies. But it couldn't be. This man was no hillbilly. He wore a gold Rolex, so how could he live in the backwoods?

A knowing smile softened the sharper planes of his face. The last time they'd met it had been pitch dark. She imagined how disappointed he must be with his damsel-in-distress in the light of day. Hailey, on the other hand, couldn't keep her eyes off every perfect inch of him.

"I'm glad you made it safely to the resort," he said and then gave her a little wink.

"What happened? You just disappeared. You didn't even tell me your name."

"My name's Darius North." He stepped into her personal space, forcing her to back up until she hit the wall in the hallway. "I haven't stopped thinking about you."

He'd tongue-tied her again. Her senses magnified—each breath and every beat of her heart. He made her feel like the only woman in the world, so much more than the shadow she was accustomed to.

Hailey kept her eyes low, a wave of shyness and insecurity creeping in when she wanted to appear suave and confident. God, his lower half looked equally impressive judging by the bulge in his slacks. Not that she was an expert in cocks. "Thank you," she squeaked out.

He tilted her chin up, impossibly slow, until they were looking eye to eye. "For what?" he asked.

She swallowed before speaking "Saving me."

"I'll do anything for you, little human. You have no idea."

Hailey could only breathe and stare into those deep, dark eyes. Her pussy pulsed, heat chasing out in every direction. If he kept staring at her like that, she'd have a spontaneous orgasm and melt into a pool by his shiny black shoes.

"I'll be waiting for you in the dining hall," he said. "I'll reserve a table for the two of us."

She nodded, in shock that he wanted to have lunch with her—Hailey Robinson. And just like that, he was gone, continuing on down the hall as if she wasn't just ready to let him take her virginity against a wall. *What the hell just happened?* She couldn't move, her breathing still labored, and body a hot mess.

All she could think about was the luncheon, not far off now, and seeing Darius again. What she needed to do was get her ass to her new room so she could make herself presentable.

Her new room was on the sixth level, the top floor of the resort. *The penthouse*, she joked to herself. She expected something more simplistic than the room she'd reserved for herself and George. Since the hotel had to foot the bill for the road closure rooms and luncheon, she didn't expect much. And she wasn't picky.

After opening the door, she dropped her bag and

stared in awe. The rear wall had floor-to-ceiling glass with a breathtaking view of the forest out back. She walked in a trance, taking in everything from the king-size bed, red roses, and chocolate-covered strawberries. This wasn't possible. When she neared the glass wall, she noticed the Jacuzzi tub set into the floor, a bottle of wine on ice nearby. This had to be a mistake.

****

Darius waited in the lobby for his mate. He kept checking his watch, his nerves on edge being away from her. Being stuffed into a suit didn't help his discomfort. The luncheon was filling up with human socialites, and if it weren't for Hailey, he'd be anywhere but here. How ironic that a little human had stolen his heart. When he saw her coming, his cock reacted immediately. He watched each step she took, capturing every detail to memory. His wolf wanted him to snatch her away, claim her, and fuck her. It was his human side that gave him the composure he desperately needed to do things right.

Before she reached him, Hailey was flanked by three males, blocking her from his view. He growled his irritation.

"Problem, boss?" asked Thorn. His beta had been patrolling the resort, ready to assist Darius with his plan.

"Maybe."

He wanted to give his woman the fairy-tale experience, and he hoped it would be enough for her to choose him as a life mate. What he hadn't anticipated were outside complications.

"Hailey, let me explain," said the blond man. "I promise it's not what you think."

Darius could sense his mate's discomfort, and his fangs lengthened in response. At any moment, he'd lose all composure and make a scene he'd regret. "Thorn, you better deal with this."

His beta didn't hesitate, walking directly towards the group. "Is there a problem here?"

"No, there's no problem, Sheriff. I'm just talking with my fiancée."

"You're not my fiancé," Hailey snapped. "Why don't you go back to your girlfriend?"

"There's no one else," he said. "I was just delayed."

"Look, I'm not stupid, and I'm not doing this again. I'm done." Hailey whirled around and headed back to the elevators.

When the male attempted to chase after her, Thorn used an outstretched arm as a road block. "I don't think so, lover boy. She said she's done, so be smart and stay away from her."

"Excuse me? Have I broken the law?"

The little shit was one of those cocky bastards who came to the resort to play golf and boast about their toys. And he thought he had a chance with Darius's mate. Big fucking mistake.

"If I see you near that woman again, we're going to have a serious problem." Thorn walked away from the group with no further discussion.

Darius stayed in the lobby, shattered that his plans had been ruined. He had the best seat in the house reserved, and he looked forward to having a romantic lunch with Hailey. His pack wouldn't be able to keep up the roadblock ploy much longer, so he'd soon lose his window of opportunity to prove himself as a worthy mate in the human way. He didn't think hunting her down werewolf-style would be a hit.

He met up with his packmates at the rear of the resort. "Where the fuck did that asshole come from?"

Jacob shrugged. "We won't let him near your human."

This had to be the male who'd dumped Hailey. He was a fool, and he'd lost his chance.

Darius wanted to rip the human to unrecognizable shreds, and it wasn't out of the realm of possibility. Maybe the prick would take a walk in the woods.

"You should make your move, Darius. That guy looks like trouble," said Thorn.

"Do you think I'll let him have her? That I'll stand on the sidelines while he takes what's mine?"

Thorn tugged at the collar of his uniform. "Are you sure it's the mating call? Maybe you just need to get laid."

He was losing patience with his pack. They probably wanted to hit up the single females at the luncheon, but their libidos had to take a backseat until Darius had his woman.

"The only female I'll be fucking is my mate. Now that the lunch has gone to shit, I only have the dinner to get this right. Keep an eye on that male. He gets nowhere near Hailey."

Darius needed to let off some steam, which meant getting out of his suit so he could shift into his alpha wolf. But even that would have to wait. He'd never felt such aggression for another living thing until he set his eyes on Hailey's ex.

****

Why am I crying? Hailey blamed her emotional breakdown on the hurt and stress George had caused her, not just this weekend, but their entire relationship. Seeing him in the flesh again brought back a plethora of negative feelings. She'd put up with his bullshit because she didn't think she deserved anything better, and she desperately wanted to be loved. But it only took one man for her to consider the possibility that real love wasn't out of the question.

Her thoughts drifted to that deep voice and those fuck-me eyes. Darius had literally saved her life, and promised her the world. It only took a few words from him to make her spineless with desire. But as much as she wanted to run headlong into Darius's arms, she had to be cautious. It all seemed too good to be true. And she couldn't survive being burned again.

She flopped on her bed and stared at the ceiling. "I've lost my chance because of that idiot." Hailey had ditched her dream man at the luncheon because of George. She wanted to scream.

A knock at her door made her bolt up in the bed. Was it Darius? George? Her heart raced as she tiptoed to the door.

"Who is it?"

"I have a delivery from the front desk."

She exhaled before opening the door. A hotel staff member handed her a large pink box with matching bow. It wasn't too heavy. What the hell was it?

Hailey set the box on a chair and carefully lifted the lid. She wasn't used to getting surprises. Inside was a full-length black dress, one she'd never be able to afford. She held it up against herself and did a little spin. It was so extravagant, and she doubted she'd have the nerve to wear it in public. Without a note, she had no clue who'd sent it—and the possibilities excited and terrified her.

Chapter Five

As evening settled over his land, the moon barely revealing itself in the darkening sky, Darius felt his wolf coming to life. It would be a full moon tonight, the peak of his virility. It would take a herculean effort to play the gentleman tonight when all he wanted to do was hunt down Hailey and mark her as his mate. He stood in the shadows far outside the resort, watching the crowds of well-dressed guests make their way from the parking area to the ballroom. Everyone who was anyone in the district was in attendance. He only cared about one—Hailey Robinson.

There was one person standing in his way—George Halbridge in room 211. Thorn had pulled a load of background information up for him, including phone records, bank statements, and employment history. The piece of shit was using Hailey as a marketing strategy. Apparently marrying a little orphan from the poor side of town would give him huge brownie points at the law firm he worked for. But George didn't love Hailey. He had women on the side, and they were frequently turned over. His swagger was all a façade—the man currently lived off credit, hence the desperate ploy with Hailey.

Now Darius had to court his woman, keep the asshole at bay, and do it without hurting Hailey. She didn't need to know George had used her from the beginning. Not to mention, Darius had to pull her into his world, one she could consider a horror show or a fairy tale. He hoped to the gods she thought the latter.

"Hey." Thorn sauntered across the lawn towards him. They stood in the dark shadows, side-by-side, watching the lights and glamour of the hotel and guests in the distance.

Darius had nothing to say. In one day his entire world had turned upside down. More than half his pack was away this week, leaving only the four of them on Northern Summit territory. He felt like a body without its limbs, having his pack so scattered. But it was nothing compared to the mating call. He couldn't fuck this up.

"Do you think she loves him?" asked Thorn.

Darius whirled around, suppressing his urge to punch his beta in the face. "Why would you ask me that?"

Thorn was unaffected by his explosive energy. He shrugged. "That would be the worst-case scenario."

"My nerves are on edge here as it is. I don't need to be thinking about more potential disasters," Darius said.

The drone of crickets settled him. The forest surrounding the resort was home, giving him a small measure of peace under the circumstances.

"Do *you*?" Thorn asked.

"What?"

"Love her."

Darius took a cleansing breath. He was so messed up he forgot his beta only had his best interests in mind. There was no one in the world he trusted more. "It's the mating call," he explained. "It's more than love. It's everything."

"…but a human?"

Darius could only chuckle. "The gods know what they're doing, Thorn. It's not my place to argue."

"Not everyone thinks it's a good idea."

He was well aware of the gossip within the pack. When he shifted into his fur, he could sense their warring emotions about adding a human to the Northern Summit Pack. But it wasn't a choice, it was fate. Hailey was Darius's mate. As alpha, he dared anyone, including a packmate, to challenge his choice. Darius would not tolerate disloyalty.

"What do you think?" Darius asked.

"You're like a brother to me," he said. "If you say she's your mate, I'll lay down my life to protect her."

He smiled, clapping his beta on the shoulder. "I know you would."

It was time. Darius had to find Hailey and work some magic, hoping she felt a similar spark for him. Thorn said she hadn't left her room, so he made his way up to the sixth floor.

****

Hailey jumped when someone knocked loudly at her door, the echo filling the obscenely large room. She'd been hiding out, feeling sorry for herself, and wishing things had worked out differently with Darius.

When she opened the door, there was a cop standing there. Maybe she could finally leave the resort. Then she recognized him as one of the jerks from yesterday.

"Hailey Robinson?"

She nodded.

"You need to come with me. There's someone who wants to speak with you."

Did she have to go? She wasn't sure what cops could and couldn't demand. Part of her hoped Darius was looking for her, like a knight in shining armor.

"Who is it?"

"He didn't mention his name."

"I don't know if I should…"

The cop's jaw twitched, his expression anything but friendly. "I didn't ask you, I'm telling you."

What an asshole. She couldn't risk this chance. It was not like it would be dangerous if a cop was her chaperone. Hailey grabbed her purse and key-card and followed behind him. He didn't speak, walking briskly ahead of her. She was only five feet, two inches herself, so it wasn't easy keeping up, especially when he decided to use the stairs. He led her outside to the rear of the resort, and she hadn't even brought her sweater. The sun had set, the distant bass of music from the ballroom drowning out the sounds of nature.

"He'll be here in a minute. Be smart, human, and take what he's offering." Then the cop re-entered the hotel, pulling the metal emergency door closed behind him. She stood out back, alone, like some fool. This time she was definitely going to report him.

Hailey rubbed her bare arms to stave off the chill. She walked along the rear walkway when someone turned the corner. "Hailey?"

No, no, no! It was that two-timing, engagement-breaking George. "I said I don't want to talk to you."

"When you invited me out here, I assumed you wanted to talk," he said. "But that's okay, I can do the talking."

"But—"

"Look, I'm sorry. It won't happen again. It was just cold-feet jitters."

Her mouth fell open. An admission of guilt? He actually expected her to forgive him? If she stayed single for the rest of her life, it would have been better than looking in George's lying eyes again.

"We can move on, celebrate, have your dream wedding. Nothing has to change."

She couldn't speak because too many expletives were crowding her thoughts.

"Let's go inside, Hailey. There're a lot of important people here we can rub elbows with. I think there's a news crew, too. Did you bring something nicer to wear?"

She was about to boil over, her cheeks flushing with her rising frustration. "Go home, George. I never said I was taking you back. It's over. I won't date a cheater, and certainly won't marry one."

"It never bothered you before," he said, anger seeping into his words.

"Of course it did! But I'm not going to live like this anymore. I deserve better." It was the first time she'd said it aloud. She almost didn't believe it herself. But Darius made her feel special for a brief moment in time. Even if everything he'd said was a lie, it gave her the confidence boost she desperately needed.

"You think you can do better?" He laughed. "You work minimum wage at a coffee shop. I'm saving you, and this is how you thank me?"

"Thank you? For cheating?"

"It's not cheating if we're not even married yet. Besides, how long do you expect a man to wait? Maybe if you loosened up a bit, instead of being so damn frigid, I wouldn't have to cheat."

She gasped, tears pricking her eyes. He was so cruel. Hailey attempted to rush away, not willing to talk a second longer, but he grabbed her arm. His fingers dug so deep, he made her yelp.

"Let me go!" she shouted, but nobody would hear with the ball taking center stage inside. Where was that no-good cop? Adrenaline rushed through her veins as memories of childhood violence returned with a vengeance. She hated how the past had so much power over her.

"You were nothing when I found you," he said. "Now you want to walk away?"

She struggled to get free. The sound of his voice, his tone, his words … she wanted to block it all out. "Stop it! You're hurting me!"

Just because George was swimming in money didn't give him the right to talk down to her. He'd led her to believe she was special, different, and worth marrying. It was all smoke and mirrors, she knew that now, but why bother to deceive her when he could have any woman he wanted?

"Don't be stupid. All my fucking friends are here. Just give me another chance, Hailey."

"I can't, George. This was all a mistake. We were never meant for each other." She attempted to tug her arm away again, but his thinly-veiled anger began to reveal itself. He twisted her arm sharply behind her back and forced her chest against the brick wall. The pain lashed through her body, and she swore her elbow would break with any more pressure.

"If you're ready to walk away, then I should get something for my time." He didn't release his hold on her, but used his free hand and attempted to force her pants over one hip.

"What are you doing?" she cried.

"Taking what you should have given me months ago."

More painful memories entered her mind like an acidic rain. She was numb, cold, and unable to fight or resist. Hailey's limbs felt paralyzed and heavy, her mind drifting away to a place far, far away.

"I promise, she has nothing to give you. And I won't let you take what's *mine*."

The pain in her limb eased instantly when George spun around. "Who the hell are you?" he asked. When the man didn't answer, Hailey turned to see what was happening.

It was him. Darius North.

She didn't realize how tall and intimidating he could be until she saw him standing next to George. The shadows encircled him, his eyes pure evil.

There was a break in the music, leaving only an eerie silence.

"You put your hands on her," Darius stated. He walked forward, like a brick wall, forcing George to back away.

"What's it to you?"

"No one touches Hailey."

George frowned, looking from Darius to her. "You know him?"

"*Don't* speak to her." Darius grabbed a strong fistful of George's shirt, lifting him off the ground momentarily. "You like to hurt women?"

George shook his head.

"I protect what's mine." Darius shoved George. He stumbled backward. "I'm trying to be a gentleman tonight because a lady shouldn't have to witness what I want to do to you right now." Another shove and stumble. "Stay away from her. Do we have an understanding?"

George kept quiet.

"This is where you say 'yes'," said Darius. Then he leaned forward to whisper in George's ear. Hailey was close enough to hear. "If I see you near her again, I'll rip your fucking throat out. Now say 'yes' if you know what's good for you."

"Y-es," George stuttered.

He rushed off once Darius released him. Once he reached the corner of the building, he shouted out, "You'll pay for this!"

Hailey's faculties returned in a hurry, her mind racing to process what just happened. He'd saved her. Again. Darius's possessive words still rang in her mind. Did he mean them? She wanted him to have meant them.

It amazed her how the same jerk who'd elicited

131

such fear in her was terrified of the hulking man in front of her. God, Darius made her feel safe, feminine, and wanted. It was an addicting feeling, one she was afraid to get used to.

"How did you find me?" she whispered.

"I was looking for you," he said. "I was worried since you missed our lunch date."

She thought she'd never see him again after ditching him. This was surreal. And the sound of "date" on his lips did wild things to her body.

"I'm sorry about that. There was another incident with … him … my *ex*-fiancé." She put the emphasis on "ex" because the last thing she wanted was to scare Darius away.

He stepped closer, so close she could smell his rich cologne. "Did he hurt you?"

She wanted to say "no", but instinctively reached for her arm where he'd squeezed her too hard.

"Let me see."

She dropped her arm, trying to remember how to breathe. The music started again in the ballroom, this time a slow song, the distant bass and dreamy melody filling the night air. Darius held her arm as if she were made of porcelain. He caressed her skin with the backs of his fingers.

"A male should never harm his female." He spoke so slowly that it mesmerized her. "A mate should be treasured. Protected. Given every kind of pleasure."

She swallowed hard, falling so easily under his spell.

"I'll never hurt you, Hailey."

She could feel the promises attached to his words, and she believed them.

"All I ask is for a chance to prove I could be a worthy mate."

Hailey knew her eyes were wide. She tried to appear unaffected, but she'd never met a man like Darius North. She had a feeling he always got what he wanted. "This is so fast. You don't even know me."

"I know enough," he said. "I have very good insight when it comes to people—especially *you*." Darius braced an arm against the wall behind her, leaning in close. He took a deep breath at her neckline, releasing it in a near-growl. She couldn't help but close her eyes, the masculine sound sending delicious shivers low in her belly.

"Why me?"

His lips brushed the shell of her ear. "It's your scent. It drives me crazy."

When she felt his stubble against her cheek, she parted her lips in anticipation. Her heart raced so fast, she swore he could hear it. When his lips met hers, he proceeded slowly, deliberately. She lost herself to his ministrations, their kiss growing in intensity.

Either she was a sucker or this was the real deal because Hailey had never felt such raw passion from a man. Darius conquered her—body, mind, and soul. The entire world went away, leaving them alone in a bubble of time and space. His tongue brushed hers as he devoured her mouth, his hands cupping her face. She became breathless as she spiralled down a path she knew there was no escape from.

"You're fucking perfect, Hailey." He trailed those hot kisses down her neck, his hands roaming south. When he reached her ass, he tugged her against his hard body. She gasped, savoring this strength and brazenness. He was so ruggedly handsome, and she was certain he could get any woman he wanted. Did he want to use her like George? Would he cheat on her the same way?

"I'm scared," she dared to admit.

"Tell me." With one hand cupping her ass in a possessive grip, he combed the other through her hair. He enveloped her, lighting her body afire with need.

"I'm afraid you're going to take everything from me and walk away. I'm afraid you'll realize you can do better. I'm afraid I'll fall in love and have my heart broken." She couldn't believe she'd shared such personal fears, but what did she have to lose? Darius was everything she'd dreamed of and this time it had to be all or nothing. No more being left in the shadows.

He chuckled—a deep, honeyed sound. "I do plan to take everything from you, little one. All I can think about is your sweet, virgin pussy, and making you mine." She could feel his erection pressed against her stomach. How did he know she was a virgin? Was it that obvious? "But I won't be walking away. I mate for life, and there will *never* be another for me."

She wanted to allow him to be that man, the one who'd change her faith, make her believe in love again. Darius continued to shock her with his no-holds-barred personality, but he was also the essence of a real man— strength and masculinity in its purest form.

"Yes," she whispered, as he tugged her hair, exposing her neck.

"Yes what?"

"Make me yours," she said. What did she have to lose? Hailey was weary of life, and ready to start over. She might have been a fool, but she was going to allow herself to trust again and hope it wasn't a mistake.

Chapter Six

Darius's wolf howled within him. Those words, those three perfect words were everything he needed to hear. Hailey had freely offered herself to him and he wasn't going to fuck it up. As much as he desired to whisk her away to her suite, he used his last shred of humanity to do things right. Not only was she a human, she was more fragile than most.

"Will you be going to the ball, Hailey?"

She shook her head. "I'm not used to fancy events."

He couldn't help but smile. Her innocence was a turn-on he never expected. He'd set out to claim a human, an unprecedented task, and succeeded. "I want to show you off."

"Darius, I'm sorry. I want to believe you, but…"

He felt her pulling away. Little did she know he was as damaged as her, fighting for survival since he was abandoned as a pup. He'd started out weak and alone, now he was alpha of a powerful wolf pack and dared anyone to challenge him.

"You can't find happiness if you don't take chances, Hailey." He smoothed the pad of his thumb along her lower lip. "I can take care of you, baby girl, and I plan to do just that."

Darius held her hand and escorted her back to her room. His werewolf libido was making itself painfully known. The full moon taunted him. When she opened the door to her suite, he couldn't hold back, crushing his lips to hers. Her hair was soft and smelled of subtle vanilla. He savored her taste and the soft mewling sounds she made. She drove him fucking crazy.

"I'll wait for you downstairs in the ballroom," he

said, pulling away.

"Don't go."

He narrowed his eyes. "I need to get ready for our date."

"Can't you stay a little longer?"

She shouldn't have asked him that. The full moon shone in from the glass wall of the penthouse suite, making his cock heavy as lead. The heady scent of her lust wasn't lost on him. "Hailey, I'm not sure you're ready for this."

The mating call was instinctive, a constant urge he held at bay for the sake of his human mate. Now she was giving him permission to take what he wanted. How could he refuse?

She kissed him, tentatively, wrapping her arms around his shoulders. "I want you, Darius. I want you to love me."

"I do," he said honestly. He stepped into the room, kicking the door shut behind them. He backed her up to the king-size bed until she sat on the edge. "I want to make you mine. Forever."

Hailey nodded. Her lips quivered slightly. His little virgin was afraid, and he was a werewolf alpha not used to playing nice. He didn't want to hurt her, but also couldn't deny what they both wanted.

He unbuttoned his shirt and tossed it. "Your desire is driving me crazy, little one. You're wet for me, too. Only me." Darius tugged off her pants, and she fell back onto the lush bedding.

"Darius…"

She squirmed on the bed, practically begging for his cock. Tonight he wished he wasn't so damn big. He didn't want to hurt her. "Tell me if you want me to stop."

"I've saved myself for a long time. I'm choosing you."

He growled, falling over her, bracing his weight on his forearms. He kissed her gently at first, but her ripe scent was his undoing. He slipped off her t-shirt and unclasped her bra before taking her nipple in his mouth. Her curves were addicting. Darius suckled her tits, using a free hand to tear away her panties. His cock jumped, never so primed for a woman before. The full moon cast its glow throughout the entire suite, demanding he complete the bond—sex and blood.

****

Hailey could scarcely breathe, her mouth dry and heart racing. Darius's body was hard, muscled perfection. The fibres of his golden muscles strained as he held back. She didn't want him to hold back.

She'd waited long enough to give herself to a man. Darius had to be the one, that knight in shining armor she never thought existed. There was something unique and powerful growing between them. She'd felt the first spark when she was lost in the forest. Now she was completely wanton, her muscles relaxing, her pussy pulsing.

"Tell me what you want," he said, his voice deeper, a man on the edge.

"You."

He took her hand, pulling it between them. She wrapped her fingers around his erection. It was as impressive as she'd imagined, hard as granite and thicker than she thought possible.

"What do you want? Tell me, Hailey."

"Your cock," she dared to say. Just talking dirty made her clit spasm, her back arching up instinctively. "Please, Darius. Give it to me."

He shifted down her body, kissing every inch as he went, even her pudgy stomach and stretch marks. When his hot tongue swiped up her folds, she screamed out loud.

"Such a good girl," he said. "Scream all you want, baby."

He delved in, suckling and licking, fucking her with his tongue until she was writhing like a mad woman. Never in her wildest dreams did she expect sex to be like this. He was claiming her, body and soul, and there was nothing she wanted more.

When she hung on a precipice, about to explode from the inside out, he pulled away.

She could scarcely catch her breath. They were both naked and sweat-glistened, only the sound of their combined breathing disturbing the quiet, moonlit room.

"Don't stop," she said.

"Another time, baby girl. Right now I need to claim you."

He moved up her body like a predator, every muscle toned and flexed. When he settled over her, she wrapped her legs and arms around him, needing him closer. He smelled all male, clean sweat and musk. Darius kissed her, their mouths devouring one another until it was impossible to distinguish one from the other.

When she felt the smooth, moist tip of his cock against her pussy, she tensed. Darius was hung like a fucking horse, so she didn't anticipate a gentle popping of her cherry. But she wanted him, regardless.

"Relax, Hailey. I'll go slow for you. This time."

He pushed in, a gentle inch at a time, filling her virgin pussy so full of cock there wasn't a cell untouched. Although it was overwhelming at first, his size sated her effortlessly. Once fully seated, he began to pump his hips slowly, a gentle rocking to get her accustomed to his girth.

"Fuck, you're tight." Darius groaned, a deliciously masculine sound. She held his massive shoulders, corded with muscle, waiting for him to unleash the beast she could sense waiting under the surface. "You're mine now, Hailey. How do you feel?"

"Full. Full of your cock."

He growled and started really fucking her. She held on for the ride, her cunt spasming in powerful waves. God, he was good at this. He dominated her completely. She'd given him her everything, leaving her completely vulnerable. It was as liberating as it was terrifying.

"I'll never get enough of you," he grated as he pumped his hips, making the bed quake. "Come for me, little one. Let me hear you scream."

Darius tongued the shell of her ear as he toyed with a nipple. He knew exactly how to fuck her, the perfect angle, perfect amount of pressure. Within seconds of his order, it built inside of her like a covered pot ready to boil over. Her eyes lolled back in her head as her orgasm reached its peak—*growing, growing, growing*. Then she detonated. She screamed louder than she'd ever screamed, yelling his name and scratching his back as she gasped like a fish out of water.

She could feel Darius fill her with his hot seed, the moisture seeping between her thighs. Hailey had done it, lost her virginity at thirty-two, on her own terms.

He collapsed briefly before rolling to the side, taking her with him. "Thank you," he said between breaths.

"For what?"

"Trusting me. Giving me a beautiful gift."

She rested her head against his chest, listening to the strong beat of his heart. "You make me feel special, Darius. I've never felt this way before."

"You are special, and you need to start believing it. Don't let the past control you. I know how it feels to live that life, and it leads nowhere. Today's a new beginning for us."

She painted lazy patterns over his chest with her finger. "I like the sound of that."

****

As a shifter, his heart already beat Hailey's name. There was no turning back, especially now that he'd claimed her body. After resting in each other's arms, Darius excused himself to get ready for the ball. He couldn't wait to show the world his new mate, and he was determined to give her the fairy-tale experience she deserved.

He made his way to the rear of the resort first. Things weren't as simple as they appeared. Darius had used all his resolve not to follow that asshole George Halbridge and beat him within an inch of his life. When he'd sensed Hailey's fear and saw that bastard's hands on her, he only saw red. His wolf howled within him to shift. To kill.

Darius shifted into his black wolf once he reached the edge of the old growth forest.

"You all had one job. Why the fuck was my mate out here alone with that male?"

Jacob emerged from the darkness. *"It won't happen again."*

"You're damn right it won't happen again! Hailey's delicate, even for a human. It's hard enough convincing her I'm not a bastard like her ex, so I don't need him fucking things up more."

"You wouldn't have to play games with a she-wolf. She'd already have her ass in the air," said Jacob. *"Is your human worth the trouble?"*

Darius lunged forward, sinking his fangs into Jacob's haunch, giving him a firm shake. His packmate yelped and submitted, laying his head on the ground. Darius felt like a lone wolf, and it was seriously pissing him off.

"There's a problem, boss." Thorn's wolf paced in front of him.

"Well, fuck. Spit it out."

"The male is already asking around about you. I don't like it," said Thorn.

"I'm not afraid of that little shit. I just don't want him near my woman."

"There's more," said Thorn. *"I tracked the scent. Brass set them up. Security cameras caught him visiting the male and your woman."*

Darius attempted to settle his raging emotions, trying to comprehend one of his own packmates going against his orders. The weight of that reality crushed the air from his lungs. As a shifter, he trusted his pack with his life. They were his eyes, ears, and limbs. This betrayal was too much, especially at the most pivotal time of his life. This mating felt like an uphill battle.

"I caught him revealing his wolf to Hailey earlier," said Darius. It was a warning sign he shouldn't have ignored.

"I know he's having a hard time accepting the whole human thing, but that still doesn't give him the right—"

"Find him! Bring him to me," Darius said.

He wanted to fault Brass, to banish him or worse, but only days ago Darius hated humans just as much as his packmate. Maybe more so. That still didn't mean he'd allow Brass to fuck up his entire courting. His mating was happening regardless of who approved or not.

****

Hailey stared at herself in the hall mirror. "What just happened?"

She paced her luxury suite, remembering Darius's complete domination of her body, and the words that still left her dizzy. And he was waiting for her.

After a shower, she approached the box still sitting on the chair by the bed. Did she dare to wear such a revealing dress? Her curves were explosive, and she'd always hidden them as best she could. But she was a new Hailey now, with renewed faith and optimism. *I can do this.*

The walk to the ballroom was difficult enough in heels, not to mention having so much skin exposed. The long black dress hugged her body and created mountainous cleavage.

When she entered the open double doors, the music, lighting, and glamorous atmosphere took her by surprise. She stood there in awe, feeling like Cinderella. The women attending were drop-dead gorgeous with bodies that looked like they belonged on a magazine cover. She felt immediately out of place and wanted to retreat to her room.

Then his strong hands were on her hips as he whispered in her ear. "You look good enough to eat." Those words made her tremble, a cascade of tingles making her needy all over again.

She turned around in his arms. He wore a new suit, his hair slightly slicked back off his face. Hailey could stare at him all night long.

"How about I get us a drink?"

Hailey nodded. She took her time walking on the tile floor to the large windows along the side of the ballroom. The darkness outside allowed her to see her own reflection—then his.

"Here with your new boyfriend?"

She didn't turn around. Why couldn't George stay the hell away?

"I did a little research, and apparently lover boy works at the resort. I guarantee you he won't have a job come Monday."

This time she whirled around, nearly losing her balance. "Leave him alone!"

George smirked, a conspiratorial look in his eyes. "You fuck up my plans, I fuck up yours. It's only fair, right?"

"This was all your fault. Not mine."

"Well, like you said, it's for the best. I don't think I could have stomached being married to you anyway." A tall, slim woman sauntered up behind him and took his arm.

"You said you'd dance the next song," she said, giving Hailey the once over.

"Of course, babe. I was just coming."

He glared at her before leaving with his date. Hailey stood there feeling like a cow, and worried she'd ruined Darius's life after he'd saved hers twice. She knew how ruthless George and his friends from the legal practice could be.

Darius returned, handing her a glass of bubbly champagne. "I think I'll keep you close for the rest of the night."

"Darius, maybe this isn't a good idea..."

He appeared so confident, but little did he know George was working hard to ruin his career or more. Guilt continued to grow inside of her. She stared at the bubbles in her glass. There was nothing she wanted more than to live this fairy tale, but she had a feeling her dreams would come crashing down at midnight.

"There's nothing to worry about, Hailey. All I want to focus on tonight is us. You've made me the happiest man in the world." He set his glass down on a ledge and pulled her unceremoniously against his body, not appearing to care what anyone thought. "And I've never seen a woman more beautiful."

She smiled.

He leaned down and kissed her cheek, and then her neck. "Such a pretty little thing. You smell so fucking good." She was afraid he'd try to do more in a very public place, but that voice from her nightmares pulled Darius from his reverie.

"I didn't know they let the help attend these kind of functions." George stood several feet away with his arms crossed. His wingman, Karl, and several friends flanked his sides. She knew he'd want revenge for being bested by Darius. "Should you be returning to the kitchen, or is it a desk in the back room?"

Darius said nothing.

"And your choice for a date? Kind of embarrassing for you, bro," said George. "Or maybe you're a chubby-chaser. Whatever, it's all good. I'm just glad you took that dead weight off my hands."

Hailey didn't think she'd breathed since George appeared. The entire ballroom of people had stopped what they were doing to turn and stare. She felt humiliated, but even more upset that Darius was put in the middle of this shitstorm. She expected him to remain quiet again, after all, there were five men to one and several more of George's friends in the ballroom.

Darius turned to face her. "I'm sorry, baby girl. I'll make things up to you when I come back." Something dark swirled in his eyes, something animalistic. Then he squared his shoulders and approached George.

"Watch how you talk about my woman," Darius said.

Oh my God, he's going to get himself killed.

"She was *my* fiancée up until a couple days ago."

"Yeah, well, finders keepers, asshole."

"You think you're a tough guy?" asked George, his voice and bravado rising thanks to his support system. "I can destroy a low-life like you."

"Let's see you try that." Darius removed his designer jacket, carefully folding it and placing it on the back of a chair. His muscles strained against the material of his maroon-colored suit shirt. God, he had a gorgeous body and shoulders so broad he'd put a linebacker to shame.

Officer Jacob from the other night entered the ballroom. Finally … security. "I'll need you guys to take this out back. This is not the place for a fight."

What the hell? Why wasn't he stopping this from escalating? He wanted the five of them to beat the crap out of Darius outside? These cops were out of their ever-loving minds.

They all began to leave the ballroom. Hailey chased after Darius, her heels clicking against the tile. "Don't do this. *Please!"*

"I won't allow him to insult you."

"It's okay. I don't care."

Darius frowned. "You should."

She grabbed his sleeve and whispered, tears stinging her eyes. "I don't want you to get hurt."

He winked. "You don't know *me* at all."
****

Darius couldn't wipe the goofy smile off his face. His mate was worried about him. She didn't want him to get hurt. He stifled a chuckle. She was so fucking adorable, and that piece of shit would pay for embarrassing her. Of all the females at the ball, Hailey was his prize. Her dress barely contained her tits, and all he could think about was drowning in her softness again. As unorthodox as their mating was, the gods had chosen

145

right. Even the thought of another woman made him bristle in distaste.

He burst out the back doors, the darkness and scent of pine instantly soothing him. The full moon was high in the sky, reminding him he needed to get his ass back to Hailey to complete the mating bond tonight—sex and *blood.*

George and his friends were raring to go, likely thinking this would be a cakewalk.

They all laughed. "Well, well, he actually showed his face…"

Darius barrelled forward, straight to George, and punched him square in the face. It felt so damn good. He dropped like an oak. Darius had no time for drama, not when he was solely focused on his woman.

"Can we join in the party?" asked Thorn, rubbing his hands together. He moved in from behind with Jacob. *About fucking time.*

Darius shrugged, already bored with the exchange. Human males were weak and puny compared to shifters. This was all a joke.

Within minutes, crowds flooded out into the night, curious onlookers wanting a glimpse of bloodshed. They'd be disappointed, especially when the blond couldn't even take a punch. He pushed through the throngs of people, trying to get back to Hailey when he saw Brass in the distance. His nerves flared up because he couldn't trust his wayward packmate.

"Jacob said your female is MIA," said Thorn, bumping shoulders with him. He had one of George's friends in a headlock.

"Fuck."

He retreated out of sight to the dark shadows and shifted. He savored the power of his alpha wolf, immediately picking up Hailey's scent. Why would she go to the forest? Would Brass kill her if he truly believed a human-shifter mating was an abomination? Darius used all the power in his legs to reach the tree line in record time. If anything happened to Hailey, his life would be a forfeit.

It was his worst-case scenario—Brass had Hailey. Did he plan to use her as a fucking hostage? To what end? Darius would tear him apart, piece by piece, if he'd harmed her. If Brass thought he could defeat Darius's alpha wolf, he was more deluded than the group of human males. He moved in slow and steady—he lived for the hunt.

He couldn't sense any fear from Hailey, and she appeared untouched, so his sense of urgency settled slightly. Once he knew he could strike without harm coming to his mate, he leaped out of hiding, knocking Brass's human form to the ground.

"Boss, wait!"

Hailey screamed.

His fangs were bared, his heart racing. Darius was ready to kill.

"It's not what you think. I was protecting her, keeping her safe."

Darius's hackles eased. Could he be telling the truth? As alpha, nothing would make him happier than keeping the Northern Summit Pack intact. But he had to be one hundred percent sure when it came to Hailey's safety.

He backed off, putting himself between Hailey and Brass.

"What's going on? Who are you talking to?" cried Hailey.

Brass got to his feet, brushing off the leaf litter from his pants. "I was talking to Darius, your mate. And he needs to complete the blood bond tonight."

147

What the fuck is he doing?

"Get away from me," said Hailey. "You're that crazy cop."

Brass shook his head. "There's a lot more going on than you can image, human. I was a fool because it's not my place to question my alpha. I swear to respect your blood bond."

Darius realized what his packmate was doing. He was helping him, a peace offering. The blood bond had to be completed during the same full moon as the claiming. With all the chaos, it would have been so easy to miss the small window of opportunity. This unique mating would be a learning curve for all of them—especially Hailey. He shifted into his skin, terrified of his mate's reaction. They'd declared their feelings for each other, and he wouldn't be able to handle her rejection.

Brass shifted and returned to the melee, leaving them alone in the hush of the forest.

Hailey stared. "This can't be real," she said. She reached out and touched Darius, running her fingers along his abs. "Is it real?"

He nodded.

"I thought the wolf this morning was tame. I knew it was too good to be true." She walked around his naked body, feeling him, pinching him. "How is this possible, Darius? I have way too many questions right now. Please talk to me."

"I'm a werewolf. No less a man, but with some extra perks…"

"I don't know what to say, what to think."

Darius couldn't lose his mate. He'd just opened her eyes to a world she never knew existed. He hoped to the gods she still wanted him once the shock settled.

"It's still me, Darius North, the man who loves you."

Hailey kept quiet. She stared, and he wondered what she was thinking. Did he disgust her? Was she ready to run and never look back?

"I'm scared," he said, tears threatening to cloud his vision.

"Tell me."

"I'm afraid you're going to take everything from me and walk away. I'm afraid you'll realize you can do better. I'm afraid I'll fall in love and have my heart broken."

Hailey smiled as tears ran down her cheeks. "So, you're a werewolf?" She shrugged. "I guess I can live with that."

He pulled her into his arms, holding her tight, never wanting to let go. "Everything will be okay as long as I have you. I love you, Hailey Robinson. Please tell me you want forever with me."

"Forever sounds good."

Darius admired the smooth plane of her neck and couldn't wait to sink his fangs into the tender flesh, bonding them for life. Tonight he'd show Hailey the power of the blood bond. A werewolf bite was legendary for its aphrodisiac effects. It would be a wild ride. "I have a lot to teach you, little one, and a lifetime to do it."

A wave of panic suddenly twisted her features. "What about George?"

He stifled a growl. "He's of no concern to either of us now."

"But he threatened you, threatened to take your job at the hotel away."

His worry faded to nothing, his world finally whole. Darius swooped his beautiful woman into his arms. "Sweetheart, I own the hotel."

The End

THE HUNT

Doris O'Connor

Copyright © 2017

Chapter One

Raphael raised his head toward the dark sky. Steam curled around his nostrils as his long drawn-out howl signaled the start. The hunt was on. Around him, his pack yipped their excitement into the crisp winter air. The forest they called home whizzed past at dizzying speed, and Raphael gave his wolf free rein.

Nothing felt as good as letting his beast run free, the animal's instincts taking over to hunt, to claim his prize. Adrenaline coursed through his veins, urging him to run faster, their target for the evening just ahead.

She was clever, the little wolf chosen for this full moon's activities. Knowing that she couldn't outrun them, she'd chosen to hide, but she hadn't counted on his beta's need to find her. Collins had asked permission for the mating to take place earlier today, and Raphael had gladly given it. The pack needed fresh blood, and it had been a while since cubs had arrived.

Besides, it would take the heat off him. He knew the pack was getting restless, impatient for their Alpha to choose his mate, but none of the females who presented themselves appealed to his wolf for anything other than a quick fuck.

Even that had gotten old fast. Between his duties

as Alpha and his work for the forestry commission, it didn't leave much room for any kind of fun. Raphael couldn't even recall the last time he'd set foot in the human village which nestled smack bang between his territory and the southern wolves.

Collins streaked past him, the scent of his soon-to-be mate in his nostrils, and grinning, Raphael hung back. At his signal, the pack disbursed, pairing off as they went.

There would be plenty of fun to be had between them tonight. Raphael shook his head at the pretty young wolf who bowed low in front of him.

Barely out of puberty, she was far too young and innocent for his battle-weary wolf. Her mother nudged her, to urge her on, and Raphael growled a warning low in his throat.

That, at least, had the desired effect, and mother and daughter bounded off into the forest. Nose in the air, Raphael took in the various scents. Something was bothering his animal. It snarled and prowled, and giving into his wolf's restlessness, he decided to wander. It wouldn't hurt to check out their territory lines. The rival pack was also hunting if their excited yowls were any indication, but they didn't hunt for sport and their prey... No, it couldn't be. How dare they?

Hackles raised, Raphael went on the attack when the terrified and bloodied deer broke through the underbrush. Her scent wrapped around him, made ten times more potent by her fear. Man and wolf inhaled as one and the knowledge of who this was to them slammed into Raphael's consciousness, imprinted itself on him in that instant their gazes connected before she hobbled away as fast as her injured legs would let her.

Mate.

Not that Raphael had any time to act on that

instant knowledge because the three young wolves that'd been chasing the deer leaped through the foliage, teeth bared. How fucking dare they hunt down a defenseless deer, let alone his *mate*.

Fury coursed through Raphael's veins and with it the ice-cold determination to make them pay. The biggest of the trio charged at Raphael, while the other two went for his sides. Laughable, really, how easy they were to read. Raphael ducked and rolled to get underneath their leader, as that idiot jumped, exposing his soft underbelly—a classic youngster mistake—which would cost the pup his life. Raphael's wolf was in no mood to show mercy, not with his mate's scent still in his nostrils. Her palpable fear, pain, and despair made his wolf deadlier than normal.

Blood sprayed, turning the snow on the ground crimson, as he opened up his opponent's guts with one swipe of his sharp claws. The youngster wailed in agony and collapsed in a heap. His cronies almost collided with him, turning at the last second. One of them took off, tail between his legs, back in the direction they'd arrived from, but the other one...

Stupid young fool growled and charged at Raphael. At least he didn't jump, but kept low. Teeth bared, he lunged for Raphael's throat, but missed when Raphael swung around and kicked out at him. The smaller animal went flying through the air and crashed into the nearest tree with a back-breaking crunch. Instantly paralyzed, he slid into the churned-up snow. It turned yellow under his broken form, and Raphael shook his head in disgust.

This was his territory, and the foul stench of the southern wolves would not be allowed to permeate his home. Blood-filled gurgles came from the fucker slowly bleeding out at his feet, and bending his head, Raphael ripped his throat out with one bite. The youngster's eyes dimmed and he breathed his last breath as Raphael spit out a mouthful of blood.

The wolf by the tree whined, his still-working front paws desperately trying to drag himself away and back to safety.

Raphael growled his fury and jumped in front of him to stop his progress. Their disgusting scent was everywhere, and cocking his leg, Raphael made sure that was obliterated with his own.

He recognized who these two were now. The hapless youngest sons of the southern pack's alpha. Raphael's actions might have just started a war, but the bloody prints his mate left behind in her flight left no room for doubt.

Grabbing a mouthful of the crippled teenager's fur, he dragged him back through the brush and to the edge of the stream which signaled the end of his territory. A sharp flick of his head and the youngster tumbled down into the icy waters. He could drown there for all Raphael cared. Would serve the asshole right.

By the time he dragged the lifeless, bloody remains of the other wolf's brother down to the edge, the fucker had gone. Good riddance to bad rubbish.

Raphael had a skittish deer to find. After what she must have suffered at the hands of the southern wolves, he highly doubted she would welcome this wolf with open arms.

A whine rose from his throat, and, nose to the ground, he followed her scent.

****

Aubrey struggled on, her sole aim to get away, but she'd long since lost her sense of direction. Where the hell was the village and the sanctuary of her little house? She should never have given in to the restless urges of her usually-so-gentle animal, especially not at the full moon.

Everyone knew the wolves hunted then, but she'd been so sure she was on the right side of the territory line. She was only going to go for a quick run along the stream. That was usually all it took to calm her deer down when she'd had one of her rare turns of simply *needing* to be in her animal form.

Unlike the wolves, she didn't need to stay out of sight in her animal form. Deer were everywhere after all, and from what she could gather, it was getting easier for the wolves, too. The forestry commission was in the process of reintroducing wild wolves into the forests in England under strictly controlled experimental conditions.

So, if a wolf shifter was spotted now, it wasn't too big a deal, though most folks always just assumed they were wild dogs. Aubrey stumbled as her hoof slipped into a rutted groove and pain shot up her leg. Bracing herself against the fall as best she could, she slid down the embankment until a fallen tree's overturned roots stopped her. Winded, she lay on her side, panting, as she mentally took stock of her injuries.

Just cuts and bruises, though the chunk of flesh torn off her flank by the smallest of the wolves she'd run into on her sprint, bled profusely and hurt like crazy. Now the immediate surge of adrenaline had worn off, Aubrey shivered in the cold air. She needed to shift back into her human form, to attempt to heal, but she would freeze her ample butt off out here without her clothes. Not to mention the small matter of that black, menacing wolf she'd almost run into in her desperate flight away from the trio.

She knew who he was, of course. The Alpha of the dominant wolf pack around these parts was something of a legend in shifter circles. Fifteen years her senior, he was way, way out of her league, no matter how much her inner animal lusted after him from afar. He'd brought peace to this corner of Northumberland, uniting the packs under his leadership, with the exception of the southern wolves who seemed intent on causing trouble.

A gang of them had caused untold havoc in the village square only last week. In their human forms, they'd driven their dirt bikes through the memorial garden, uprooting plants and turning over a bench. No one quite knew what to do with the gang of bikers in their midst, because they disappeared as quickly as they appeared, and Aubrey was certainly not going to tell what she knew. She liked the quiet, unassuming life, nestled away between the humans who had no idea what was going on.

At least the humans didn't judge her for her complete inability to be more deer-like. She glared into the darkness surrounding her. She was not going to be some stag's doormat, thank you very much. The best thing she ever did was move away from Scotland and take the job as school teacher in this tiny village. Her refusal to mate with the head stag had gotten her ostracized from the deer-shifting community. Her parents, in particular, her mother, had been the most disparaging.

"Why can't you be more like your sisters?"

That comment still stung. Both her younger sisters were willow-like and thought the sun shone out of their mates' hoofs and asses. They also didn't have one original thought in their heads. Aubrey would rather shoot herself than be like them. She had a brain to go with the extra weight she carried, and she had every intention of using it.

Mind you, she mused to herself, as she shifted and

cried out in agony, she seemed to have entirely misplaced her brain tonight. While the shift had stopped the bleeding on her thigh, her teeth were now chattering and she still had no idea where she was. She ought to move, but with the howls of angry wolves far too close by, she daren't risk it.

As she shifted so rarely these days, she didn't have the finely honed instincts needed to stay off their radar, which had gotten her into this mess in the first place. She didn't even want to think what the big black wolf might have done to the trio who'd pursued her. The sounds of fighting had been utterly terrifying. No doubt he would be furious with her for putting him in the situation of defending her.

That moment she'd looked into his glowing eyes … the way he'd growled as though she meant something to him… Her deer had been all but ready to throw herself at his mercy and that was insane. Wolves ate deer, she had to remember. And it didn't seem to matter one iota to them that she was indeed a shifter and thus not food, as so aptly illustrated by the terrible trio.

Aubrey pulled her knees to her chest and wrapped her arms around herself in a vain effort to retain some body heat. Thoughts of what else those three might have done to her when they finally realized she was a woman didn't bear thinking about.

The shivers started in earnest now, and Aubrey swallowed down her rising panic when she couldn't rouse her deer to shift back into animal form. While she didn't have an inbuilt fur coat, like the wolves, she would be warmer as her deer.

It seemed her animal was too frightened to come out and play, however, and who could have blamed her? Aubrey suspected her shy deer half would take a very long time indeed to recover from this ordeal, if she ever did. Aubrey hadn't exactly relished becoming part of the hunt herself. She needed to move or she would freeze right here.

A menacing growl just above her hiding place made her jump in fright. She banged her head on the trunk of the tree in the process and stuffed her hand in her mouth to stop herself from crying out in pain. As it was, she saw freaking stars. That was all she needed: to knock herself out. Dirt and stones dislodged from under her as the whole tree shifted, and the ground gave way.

This time Aubrey did scream as she tumbled down the frozen incline and into the ice-cold waters of the stream.

She fought to breathe as a heavy weight pinned her down before pain sliced up her neck, and her head was out of the water. A pair of glowing yellow eyes was her last view before her vision dimmed.

Chapter Two

His mate tumbled down the embankment in a heap of white limbs. One of the most terrifying sights Raphael had had to endure in a long time, and he'd seen some shit in his time. However, all that paled into insignificance at the realization that she was in human form and thus far more vulnerable.

Any she-wolf would have shifted mid-fall and escaped the melee, but her deer was either not capable, or too terrified to try. Perhaps a combination of both. Her terror was a palpable force in the air, and it made his wolf want to kill those bastards who'd touched her all over again.

He zigzagged his way down the steep incline and did the only thing he could do, bite the back of her neck to yank her head out of the water, while he put all his weight on the log which had half fallen on top of her. That action shifted it enough for her to twist her upper torso and to take a deep gulp of air. Her terrified brown eyes connected with his before she lost consciousness, which was probably just as well. With her legs effectively pinned under the rest of the tree, she had to be in an awful lot of pain. Raphael shifted into his human form with a bone-crunching roar which would have also served to warn away anyone else. He didn't even want his pack to see his mate so broken and vulnerable. There would be enough explaining to do when they realized their Alpha had chosen a deer for his mate.

Raphael shook his long, dark-brown hair out of his eyes and proceeded to extricate the young woman from the debris surrounding her. The more of her his actions revealed to him, the more she took his breath away. His mate was all woman with curves to die for, and his wolf positively salivated at the sight of her wide hips, rounded tummy, and large tits, not to mention the bare cunt he caught glimpses of as he turned her over and lifted her out of the icy water in one fell swoop. Not that now was the time to have those thoughts, because his little doe was barely breathing and far too cold. The cut on her nape was also bleeding quite heavily and Raphael cursed under his breath, while he half shifted and licked the wounds to help clean them. The sweet essence of his mate exploded on his tongue, and his wolf whined his need.

If he needed any more proof that he'd finally found the one female he was destined to be with, seeing those wounds close in front of his eyes was all the confirmation he needed. Throwing his head back, he gave a long mournful howl into the night air. The echoing howls of his pack filled the air, among them one from Collins.

No, I do not need help. I'll explain when I see you. Take charge in my absence.

Absence?

Where are you going?

Boss, are you sure?

A cacophony of howls filled the night air, and the confusion of his pack set heavy in his gut, but Raphael's mind was made up. He roared his confirmation to the moon, and his pack fell silent.

One lone howl brought him peace.

I've got this, boss.

The woman in his arms coughed and her eyes briefly fluttered open. He forced a grim smile on his face and the most delightful blush spread over her pale skin. It was hard to tell in this light and with her long tresses all matted and dirty from the water, but if he had to guess, he'd say she was a natural strawberry blonde.

"Hey, little doe. It's all right, I've got you."

She blinked and the most delightful blush stole across her far too pale, heart-shaped face. Her little nose wrinkled up, her brows drew together, and she inhaled deeply. That blush deepened, her breathing sped up, and her sweet musk increased. Sensing her body's immediate response to his nearness did nothing to help Raphael control his wolf. His jaw ached with the need to bite her shoulder and to cement this bond between them, and he knew his incisors had grown more prominent. His cock hardened and the little bundle of curves in his arms gasped when she noticed that body part of his nudging her hip.

"No, please, I can't. No."

She struggled in his arms, or tried to. As ineffective as a newborn's mewls, her voice barely carried and her hand pushing against his chest simply served to inflame his wolf. His animal didn't care about the circumstances. All he wanted was to pin this woman down right here and now, fill her with his cum, and listen to her screams of ecstasy as she came all over his dick with his teeth buried in her neck.

Raphael closed his eyes, took a deep breath in to draw her sweet scent into his lungs, and to appease his wolf. Even so, he knew his voice came out distorted when he spoke to her again.

"You can, and you will, little doe, but not here and not now. Where do you live? Let me take you home."

His mate jerked in his arms, and she frantically shook her head.

"No, you … mph."

Kissing her seemed the most expedient way to shut up her protests, if not the wisest to help his control.

Her gasp of surprise granted him access, and Raphael took full advantage of that fact. He took charge of the kiss, letting his animal take over and do the talking for him. His wolf's low growls filled the night air when she kissed him back. Tentatively at first, as though she was afraid of his response, and then bolder. Her hands wrapped around his neck, fisted in his long hair, and the sweet scent of aroused woman hit him in the gut.

It would have been so easy to pin her against a tree, bury himself balls-deep inside her sweet body, and fuck her brains out. In the past, that was exactly what Raphael would have done, but this woman setting his blood alight with lust was not just any woman. She was his *mate*, and she deserved better than an animalistic fuck against a tree. As he breathed in her scent, imprinting the feel and taste of her onto his brain, he also pulled back.

All flushed and warm now, she clung to him, and when she tried to pull his head back down to kiss him, he smiled and shook his head.

"Your address, my sweet. Let's get you home and then we can finish this."

She blinked again in that sweet confused way she had, but she did whisper her response.

"The teacher's cottage in the village, but…" She stopped speaking and her terrified deer briefly appeared in her eyes.

He sensed the reason for her flight response before he heard them. Furious growls vibrated through the air.

Southern wolves on the opposite bank. Fuck it all to hell and back. They were exposed and he was on his own with his fragile mate to protect.

Pushing her away from him, he shifted and put his large bulk between his mate and the other wolves.

****

Aubrey gasped as she landed butt first in the snow. Seeing him morph into his big black wolf had to be the most awesome sight ever. As a man, he towered over her, his strength apparent in the effortless way he carried her. Aubrey was no lightweight, yet he hadn't seemed fazed at all, manhandling her with an assured ease, which should have pissed her off, yet had the opposite effect on her. His amber eyes seemed to look directly into her soul when she'd struggled to shrug off the last membranes of fog claiming her brain after that fall. Her deer had screeched just one word over and over.

Mate.

It couldn't be, however. He was a wolf, an Alpha at that. He would never take a mere deer shifter as his mate. Even if by some miracle he did, his pack wouldn't let him, and an Alpha was ruled by the best interests of his pack. Everyone knew that, and Raphael Taylor was one of the best Alphas there was. She would be a hindrance to him at best, a liability at worst, just like she was now.

Terror held her firmly in its grip, as she watched the growling exchange between him and the other wolves. She couldn't understand a word they were saying to each other, of course, but she got the meaning loud and clear.

If ever she'd seen a declaration of war, this was it. Her deer at long last erupted, and not wishing to hang around, she took off as fast as she could. Following the stream, she eventually found her bearings and sprinted for home, all too aware of the wolves running alongside on the other side of the stream, taunting her.

Of Raphael, there was no sight, and she'd never been so grateful to leap over her back fence than she was at that moment. Safety, at last. The familiar scents of home surrounded her. Taking a furtive look around to make sure the old dear in the cottage next to her hadn't woken up and was taking a stroll like she was wont to do,

Aubrey shifted back into her human form and pulled the tattered old bathrobe she'd left on the deck over her naked form.

Everything hurt back in her human form, and she gingerly put one step in front of the other. What she needed was some painkillers and a good long soak in the bath. She might even finish that bottle of wine. Aubrey typically didn't drink on a school night, but these were hardly ordinary circumstances. Not every night she was hunted by wolves, met her mate and then run out on him.

The bite on her nape throbbed as she thought of Raphael. He must have bitten her there when he pulled her out of the water. Fear gripped her anew as she lifted her back door key out from under the flowerpot and unlocked her little place.

He had *bitten* her. Not the usual place a wolf marked his mate, but did it count anyway? Were they in fact now mated? That didn't bear thinking about.

Aubrey only had her parents and sisters, and the rest of the mated deer she had encountered to hold up as a yardstick, but there was no way in hell she was ready for that.

Being mated meant subjugating herself to your mate and hell would freeze over before Aubrey would ever do that.

She purposely ignored the little devil on her shoulder calling her a liar. Would submitting to Raphael be that terrible? After all, her body had come alive in his arms. His warmth, his strength, his sheer overwhelming masculine presence had made her forget where they were and she'd simply acted on instinct. His kiss—boy, could that man kiss—had been a brand, a claim on her very soul, and she had responded.

Aubrey pulled the chilled wine bottle out of the fridge and held it to her overheated cheeks. Just remembering that kiss made her body react. Her nipples did their best to poke their way through the terry of her robe, her clit tingled, and she grew wet between her legs. If he burst through that door right now, then…

Oh my God, the door, the wolves.

The wine bottle slipped through her fingers and smashed on the stone tiles which made up the floor of her kitchen. She jumped over the shards of glass, her only aim to secure all the doors and windows. By the time she checked the last one, she had trouble pulling breaths into her lungs, and then she saw him.

One lone, big massive wolf on the edge of the forest her cottage backed up to. Blood marred his fur, and he limped. The deer inside of her wanted to leap through the window and help him, but her rational side urged caution. Sure enough, more wolves appeared and surrounded him. One almost as tall as him nudged his side and then looked straight at her.

Aubrey quickly let the nets fall and stepped back. That had to be his pack, and if she had to guess, that wolf had been his beta. He, too, had been covered in blood, and the look he'd thrown her way had been almost menacing.

No, they would never approve of her.

One by one, the wolves retreated until only Raphael remained. Their gazes connected and even across the distance separating them she could feel the connection between them. Tears streamed down her face as she pulled the nets away and rested her hand on the windowpane.

Raphael raised his head and his long, mournful howl echoed through the night air. Aubrey blinked and he was gone, as though he'd never existed.

Chapter Three

"Miss, Miss, that strange man is here again." Timmy jumped up and down, and taking her hand, pulled Aubrey to the window.

The five-year-old was prone to flights of fancy, so Aubrey didn't expect to see anyone. Not like the first time he'd said that a week ago when she'd rushed out of the classroom only to find no one there.

After all, it had been almost a month since that fateful night, and Raphael hadn't sought her out like she might have thought.

That seemed to be reserved for her dreams. Every night, without fail, she would wake up, hot, sticky, and on the edge of release, gasping his name after yet another erotic dream which left her reaching for her little battery-operated friend. Lately, she hadn't even bothered to do that. The weak orgasms she achieved that way barely took the edge off. What she wanted, and needed, was to seek out Raphael, and that she couldn't do.

Despite the intense moments they'd shared in the forest, he clearly didn't feel the same way, which left her horny and frustrated, and liable to snap at her pupils like she was wont to do to Timmy now.

Oh, for goodness' sake. This is pointless. Pull yourself together.

"Look, Timmy, we've talked about this, there's no one there, oh…"

The rest of whatever she was going to say fled her brain in a puff of smoke, because the man dressed all in black was none other than Raphael, and he looked good enough to eat. He'd left his long hair loose to fall around his head. He ran a hand through his beard as she watched. The action made his long coat gape open and she swallowed hard when his top rode up, exposing a thin strip of his hairy muscled abdomen. Not an ounce of fat on that man, for sure.

Black jeans hugged his muscular thighs, and she couldn't tear her gaze away from the bulge they so perfectly outlined. Heat flooded her panties and she was beyond grateful the windows were shut, otherwise, Raphael would have no doubt smelled her instantly. How mortifying that would have been. As it was, he raised his nose in the air, and then looked straight at her. A somewhat uncertain smile kicked up the corners of his mouth, even as his eyes bled to the golden yellow of his wolf's and back again. Belatedly, she noticed the beautiful bunch of flowers in his other hand.

"Miss, who is that?"

Timmy's tug on her arm broke the spell, and she focused her attention on the little boy, who regarded her through eyes the color of the deepest ocean, his little brows drawn together in a frown.

"A friend, Timmy, that's all." The lie stuck in her throat, but she could hardly tell the boy the truth, even if she knew what, exactly, she was to Raphael.

"If he's your friend, Miss, why is he not coming in?" Timmy asked. "He keeps going away again."

Aubrey's heart gave a very suspicious lurch in her chest at that innocent question.

"He's the man you've been seeing, Timmy?"

"Yep, and look, I think he's coming in this time."

Sure enough, Raphael unlatched the little gate and strolled up the path in the long loose-limbed stride so typical of a male, predatory shifter. She sure felt like his prey, as she somehow got her limbs to move to intercept him.

"Right, let me just..." Flustered, she pushed a strand of hair behind her ear. As usual, it was escaping the bun she tried to contain the bane of her existence in. She really ought to just cut it, but somehow she always chickened out at the last moment.

She flicked on the smart board on the wall—the school's newest and high-tech teaching tool—and selected an educational video for the class to watch.

"I just have to pop out. Watch this in the meantime."

A chorus of happy *whoops* greeted that announcement, and taking a deep breath in for courage, Aubrey reached the front door just as his heavy knock heralded his arrival.

The part-time secretary the educational board employed stuck her head out of the tiny office at the same time.

"I've got this, Brenda," Aubrey said. "I won't be a minute."

"Sure thing, my dear."

Brenda smiled at her and shut the door to her office behind her. Before she could lose her courage and change her mind, she yanked the door open. Raphael must have been in the process of bashing on it because his fist missed her nose by inches, and he fell forward only to catch himself at the last minute.

"Jesus, don't do that. I almost hit you."

His deep gravelly voice did strange things to her insides, as did the way he now shuffled from foot to foot and then thrust the bouquet of flowers at her.

"Here, I didn't know what you liked, so there's one of everything in there. I'm sure the local florist thought I'd lost the plot. Anyway—" He stopped speaking, inhaled sharply, and grinned. "Will you please take this and let me in? I fear we're attracting an audience."

Sure enough, a peek past his huge shoulders

showed several of the mothers arriving to pick up their kids, staring at them both, open-mouthed. No doubt wondering why such a hunk was delivering flowers to the spinster teacher.

"You can't come in. I work here, and it's almost pick-up time. What are you thinking?" She tried for her best schoolteacher tone, but just a husky imitation of her usual voice came out. What the hell was that about? To add insult to injury, her nape started tingling the more his spicy scent enveloped her, and her hand went up to that mark without any conscious thought. Raphael's low growl at her action made her gasp. She hastily dropped her hand, but the damage was done because she looked into the softly glowing eyes of his wolf.

"Little doe."

Two little words, delivered in that deep, dark delicious growl, made her want to forget everything and jump him like a wanton woman.

"Don't call me that. Please, just leave. I can't do this now." She put her hand out to push him back, but the minute her palm touched his chest, his heat scorched her skin. Tingles of awareness traveled up from that point of contact, raced each other over her skin until they settled in her pussy. There was nothing at all she could do about the way her body reacted to being this close to her mate. Instead of pushing him away, her fingers curled in the fabric of his t-shirt to pull him closer.

Not that she could move him either way.

"I know. I just came to give you these." Raphael uncurled her fingers and pushed the bouquet of flowers into her hand. It served as a wonderful distraction to bury her flaming face inside them, as his free hand briefly caressed his mark.

"Go, work, I'll see you later. We're sorting this tonight."

With those ominous words, he shut the front door for her and Aubrey blinked as she slowly came to her senses.

Oh Lordy, was that a promise or a threat?
****

Raphael forced his feet to keep on moving, one step in front of the other, away from his mate. He hadn't dared hope for this, had half-expected her to throw his flowers back in his face, which was why he'd chosen to come to her place of work instead of her home. He'd counted on the fact that she wouldn't want to make a scene in front of her pupils.

What he hadn't counted on was his wolf's reaction to seeing her in person. The sensible blouse and long pencil skirt shouldn't have looked sexy, yet all he could think about was what she might be hiding under there. From the barely-there makeup, to the strawberry-blonde hair, which she'd tried and failed to contain in a bun at her nape, to the sensible flat court shoes on her feet, she'd dressed to convey the image of the quintessential schoolteacher.

Yet her reaction to him had been anything but.

Raphael nodded toward the bundle of human mothers who didn't even attempt to hide their ogling of him. They couldn't really help themselves, reacting to the pheromones his wolf sent out without even trying. In his younger years, Raphael had taken full advantage of this phenomenon. Newly mated, however, the attention simply made him uncomfortable.

There was only ever going to be one woman for him, and that was the curvy little deer he'd left behind in the school house.

Aubrey Verene. Her name rolled off the tongue. Not that she would be Verene for much longer if he had anything to do with it. For starters, that deer-shifting clan

169

were a pain in the hoofs, lost in outdated ideas of what a mating ought to be.

Raphael didn't want or need a blindly obedient mate. No wolf shifter had ever favored one of those. She-wolves simply weren't docile like does were, which was why his pack had been outraged when they found out he'd mated with a deer.

They might have united with him in the attack of the southern wolves. That had been an attack on their territory, after all, and a threat to one of them was a threat to them all, but they sure as fuck hadn't appreciated the reason for it.

Serena, the highest-ranking female of their pack, and mother of the young she-wolf, who'd been trying to push her daughter onto him for weeks now, had been the most vocal of them all.

"This is preposterous. No wolf can be mated to a deer. You need a strong female by your side."

Raphael had challenged her, hackles drawn, teeth bared, and, eventually she had grudgingly bowed her head in submission.

Collins, as ever the peacemaker, had stepped in.

"Our Alpha has chosen."

While Collins had sided with Raphael in public, he'd had plenty to say to him in private.

"She is right. You need a strong female by your side. Deer are not known for their strengths and she's a Verene."

Collins had spat that name out as though it was an insult. His wolf had wanted to tear the other man's throat out for disrespecting their mate. His animal didn't care about any of that. Aubrey was his, and that was all there was to it. The man knew better, of course.

"She also left the community and has chosen to live in the village."

"Among humans. What does that tell you, boss? And she hasn't been back, has she? A she-wolf would have fought by your side, not hidden away in the one place we can't enter in our wolf forms. Are you sure about this?"

Raphael sighed, remembering that conversation, just as he had done then, and glared at the neat little cottage his mate called home.

She had green fingers, as one might have expected of her. Neatly trimmed flower beds lined the path up to her front door. With the snow having melted and spring in the air, the first shoots of whatever bulbs she'd planted were pushing through the earth. An equally impressive vegetable garden slumbered away by the side of the cottage. Her scent was everywhere, calming his agitated wolf. One sniff was all it took to locate her spare key inside the fake rock by the porch steps, and having scanned the area to make sure no one was watching him, he let himself in.

His wolf whined low in his throat because being surrounded by all the things she touched on a daily basis was bliss and hell all rolled into one. It also made him doubt what in the hell he was doing here.

This was her home, he could tell that from all the little personal touches, from the crocheted throws over the old settees nestled around the fireplace to the many sketches on her wall, which had clearly been drawn by her.

He stopped the longest at the picture of a black wolf. Teeth bared, he was staring right out of the sketch, silhouetted against the night sky, menacing, and dark. Was that how she saw him?

Prowling around her place and snooping in her things would not get him the answers he sought. It would no doubt just piss her off, and he hadn't come here to argue with her.

Raphael had enough arguments to last him a lifetime.

Wincing, he bent down to rummage around in her fridge. Barely healed, his side still hurt like the fucking bitch. The fight to the death the southern wolves' Alpha had challenged him to, the one he'd agreed to in order save his pack and to stop all-out war, had been hard won.

Driven by the need to avenge his sons' demise, the old timer had fought dirty. Manson Southern hadn't ruled his notorious pack and gotten away with their misdeeds for all that time without knowing how to fight.

It had taken all of Raphael's strength to bring the older wolf to its knees. The death of Manson meant Raphael was now in charge of them all, which placed the human village containing his mate smack bang in the middle of his territory.

He could just imagine his mate's face when he imparted that bit of knowledge. A deer surrounded by wolves.

Would she run, or would she stay? That was the question which sat heavily in his gut, as he set about preparing a meal for them both, with the few ingredients he'd found in the fridge.

Only one way to find out and he was going to settle this tonight, once and for all.

Aubrey was his and he would make her see that, come what may.

Chapter Four

Darkness had fallen in earnest by the time Aubrey left the school, having straightened everything she could think of, and she really couldn't dilly dally any longer. Besides, she wouldn't put it past him to come looking for her and to drag her off like some sort of caveman.

While the thought of being at his mercy had her pussy clenching in need—really, what was that about—she hadn't come this far to meekly submit. Alpha or not, mate or not, she wouldn't make this easy for him. How dare he show up at her place of work like that, as though it was his God-given right to do so.

And with flowers to boot.

Damn the man.

Aubrey grabbed the beautiful, extremely colorful bunch she'd left in the sink to water them, and made for home. It was only a short walk to her cottage. Normally speaking, having to cut across the church cemetery which stood between the school and her cottage didn't bother her, but tonight the fine hair on her arms rose. Her deer raised her nose in the air and froze. The unmistakable scent of wolves was in the air, and it wasn't the reassuring spicy scent of her mate's. Like it always did when she thought of him, the mark just under her hairline throbbed, and she took strength from that connection. Besides, this was her domain, and she'd be damned if she let some she-wolf frighten her on her own turf.

The sickly sweet smell, which had decidedly wet dog undertones—a thought, which made Aubrey grin despite the malicious intent she sensed from the shadows surrounding her—intensified. Had she not been so hyper-aware tonight, she would have screeched and dropped the flowers in her hand, when the big gray wolf jumped into her path.

Not as big as Raphael by any means, and clearly female, this she-wolf was still a formidable presence as she growled low in her throat and barred Aubrey's path. Other smaller wolves appeared until she was surrounded. Deathly quiet in their approach, they sniffed the air. Aubrey swallowed hard and tried her best to stare down the myriad of glowing eyes around her.

She wouldn't show them fear. They might smell it on her, but she would conquer this. How fucking dare they do this? Aubrey had left all this intimidation shit behind when she left the Verene deer, and hell would freeze over before she gave in to these wolves.

"Get out of my way, wolf."

She spun round in a circle holding that blessed bunch of flowers in front of her like some sort of shield. Not that it would do her any good if they chose to attack. To do so would break countless rules, however, and she could only hope they'd simply come to intimidate her.

This was the very reason she'd stayed out of the forest, after all. She'd known the wolves wouldn't be happy about her mating to Raphael.

At least that answered one question she'd been pondering. His bite on her neck clearly did mark her as his, otherwise they wouldn't have been here.

How fucking typical that was? She might very well be torn to pieces by a mob of angry wolves for being mated to their hot-as-hades Alpha, and she only had one kiss and erotic dreams for her trouble. One would think if she were to snuff it, the universe would at least have granted her a good shag with him first.

Aubrey couldn't help it. A somewhat hysterical laugh bubbled up and burst forth. Once she started, she couldn't stop laughing, and the wolf directly in front of her shifted into an athletic, middle-aged woman. She glared at her, arms crossed under her still far-too-perky boobs. She had to be in her fifties if the streaks of gray in her dark hair were any indication, but she was in excellent physical shape for a woman her age. Of course, she would be. Aubrey mentally rolled her eyes and sobered.

Damn bitch. That just wasn't fair. Here Aubrey was all soft and wobbly in places she could do without, and this woman, a good thirty years her senior, was all trim and bloody perfect.

"What's so funny, little doe?" The woman snarled that question, her eyes glowing menacingly in the dark.

Hearing those words come from her, made Aubrey see red. "Don't you call me that, bitch."

The older woman growled and advanced on her. Hands formed into claws, she made a menacing sight, one that would normally have made her deer cower in the corner. Sure enough, there was no way her animal was inclined to come out and play, but that was a good thing in the circumstances.

She didn't want to taunt the wolves with venison a la carte, so to speak.

Aubrey threw the flowers at her, not that they made contact due to the she-wolf's fast reflexes, but she had to do something.

The she-wolf laughed.

"That the best you got, you frightened little soul?"

Her handbag was next, and as the blasted woman clearly hadn't been expecting that, it made heavy contact with her shoulder, before it clunked on the ground.

Should have put an extra brick in that.

The wolf snarled in anger, but Aubrey wasn't done. What possessed her, she would never know, but instead of backing away, she advanced on the other woman. Hands on hips, she got right in her face until her sickly scent almost made her gag.

"I haven't even started yet. Get out my way. This is my home, and you have no business being here, let alone try and threaten me. I'm your Alpha's mate."

Surprise registered briefly in the she-wolf's eyes before she growled right in Aubrey's face. It was enough to make her want to gag, but she forced herself not to react.

Around her, the mood shifted. It was an almost imperceptible change of surprise and grudging respect.

The wolf tried again, but a menacing and all too familiar growl from behind her made her drop her head in submission.

Raphael appeared, looking edible and murderous all rolled into one. Aubrey breathed a sigh of relief at his appearance.

"Serena, what the fuck do you think you're doing?" He gave the woman a shove as he went past her, and placing his hand on Aubrey's nape, he took up a protective stance next to her. She couldn't help but lean into him a little, and his wolf growled low in his throat as the man's hold on her softened. Hells bells, the way his thumb caressed the sensitive skin under her ear... It sent all sorts of delicious shivers across her skin.

"She's not worthy to be your mate." Serena drew herself up to her full height and did her best to glare Aubrey into submission.

Too bad the bitch was straight out of luck, because with the scent of her mate surrounding her, his strength, warmth, and protection enveloping her, even her deer stopped being frightened.

Aubrey shook Raphael's hand off and took a step toward Serena.

"Says the bitch who needs a breath mint and a good wash. You smell, and not in a good way. Eau de wet dog doesn't work for canines let alone wolves."

Serena reared back at the insult, but Aubrey wasn't done yet.

"I told you once, and I'm not going to tell you again. Get. Out. Of. My. Way. I'm your Alpha's mate and I demand the respect due to me. Now move."

Heart pumping inside her chest so fast, Aubrey wasn't at all sure she might not be in danger of fainting—which would have completely ruined what she was going for here—she waited. Much to her surprise, Raphael hung back and didn't intervene.

His intense focus on her made her skin tingle, and she sensed his silent approval of her actions loud and clear, but he must have decided that she could handle this. In truth, Aubrey knew she had to get the other woman to back down, or this would never work, and she desperately wanted it to work.

Like it or not, she was his mate, and that meant something.

It seemed to take an interminably long time before Serena dropped her head and stepped out of the way.

Aubrey offered her a tight smile and bent down to pick up her bag and rescue her bunch of flowers, but a pretty young girl, who bore a remarkable resemblance to Serena, beat her to it. She handed her the items, bowed her head, and smiled at her.

"Here, let me, ma'am. Forgive my mother. She doesn't take to change well. For what's it worth, I think our Alpha chose well."

A loud huff came from Serena before the air around her shimmered and she changed back into her wolf. The pretty young thing, too, changed back. Clutching her possessions to herself, Aubrey resumed her journey to her cottage. If she walked much faster than she normally would have done, then surely she was allowed.

There was only so much confrontation and nakedness she could take on an empty stomach, especially when every one of those damn wolves was such a perfect specimen in their human form.

It just wasn't fair and, holy crap, she was *mated* to one of them. After her very public declaration, she would never get rid of him now. Far more worrying was the fact that she didn't really want to.

****

Raphael watched his mate sprint away with mixed feelings. He was so damn proud of her he thought his heart might just burst. He was also itching to tear a strip of Serena's hide, but that would have to wait.

He had a mating to complete.

Serena bowed to her knees and presented her throat in a clear sign of submission which calmed his agitated wolf. He waved her away with a snarl, and one by one, his pack disappeared until only Collins remained behind with his new mate.

He approached head down in his wolf form and nudged Raphael's leg.

This wasn't my idea, boss, just so you know.

Raphael responded to him as his wolf.

I know, it's done now. She did well, my little doe, did she not?

Raphael couldn't keep his pride out of his response and Collins laughed, while his mate sighed.

Aye, boss, that's she did. I take it we will not see you until the Hunt?

Raphael laughed and shook his head.

Maybe not even then. It might be too much for her yet.

Collins's mate cleared her throat.

Speaking as a mated female, Alpha, I think she may well surprise you.

Raphael grinned and once the two wolves had sprinted off, nudging each other in the playful way only newly mated and in-love wolves were apt to, he slowly retraced his own mate's steps.

She was silhouetted in the light spilling out from her windows and Raphael grinned to himself at the astonished expression on her face. Laying the table and adding candles to give it that romantic feel sure had been good moves on his part.

He shut the front door behind him with much more force than he needed to give her fair warning of his arrival. Even so, she still stood there, staring at the table he'd pushed in front of her open fireplace as though she'd never seen it before. The fire had gotten a good burn on it in the time that had passed for him to find out what was taking his mate so long and to get back here. She had to be too warm in the duffle coat she was still wearing over her clothes, and sure enough, beads of perspiration dotted her nose when he stepped up behind her.

"Let's get you out of this, and I'll put the flowers in water for you, too." He tugged the now rather disheveled-looking bunch out of the death grip she held them in, placed them on the table with her handbag, and reached around her to undo the buttons on her coat.

She looked up at him briefly with the startled eyes of her doe and then continued to stare into the flickering flames. They threw shadows across her face, and Raphael wished he knew what she was thinking. He let his fingers linger over the buttons by her breasts, satisfied beyond measure to hear her soft inhale. The coat gave way and she helped him shrug it off her shoulders. He flung it over the back of the settee and, turning her by her shoulders, brought his hands into her hair. Another one of those soft inhales, almost a moan, came from his mate as he removed the hairpins one by one, until her glorious tresses tumbled half way down her back and hung into her cleavage. At some point, since he'd left her at the school, she must have undone the top buttons of her blouse. The creamy skin he could see, the glimpse of a shadow in her impressive cleavage, made his wolf salivate with the need to taste her. To truly make her his, until she was in no doubt that she was owned by this Alpha.

However, knowing the examples of mated ownership she would have grown up within the Verene deer, he forced the possessive animal to stand down and gently steered her to the table instead. She fell, rather than sat, in the chair he pulled out for her, and when he poured her a glass of wine which he'd left in a cooler on the table, she finally spoke.

"What is all this?"

Raphael filled his own glass and clinked it to hers.

"I would have thought that was obvious, little doe. You clearly had a hard day, and that was before that stunt Serena pulled on you." He paused and smiled at her. It was beyond satisfying to see her this rattled. "So, I thought I would cook you some dinner and help you relax."

He took a long swallow of the Sauvignon Blanc, and his wolf positively strutted at the way her eyes followed his every move.

"You cook, too?"

"You'd be amazed at my talents, little doe."

Raphael winked at her, and the most endearing blush spread over her cheeks and into her cleavage. It made his fingers itch with the need to see how far down that blush went. Her breathing sped up under his silent scrutiny, and her nipples pushed against the cotton of her blouse. His dick, already at half-mast, gave up any pretense of behaving itself and punched forward with a speed that made him feel a little light headed. She noticed almost straight away, being that his crotch was in direct line with her face. Her little pink tongue darted out to wet her bottom lip, and Raphael growled a warning. Her eyes widened and her sweet musk increased, making his wolf want to explore the wetness he sensed between her legs.

The grip on the stem of his wine glass grew white-knuckled, and he forced himself to put that receptacle onto the table and take a step back, lest he gave in to the instinct to devour his mate.

"I'm going to check on our stew. It should be ready by now. Vegetable, of course, as that's the only thing you had in."

Aubrey's mouth fell open in surprise, and she shook her head. "You cooked me vegetable stew, but that … surely you're not a vegetarian?"

His wolf groaned in disgust, and Raphael forced a grim smile on his face.

"Of course not, but you are. Forcing you to eat meat would be as counterproductive as giving in to the urge I have to say "fuck the food", bend you over this table, and bury myself balls-deep inside that nice, juicy pussy I smell all wet and ready for me."

She gasped and went a little cross-eyed as he adjusted his dick away from his zipper with a groan of his own.

"However, that would make me a complete ass like the Verene Stags are to their mates, and I would never treat you like that."

Aubrey blinked and went very still at that grudging admission.

"You won't?" Her voice was barely above a whisper, but he heard her loud and clear, sensed her relief, and, if it wouldn't completely blow his street cred, he'd have punched the air in triumph. He had read her

181

reluctance right then.

"No, I won't. I want an equal partner as my mate. One I can proudly call my own. A woman who gives me her submission freely because she wants to. One who challenges me at every step. One with intelligence and the inner strength to stand up to my pack and demand the respect due to her. In other words, I want you, little doe."

Chapter Five

Aubrey knew she was doing goldfish impressions, but, really, she couldn't have heard him right, could she? She couldn't think of one thing to say, so she simply stared at him.

Raphael's smile was a little forced as he nodded, and then, having picked up the bunch of flowers on the table, turned on his heel and disappeared into her kitchen.

She could hear him open and shut the Aga, and the most delicious smell wafted into the living room. Her stomach promptly growled, reminding her how long it had been since she'd had something to eat. Raphael reappeared at that moment with her vase filled with what was left of the myriad of flowers he'd brought her.

"I shouldn't have thrown them at her. So many got broken." She reached out to touch the delicate stem of a violet and risked a look up at him.

Brows drawn together in a frown, Raphael seemed miles away. His wolf's low menacing growls sent a shiver of apprehension down her spine. Acting on instinct, she put her hand on his forearm and that incessant growling stopped.

His harsh features softened as he looked down on her. "I should make her leave the pack for daring to challenge you."

Aubrey shook her head so hard strands of her hair whipped around her face.

"No, you can't do that. She was only, well, I mean it's only natural to be wary. She doesn't know me, and on paper, the whole thing is ludicrous. Wolves eat deer, after all."

She recognized her mistake the minute the words came out of her mouth, because Raphael's eyes bled to the glowing yellow of his beast's, and when he smiled, she gasped at the sight of his razor-sharp incisors. The mark on her nape throbbed, her pussy clenched, and she couldn't stop her deep-throated moan in response to him.

"Oh, this wolf has every intention to eat you, little doe."

"Oh."

He smirked, shut her open mouth with his large index finger, and traced the contours of her lips almost absentmindedly before he shook himself and stepped back.

"Food first, though." He walked off, adjusting himself as he went, and Aubrey downed half of her glass of wine in one go. It warmed up her insides and caused an immediate nice buzz in her system.

She was in the process of refilling her wine glass when Raphael reappeared with two steaming bowls of vegetable stew in his large hands.

"Go easy on that until you've eaten something, sweetheart. I want you conscious when we make love later, not comatose."

He placed her bowl in front of her and sat down opposite her with his own food.

"Is that what we're going to do, then, make love?" she asked. "I thought you wolves just fucked doggy style." Lord only knew why she was goading him. It had to be the wine talking, or maybe she was just high on his presence, because she was so aroused, that the slightest friction against her clit would be enough to send her over the edge.

With that in mind, she clenched her thighs together and buried her gasp of delight in the mouthful of stew she'd just taken. "Oh God, this is so good."

She mumbled around the food in her mouth as countless flavors exploded on her taste buds. So engrossed was she in eating that she completely missed the fact that Raphael had gone very quiet. Only when she pushed her empty bowl away did she notice he'd hardly eaten anything. His hungry gaze devoured her instead, and she froze as she looked into the eyes of his wolf.

Everything south clenched in need, and he inhaled sharply.

"If you come now, I'll have to spank that luscious ass. Your orgasms are mine, little doe, and don't you forget it." He reached under the table to pry her legs apart, and he groaned as his nostrils flared. "You smell so fucking good. I want you."

The raw need in those growled words echoed her own feelings. "I wish you'd take me then, mate."

In the blink of an eye, he was on top of her, and Aubrey could only hold on for dear life as he lifted her up, chair and all, and proceeded to kiss her senseless. His sheer strength took her breath away, and burying her hands in his long hair, she kissed him back with all the pent-up sexual frustration she felt.

His hands shifted to her ass, and the chair crashed to the floor as she brought her legs around his waist and clung.

The heat of his solid erection branded her, even through the layers of clothing still separating her from her prize, and she moaned her need as her hips took on a life of their own.

Her back hit the wall with a thump when Raphael crowded her against it, not once breaking his fevered kisses. Grasping her hips, he rubbed her pussy up and down his cock while he ran his lethal teeth up and down her neck.

Shivers raced over her skin, and she didn't even know what she was pleading for, as the delicious friction his denim fly created against her clit threatened to send her over that edge.

"That's my girl, come for me, like this, right now. You're so fucking hot."

That growled command did it. Aubrey's climax raced through her, made ten times more potent by Raphael sinking his teeth into her neck. She screamed as waves of bliss pulled her under. They radiated out from his bite in ever wider circles until they all came together in her clit. That little bundle of nerves contracted, and her internal muscles clenched and released with the desperate need to be filled, stretched by her mate.

Lights flashed behind her eyes, and she was dimly aware of Raphael carrying her upstairs before she flew through the air and onto her bed. He was on top of her before she'd even stopped bouncing, and together they somehow managed to rid each other of their remaining clothes until they were both gloriously naked, with Raphael positioned between her splayed legs. So close, yet so far. One hand by her head he kept his weight off of her, while his fingers dug into her hip to stop her attempts to wriggle closer to his cock.

His claws ran out as she continued to struggle, and she gasped at the pain, which only served to make her more determined to have him inside of her.

"Stop it, little doe. Just let me look at you."

His deep voice had dropped a further octave and held that steel of command which simply meant she had to obey him. With his eyes glowing softly in the dim light of her bedroom, and his long hair hanging down, enveloping them both in a cocoon of intimacy, she could do nothing else but stare up at her mate.

Oh my God, he really is my mate.

Raphael's stern features softened as though he could read her mind, and who knew, maybe he could. After all, she read his emotions loud and clear. The waves of possessiveness should have been a turn-off, yet with Raphael looking at her as though she was the most precious thing to him, they were anything but.

"Have I told you how beautiful you are, mate?" he asked, dipped his head, and then inhaled deeply next to her ear. His beard tickled, and Aubrey giggled. His growl shook the bed, and in the next instant, he flexed his hips and thrust into her waiting body in one long, measured move. Despite how wet she was for him, his move hurt as her body struggled to accept his size. Already his cock swelled, thickened in the knot which would keep him locked to her as they rode out this, their first proper joining.

"Fuck, you feel so good. Relax for me, breathe, and let me in. That's my very good girl.

Raphael shifted so that he could grasp her breasts. He buried his head between them, breathed in, and then licked a path of fire over her skin with his raspy tongue until he could suck her nipple into his mouth. Aubrey groaned under the onslaught of his mouth and fingers, and she lifted her hips. That move meant he slipped further into her body until she was so utterly filled by him she didn't know where he ended and she began. Gasping for breath, pinned in place by his considerable bulk, she couldn't move, could barely breathe, truth be told. Not that it mattered, not when every fiber of her being was on fire for this man, as he grew even bigger inside her.

A high keening sound filled the air, and it took a moment to register it was coming from her, and then, Raphael raised his head and slowly ran his clawed fingers down her body until he could grasp handfuls of her ass.

He groaned deep in his throat, and lifting her ass up, he shifted to his knees. It made him gain even deeper penetration, his balls hit her ass, and Aubrey gasped and tried to shut her eyes against the sensation overload she was subjected to.

Open your eyes, sweetheart. I want you to see how my cock stretches you. You're mine now, little doe, and I shan't ever let you go.

His voice in her head carried the deep growl of his wolf, and if she'd needed any more proof that they were meant to be, this was *it*.

I can hear you. I can hear your wolf.

Aubrey opened her eyes and gasped anew when she looked into the eyes of his animal. Right now, here in this moment, it all fell into place. There was no room for doubt, only this overwhelming feeling of belonging, of having found her safe haven, the one place in all this earth she was meant to be.

Raphael's lopsided grin in response to her as he pulled almost all the way out of her, made her fall in love with him all over again, and she blurted out the feelings of her heart.

"I love you."

Raphael threw his head back and howled while sliding back inside her pussy. That move sent every one of her nerve endings alight with the need for this man, her destiny, her mate.

Of course you can hear him, you're ours. I love you, little doe.

Aubrey clenched around his cock, and it seemed to be the signal Raphael had needed because he allowed his wolf to take over. Aubrey stopped thinking and simply felt as Raphael thrust in and out of her like a madman. The bed bashed against the wall, and Aubrey met her mate thrust for glorious thrust as the pressure built between them to unbearable levels with Raphael shouting his possession of her with every push into her.

"You. Are. Mine."

"Yes, yes, I am. Oh God, I'm going to…"

Aubrey screamed as her orgasm hit, and Raphael pulled out of her. He flipped her over and then surged back into her pussy while sinking his teeth into her shoulder.

That sharp pain morphed into bliss so intense, Aubrey couldn't breathe, couldn't do anything but absorb the incredible feeling of being owned body and soul by this man, as he stiffened above her. Raphael roared his release, heat bathed her insides, and she came again as his cock expanded to impossible dimensions, and he knotted in place. Her vision dimmed and the world narrowed as she became one with man and wolf, her deer wrapping itself around his wolf, as he stood over her to protect her always.

By the time she could breathe with any degree of normalcy, Raphael had rolled them so that they were on their sides, still joined together in the most intimate of embraces. His rough tongue licked his mark, and he nuzzled in when he noticed she was with him again.

"Hey, mate."

Propping himself up on one elbow, he looked down on her and the tenderness in his gaze proved her complete undoing. Tears sprang into her eyes, and try as she might, she couldn't stop them from falling. His wolf's whine echoed in her head while the man pulled her closer and kissed the tears off her face.

I'm okay, it's all right, really.
Then why are you crying, my love?
I don't know. I'm just so happy I guess.

Raphael's sharp exhale ghosted across her face, and she could feel his relief as he relaxed around her and kissed her nose. His knot slowly lessened and, their bodies thus released, he rolled over, taking her with him so that she half rested on his chest. Closing her eyes, she nestled in, loving the way his chest hair made the comfiest cushion ever. Aubrey let her hands explore the dips and valleys of his abdomen. She frowned when her questing digits encountered the raised scar tissue just above his hip. His wolf whined, and the man took a deep breath in.

"What happened?" she asked, even as horrific images of Raphael in wolf form, fighting for his life, flooded her mind.

Oh my God, you fought. For me?

She tried to push away, but Raphael rolled them again until he was back on top of her. Raising her arms above her head, he pinned them down, and Aubrey mewled in need when she felt his cock harden anew. It nudged her mound, and Raphael's grin grew sinful as he looked down on her.

"Again? So soon?"

In answer, he simply lifted one of her legs over his shoulder and seated himself in her pussy in one slow measured thrust that made her internal muscles quiver around him.

"Yes, I want you, and I've waited a long time."

Whatever protest she might have had was stopped by his kiss, and Aubrey simply gave up and made love with him. There was no other way to describe it really, as they brought each other to release time and time again. By the time she finally fell into exhausted sleep, the first rays of sunshine were turning the sky orange.

****

Raphael woke up to the smell of coffee. He smiled and promptly frowned when he reached across the bed to find it empty. His wolf growled his annoyance and immediately scanned their surroundings for his mate. She wasn't far. He could sense her presence in his mind. Gentle humming filled it, and Raphael threw the covers off and stretched. The sharp pain that action usually evoked in his side didn't materialize this morning. The scars were still there and always would be, but they didn't hurt anymore. Sex with his mate had healed the last of his injuries.

My mate.

His grin deepened as he padded across to the bathroom, used the facilities, and then made his way downstairs.

Aubrey was standing at the kitchen sink, hands clasped around a mug of coffee, staring across at the forest and seemingly miles away. A deep-throated moan escaped her when he came up behind her, pulled her flush against him, and rubbed his morning wood, made ten times more prominent by the sight of her wearing nothing but his t-shirt, into her ass cheeks. He had to bend his knees to do so because she was a good head shorter than him in her bare feet. The fact that she immediately grew wet for him, the sweet musk of her arousal hitting his nostrils, did not help his stiffy one bit.

To distract himself from visions of bending her over right here and now and taking her from behind, he nuzzled into her neck, and then snatched the coffee cup from her.

"Oi, you, that's mine. Get your own, wolf."

Laughter tinged her voice, and sure enough, when he pushed away from her, shrugged, and downed the coffee in one go, she mock-glared at him.

Her gaze traveled up and down his body, snared on his erection, which made her bite her lips and groan and then settled on his side. Her eyes widened, and reaching out, she ran the tips of her fingers over the scars.

"They look better," she said.

"The best sex a wolf ever had will do that to the man," he said, and linking his fingers with hers, he lifted them up to kiss her knuckles. "Good morning, beautiful."

Aubrey cocked her head to one side and narrowed her eyes.

"Really, the best sex ever?" Her tone of voice told of her doubts, and his wolf snarled at her. His little doe stuck her tongue out at him.

"Yes, really, you're my mate and wolves mate for life."

Her face fell and Raphael silently cursed the doubts he still sensed from her. To put his point across, he put her hand back on his scars, cupped her nape with his free hand, and pulled her closer so that he could rest his forehead on hers. Their scents mingled, their respective animals reaching out to each other at the same time until they became one.

These scars will always serve as a reminder of the day you came into my life. I killed for you then, and I will do so in future if I have to.

Aubrey pushed against his chest as though to pull away, but he was having none of that.

"No, no regrets, my sweet. The southern wolves had it coming. Killing their Alpha has put me in charge. It will take time, but I have every intention of getting them to clean up their act. There were many who came forward after the fight to pledge their allegiance to me and my mate."

Aubrey's surprised inhale gave him access, and he claimed her mouth in a passionate kiss which served to tell her all he couldn't put into words.

By the time he broke the kiss to take a much-needed gulp of air, Aubrey's doubts had lessened in his mind.

"Can we really make this work?" she asked.

Raphael sighed and pulled her in close. The instinctive way in which she snuggled into his embrace as he rested his chin on the top of her head meant his love for her expanded and grew until he thought he might burst.

"We can and we will. Anything else is not an option, little doe."

Epilogue

Raphael raised his nose into the air and howled at the full moon. The heavy ball of pale light hung low in the night sky, so close that one could almost touch it.

Around him, the answering howls of his pack came from all corners of the forest. The Hunt was on. Adrenaline surged through him as he ran through the trees in search of the one scent that meant the world to him. She was clever, his mate. Knowing that she could never outrun him, especially not now, she'd chosen to hide. He zigzagged here and there, hot on her trail. Her time was close and no one in the pack would have thought any less of her had she sat this hunt out, but not so his mate.

From the very first hunt she had joined, her beautiful deer form had become a familiar figure at the pack hunt. Sticking close to his side at first, and then, as her confidence grew sprinting side by side with the she-wolves and the cubs.

A true leader and guide to the younger females as they came to her with their troubles, always a hug for the little ones, and not too proud to listen to the advice of the older and wiser females of the group, she had proven her place by his side time and time again. The little cottage she had refused to leave because she was still very much the local and much-loved teacher, had become a second pack house.

Recent additions had made it bigger, better able to accommodate the meetings they held and their growing numbers.

The plaintive mewl brought him up short as he crested the hill. Followed by the cutest attempt of a growl, it came from the secluded meadow where they'd made love many times this summer. Of course, she would go there for this most precious of occasions. Belly to the ground, so as not to startle them, Raphael inched forward. The view that greeted him took his breath away. His little doe curled up on her side, licking the fawn while the wolf cub blindly nudged his mother's belly to find the milk he sought.

Aubrey looked up from her task and smiled at him.

Meet your son and daughter, Raphael.

The End

ALPHA AT ALTITUDE

Lily Harlem

Copyright © 2017

Chapter One

Chloe Burton reached for her bottle of beer and glanced around the crowded bar. At seven thousand feet above sea level, it wasn't a usual drinking hole. It wasn't only the thin air that gave the game away, it was also the dirt floor, the scruffily dressed clientele and the snow which skittered in whenever the rickety door was opened.

But the beer was cold—like everything else—and the all-male faces friendly, so she wasn't complaining.

All except one face. She knew him only as Aaron and he was one of the few white men who lived in the remote Nepalese village of Nagasti. She'd spoken to him several times over the last few days as she'd waited for her colleague, Jim, to recover, and each time his gaze had been so intense she'd felt like he was drinking her in, memorizing her features … imagining her naked and spread before him.

Phew, what a way to heat up!

Because she'd be willing. He was handsome in a rough-and-ready kind of way. His blond hair, streaked with unusual black strands, hung over his ears and down his neck and appeared perfect for gripping. His eyes were the palest green, reminding her of the delicate moss coating tree trunks back home in England. And his jawline and neck were coated with the dense facial hair all the local men favored, no doubt it kept them warm when checking their animals on the mountain and tending the meager crops growing on the slopes.

She glanced his way. It had become a habit to know where he was.

As usual, he was looking at her from a seat in the corner. He didn't drink alcohol, she'd noticed, and a glass of iced water sat before him. Iced water? A cold beer was fine, it was the only way to drink beer, but really … ice in his water? Up here where the temperature had been sub-zero for months?

He inclined his head, acknowledging her, and kept his gaze steady.

A small shiver ran up her back and tickled over her scalp. It was more than just his looks she found fascinating. It was the whole package. He wasn't a man of many words, she'd found, but what he did say was to the point. And he knew the mountains better than the locals, so she'd been told. He was also tough, the freezing temperatures and bitterly cold winds barely seeming to affect him. And while everyone else huddled beneath several layers of wool, fur, and leather, he wore only dark pants and a black sweater, even when outside.

She took a sip of beer and studied the map in front of her. Two weeks ago, along with Jim, she'd set several motion sensor cameras a few kilometers from the village and spread over a wide area of the mountains. They were hoping to catch footage of snow leopards in the wild, hopefully a mother and cubs. Eager to prove herself, even though only twenty-five, as a wildlife documentary producer, Chloe had a good feeling about this place. Stories amongst the locals were rife. It seemed the leopards were around, as a couple of sheep had been taken over the last year. Sadly this made the beautiful creatures unpopular with their human neighbors, and this situation didn't help their dwindling numbers. Add in poachers who wanted their fur, and it was no wonder these rare animals were so keen to hide away from people.

She rubbed her lips with the tip of her finger, a nervous habit, and hoped Jim would soon recover from his bad stomach. He'd been laid up since they'd returned from setting the cameras, which had meant staying in the village. He'd been too weak to travel down the mountain and he refused to be carried by Sherpa. She couldn't blame him, because that would be a perilous and nausea-inducing way to travel.

But if she didn't get the motion cameras back soon, she'd be going over schedule, something her boss would frown upon. And more to the point, if she hadn't captured any footage, she wouldn't have time to reset the cameras in different locations.

Again she glanced at Aaron.

He'd sat back and crossed his arms, his biceps straining against the material of his sweater. He was still staring straight at her.

Damn, those eyes. If only she could read them, find out what he was thinking. Sometimes she wondered if her presence annoyed him, other times it seemed as if he wanted to flip her over the table and fuck her.

Perhaps if Jim was still unwell in the morning she could ask Aaron to go with her to retrieve the cameras.

No. That was a crazy thought. Why would he help? As a carpenter, he surely always had work to do. She could pay him, but money didn't appear to be a driving force in his life.

She tore her gaze from his and folded the map. No, she wouldn't ask him. And she also wouldn't wait for Jim. The forecast predicted a break in the weather for the next few days, so she'd go alone. It wasn't as if she didn't have the gear or the training to survive in the mountains. And retrieving a few cameras was hardly scaling Everest.

Standing, and feeling pleased she'd made a decision, she finished her beer and then headed out of the bar.

Several of the men, young and old, bid her goodnight, smiling and showing various dental issues. Her unplanned stay had been made pleasant by the friendliness of the people. Men and women were happy to chat the best they could given the language barrier, and she'd been made to feel welcome.

The night air was bitterly cold and freezing fog shimmered before her. She retrieved her flashlight and turned it on. The small room she'd rented was only a hundred yards away, but with no street lamps and a moonless sky, she needed to light her way.

She trudged along, a fresh layer of snow squeaking underfoot. She tugged up her zipper, protecting the lower half of her face from the chill, and was glad of the snow reflecting the flashlight.

She reached her low, shack-like building and pulled out the key. Fumbling a little in the dark, she suppressed a shiver. She'd be glad to light a fire and get into bed.

A soft thud came from behind her.

Turning, she raised the flashlight, her heart rate picking up.

Aaron stood only a meter from her.

"Bloody hell. What are you doing?" she asked. "You scared me."

"I apologize."

She pressed her hand to her chest, willing her heart to settle.

He watched her movement, his eyelids heavy and

199

his breath collecting in the air before him.

"It's not polite to sneak up on women in the dark."

"Maybe you shouldn't be out on your own in the dark."

"This place is safe enough." She lowered the torch down his body and rested the ring of light on his clumpy leather boots.

"It's not safe for you."

"What does that mean?" She raised the light to his face again.

He didn't blink. "It means I don't want you out alone."

She bristled. He had no claim on her. No right to tell her what she could and couldn't do. "I walk around London all the time."

"This isn't London." He paused. "Or hadn't you noticed?"

She frowned. His question didn't deserve an answer. Besides, she was fascinated by the way the freezing fog had settled in his facial hair and the bangs hanging around his temples. It sparkled, as though he'd had glitter shaken over him, and it made him appear almost ethereal.

"There is more danger here than you realize," he said.

"Like what?"

He stepped closer and cupped her elbows in his palms.

It was the first time he'd touched her, and the sensation of his fingers applying pressure to the material of her jacket sent tremors up her arms, over her shoulders, and across her back.

"I am concerned for you," he said, lowering his face to hers.

"Why?"

"You are a white female high in the Himalayas. Your sort is not found here often."

"Is that why you keep staring at me?"

"No." He shook his head.

"So why?"

"Why do I stare at you, or why are you in danger?"

She wanted the answer to both questions, but chose the one her mother would opt for. "Why am I in danger?"

"The Shaman have been here. To your home."

"I don't know what you mean."

He tugged her to the left and reached above her door to the frame. "They've left this?" He plucked a feathered-covered object, the size of his thumb, from a length of string.

"What is it?" Chloe asked. She peered at it and then quickly recoiled. "Oh, yuck!"

"It's a chicken foot." He paused. "It's a warning."

"But ... why?"

"You have been here too long for their comfort. You have been too familiar amongst the men of the village."

"Hey, I resent that. Apart from some friendly chat in the bar ... if you can call it that ... I've stuck to myself."

"That's exactly it. How many women do you see in that place?"

"Er ... well ... none."

"Exactly. It is not the way of the village."

"But no one said I couldn't go in." Her mind was spinning. She'd felt welcomed, comfortable. Had she really overstepped the mark?

"They have now." He stepped back and then

hurled the offending clawed foot into the air. It was quickly engulfed in darkness and Chloe knew it would land somewhere down the steep slope to the right of her shack.

"Well." She set down her shoulders. "They don't have to worry anymore. I'm heading into the mountains at first light to retrieve my cameras. Then, I'll be on my way."

He raised his eyebrows. "Your colleague is better?"

"I don't need Jim. I can manage alone."

"And you're not worried about the storm?" He folded his arms and frowned.

"There's no storm. The forecast is settled for the next few days."

He tipped his head and huffed.

"What's that noise for?" She didn't think Aaron would have the access to meteorological information the way she did.

"I disagree. There is a storm coming."

She spun her key in her gloved hand. "I'll take my chances."

"That's my point." He wrapped his hand over hers, stilling the key. "I don't want you taking chances."

His gaze was intense, and heat from his body poured onto her.

"Get off me."

He didn't move, just made a low growling sound.

"Aaron." She tugged her hand away. "I appreciate your concern. But I'm a big girl. I'm perfectly capable of taking care of myself in the mountains, even if I come across Shaman, storms, and snow leopards."

"You really think so?"

"Yes. I do." She turned, unlocked her door, and quickly let herself into her room.

As she closed the door, she had one last glance at the man who seemed to be tailing her. What was it with him? Why did he care about her safety so much? He hardly knew her and certainly not enough to tell her what to do.

But damn it, the guy was cute. Her heart rate had rocketed by being close to him. And when he'd touched her...

Chapter Two

At first light, Chloe slipped a note under Jim's door, telling him her plans. She then hoisted her heavy rucksack onto her back, locked up, and followed the small gravel trail heading west from the village.

It was barely trodden as the locals preferred the southerly slopes for their crops. The air was still and sunlight reflected off the snow, making her glad of her shades.

Chloe didn't usually mind being on her own, but thoughts of the chicken claw and Shaman kept sneaking into her brain. Had she really annoyed some of the village elders? And if so, why not say something to her? No need for mangled animal parts to be left dangling from her doorframe for her to find.

Or rather for Aaron to find.

She stomped onward, navigating past a steep drop, then up a slope with sharp gray rocks jutting from it. She had two miles to go before she reached the first of four cameras. Then it would be another mile to the second. She planned on sleeping in the small sheltered valley she and Jim had used before, then retrieving the other two cameras and heading back to the village. The distances she needed to cover weren't huge, but with difficult terrain, it could take several hours to travel a mile or two.

She paused and had a sip from her water bottle, took a moment to enjoy the beautiful view. It really was like being on the top of the world. Below her, clouds hovered, and level with her, an eagle soared.

She heard a sound from behind and turned, but there was nothing there, not even a Himalayan rabbit.

"Stop it." She frowned. The last thing she needed

was her imagination going into overdrive. There were no Shaman around.

But what about poachers?

If there were, she was sure they'd stay well out of her way. Or at least that was what she was telling herself.

She carried on, warming as the sun rose, and keeping a watch out for leopard tracks.

There were none.

Several times she checked behind herself. A strange sense of being followed was bugging her.

It's only what Aaron said that's put me on edge.

Finally, and with the help of her compass, she came to the first motion sensor camera.

"I hope you've come out to play, snow leopards," she said, dismantling it. There were no tracks around it, but the snow here was deep and fresh and could be covering evidence.

After securing the camera safely in her rucksack and munching a protein bar, she took a northeasterly course.

A shadow slipped over her, engulfing the surrounding rocks. She glanced upward. A large, fluffy white cloud covered the sun.

"Mmm … don't get any ideas," she said. Aaron's words came back to her. *Aren't you worried about the storm?* "One cloud does not make a storm."

Even so, she sped up and made good progress to the next camera.

Here there were large feline tracks in the snow. She couldn't be sure if they were leopard, as pallas cats also inhabited the area. Though if anything, they were even harder to come across than leopards, so she hoped it would be the creature she was after.

Feeling more positive, Chloe glanced at the sky. The clouds had gathered, but there was no wind. She'd carry out her plan and stay in the mountains overnight. She probably didn't have enough daylight hours to get back to the village anyway. And she did need those other cameras. Plus, apart from anything else, she was tired.

Half an hour later, she was in the small sheltered valley. It wasn't exactly hospitable, but with the right equipment, which she had, it would be sufficient for the night.

She set about erecting her orange tent against the side of a huge pyramid-shaped rock clinging to the edge of the mountain.

Once the tent was up, she stepped back and gave it a visual check. A sudden clunking noise to her right caught her attention. It was a small stone running down the side of the rock. She glanced upward, wondering what had disturbed it, but could see nothing.

Again, an uneasy feeling swirled in her belly. She was all alone, miles from anywhere.

She shook her head. It was probably a bird or a rabbit, nothing more sinister.

Needing water, which flowed down the rocks at the far end of the gully, she headed off with her bottle. She'd make herself a cup of tea and a hot meal. The best way to ensure she stayed warm was to heat from the inside.

After collecting icy water, she returned to her tent. But as she approached, the niggling feeling rushed into something more. Fear.

Hanging from her tent, by its feet, was a dead chicken. The whole thing this time, not just a foot, and it appeared freshly killed—it's throat slit, blood dripping onto the virgin-white snow.

She clasped her hand over mouth, held in a scream. Spinning, she searched the small valley.

There was no one there.

But there *had* to be someone.

She needed to get back to the village. Aaron had been right. She shouldn't have come alone. There was much more danger up here than the elements.

Thinking of the weather, she glanced up. The clouds had taken on a dark hue, and as she looked, a gust of wind pressed her jacket to her body.

"Shit," she muttered, turning back to the tent.

She gasped and a burst of terror shot into her veins. She dropped her water bottle.

Standing at the entrance to her tent was a man. He wore a long black coat with strapping binding it to him, and his boots were the same as the locals wore. His face was partly covered by his fur-lined hood, but what she could see had been painted with vertical red stripes.

He stared at her, and at his side, he held a knife dripping with blood.

Adrenaline pulsed through her. Did he mean to slash her throat the same way he had the chicken? Was she about to meet her maker?

"What do you want?" she shouted, clenching her fists and hoping she sounded braver than she felt.

He began to chant and walk toward her, leaving a trail of bright red droplets in his wake. His eyes were dark and manic, as if he were in some kind of trance.

She turned, stifling a scream. She had to get out of there. Run. Find a way down the mountain however she could.

But I'll die trying.

She stilled and a fresh wave of panic swarmed over her skin. Pacing toward her, its shoulders shifting and its green gaze fixed on hers, was a huge snow leopard. If she'd been scared before, now she was terrified.

The beast was baring its teeth, the canines

enormous. A low purring noise, more like a growl, emanated from it, and its huge paws sank into the snow.

Chloe didn't know what to do. Nausea twisted her guts and her legs threatened to give way.

The creature grew closer, its eyes flashing.

There was nothing for it. She'd have to take her chances with the Shaman and run back that way. Maybe she could fight him, because she didn't have a hope against the powerful beast stalking her. It would knock her out with one swipe of its paw.

But just as she'd made her decision, the leopard broke into a run.

She screamed and shut her eyes, waiting for impact and for its teeth to sink into her neck.

But there was nothing more than a rush of air and a flurry of snow against her cheek.

A yelp echoed against the rocky cliff, and she spun to see the Shaman drop his knife and run.

The leopard was after him, its tail rod-straight and a cascade of snow puffing up behind it.

The Shaman made for the narrow gap in the cliff leading from the shelter of the valley. He went out of sight a second before the leopard did.

Chloe rushed to her tent, ignoring the gruesome blood splatters on the snow, dived inside, and zipped it up.

What if the Shaman outsmarted the leopard and came back for her? What if the leopard doubled around, still hungry, and dragged its claws through the flimsy material of the tent, sank its teeth into her, made *her* its supper?

She drew up her knees and hugged them, barely suppressing a whimper as a loud rumble of thunder bellowed overhead.

Tears flowed down her cheeks. She hated herself

for crying. It wasn't who she was. She was tough, independent. A modern woman making a profession for herself and perfectly capable of surviving the elements.

But leopards and mad men?

The gusting wind pushed the sides of the tent and yanked at the ropes she'd used to secure it.

Her shelter for the night would be no help to her if the leopard came back still hungry. But it gave her some kind of mental protection. It wouldn't be able to see her, and she wouldn't be able to see it.

Chloe didn't know how long she sat there. It became dark. The storm continued. She was cold. She wanted to make food and a drink but was too scared to move. What if the leopard was prowling around outside? What if it was waiting for her to show herself?

And then pounce.

As she stared at the shadowed zipper on the tent, watching the material billow, it suddenly pulled upward. The noise of it seared through her eardrums and she scooted to the farthest corner of the tent, pressing herself against it. Once again terror twisted her guts.

The Shaman was back. He must have outrun the leopard somehow, used his magic and tricks to escape. And now he'd come to kill her, stab her with his rusty knife and bleed her dry

She held in a scream as a face appeared, the features lit by the weak reflection of the snow on the tent.

But it wasn't the Shaman.

"Aaron?"

Chapter Three

Is it really him? Is Aaron really here?

She wasn't sure if fear was playing tricks on her brain.

"Are you unharmed?" he asked, his familiar deep voice was like a song to her ears.

She pressed her fingers to her lips, holding in a sob of relief.

Concern flashed over his eyes and he quickly let himself into the tent, securing the zipper behind himself. He then flicked on the small light she'd been too afraid to illuminate.

As soon as he turned back to her, Chloe hurled herself at him.

"Hey, hey, it's all right," he said, wrapping his arms around her and holding her tight. "I'm here. Nothing will hurt you now. I promise."

"Oh God, it was so awful." She pressed her face against his sweater and closed her eyes. "First the Shaman, and there was … a chicken … and blood." A sob bubbled up. "And then he was chasing me with a knife … and there was a … leopard."

"I thought you liked snow leopards?" He spoke against her hair, his breath heating her scalp.

"I do … from a distance."

"He wouldn't have hurt you. Maybe lick you a little."

"He was looking at me like he … wanted to do more … than lick me."

Aaron chuckled and tipped her chin with his finger. "You think he wanted to eat you?"

"Yes. But luckily he chased the Shaman and not me." She looked into his pale eyes which were somehow familiar. "Do you think he's killed him?"

"I doubt it, maybe just scared him away."

"Well, I'm grateful, but what if he comes back?"

"The Shaman?"

"No, the leopard." She nodded at the tent walls. "These won't keep him out if he's hungry. You should have seen the size of his teeth. And he'll have enormous claws, too."

"He's not hungry."

Chloe frowned. "How can you know?"

"There's plenty of food up here for leopards, plus there's the chicken."

"Oh, yes … I suppose." She sat back a little and smoothed his sweater. It had rumpled over his chest where she'd clutched it. "Sorry."

"It's okay." He seemed in no hurry to release her and kept his arms around her torso.

"But … but what are you doing here?" She frowned. "And where is your coat and your equipment?"

He smiled, just a tiny tilt of his lips, and gave her a squeeze. "I've got everything I need."

She raised her eyebrows and sniffed, pleased her embarrassing crying had passed. "But where?"

"In this tent." He tipped his head, studying her with the small smile still in place. "I have everything I need right here."

"Ah, you knew I'd have all the equipment, right." She paused. "When you followed me."

"I can't deny I followed you." He nodded. "And it is a good job I did."

She pressed her lips together and nodded. Seeing Aaron stick his head through the tent had been one of the best things to have ever happened to her. "But why *did* you follow me?"

"I was concerned for your safety and wellbeing."

"But what concern is it of yours?"

His smile fell away. "More than you could possibly know." He'd spoken in a low, firm voice, the heat of his words washing over her face.

She reached up and pressed her palms to his cheeks, his facial hair tickling her skin. "I'm glad you did."

"Good." His eyes darkened and a crease plowed over his brow.

He is so damn sexy.

"But right now," he said, and rubbed his hands up her back and drew her a fraction nearer, "we need to get you warmed up."

She shivered and realized he was right, though being so close to him was very pleasant. Despite him not wearing much clothing, heat radiated from his body. And also his scent had wrapped around her, a dark musky smell that seeped into her nostrils and filled her lungs with need—a need for what, she didn't know.

She swallowed.

Yes. I do know.

She wanted him. She had from the first minute she'd seen him. She could admit it to herself now. His brooding demeanor, the way he seemed to devour her with his gaze, had made him the most irresistible man she'd ever met.

Or at least that was how it felt right now.

She threw herself at him, connecting her mouth was his.

He tensed, his mouth unmoving, his limbs stiff.

For a split second.

Then he took full control of the kiss. Groaning, he slanted his head and drove his tongue into her mouth. He slotted his hands into her hair, holding her firm as he deepened the kiss.

She gasped for breath as lust infused her system. He tasted divine, of man and desire and everything she needed in her life and thought she'd never have again when death had knocked on her door.

He slipped his hands to her jacket and began to remove it. She helped by shrugging her shoulders, then once it was free, she tugged at his sweater.

Their kiss broke briefly as they pulled it over his head.

For a moment she paused and took in the sight of his broad chest. It was tan with the same combination of blond hair with black patches as he had on his head. His nipples were small and hard and his pecs broad—he had three raised scars on the left one, equal distance apart.

She gripped the roundness of his shoulders and kissed him again, loving the scratch of his beard on her face.

He was fiddling with her sweater, and within seconds, it was off, revealing her thermal layer.

"You have too much on," he murmured.

"So take it off."

"I intend to." He whipped off her black underlayer, exposing her bra, and then snapped apart the buttons on her trousers.

Her heart hammered, her breaths came fast. She no longer felt cold, and heat blasted through her. As he kneeled back and deftly set to undoing the laces of her clumpy boots, she stared at his wide torso and the way the muscles in his arms danced under his skin as he worked. There was another scar, on his right forearm, three lines, like the one on his chest.

Soon one boot was off, and then the other.

He gave her a dark look, one that oozed lust and desire, and then pulled at her trousers, dragging them down her legs, her knickers going with them.

"Aaron." She gasped as the force of his actions knocked her back onto the sleeping bag she'd set out earlier.

"I want you to be mine." He whisked her clothing from her ankles and tossed the bunch of material aside. It hit the lining of the tent and slid down. "I have wanted you from the moment I saw you."

"I didn't think you even liked me."

Confusion crossed his face. "The first time I saw you, smelled you … I wanted you."

She smiled and spread her legs. "So have me."

God, when had she gotten so brazen? It must have been her close shave with a Shaman and a leopard that had done it.

He scanned her body, his gaze settling on her pussy, and licked his lips.

A tremor went through her. For a second, her power slipped away and she felt almost sacrificial lying before him. But she wanted to be his, she wanted him more than she'd ever wanted any man.

He raised so he was on his knees and undid his black pants. He pushed them to his thighs. Apparently absent of underwear, his cock jutted out, hard and thick.

Chloe squeezed her internal muscles. Damn, the guy was well-hung. But she shouldn't be surprised, the rest of him was huge, too.

"This first time, as I claim you," he said, resting over her, his chest touching her bra and his cock tapping her thigh, "will be amazing."

"Claim me?" That was an odd expression.

He smiled. "Yes. Claim you." As he'd spoken, he'd pushed two fingers into her pussy. A firm drive until he was knuckle deep.

She whimpered and arched her back.

"You're so soft and hot," he said against her lips.

"And so ready for it."

"Yes. Fuck me. Aaron, fuck me."

"You are keen to mate?"

"Mate, fuck, shag, screw, whatever you want to call it." She reached for his cock and wrapped her fingers around his heated flesh. "Make me forget about everything except you."

"I can do that." He pumped his fingers in and out of her.

She groaned. She'd meant to work his erection, caress him, too, but all she could concentrate on was Aaron's touch, his fingers working her internally and the heel of his hand catching on her clit.

She closed her eyes, the first spark of an orgasm growing.

After a few minutes, he withdrew. His weight settled heavier over her and his nose touched hers.

Staring into his eyes, she cupped his cheeks.

He sought her entrance with the tip of his cock and stilled. "I want you."

"You've got me."

"Have I?"

"Yes." She tilted her hips, trying to seat herself on him.

"Oh, to the gods above," he murmured and then pushed in.

His wide cock parted her delicate flesh as he took a slow ride to full depth.

Chloe held her breath and didn't take her attention from his eyes as he filled her. It was exquisite to be so stretched, so invaded.

She curled her toes in their socks and hooked her legs behind his. She was panting, her chest rubbing up against his.

"I'm going to make you feel so good," he said,

kissing over her cheek to her ear. "Full of pleasure."

"Yes, make me come, now."

"But you have to keep breathing, you're at altitude."

"So are you."

"It doesn't affect me."

She wondered about asking him why, but her need for fucking was stronger than her need to know what he was talking about. Altitude affected everyone. "Make me come. Come with me. Please."

He buried his face in her neck and began to rock his hips.

The way he moved caught her clitoris perfectly and rubbed her internal hot spots exactly the way she needed. She clung to him, straining up to meet his thrusts. Her limbs were tingling, her belly tight. The pressure grew.

And damn, his cock was rock hard. Could it get any more so?

"Let the pleasure take you," he said, suddenly lifting and straightening his arms so he could look down at where they joined.

"Yes, yes, I'm coming, it's here, the pleasure…"

"Come for me, Chloe."

She gripped his biceps and cast her gaze downward. Watching his cock shunt in and out and his body drag against her clit, tipped her over the edge.

"And breathe," he demanded. "Keep breathing."

She did her best to keep dragging in oxygen as her pussy went into a series of delicious spasms. But it was difficult. Her body barely felt like her own. She was a mass of bliss spreading from her pelvis to her fingers, delighting every nerve along the way.

He caught her chin in his hand and lowered his face. "Breathe."

She pulled in a great lungful of air and blew it out.

He kissed her, withdrew, and then plunged back in.

Another wave of pleasure shot through her pussy. *When has it ever felt so good?*

He stayed with her, pumping his cock in and out until her orgasm faded. He then stilled, buried deep, with his breaths slow and controlled.

"You … you didn't," she said, running her fingers through her hair.

"No."

"But I want you to."

"I will." He pulled out and slipped his arm around her waist. "But this way. I do it this way."

He flipped her over onto her stomach, and then tugged her to her hands and knees.

She gasped as her hair fell forward, and she clutched the shiny material of the sleeping bag.

So he's a take-it-from behind guy.

"You're so sexy," he said, palming her buttocks. "All I ever wanted." He slid his touch to her hips and held them tight.

She braced as his cock nudged her pussy. She had a feeling he'd be letting go of some of the fierce control he always seemed to have over himself. She wasn't complaining.

He sank deep, his way eased by the moisture of her pleasure moments ago.

He groaned. A low-throated, rumbling sound that made her think of an animal, which one, she wasn't sure. Lion perhaps, or tiger.

Seated deep, his balls pressed against her labia, he gave another shunt and pulled her back onto him.

"Oh…" She gasped. From this angle, taking him so high was amazing. She was sure he was nudging her cervix.

"Yes, mate of mine…" He pulled almost out and then thrust back in. He was in control of her body, holding her exactly where he wanted her. "I'm going to take you now."

She didn't answer because he'd set up a wild, primitive pace, fucking her hard and fast. His flesh slapped against hers. His fingers were like pincers on her hips. His cock speared in and out of her.

Chloe shut her eyes and succumbed to the moment of being his. Surrendering her body so he could take his pleasure was so erotic. To think this big, tough guy, who fascinated her so much, was only thinking of her, needing her in this moment…

"Yes. Yes." He sank deep and came, filling her with his seed.

Chloe pushed back onto him and clenched her internal muscles around his cock.

A long, dense growling sound erupted from him and he released her hips and rested over her, his chest hot on her back.

Unable to take his weight, she slid to her belly, taking him with her.

He kissed her ear, his breaths competing with the sound of the storm outside, and propped onto his elbows a little.

"You enjoyed it?" she asked, twisting her head to the side where his face was.

"Do you even need to ask?" He curled his hips under, reminding her he was still deep inside.

Not that she could ever forget.

"You fuck like a wild beast," she said and then giggled.

"Maybe that's what I am."

Chapter Four

Aaron kissed her temple and then withdrew. "Are you warmer now?"

"Yes, much." She felt empty without him, but pleasantly aching, too.

He reached around, unzipped the sleeping bag, and then moved to sitting. "Get in."

"I'm okay."

"You won't be warm for long." He bent and kissed her bare shoulder. "Your sexy layer of sweat will freeze if we're not careful."

"Okay." She knew he was speaking the truth. She'd normally have spent the night fully clothed in a situation like this, and in the sleeping bag. Yet here she was, pressed up against Aaron, and feeling as warm as if she'd been sitting by a roaring fire back home.

She put her feet, still in socks, into the bag and slid down it. "You coming in?" She wasn't sure there was room, but they'd figure a way.

"No, I'm fine."

"But—"

"Trust me." He tucked his cock into his pants, and then wrapped his arm over the sleeping bag and pulled her to him.

She was aware of his body pressing against the length of hers and the heat from him penetrating the high-tech material. Glancing up at his face, she found him staring down at her.

"You are so beautiful," he whispered, stroking her cheek and pushing a lock of hair behind her ear.

She smiled. "I look better when I haven't spent the day being chased around the mountains."

"You couldn't look any more beautiful than you

do at this moment."

She huffed a little, knowing it wasn't true. She likely was a mess.

"Your cheeks are flushed," he said, "from the efforts of our mating. Your pupils are wide with satisfaction, and your lips…" He paused and swept his mouth over hers. "Swollen from our kisses." He shook his head. "A woman couldn't be more beautiful to a man as when she's fresh from being his."

Her heart tripped over itself. Damn, the guy was good. He might not be a guy of many words, but when he did speak, well … she was almost in danger of thinking he could get right into her heart.

She smiled. "I'm worried you'll be cold."

"Can't you feel my heat?"

"Yes." She paused. "But how come you are so hot? The temperature is well below freezing up here."

He said nothing.

"And you never wear a coat or thermals."

"I guess my body temperature runs higher than everyone else's."

"Isn't that a bit odd?"

"Not to me." He pressed a kiss to her lips. "Shh, now. Try to sleep. You've had a long day and there is much to do tomorrow."

"Yes. I need to collect the other two cameras."

He moved closer, tucking her head beneath his chin and stroking her hair.

Chloe shut her eyes and sighed. Within the hour, she'd gone from fearing for her life to being utterly satisfied and content.

And it was all because of Aaron.

She soon fell into a deep sleep. Dreams stole up on her. The leopard was on her mind, its graceful body moving through the snow. She imagined she could smell it. At one point, she even thought of its black-dotted fur pressed against her cheek—soft, warm, and dense.

Aaron was in her dream too, with the snow leopard. His eyes so knowing and seductive, staring at her in a way that made her think he wanted to fuck her again.

She squirmed within the bag and stretched her legs out. She was cooler and she realized it was morning. The orange glow from the tent penetrated her eyelids. She opened them, knowing as she did so Aaron wasn't there.

Disappointed, she sat. The zipper was open and the startling white of the snow told her it was a blue-skied day.

Next to her, on the base of the tent, was a dent where Aaron had lain.

She brushed her hand over it and collected several coarse hairs sitting there. They were golden mainly, and long and thick. But they weren't where his head had been when they'd gone to sleep. They covered the whole length of where he'd stretched out.

Puzzled, she reached for her thermals and dragged them on. Then her sweater and jacket. After retrieving and donning her knickers, trousers, and boots, she moved to the edge of the tent.

A fresh layer of snow had covered the hideous chicken blood. *Thank goodness.* And there was no sign of the poor creature's body.

She licked her lips and her stomach rumbled. She needed a hot drink and food. She'd expended a lot of energy the evening before.

With a smile at the memory of Aaron's enthusiastic lovemaking, she flicked the tent open with the intention of finding a flat rock to set her small gas stove on.

She paused and glanced around, wondering if

Aaron had beaten her to it and set up for breakfast already.

Nothing.

She couldn't see him.

Stepping out, she placed her booted foot next to a print in the snow.

A paw print—a *huge* paw print.

She gasped and drew her hand to her mouth. The snow leopard had returned. It had been right there. At the entrance to her tent. It had likely taken the chicken.

Fear swarmed within her. Where the hell was Aaron? The creature could still be nearby. Oh, God, what if he'd gone for a pee and it had followed him? Eaten him for its breakfast.

She took a few more steps away from the tent, searching desperately for Aaron's footprints. She needed to follow them, to see if he was okay.

But there was nothing—only the paw prints sinking deep and heading away from the tent.

She frowned, confusion swamping her brain. Surely Aaron hadn't left her side so long ago the snow had covered his prints. It didn't feel, though she'd been sleeping, as if he'd been gone for any length of time.

She had a moment of warring with herself, wondering what to do. Should she follow the leopard prints, see where they took her? Should she lock herself back in her tent and hope the creature didn't find her?

Her concern for Aaron won out, and she moved cautiously toward the gap in the rocks the Shaman had darted through. The paw prints were clear to see, right down the middle of it.

Emerging on the other side, with the view of the mountains stretching before her, she stopped, her palm pressed against the cool cliff face.

Standing, with his back to her, was Aaron.

He was about ten meters away, staring at the stunning vista.

Her heart rate picked up. He appeared unharmed. Though how he was tolerating standing in the snow totally naked, she had no idea.

"Aaron!"

He turned.

For a moment, she drank in the sight of him. He was a truly gorgeous specimen of a man. Tall, lean, strong. His body hair making him appear a little wild. His cock hung heavily and his legs bulged with muscle.

"Come and put some clothes on, before you get frostbite," she called.

He said nothing, but started to walk toward her.

"And the leopard is about," she said, checking her surroundings again. "I've seen its prints, near the tent."

"Shame you didn't have a camera set up," he said, reaching her and cupping her cheeks. His hands were perfectly warm.

Thoughts of the leopard vanished as she looked up into his eyes. Instead she allowed memories of him kissing her, stripping her naked, sinking deep, to flood her brain.

"Good morning," he said quietly and then kissed her.

She held onto his forearms and melted toward him.

After a minute of exploring her mouth and making her giddy with longing, he pulled back. "We should get some warm food and drink inside you."

"I can think of something else I'd like inside me."

A smile tugged at his mouth. "I like how your mind works." He reached between them and took hold of his cock. It was semi-erect now, and he gave it a few languid strokes. "But I am worried about you getting cold. And the light won't last long today. We have four kilometers to cover, right? To get the cameras and get back to the village."

How does he know?

Only she and Jim had been privy to the information.

He must have seen her frown. "I'm guessing," he said. "It's where I'd put them if I were you."

"Oh, well, yes, you've guessed about right."

He released his cock and took her hand. "Come on."

She followed behind him, enjoying the view of his naked ass. It was high and pert, but like his chest and arm, had a set of parallel scars on the left buttock.

"How'd you get those scars?" she asked.

"Which ones?" He kept on walking and tugged her through the gap in the rocks.

"All of them. They're all the same."

He shrugged. "Fighting."

Fighting?

"Who with?" she asked, horrified at the sort of weapon that must have been used on him.

"Males." His tone was curt.

"Men. Why?"

He kept on going, pulling her toward the tent.

"It's a territory thing."

She frowned. What did he mean? Was it a jealous fight? Was territory a word he used for his lovers? "Do you mean you fought over a woman?"

"Kind of."

They reached the tent and he pulled on his clothes and boots.

"I couldn't see your footprints," she said, indicating the paw prints leading from the tent and now interrupted by theirs.

"No?"

"No." She hesitated. "It's strange."

"Lots of strange things happen on the mountain, Chloe. You must know that. You've spent enough time here."

"I guess."

"So where is your gas canister?"

"It's here." Reaching into her rucksack, she decided to let the matter drop, for now. Aaron really was the most unusual guy she'd ever come across. As much as he was totally heart-stoppingly, drop-dead gorgeous, he was also an enigma with a tendency to speak in riddles.

****

Within the hour, they'd left the small valley and were nearing the first camera point.

As they approached, a familiar sense of anticipation welled within her. She hoped she'd been successful in retrieving footage of the shy leopards. Though the one she'd encountered didn't exactly appear timid.

"It's here," she said, checking her map. "Behind this rock."

The wind had picked up, but the sky was still a stunning, rich blue. Chloe edged around the rock and was relieved to see her camera intact.

"You've been lucky." Aaron pointed to the ground. "A mother and cubs."

"Really?" She studied where he was pointing. "That's incredible. Oh, I hope the footage is good."

"Should be." He shrugged. "Three cubs, all milling about."

She took the camera and carefully put it in her rucksack. The thought of getting back to her room and checking out what had been captured was very exciting.

She wondered if Aaron would like to join her.

"And the next one. To the east, right?"

"Er, yes." She glanced east, the way he was indicating, and the vertigo-inducing track they'd have to negotiate.

"About an hours' trek?"

"I believe that's how long it took us last time." She paused. "But how...?"

"Like I said, they're the areas I would search for snow leopards. Good hang out places."

"You know a lot about snow leopards."

"More than you do." He leaned in and pressed a kiss over her lips. "Come on."

He set off at a brisk pace, seeming every bit at home on the perilous path as a mountain goat would.

Chloe was more hesitant. One slip and she'd plunge to her death.

He must have noticed because he turned and reached for her hand. "It's okay. Stick close. I won't let you fall."

"Thanks."

He smiled and carried on. She was more confident with his firm grip and glad she wasn't doing this part of the trip alone.

In fact, she was glad she wasn't doing any of it alone. The mountain might be visually beautiful, but it was as fierce as the weather and the creatures it was home to.

Chapter Five

There'd been more prints around the final camera which meant Chloe had spent the journey back to the village in a jubilant mood. Surely she had enough to make the documentary. Jim would be ecstatic.

"How about I buy you a beer to celebrate?" she said as they trudged into the village at nightfall.

"Kind of you, but I don't drink beer."

"Oh, yes, of course. Well, an iced water then?"

He chuckled. "That would be good."

"Do you think…" She hesitated. "You know with the Shaman about, the chicken and …" She looked up at his face, now doused in shadows. "Will it be okay for me to go in there?"

"Yes. With me, no one, or anything, will hurt you."

"Okay. If you're sure."

"More than sure. It's a promise."

The vehement tone of his voice made her feel as though she'd been wrapped in a warm security blanket. She couldn't remember anyone being so determined about keeping her safe. It was a nice feeling, especially being so far from home and in such an alien environment.

When they reached the bar, Aaron pushed the rickety door open.

The smell of warm smoke, from tobacco and a fire in an empty oil drum, filled her nose.

The sound of men in conversation didn't alter as they walked in, but still, Chloe couldn't help a glance about, wondering if the Shaman was there. Would she recognize him without his strange face paint and his hood down? Perhaps he wasn't from the local area at all.

Most of the men were familiar. The village had a

227

tiny population, and although she didn't know them all by name, she did know their faces. But in the corner, farthest from the fire, sat two men she definitely hadn't seen before.

Aaron indicated for her to take a seat while he got drinks.

"Here, take this." She handed him some money.

"Thanks." He took it.

She was a little surprised, but shrugged it off. Instead, as she sat, her attention returned to the two strangers. They had a map spread out in front of them and one wore a furry hat which was cream-colored with black spots.

When Aaron sat next to her and placed their drinks down, she was still studying them.

He followed her line of sight. His body tensed and he sucked in a breath. "Damn it."

"What's the matter?" she asked, taking in the hard line of his jaw and the flash of displeasure in his eyes.

"Poachers."

"What?" How the hell did he know?

"See his hat. It's leopard."

"Oh, God, no." A sick feeling burned in her stomach. "Really?"

"Yes. Only poachers would dare to wear their crimes like a badge."

"What can we do? Report them?"

He took a sip of his drink. "Yes, it will need to be made clear they're here."

Chloe swung her gaze around the room. "To the villagers?"

"No." He shook his head and set his hands on the gnarled wood of the table, clenched his fists. "The leopards."

"But how…?"

"At first light, I will leave warning scents and give a shout out."

She held out her hands. "Aaron, what are you talking about?"

He bit on his bottom lip and cupped her chin. "It will all become clear. Please stop concerning yourself with details."

"But I can't get my head around the details."

"Do you want to be mine?" He narrowed his eyes and a curl of hair fell over his cheek.

"Well … yes."

"So trust me."

"I do."

He tipped his head and the lock of hair moved. "Trust me when I say what you think is strange, is perfectly normal here."

"I'm trying." She stroked her hand over his forearm. "But it's a big ask when I'm trained to ask questions, investigate."

"I accept this about you." He released her chin and pressed his hand over his chest. "And I must ask you to accept things about me."

"I do. I want to." She didn't know what it was she was supposed to be accepting.

"Come on, drink up." He nodded at her beer. "I thought you wanted to check your footage."

She took a few slugs, the malty liquid coating her tongue. "You're right. I'm dying to see what set off the motion sensors. I'm hoping it's something to brighten Jim's mood when I tell him tomorrow."

Aaron stood. He gave the poachers one last glance, hate flashing over his pupils, and then rested his hand at the small of her back.

She allowed him to steer her from the bar, and once in the open, down the small walkway to her room.

She opened the door and held it wide, inviting him in without words.

He took the invitation.

The place was small and functional. A bed, a chair and desk, and a wardrobe. There was a grate for a much-needed fire and a stack of logs replenished regularly by her landlord. A small room at the back held a toilet with an onerous flushing system and a shower which was little more than a trickle of lukewarm water.

After closing the door and drawing the thin curtains, Chloe quickly set to lighting the fire.

Aaron sat on the end of the bed, watching her.

"Not something I was particularly skilled at before I came here," she confessed as the kindling caught. "But needs must."

"You seem very proficient now."

"I'm getting there." She watched the flames lick upward and then added a small log. It would need tending over the next few hours, but that was okay.

Aaron slipped off his boots and set them by the desk. "Is this what you look at footage on?" He nodded at her laptop.

"Yes." She reached for it, enjoying how he'd settled himself into her room. She hoped he'd stay the night, and be up for a repeat performance of their sexy time on the mountain.

She copied him and removed her boots, sat in the middle of the bed, the memory sticks from the cameras now in her hand. "Here goes."

He moved in close. Again, heat radiated from him, much the same way as the fire's warmth was hitting her.

"Let's check the first one." She slipped it in and clicked 'open.'

The screen filled with the view of the mountains

from a small flat space flanked by gray rocks.

"The sensor has been triggered eighteen times," she said, pointing to the data in the corner of the screen. "But it won't be all leopards."

"Mmm…" he said, peering forward and his shoulder brushing hers.

For a moment, she wondered about forgetting the cameras and getting down and dirty and sweaty and naked with the hot man at her side. But the producer in her won out and she flicked through the images.

As she reached the last one, her heart sagged in disappointment. All that had been recorded were rabbits and a solitary musk deer. On two occasions, it wasn't clear what had set off the sensor.

She switched to the second memory stick. This one had been turned on four times. Each one showed a pallas cat. Great, if they'd been what she was making a program about, but not so much when it was leopards she wanted.

"Right in the middle of pallas cat territory," Aaron said.

"Yes, must be."

Frustrated, but hopeful the third stick would offer more, Chloe switched them over.

"Now that's much better," she said, rubbing her hands together and grinning as a mother snow leopard and three cubs walked past the lens.

Aaron chuckled. "Cute, huh?"

"Very. But I bet the mother wouldn't be if she came across us. Thank goodness for these cameras."

Aaron stroked his hand down her hair. "Instinct is a powerful thing. Especially a mother's."

She turned to look at him.

He continued to caress her hair. "Do you desire offspring?"

"Maybe one day I'll come off my contraceptive pill."

He raised his eyebrows. "The sooner the better."

"I take it that means you want a family."

His attention left hers and he concentrated on the freeze frame of the cubs. "I have family. They're beautiful."

"You already have children?" She paused. "Don't tell me you have a wife hidden away somewhere, too."

"No, nothing of the sort." He looked at her again. "There is only you."

Was this another one of the things about him she had to let go? It was getting kind of hard to.

"Check the footage from the last camera." He nodded at the screen.

"Okay."

This one showed a single male leopard out in a storm. She knew it was male because of its size, and it came right up to the lens, sniffing and peering at it with its pale eyes.

A layer of snow covered its head, collecting around its ears. For several minutes, it stayed in shot, checking out the area and giving her numerous wonderful pieces of material to use.

"He's beautiful," she whispered when the animal finally disappeared from view on the last clip.

"You think so?" Aaron asked, taking the laptop and setting it on her desk.

"Yes, totally breathtaking."

He looked at her and smiled, and then added another log to the fire. When he turned back to face her, he removed his top.

"And I think *you're* beautiful, too," she said, enjoying how his body almost glowed as it was caressed by the dancing shadows of the fire.

"As beautiful as a snow leopard?" he asked, crawling onto the bed.

"I…" She couldn't compare the two. They were so different, but both equally majestic.

"It's good you can't answer that. The snow leopards need people in the world who are mesmerized by them. It will help keep them safe." He leaned over her so she was forced to lie flat.

"Yes, I want to help them."

"You already are." He kissed her, the same deep, passionate kiss as he'd given her on the mountain.

She hooked her hands behind his neck and pulled him closer so their bodies were in alignment. Through clothing, his cock pressed against her mound.

She had a sudden urge to get up close and personal with his dick again. So with a shove, she pushed him to his back.

"What are you doing?" he asked, looking up at her as his head hit the pillow. Surprise washed over his face.

"You gonna let me have some fun?" she asked, waggling her eyebrows and reaching for his waistband.

"Will it be fun for me, too?"

"Of course." She popped open the button. "If you like having your dick sucked, that is."

His mouth fell open and he half sat, reaching for her wrist as he did so.

A shard of alarm went though her. He didn't like blowjobs?

"What's up?" she asked, stilling.

"I…" He shook his head. "I don't know."

"What don't you know?"

"I mean, I've never…"

"You've never had a blowjob?"

Really?

"You blow?" He appeared slightly alarmed.

"No." God, who was this wild sexy man, full of mystery and passion, but also infused with innocence? "Of course I won't blow." She tugged and he released her wrist. "Why don't I show you?" She pressed him flat and was pleased when he stayed on his back. "Relax, enjoy. Most men would sell their soul for it."

"I'm not your average male."

"Don't I know it?" She undid his pants and then wriggled them down to his thighs.

His erection released, hard and long, and she took it in her hand. "Close your eyes." She slid down the bed so her face was level with his groin.

He did as instructed.

"Just feel."

He blew out a long low breath, his chest deflating and his abdominal muscles tensing.

Watching his expression, she flicked out her tongue and licked the head.

"Oh fuck..." he muttered, his belly tensing further.

"Not yet." She circled his glans, stroking the point of her tongue into the groove and then concentrating on his frenulum.

Again, he groaned. A low deep rumbling sound telling her he liked what he was experiencing.

Gently, she began to work his shaft within the clasp of her hand.

It was like satin on steel, and so damn hot. He grew more erect and his cock twitched.

She decided it was time to take him deep, show him for real there was no blowing involved, only a bit of sucking.

Stretching her mouth wide, she circled his head, then slowly, so slowly, dropped down so his shaft smoothed over her tongue and filled her mouth.

"Oh, gods above." He rammed his fingers into her hair and coiled forward. "Chloe, mate, oh…"

Her pussy dampened, her nipples were tight. Hearing his pleasure was a massive turn on in itself.

She withdrew and balanced his glans on her bottom lip so she could caress his slit with her tongue.

Again he groaned, dropping back and releasing her hair as he did so.

She glanced up at him. His spine was arched, his chest rising and falling rapidly, and his eyes closed. He was gripping the wooden slats of the bamboo headboard and exposing his underarm hair.

Again she sank deep, taking him to the back of her throat. A strange growling sound erupted from him and a slick of pre-cum coated her tongue.

God, he's close.

She quickly decided she wanted him to have the full experience. To come in her mouth. She was honored to be giving Aaron this pleasure for the first time.

She set up a relentless pace, using every trick in the book with her tongue and lips.

Soon he was bucking his hips to meet her. His fingers were clasped tight in her hair again, and he was gasping and moaning.

With her free hand, she cupped his balls and gently squeezed.

Then it was there. His orgasm rushed from him. Salty fluid filled her mouth and she swallowed it down quickly.

More came and his cock pulsed against her tongue.

"Chloe, oh, yes…"

His balls were packed tight, but still she held them and was rewarded with another shot of cum.

Finally he stilled. He released her hair and flopped back on the bed. The sound of his rapid breaths filled the room.

She let him fall from her mouth and caught his shaft in her hand. "You see, no blowing involved."

He rested his forearm over his eyes and laid his opposite hand on his chest. "That was…"

"Awesome, incredible?"

"All of those and … wow, when can you do it again?"

"As soon as you've recovered."

Suddenly he reached for her and dragged her up his body so she was on top of him. "It won't take me long to recover. Not with you around."

Chapter Six

"Are we nearly there?" Chloe asked as they trekked up the west side of the mountain.

"Yes. Not far now." Aaron stomped ahead, seemingly uncaring his black sweater was now coated in a thin film of snow.

Chloe curled her hands in her gloves and followed him. It seemed to her she'd follow him anywhere now. He'd gotten under her skin and unbolted the door to her heart.

The night before had been incredible. He hadn't opted for another blowjob when he'd recovered. Instead, once again, he'd taken her from behind, this time providing her with a wonderful deep G-spot orgasm which had left her boneless with satisfaction.

But she would have his cock in her mouth again … soon. Perhaps here, up on the mountain. She knew damn well he wouldn't complain about the cold.

As they rounded a corner, she pushed away thoughts of going back to England. She didn't want to leave Aaron or the village. It had quickly become home.

But her job, her ambitions, her small flat, it was all back there.

An eagle screeched overhead and she resolved to live for the moment and trust it would all work out. Perhaps Aaron would come back with her?

Who was she kidding? The man was made for living in the mountains. She was sure he'd die if he had to cope with a commute through London traffic. It wouldn't suit him.

He held up his hand. Indicating for her to stop. She did. "What is it?"

"I heard something." He raised his nose and

appeared to sniff the air.

"You smell something, too?"

"I'm not sure." He turned to her. "I want you to stay here. This is a safe place on this path." He glanced upward. "No avalanche danger, and if you stay away from the edge, you'll be okay."

"Where are you going?"

"Up another hundred yards or so. To deliver my warning."

"Which is?" She held up her palms.

"Please. Wait here." He turned and disappeared around the corner.

Chloe huffed. How come she'd been left alone? And what the hell was the warning he kept talking about?

A coil of annoyance wound through her. She wanted answers, and she wanted them now. Too many things didn't add up about Aaron. She didn't know what they were supposed to add up to, but she wanted to know.

She decided to follow him. He couldn't tell her to wait on the side of the mountain like a good little girl and expect her to obey.

With dogged determination, she marched ahead, being careful to stay away from the dangerous edge. The snow became deeper as she went into a shadowed area.

Picking her way carefully, she paused.

Fresh leopard prints.

They led forward as if the creature had been in the area very recently.

"What the…?"

How come they hadn't seen it? Or maybe Aaron had.

She took another three steps and then froze.

Her heart clattered and she gripped the rock to her right.

An eerie roar filled the air. It was more like a deep

mewling shout. And it was very close.

Snow leopard.

Half of her wanted to turn and run, and the other half of her wanted to see it.

Aaron. Where are you?

Her need to find him was too great. She edged around the next bend, knowing the creature wouldn't be far from her.

She was right. Standing majestically on a rock was a huge male snow leopard. Its paws were massive, its thick neck outstretched as it sent its strange cry into the snow-filled sky.

On and on it made the noise, transmitting it down valleys, and over the mountain tops.

Chloe marveled at its beauty. So few people were lucky enough to catch even a fleeting glimpse, yet here she was feasting on the sight of one for the second time.

Suddenly, it stopped making its strange nose and turned to stare at her.

Admiration turned to fear.

She quickly backed up. And once around the corner, turned and hastened her pace.

She wanted to shout for Aaron, but she was worried doing so wouldn't help her situation with the leopard.

But a noise behind her warned it was too late, and as she arrived back at the place Aaron had left her, the snow leopard appeared.

She pressed herself against the cliff.

The leopard approached her, its paws sinking deep, its gaze set on hers.

She was about to die. This time, for sure, she was going to be snow leopard dinner.

A sudden movement to her right caught her attention. She fixed her fear-fuzzed vision on it.

A man appeared through the snow.

Not any man. It was the poacher she'd seen in the bar the night before—the one with the fur hat—and he held a gun aloft, aimed at the leopard.

"No," she shouted. She didn't want to die, but she definitely didn't want the leopard to die and the poacher to win. Besides, he'd probably shoot her afterward for being a witness.

Her cry alerted the leopard who turned. Its body dipped backward, as if harnessing power. Then in a flash, it pounced on the man, knocking his gun from his hand. The weapon flipped, cartwheel style, and landed at her feet.

"Agh!" The man yelled as the leopard hurled itself over him, its head shaking as it took a bite from his jacket.

"Help," the man shouted. "Help me."

Chloe stood stock-still, watching the terrifying scene.

The leopard stepped back a fraction. It lifted its front leg, and with one powerful sweep of its paw, it sent the man over the side of the cliff.

His scream echoed for a full five seconds before it was silenced by his brutal landing.

"Oh, my God," Chloe said. She came out of her shocked frozen state and grabbed the gun. She then squeezed up against the cliff and pointed it forward.

The snow leopard turned to her again, its green eyes flashing as it breathed heavily.

Okay, so now it was up to her. She could shoot the creature and live, or die at its hands.

She waggled the gun. "Go away."

Strangely the creature hesitated, as if it knew what she held was dangerous.

"Please, go away. I don't want to hurt you," she

said in a croaky voice.

"I'll take the beast away for you." Behind the leopard, another man appeared. He, too, was holding a gun aimed at the creature approaching her. "And I'll make a hefty profit in the process." He cackled.

The leopard spun around, making its head an easy target.

"No. You can't do that." Fury raged in Chloe and she took aim. "You and your sort are evil." She shot at the man.

She'd intended to hit his chest, but got his right leg. Blood spurted onto the snow and the impact caused him to jolt backward, his gun falling from his hand. It clattered over the cliff edge, going the same way as his friend.

The man screamed and clutched his shin.

"Get out of here or I'll finish you off," Chloe shouted. "Then I'll kick you over the mountain to land with your buddy."

The man flashed her a look of hate and hopped backward, quickly disappearing from view. All that remained were his splashes of blood.

Chloe looked at the leopard again. It was breathing hard, its breath collecting in the air in front of it.

Slowly it turned to face her.

She still held the gun aloft, but it was aimed at the side of the rock where the poacher had fled.

He might come back.

A tremble went through her belly as the leopard approached.

"Go eat him," she said with a quiver in her voice. "Go eat the bad guys." She directed the gun at the leopard. But she knew she couldn't and wouldn't shoot it. She'd die before she hurt it. "Go eat him, he deserves it."

Still the leopard neared.

A brief image of newspaper headlines at home flashed in her mind. *Snow leopard eats female wildlife producer while filming in Himalayas.* Her poor parents would be distraught.

"Please no." She shook her head and beat down a wave of nausea. Would it be a quick death? How much pain should she expect? Would it wait until she was dead before it started eating her?

Chapter Seven

Chloe stared into the leopard's eyes, pleading with it to have mercy and leave her be.

Where is Aaron?

He was her last chance. Her only hope.

But it was too late. The creature was right in front of her now.

It sprang back onto its rear legs and rose upward, stretching its body to a standing position. It placed its paws, each as big as her head, on the cliff wall on either side of her face.

Its wet nose almost touched hers. Its eyes, so beautiful and flecked with gold, stared at her.

What is it doing?

She was sure it was playing with her. Toying with the human it had found.

She dropped the gun. Trembling so much, she was unable to hold it.

She prayed it would be quick.

But as she stared at the leopard's face, it began to change. The nose retracted, the eyes became smaller, and in place of a fur-covered brow, human skin and blond tousled hair.

The wide animal shoulders turned to broad male shoulders, and a near hairless torso was revealed. The arms, in her peripheral vision, also lost their fur, and flesh thick with muscle and tendon appeared.

"Don't be scared," the creature said.

But it wasn't a creature, it was Aaron.

She shook. A full body shake that started in her core and traveled outward.

What the hell is happening? I'm seeing things.

She shut her eyes and opened them again, fully

expecting to see the leopard still standing in front of her. Her mind was surely playing tricks on her at the moment of her death.

But it was Aaron staring back at her with the exact same eyes the leopard had.

"It's me," he said, studying her intently. "I won't hurt you. You're safe. I promised you always would be."

"I … I don't understand."

"I'm a shifter. I move between two bodies. Snow leopard and human."

She hadn't heard him right. She was dreaming. It was the only explanation.

"Chloe." He frowned.

"But that's not real." Shifter? It was the stuff of teen movies, fiction … wasn't it?

"Do I feel real?" He took her hand and pressed it over his chest. "Tell me. Do I feel real?"

Beneath the warm flesh his heart beat rapidly.

"Yes, yes, you feel real." He did. God, he did. As real as when he'd been making love to her.

"Shh…" he said. "Calm yourself. It's okay. It will all be okay."

"I don't understand. How can it be?" She pressed her other hand to his chest, absorbing his heat. Glancing down, she saw he was naked.

"It's the way I was born."

"But…"

"I am destined to mate for life with a human woman, and that's you." He paused. "If I have human children, they will be with you. Only you. There is only you now, for me."

"Aaron." She went to move away, trying to gather her thoughts. But he kept her trapped against the cliff edge with his body.

"You have to understand, Chloe."

"I don't know if I can." She shook her head. "It's all too much. I just watched a man fall to his death, shot another, and then believed I was about to be eaten alive." She suppressed a sob. "And now you … you're a … snow leopard."

"Come here." He tugged her close.

She allowed him to wrap her in his arms. Her thoughts were muddled. Common sense and logic at battle with what she'd seen with her own eyes. But still, his embrace was welcome and comforting, as were his scent and the way he rubbed a soothing circle on her back.

"My beautiful mate," he murmured. "Calm yourself. No need for tears. You know the truth now. From here we can move forward."

"Forward," she repeated.

"Yes. I can show you everything. Tell you everything."

"What else is there to show me?" She pulled back. "No, don't tell me, you can turn into an eagle as well."

"No." He huffed. "I only have one alternative body."

"Of course, silly me."

With a frown, he held her at arm's length and stooped a little to look into her face. "I want to show you my home. So you can see what I will provide you with, forever."

"Forever is a long time."

"It is the perfect amount of time to love someone the way I love you."

So there it was, the 'L' word. Sure she'd toyed with it herself. Aaron was one hell of a man and lover. But now … could she love a shifter?

She stared at him. He was still Aaron. Nothing had changed about him from when they'd stood in the mountains the day before, he stark naked and kissing her like he'd never stop.

I have a shifter for a lover?

"Wait here," he said, releasing her. "Then I will take you down the mountain and as we go, you must settle your thoughts."

She didn't answer, instead she waited as he went out of sight for a moment and then came back dressed in his usual boots, dark pants, and black sweater.

He took her hand, and, in silence, they began to navigate their way down the mountain.

She stared at the back of his head, his unusual hair, she now realized, matched a snow leopard's markings. Her gaze drifted down his body. No wonder he was so strong and lean. And heat always poured off him, his lack of needing a coat, it was all explained now. His DNA was clearly nothing science had seen before. And the footprints from the tent, the hairs where he'd slept…

She hadn't dreamed of being snuggled up with a leopard that night on the mountain. She really had been, and he'd walked out of the tent on four feet, or rather, on four paws.

"Are there many of you?" she asked suddenly. "Shifters, I mean. Up here?"

"I am the only male snow leopard shifter in this territory. It is my territory."

"How can it be?"

"I fought for it and the females within it." He tapped his butt, indicating his claw mark scars through his pants. "Many fights over the years."

"The females." She tugged his hand. "So you … you mate with them, when you're in your leopard body."

He stopped and turned. "Don't be so shocked. It is the instinct of animals to procreate, and we are an endangered species." He paused and stroked the back of his thumb down her cold cheek. His voice softened. "But that's all it is, instinct, an urge, nothing like when *we* make love, then it is desire and passion and love. My human body is very different when it comes to the erotic. I'm sure you discovered that last night when you took me in your mouth and left me giddy with ecstasy."

Will I ever get used to this? I have to try.

"I think I understand." She paused. "So those cubs, the ones we filmed. They're in your territory?"

"Yes, they will be mine." He shrugged. "She is a good mother, which is just as well because I never have anything to do with my animal offspring."

"But you would your children … our children."

He smiled as though enjoying her saying 'our children'. "Of course. I am a man who wishes to be a father. A father to *your* children."

He turned and carried on walking.

Well, at least I know what I'm getting now.

Soon the village came into view. Chloe tried to imagine leaving now. Should she make a quick exit and run from such an unusual relationship with such an unusual guy? Or should she go with her instinct, the one telling her he was the best she'd ever come across or was likely to, and stay here in Nepal?

She didn't know, but as the air became richer with oxygen, she found her nerves settling and her jumbled emotions beginning to untangle.

She had deep, profound feelings for Aaron—she had for a while. And now he'd shown her what he really was, it had brought them closer … hadn't it?

He led her to the south of the village and then up a steep slope littered with rocks and away from the other homes. A yak scrabbled to avoid them.

"You live up here?"

"I prefer to be slightly out of the way of the

villagers."

"Does anyone else know what you are?"

"The elders do."

"And they're okay with you being half man, half snow leopard?"

"Chloe, I'm *all* man, or hadn't you noticed?" He turned and raised his eyebrows.

"Well, yes ... but you know what I mean." A heated flush traveled over her chest and up her neck. Damn, he certainly was all man.

"Shifters are as ancient as the mountains themselves," he said, continuing to lead her up the track. "It is the way of the land for the elders to be trusted with that knowledge, and it is how I live here, in harmony, doing my work."

She shook her head. It was a lot to take in.

"They all know and support me," Aaron went on. "My protection of the leopards is important to them, mainly for superstitious reasons, but it doesn't matter, as long as it's important. Plus, as this is scented as my territory. It keeps other leopards away from livestock, most of the time, at least. So I'm doing the locals a favor *and* acting as a caretaker and contributor to my species."

She was quiet for a moment, and then said, "So they'll know, me with you ... that you and I are ... that I'm with a shifter?"

"Yes, and they'll accept you as my one and only mate."

"Aaron, I don't understand. You're what, nearly thirty? How come you've never been with a woman?" She hesitated. "At least I'm guessing that's the case from what you've said."

"I'm twenty-five, and shifters, well, in our human form, we wait for the right one to come along so we can give with all of our heart and soul. The opposite as when we mate as animals which is purely for procreation and without emotion." He paused in front of a large wooden house, much bigger than the others in the village. "And you have, finally. Come along, that is." He wrapped his arm around her waist. "Welcome home, mate."

Chapter Eight

"Wow, it's impressive," Chloe said.

"Built with my own hands."

"It must have taken years."

"I had time to kill as I was waiting." He pressed a kiss to her temple. "Waiting for you as it turns out."

Have I been waiting for him?

She looked into his eyes. They were full of love and desire and brimming with excitement and passion.

Yes. It's him I've been searching for.

The sudden knowledge was like a light coming on in her mind and heart. She *could* see a future with him. She wasn't sure of the details, but it was Aaron she needed to be with. Her soul was content when he was near, her future secure and warm.

"Chloe." He cupped her face, the way he often did. "I want to take you inside our home, strip off your clothes, and show you how much you mean to me. Show you how you've completed my life and how I will spend the rest of my days making you, my mate, happy."

"You move fast, Aaron."

Too fast?

"Only when I'm determined to get what I want."

He stooped and the next thing she knew, she'd been lifted into the air and was pressed against his chest.

"Aaron." A giggle erupted from her. It was a release of tension, a bubble of joy. She liked the sound of him stripping her naked and being his mate. Hell, what girl wouldn't?

But he's a snow leopard.

She pushed the thought aside. How much did that fact about him really matter?

He marched up the two steps and then kicked the

door open. It whacked against a wall with a hefty thud.

What greeted her wasn't what she'd expected. A large room with a huge fireplace was set before her. There was a kitchen area to the right, huge windows making the most of the spectacular view. And the furniture was elegant and polished. Pictures hung on the wall and the room smelled of flowers.

"Do you like it?"

"It's nothing like the meager shack I've been staying in. I like it very much. It's positively five star."

"Good." He stepped over the threshold, still carrying her, and back-kicked the door shut. "But you can study it more later. Right now, we're going to the bedroom. I want to hear the cute little noises you make when you come again."

"Aaron." She swung her legs, but clung tighter to him.

"Don't pretend you don't want it." He chuckled and then tipped her onto a huge four-poster bed.

"Wow," she said again, staring up at the thick scarlet material billowing above her. "This is lovely."

"Only the best for my woman." He pulled off his sweater. "And as a Western woman, I know you'll appreciate all the modern comforts I've added to make life easier." He stooped and removed his boots. Then he stood and pushed his pants down his legs, and kicked them aside.

Chloe propped herself onto her elbows and feasted her gaze on him. Her whole body reacted to seeing him naked and aroused. Her pussy dampened, and her nipples tingled.

He placed his hands on his hips. His erection bobbed, the head shiny and domed. "Take your clothes off."

She swallowed. "Yes."

Hurriedly, she fumbled with her boots, and then tugged at her jacket and undergarments. A minute later, she was also naked.

He hadn't moved, watching her intently. "Your body is so soft and pretty," he said.

She lay flat and cupped her breasts, trapped her nipples between her fingers and tugged. "My body wants your body."

He smiled and crawled onto the bed, his face level with hers. "I want to do something."

"Tell me."

He moved so his lips were brushing her mouth. "I want to taste you … down there."

She clenched the muscles in her belly and tweaked her nipples harder.

"I want to taste you the way you did me." He paused. "Can I?"

"Yes."

He grinned and slithered downward, his skin heating hers. Pausing at her chest, he took her hand away from her right nipple and flicked it with his tongue.

She moaned and closed her eyes. Her nipples were so sensitive.

He repeated the action, scooping her breast into his palm and gently massaging.

"Aaron," she said, slotting her fingers into his hair. "Yes, like that."

He sucked and nibbled, and then switched his attention to her other breast, treated it to the same caress.

After a few minutes, she needed more. "Please … lick me."

"With pleasure." He kissed his way down her belly.

She spread her legs, allowing him to settle between them. There was something so erotic about being with a man with limited experience. Not that she was overloaded with sexual history, but still...

"Ohh..." She gasped as he ran his tongue over her labia and settled it on her clit.

Clutching the bed sheet, she curled her toes and arched her back.

He set up a steady rhythm on her clitoris.

Oh, God, it must be instinctual. He's spot on.

He worked her with his tongue, building her up.

Soon the pressure was at overspill point. "Aaron, oh ... yes. Now..."

He lifted up and gripped her waist. His expression was dark, his cock thick and engorged. "Turn over. I want you from behind."

"No, please, like this, over me. I want us to come together, face to face."

"You do?"

"Yes, there are lots of ways for us to come, not just with you behind." She tugged his arms. "Please, come here, the way we did in the tent the first time, but until we climax, together."

He hesitated.

For a moment, she thought he was going to flip her over and fuck her despite her request, but he didn't. He slid up her and eased his cock into her pussy.

"Oh..." Her mouth hung open as she stared up at him. She was wet and ready for his girth, but still the combination of pleasure and discomfort was breathtaking.

"I'm hurting you?" Concern crossed his face.

"No, no, it's wonderful. *You're* wonderful."

"So you'll stay?" He hit full depth and captured her face in his hands. "Here with me?"

"Yes. I really want to."

His eyes softened. "That's all I need to know. The

rest we can work out."

"Can we?" There was so much to work out.

"Yes. We are mates now."

"But my work?" Could she give it up? She'd strived to become a wildlife documentary producer for years.

"Your filming will reach new levels here with me. You will be an ambassador for the mountain animals as well as contributing to the species." He paused. "There could be no better way to use your talents."

"Contribute to the species?"

"Yes. We will have children, the males will become shifters in their teens. You are my destiny." He withdrew and pushed back in. "You are also the destiny of the snow leopards."

His words spun in her mind. Her children, the boys, would become shifters. They'd help populate a dwindling species. She and Aaron, together forever … here in this beautiful, but dangerous land where the earth met the sky. And what was more, she'd get to film it all.

"I love you," he whispered against her lips.

"I love you, too." She paused. "My beautiful, handsome, mate."

He groaned and captured her mouth in a deep, passionate kiss, began to rock his hips, rubbing against her clit and building up her orgasm.

After a few minutes, she broke the kiss. "Come with me, Aaron. Like this, two humans finding satisfaction together, face to face."

"I'm … going to … it's too good." His eyes glazed slightly and he pulled back his lips. "It's here, my seed."

As he toppled into his release, Chloe allowed hers to ravage her. She clung to him, watching his expression as he succumbed to pleasure.

On the final throe, he released a primitive growl that dragged another luscious spasm of bliss from her. Heat washed through her. Happiness filled her heart and soul.

Never in a million years did Chloe Burton think she'd make a life for herself in the Himalayas, with a beautiful man who could shift into a snow leopard. But it seemed that was what her future held, and she couldn't be more excited about what a life at altitude held in store for her and her mate.

The End

FATED TO THE RAZORBACK DEMON

Maia Dylan

Copyright © 2017

Chapter One

Demon Kane watched his opponent step sideways, and he countered it with a move of his own. Both men bled from various wounds. The swell of dominance that filled the cage they fought in told him that their animals drifted close to the surface. But Demon had a distinct advantage over the wolf shifter he faced off against. His animal was calmest, and his control over the beast never stronger than when he was fighting, no matter what form he took to do it.

"How does it feel knowing you are the last of your crew?" the wolf shifter said in a garbled voice, another sign his wolf pushed forward.

Demon remained quiet. The wolf wasn't the first to try to goad him into making a mistake.

"When I end you, pig," the wolf spat, "I'll be fucking famous. I will go down in history as the man who killed the legendary Razorback Demon."

Again Demon refused to rise to the taunt, simply tracking him as he moved around the cage. The wolf was tiring. Hell, if truth be told, Demon was feeling pretty fucking tired himself, but the wolf's fatigue fueled his frustration, and that meant it would only be a matter of time.

Demon saw when the wolf tensed as he prepared to move to strike out at him, and stepped in to counter it. They came together in a flurry of punches and roundhouse kicks that whipped the crowd into a frenzy. As sick as it might sound to many, Demon thrived on the crowd's reaction to the fight. He enjoyed the roars of approval when his opponent scored a direct hit, but he lived for their groans of disappointment when he inevitably fought back.

Demon was lost in the fierce dance of battle, watching and countering the moves of the wolf. He felt each blow that connected, but as if from a distance. His beast wallowed in the pain and reveled in the scent of blood filling the arena. This was what they lived for. Razorbacks were a vicious breed, thriving on violence, and Demon was the worst of them all. He had nothing to lose when he stepped into the ring.

He saw the wolf's left foot slip in the blood that pooled on the floor of the cage. Inside, his beast roared with triumph, knowing that victory was within his grasp. Demon inhaled, readying himself to step in and strike, using the side of his right hand to crush the wolf's windpipe. This would give Demon the seconds he would need to step quickly behind his opponent, and snap his neck. But the scent he drew in gave him pause.

Mate.

He knew it as soon as he scented her. The one woman the Fates had destined would be his was here in the arena. His heart sank even as it began to pound in anticipation. He had never expected to meet his mate. Never wanted to curse a woman with who he was as a man, let alone the beast that lived within him. He had lived his life believing that surely the Fates wouldn't be so cruel as to tie a woman to him, and yet here she was.

His opponent forgotten, he turned to search the crowd through the electrified mesh of the cage walls. It was a Friday night and the place was packed with shifters and humans alike, all here to watch two men rip each other apart all in the name of entertainment. His gaze slid across the faces in the crowd with a desperation he had never felt before. He knew he would recognize his mate the moment he saw her. He—

Demon grunted as pain exploded in his right side. He dropped to the left out of instinct and avoided the elbow the wolf bastard aimed at his temple by mere millimeters. He went with his own momentum and dove to the ground, rolling over his shoulder to come back to his feet. For the first time in his life, his beast was roaring for him to forget the fight. He demanded that Demon rip the cage open and tear the crowd apart until their mate stood before them. He had always found it difficult to control the beast, but with the prospect of finding their mate, it was damn near impossible.

Against his will, his attention slipped back to the audience, scanning as he went. His gaze slid past the crowd near the entrance to the arena. There was a flash of brilliant green that caught his eye, and his gaze locked with the most alluring female he had ever seen.

Her hair was jet black, falling straight from a central part at the top of her head. He had no idea how long her hair was because the crowd blocked a lot of her from view. Her light mocha-colored skin was flawless, but it was her unusual eyes that caught his attention. And although the color was unique and beyond beautiful, it was the horror and fear he saw shimmering there that held him captive.

Those stunning, expressive eyes widened as he stared at her, and he watched her mouth move as she yelled for him to "look out", but he was too caught up in her beauty to comply completely. He did manage to tense and took some of the momentum of the kick that came his way with his arm. He didn't stop it completely and Demon crumpled to his knees as the boot he took cracked a couple more of his ribs and the pain stole whatever air he had left in his body. He grunted as he fell forward onto his hands, but his gaze remained steady on his mate. He saw the man he hadn't noticed standing behind her reach up to grip her hair from behind and wrench her head back against his shoulder. Despite the roar of pleasure from the crowd at his misfortune, he was certain he heard her cry out in pain.

All pain fled beneath the heat of his wrath, and he pushed to his feet. His woman was being mistreated, and nothing and no one was going to keep him from getting to her. Not the crowd, not the damn electric fence, and sure as fuck not the asshole who stood before him with a smirk on his face. His beast bellowed within him as a red haze of rage fell across his vision and Demon gave himself over to its fury.

Chapter Two

"Does watching two men fuck each other up get you hot, pet?" Jasper growled in her ear.

Ana had to fight the urge to flinch away. She knew from experience that wouldn't end well for her.

She stood as still as possible, wanting the concrete floor to simply open up below and swallow her whole. She didn't want to be here. She wasn't a dominant. Her wolf was as submissive as they come, and standing in a room filled with the scents of dominants and predatory males had her knees buckling with fear. The need to run was hard to resist, but with Jasper pressed against her, she had no hope of escaping.

Eight months ago, Jasper's brother Ezra had killed her Alpha and taken the pack as his own. Jasper became their pack Beta. They were both cruel, sadistic sons of bitches and for some reason, despite her submissive nature and the plethora of other female wolves all vying for his attention, Jasper had decided to take Ana as a Beta female hopeful. Ana's wolf cowered in his presence and she knew her scent filled with fear whenever he was near, but that seemed to only make him more determined to have her for his own.

"I-I don't know, Beta. I've never been to a cage fight before," she whispered. Jasper didn't like it when she didn't answer his questions. The first time he spoke to her, she couldn't manage more than a squeak. That had been the first time he'd slapped her, and the shock of it had her crying out. A sound he said was as alluring to him and his wolf as any perfume or scent could be.

"Then let's go inside and see if I can't do something that will get that hot little pussy of yours wet."

He pushed into her until she stepped further into

the crude arena. It was nothing more than an old wooden warehouse with tiered seating leading down to a circular cage at the center of the room. The walls of the enclosure were halfway to the roof of the three-story building, and two men stood within, stalking each other. The scent of dominance was thick in the air now that she was physically inside the building, but she caught the coppery tinge of blood in the room. Jasper pressed into her again. The sensation of his erection pressed against her ass had her gasping in shock and fear, and that was when she caught it.

Wrapped within the metallic scent of blood, Ana was struck with the wild scent of man, laden with a strong hint of earth and forest and just a touch of something spicy she struggled to name. It was a scent that called to her and her wolf like nothing else, and it was just as her mother had always told her it would be when she scented her mate. The woman she was and the wolf she could become both recognized the man the Fates had bound her to from the moment she was born. She had always dreamed of finding her mate. Never would she have thought it would be somewhere like here, with Jasper pressed against her like he was.

Anxiety began to build within her and she knew she was headed toward a full-blown panic attack. She took another deep breath to take comfort from the scent and froze. Her mate was dominant. Alpha dominant. More dominant than any male she had ever encountered. *What the hell were the Fates thinking?* Why would they pair a male as dominant as that with a wolf so submissive she turned tail and ran from her own damn shadow?

Jasper pushed her forward again and the crowd parted to allow them a better view of the cage. Ana's mouth opened on a silent cry of dismay when she caught sight of the two shifters in the center of the ring. Her gaze was drawn immediately to the slightly shorter of the two men who stood on the far side of the cage. He was huge, heavily muscled, with the words *angelus mortis* tattooed in an intricate cursive font across his chest. He wore the label 'angel of death' on his skin. This was what he believed he was. This was her mate. She gasped when he stepped toward his opponent and the two of them began to punch and kick each other with blurring preternatural speed that had the crowd roaring in appreciation.

By the time the two stepped apart, Ana's heart was in her throat. When his opponent, a man she knew to be a wolf shifter, seemed to slip, she thought the fight would be over in seconds, but her mate hesitated. A move that saw the wolf take advantage, and come back with a hard punch to her mate's side. She winced as she imagined she heard his ribs breaking beneath the power of the hit and he dropped to the ground. Ana caught a glimpse of more ink on his back when he rolled back to his feet, but she had no time to catch it in detail before he turned. His stare swept over the crowd methodically.

His gaze swept passed her and then slammed back until their eyes locked. Ana lost the ability to breathe. Despite the blood and sweat streaming from him, Ana could tell he was gorgeous. His dark-blond hair, lightly stubbled jaw, and piercing brown eyes held her captive and she felt her body soften with arousal at the heat in his stare.

"Damn, Ana," Jasper groaned behind her. "These fucking fights do turn you on. I can fucking smell your sweet arousal on the air and it's driving my wolf fucking crazy."

Ana was caught between her body's visceral reaction to her mate and her disgust and fear of the man behind her. She kept her eyes trained on her mate. She watched in horror as his opponent stepped to the side and whipped his body around in a hard roundhouse kick she knew was aimed again at those same ribs.

"Look out!" She saw him react a little to her warning and her heart filled with joy for a moment, before it flooded with fear as Jasper yanked her head back with a cruel hand in her hair.

"Please!" she cried out, lifting both hands to try to hold his wrist against her head, desperately trying to alleviate some of the pain he was inflicting.

"Please what, Ana?" Jasper snarled.

"P-please, Beta," she pleaded, pushing onto her tiptoes trying to ease the pain. "Please, don't hurt me. I'm sorry."

Vaguely, she was aware of the crowd roaring, but Jasper started to drag her backward out of the arena and all her focus turned to him. "You are sorry, Ana, a sorry little bitch that just fucking cost me a goddamn fortune. I had a bundle on that damn wolf. Now, you are going to pay."

Ana sobbed as she fell back, still holding onto Jasper's wrist. She cried out when her lower back slammed into the gravel of the carpark. "I'm sorry. I-I'll pay you back. Please!"

Jasper's laugh was pure evil and had Ana's skin crawling. "It's not money I want from you, Ana. I thought you might have been getting turned on by the violence, but it was that fucking razorback, wasn't it? I saw the way he looked at you, and you warned him! Well, fuck that." Jasper began to drag her through the carpark. Ana could see flames suddenly reaching out through the top of the warehouse and the crowd that had been packed within the building now poured from every exit, the air around them filled with panicked screams.

"I need to see fear in my women. The dominant females of the pack can never give me that. Like I told you, my wolf and I love it when you cower in fear. The scent of your terror makes me so fucking hard."

Ana cried out, tears streaming down her cheeks. She could feel the bite of the gravel tearing into her skin as Jasper continued to drag her toward his truck. Her cries seemed to amuse him and his crew, because all three of them laughed as she continued to beg and whimper. Jasper dragged her over a broken bottle and Ana screamed out in pain.

"Let my mate go now, and I promise to leave something recognizable about you for your next of kin to identify."

Ana's heart began to beat faster at the voice that came from nowhere, and she shivered as she caught the alluring scent of her male on the air. "You decide to keep dragging her like that then I won't leave a fucking inch of you unbroken. I will turn you inside fucking out."

Despite the increased pain from the change in angle, Ana looked up at the man who stood three feet from her staring at Jasper with deadly intent. His body was tense, his fists were clenched at his sides, and he seemed to be covered in what looked like soot and a whole lot of blood. Not all of it his.

Her mate had come for her. No doubt she should be thankful. And Ana was sure she would be, if her fear of the man with death shining in his eyes didn't have her quivering on the edge of a nervous breakdown.

Chapter Three

Demon had no clear recollection of how he got out of the cage, or how he came to be standing in the car park three feet from his mate and her tormentor. He had a vague recollection of throwing the wolf over the top of the electric fence, but after that it was a blur. He didn't really give a fuck how he did it. His focus was completely locked on the wolf with his hands on his mate.

"You think this submissive bitch is your mate?" the asshole answered, shaking the woman slightly. Demon's beast grunted in anger at the sight of her wince of pain.

"Like I said," Demon said, his voice garbled as his beast pushed forward, "unless you have a desire to inspect your own intestines up close and real fucking personal, you will let. My. *Mate.* Go."

Demon heard the sounds of car doors slamming behind him, but his focus never wavered. He saw his mate glance behind him, and he figured more of this asshole's friends had just walked up behind him.

The man who now topped his shit list grinned at him, and Demon saw his fingers tightening in the woman's hair. "This bitch is part of my pack and therefore she belongs to me."

Demon growled when the bastard used his hold on her to pull her to her feet.

"And I do not share. So, Razorback, I'll leave you with a few of my men while I take my bitch home."

Demon grunted as a chain fell over his head and pulled tight around his neck. He lifted his hands to try to pull the metal away from his windpipe, but he was grabbed by multiple hands from behind, holding him still.

"No! Don't hurt him!" his mate cried out and his beast froze at the concern in her tone. When the asshole reached a partially shifted hand to wrap around her throat, everything within him tensed. Demon growled when he watched a steady stream of blood slide down his woman's neck from where the bastard pressed a shifted claw into her skin.

"I wouldn't worry so much about what's about to happen to the pig."

His mate flinched when the prick slid his tongue down the side of her neck, tracking the blood and making obscene sounds of pleasure. "If I were you, I would be more concerned about what I am going to do to you once we get back home."

Demon remained still, watching as his mate was dragged into the truck behind them. He could taste her fear in the air, and for that alone, there would be a river of bloodshed this night. But seeing the apology lingering in her eyes and the hopelessness flashing across her expression, he would make sure her tormentor took a long while to die.

He knew there were five wolf shifters standing behind him, and he flinched as they started to pound on him, taking particular care to hit him where he was already wounded. Demon kept his gaze on the truck until he was dragged to the ground, and they started kicking him. He waited another few moments to ensure the truck was out of view before he swung both legs around in a full circle, moving the wolf pack off him enough so that he could get to his feet.

"Well, lookie here," the wolf standing directly in front of him drawled. "The Razorback wants to go a round or three. Where was this fight when the bitch was still here? What's the matter, pig, you don't want anyone to see you lose a fight?"

Demon turned to look at the mouthy wolf, and grinned, embracing the red-hazed bloodlust of his beast. "I don't want to scare my mate with the reality of the beast she has been bound to. I figured I'd wait until she was out of sight before I let my boar loose on you assholes, and he bathes in your fucking blood."

The wolves all frowned. They thought five of them could bring him down? *Fuck. No.* They should have brought the whole damn pack. When he fought as a man, he was formidable. If they faced his beast, then they'd better pray for a quick death. He was the Razorback Demon, and when it came to being an apex predator, there was no one and nothing higher than he.

Demon threw his head back with a roar as he gave himself over to his beast. In a flash of white pain, and the shimmer of ecstasy that came with a shift, he embraced the change and became his boar. He made his beast promise he would leave at least one of the fuckers alive enough for Demon to question his mate's whereabouts before they killed him. Then he slipped back and allowed his animal the destruction he had been denied too long.
****

Ana whimpered and shivered as she crouched in the corner of the concrete bunker she'd been pushed into. The cells were located a distance from the main living quarters for the pack, and Ana had always thought that was so no one would be bothered by the screams. It wasn't the first time Jasper had put her here since he and Ezra had arrived, but it was probably going to be the last. There was no way he would allow Ana to live now, and if the truth be told, if what he had threatened her with on the drive back to their pack lands came to fruition, she didn't want to survive it. She would rather drift into the arms of her ancestors.

She pressed the palm of her left hand to her chest

at the pain that had settled there. Dying would mean not seeing Demon again, and her heart ached at the thought. She had heard of the Razorback Demon, of course, but she would never have thought he would be her mate. She had no idea how a mating between one of the most dominant shifters of their time and a submissive wolf could work. All she knew was the thought of not seeing him again left her feeling bereft.

Ana flinched as the door at the top of the stairs slammed against the concrete wall, and the slow methodical sound of someone descending the stairs had fear spiraling within her. Her heart pounded and her breathing raced as Jasper stepped into view at the bottom of the stairs.

"Ahhh, there's my timid little submissive." His voice made her skin crawl and she bit off a whimper of fear. "Don't hold back those sweet sounds, Ana. You know how much I love to hear them." Jasper briefly closed his eyes as he inhaled deeply. "They are almost as big a turn on for me as the sweet aroma of your fear. If only I could bottle that shit. I would make a fucking fortune."

Jasper swaggered over to the door of her cell. "I am really looking forward to tonight. I figure by morning I would have fucked you out of my system, and ready to move on. I reckon there won't be much left of you, but whatever there is, I have promised the boys they can have at it. Especially the group on their way back now. Your mate didn't put up much of a fight in the end."

"H-he's dead?" she whispered brokenly.

"Of course he's fucking dead." Jasper sneered. "What the hell did you think was going to happen? One fucking shifter against five of our strongest wolves was not going to end any other way. Hell, perhaps the fucker welcomed death in the end. Maybe he saw what the Fates had destined for him and figured that was a much better option for him."

Ana felt tears swell at the thought her mate would rather embrace death than face a future with her. But then again, what did she have to offer him? The slide of metal against metal pulled her from her own thoughts as Jasper slid a key into the lock of her door. She scrambled to her feet as it swung open.

Jasper stepped inside with an evil grin. "You gonna put up a fight, Ana? God, I hope so. There is nothing I love more than a woman who puts up some resistance. You wanna fight, love, then do it well because I am going to love every fucking minute."

Ana made a vow to herself that, submissive or not, she would not stop fighting. She took a steadying breath as Jasper began to stalk toward her. Her wolf whimpered, urging her to run. But there was nowhere to go. When Jasper was close to her, she felt a sudden rare streak of rebellion slam through her and she slapped him as hard as she could with her right hand.

Jasper's head whipped to the left and the coppery scent of blood sparked between them. Ana wanted to cheer at the thought she might have hurt him, but when he turned to look at her, Ana saw lust shimmering in his gaze.

"First blood to you, Ana." Jasper's voice was thick with arousal. "But I assure you, the last will be to me!"

Ana screamed as Jasper lunged forward, wrapping both hands around her throat. Both froze when a low growling sound came from outside. A sound so chilling it had the hair standing up at the back of her neck.

Shouts of alarm from the men Jasper had no doubt brought with him could be heard, but they soon morphed into screams of panic and pain. All the while the continuous growl of an animal filled with rage could be heard.

Ana couldn't stop her small smile as she looked up at Jasper. "Perhaps the reports of my mate's death were, as they say, greatly exaggerated?"

Jasper's gaze narrowed and his face flushed with anger. This was the first time she had ever said anything to him that wasn't a stuttered plea.

Ana saw the back hand coming and tried to move with the blow to lessen the impact, but with Jasper's other hand still wrapped around her throat, there was no escape. The crack of his hand against her cheek echoed in the room and she fell to the side. She slumped on the concrete floor in shock, and felt the warm slide of her own blood down her chin as she watched him stride to the cage door and lock it from the inside.

"He can't fucking save you, Ana," Jasper spat. "He—"

The sound of the door upstairs exploding inward shocked them both. Demon stepped into the room a few seconds later. Ana gasped at the sight of him. There were ugly dark bruises forming along both sides of his torso. He was bleeding from at least three gunshot wounds that she could see and his face was a mass of blood and swelling.

"You wanna make a bet on that, wolf?" Demon said in a voice thick with anger as he turned to face the door of the cage. "How about this? You give her to me now, I leave your limbs attached."

Jasper growled low in this chest and Ana felt the oppressive weight of his dominance fill the room, but Demon didn't even flinch. "Like I told you, pig, she's mine. Ezra has decreed that she is mine and I can and will do anything I like to her."

As if to prove his point, Jasper strode over, pulled

back his leg and kicked her hard in the stomach. Ana cried out as she curled in on herself for protection.

"Fuck!" Demon screamed as he gripped the bars of the cage, his entire body swelling with the effort he used trying to pry the bars apart. Over the sounds of her own pained breathing, she heard the grinding noise that meant he'd actually managed to move the bars. "Open this fucking door, dog, or I swear to God I will burn this fucking pack to the motherfucking ground!"

Jasper laughed evilly as he kicked her once more and then moved with supernatural speed to the bars and slammed his fist into Demon's nose. Ana saw the eruption of blood that accompanied the hit, but Demon never stopped his efforts to bend the bars.

"I'll let the bitch go, pig, but you can watch me fuck her first." Jasper sneered as he began to pull off his shirt. "But I warn you, you may not want her when I'm done."

Demon went ballistic at the cage door, snarling and cursing, and Ana saw his eyes glow red as he suddenly stepped back from the cage.

His gaze met hers, and she thought she saw regret in his eyes. Was he just going to leave? Was Jasper right in his assumption that Demon really didn't want her as a mate? She was still grappling with that when Demon threw his head back on a roar that shifted into a snarl of rage as he exploded into his boar. The animal was huge. If she were standing, he would be taller than her five-foot-five frame. He was a dark brindle color, and his eyes were a blood red that had her wolf cowering in fear.

Jasper looked at the giant razorback in horror as the boar charged the door of the cage, slamming his huge head into the bars, bending them in the process, his massive tusks reaching through the bars and slicing a deep gash in Jasper's thigh.

Jasper cried out as he dropped to the ground, sliding back further into the cell, pressing his hands to the wound that bled furiously. Ana remained where she was, the dominance so strong in the small space she wasn't sure she would be able to stand against it.

The boar moved back, that eerie continuous growl echoing around the room. The volume escalated as the animal dragged its front right hoof through the dirt and then launched itself at the bars which buckled even further. On the next run, the boar would be in the cage with them.

Jasper cursed and he appeared to shimmer before her for a moment, and then a giant gray wolf stood in his place. Blood still dripped steadily from its hind leg. She thought perhaps Jasper would wait and engage the boar when it got into the cage, or perhaps would attempt to evade the massive animal and escape. She realized how naïve she truly was when the wolf's head turned in her direction. The arctic blue eyes of their kind locking with laser-like intensity on her.

Time slowed to a crawl. She watched the muscles in the wolf's body tense to launch itself in her direction, and when she turned to the boar, she saw the look of rage in the animal's eyes as he screamed his displeasure and threw himself toward the cage door at the same time the wolf moved in her direction.

With a calm that belied the danger she was in, she watched as both animals charged. She knew it would be a close race. Either Jasper would reach her first and she would be rushed into the arms of her ancestors, or her mate would get to her in time. She looked past Jasper and stared at her mate as he rushed the cage. Even in this form, he was breathtaking to watch. Ana lifted her arm almost absentmindedly and Jasper's teeth ripped through the tender skin and flesh of her forearm. She heard the bone snap as the wolf shook her so hard her head slammed back against the concrete wall. Ana took comfort in the fact that the last thing she saw before the darkness claimed her was her mate, charging into the cage like the harbinger of death itself and she knew she would be avenged.

Chapter Four

Ana took a deep breath as she woke, and froze at the scent that surrounded her. The unique blend of man, earth, and spice, with a heavy thread of wild sparked her arousal and her memories at the same time. Ana sat up with a gasp, crying out at the pain crashing through her at the sudden move.

"Shh, lie still," a male's voice grumped, and she looked frantically around her for the source. Her gaze landed on the figure of a man dressed in jeans and a white t-shirt, slumped in a chair against the wall next to the bed she was lying in. Despite the lack of light in the room, her shifter abilities enabled her to see the man clearly in the muted predawn light.

It was her mate. The Razorback Demon. She was immediately filled with fear and caught the acrid scent of it in the air. The scent intensified when the man growled low and leaned to prop his elbows on his knees.

"For fuck's sake, Ana," Demon grumbled. "I'm not going to fucking hurt you. Stop being scared of me."

"How do you know my name?" Her voice sounded raspier than normal.

"I heard him call you that in the bunker."

Images of the moment he exploded into his boar flashed through her mind. Ana took a few rapid breaths in an attempt to hold off the panic that was building steadily, and to keep from passing out.

"Calm. The hell. Down. All this fear is fucking with my beast. Stop being scared."

Ana flinched at the anger in his tone. She took a few deep breaths, employing the tactic her mother had encouraged her to use when the fear became crippling. When she was able to breathe without whimpering, she slid back on the bed until her back was pressed against the wall. The slight ache in her right arm reminded her of Jasper's attack and she pushed back the sleeve of the shirt she wore to look at it. The scars were still pink, but it looked relatively healed.

"He did a number on your arm," Demon said. "You being a shifter and my blood are healing it fast."

Ana frowned as she looked up at him. "Your blood? What does that mean?"

Demon scowled like he hated the question. "The wolf not only broke your arm, he managed to get your throat before I got to him." Ana lifted a hand to her throat and her fingers slid along the puckered skin of scar tissue right over her carotid artery. "You were bleeding out too damn fast. I had to seal the wound, and the only thing I had that could do that was my blood. I forced you to take my blood before you could die. I have bound you to me."

Ana nodded like she understood when really, she had no clue. "Okay, thank you."

There was a pause before Demon threw his hands up in frustration, making her flinch once more. "Really? Thank you? Is that all you can fucking say?"

Ana felt a tendril of emotion she couldn't recognize unfurl within her. "Well, yes. I would think that when a person saves the life of another, they would say thank you."

Demon leaned forward once more and glared, and that unknown emotion within her swelled. "I've just told you that I forced you to take my fucking blood and bound you to me for life and you fucking *thank* me for it!" Demon slammed his arm out to the side, punching a hole in the wall beside him, and fear spiked within her. "What the ever loving hell is that all about? And I told you to stop. Being. Scared. Of. Me!"

Ana's heart began to thump a little louder and she

suddenly knew what that emotion was within her. For the first time in her submissive existence, she was pissed. "Firstly, you arrogant pig, and yes that damn pun was intended, I was being fucking polite. Something I am sure is completely foreign to you. Secondly, I do have an issue with being bound to you. I am a submissive wolf shifter who has always imagined she would find a submissive mate and the two of us would live a quiet life together. I would serve my mate and he would love me for who I am. I knew that dream was lost to me the moment I caught your scent in that hideous arena. Thirdly, you can't simply demand that I not be scared of you when you sit in that chair and do nothing but scowl, snarl, swear, and yell at me. Your dominance rolls off you in waves and I am simply amazed that I haven't just keeled over and passed out from the power of it. So, if I am scared of you for the moment, pull your big boy panties up and accept it. I'm not sure when it's going to change, and in the meantime, you are going to have to live with it!"

At the end of her outburst, Ana breathed heavily, in shock that she had spoken so brazenly. Demon's jaw had dropped and he sat staring at her like she'd suddenly grown a second head. From the way she had just yelled at the Razorback Demon, like some kind of demented fish wife, she thought perhaps she had.

Demon sat back with a slow grin, and Ana stared in amazement at the transformation. There was no mistaking the fact he was gorgeous, but when he smiled at her like that, he was simply breathtaking.

"Damn, Ana," he drawled in a voice that had heat pooling low in her abdomen, "you sure act more dominant than any submissive I have ever met. I don't think I have ever been told off before in my life."

Ana blushed at his words. "Yeah, well, you

deserved them. Perhaps if your parents had disciplined you with a scolding or two you wouldn't be so arrogant."

Demon's expression blanked in a heartbeat. "My parents would have been more likely to beat the shit out of me."

Ana frowned at the dispassionate tone he used. "Your parents mistreated you, Demon?"

Demon flinched slightly when she used his name, but she remained silent, awaiting his answer. "They were both dominant razorbacks. They fought and bled each other more often than not. In fact, the two of them killed each other when I was seven."

Ana frowned. "I've never heard of mates capable of physically hurting each other to the point of death."

Demon frowned. "They weren't mates."

Ana tilted her head at the tone Demon used. "There's more to that isn't there?"

Demon stood up abruptly from the chair and moved toward the bedroom door. "You're too skinny. Come get something to eat."

Demon slipped from the room, and Ana gnawed at her bottom lip. She had seen the spark of hurt that crossed his face, and it pained her to think she might have caused him pain. She stepped out of the bedroom and came to a sudden stop. The floor-to-ceiling windows across from her gave her the most magnificent views of the mountains that took her breath way. She walked slowly through the living area, noting the furniture in the room screamed taste and expense.

She crossed the room, more confused than ever, and moved toward the kitchen area of the open-plan room. Demon was pulling sandwich fixings from the pantry and fridge and her tummy growled at the sight.

Demon looked up with that intense look on his face and her heart stuttered. "I guess you're hungry. Sit down and let me feed you. The thought of you being hungry makes my boar anxious and concerned. Two emotions I would have never thought I would use when referring to my beast."

Ana offered a small smile and moved to take a seat at the breakfast bar. The two of them ate in companionable silence, and Ana found herself relaxing. She even caught herself snatching sneak peeks of the man who scared her and excited her at the same time. On more than one occasion, she caught him staring back at her and that sparked flutters of excitement within her.

"You know," she said in a quiet voice as she wiped her fingers on the napkin he handed her, "I don't like you referring to your boar as a beast."

Demon looked up at her in surprise.

"He saved my life. I'd be willing to bet money that he's saved yours, too. He is no beast. He's a big, proud, dominant Alpha boar." She bit her bottom lip and noticed that his gaze latched onto the move and darkened. "And he's my mate."

Demon leaned forward, the scent of him thickening the air around her. "And what about me? Am I your mate, too?"

Ana felt herself caught in Demon's gaze. "What do you think?" she whispered.

Demon frowned. "I don't have to think, I know I am. But what I don't know is whether or not I can keep you."

Ana tilted her head to the side. "Keep me?"

"You're mine. Mine to protect," Demon's whisper rolled over her, making her shiver. "But I don't know how to do that when I scare you so damn much. I saw the fear in your eyes when I shifted. I can't be anything other than what I am, and what I am scares the shit out of you. How can that work?"

Chapter Five

"I don't know."

Demon felt his mate's words like a physical blow. A relationship between the two of them would be impossible. Ever since he had brought her to his home after laying waste to the prick who had thought to harm her, his beast had been a pain in his ass. He demanded Demon claim her, take her, mark her, fuck her, anything that would cement the mating bond that had formed as soon as he had given her his blood. If Demon had thought his beast was determined before, now the fucker was simply relentless.

Demon pushed back from the breakfast bar and turned to face the window, breathing through his disappointment and a strange ache that had formed in his chest. He flinched when he felt her small hand press against his back. The fact he hadn't heard her approach was a sure sign of how stirred up he actually was.

"Let me finish, but stay facing the window so I can get this out," she said quietly. "I'm a submissive wolf whose role in the pack was to clean up after others, and look after the pups. I'm so submissive the mere fact that I am standing this close to you ... touching you ... is amazing in itself. And it gives me hope that maybe it can work. I just don't know how it will in this moment. I feel like I am yours, too, Demon."

He closed his eyes at the breathless sound of his name on her lips.

"I'm just not sure if I can keep you, either."

Demon turned then, and pride bloomed within him when his mate stood her ground. He could feel the tremble in her hand as it now lay against his chest, but she didn't step back. *Good mate.*

"Kiss me," he said in a voice that sounded a lot harsher than he had intended.

Ana flinched.

"Ana." He desperately tried to quell his beast enough to sound like he wasn't angry. "I want to kiss you so damn bad, but I find that when I am this close to you, my control is balanced on a knife's edge. Kiss me, please. If you leave it up to me, I will consume you and I'm so fucking scared I'll scare you off."

Demon waited, tensing every muscle in his body to keep himself from pouncing on her. He watched as indecision waged in her eyes. Just when he thought she might turn or step away from him, his mate surprised him once again with how courageous she was. She lifted a visibly trembling hand to his shoulder and then leaned in, pushing up to her tiptoes, and tilted her head toward his. She was so small he had to lean down a little to meet her. When their lips touched, Demon felt his beast still within him.

Ana gave a little sigh of pleasure, and her lips moved over his with sweet gentle kisses. The effect on his beast was unimaginable. The boar growled in satisfaction and rolled over on its back, reveling in the touch of their mate, content to have her touch them. The effect on Demon was a lot more visceral. His blood thickened and his cock hardened to the point of pain, and for the first time in his life, it was the man who demanded action.

Ana pulled back a little and stared into his eyes. "Demon, I don't know how to do that … well, harder. Is that the word? I'm not sure. I want more, I want harder, but I can't—*hmph.*"

Demon swallowed the rest of her words with his mouth. He wrapped his arms around her and lifted her up and against him. He was pretty sure she was no longer standing on the ground, but he didn't give a shit. He swept his tongue into her mouth, licking deep and growling at the sweet flavor that was uniquely Ana. He felt her arms lift to grab him around his neck and he carried her over to the breakfast bar, continuing the sensual assault on her mouth, employing his teeth and his tongue to discover what made her quiver and what made her moan.

When he got to the bar, he pushed everything out of his way, and deposited her on the counter. He nudged her knees apart, and stepped between them. He growled with pleasure when her legs lifted to wrap around his hips. He placed his hands on her knees and slid them down her silky firm thighs, under the shirt of his that she wore until he could cup the firm flesh of her ass, encased in a small pair of functional panties.

He pulled back so he could look into her face, beautifully flushed with arousal. "You are mine, Ana. Never doubt that. And now that I have you, I won't be letting you go. I will also not allow you to wear panties like these."

Ana gasped when he ripped her panties and lifted her so he could throw the offending item away.

"You'll be bare for me or in a lacy thong that I can slide out of my way when I want to play with what's mine. But never will you wear cotton. You're too fucking beautiful for cotton."

Ana bit her bottom lip as she ran a hand down his chest. "Demon, I've never been with a man before."

Demon froze as a bucket of ice was poured over his arousal. His mate was a fucking virgin. The fact that information thrilled the beast within him, knowing that she would only ever he theirs, showed what a sick bastard he was. He should be scared. What the hell did he know about being with a goddamn virgin?

"Just let me make you feel good," he whispered, shocking them both. He began to rock his hips forward, grinding against her. From the way her green eyes sparked and her mouth opened on a gasp, the counter was exactly the right height.

The way he moved against her affected him just as much and flashes of pleasure began to explode within him. Leaning as his body began to tighten, he claimed her mouth, kissing her with every ounce of emotion slamming through his body. Over and over he rolled his hips against her, both of them groaning at the sensation. Demon growled when he inhaled the air around him, perfumed so sweetly with the scent of her arousal.

Ana groaned against him, tightening her grip around his shoulders. When she started to meet his thrusts with tentative circular motions of her own, he knew he wouldn't be able to hold out much longer. He pulled back from the kiss, wanting to watch her face as she went over, and his heart clenched within his chest at the sight of the arousal flushed so sweetly across her cheeks. He reached a hand down and groaned at the honey pooling in her pussy. He loved the shocked gasp she made when he ran his finger around her swollen clit.

"Come for me, my Ana," he said in a voice that rang with need. "Come for me and call my name. Tell the whole fucking world who you belong to." Demon pressed his middle finger into her pussy, sank it in as deep as he could, and pressed his thumb against her clit.

Ana's reaction was instant. She jolted hard as her release hit her, shuddering and jerking against his body. He basked in the sound of her screaming his name to the heavens, her head thrown back in ecstasy. When she ground herself against his hand and his cock, she inadvertently threw him into the maelstrom of his release. Helpless to stop, he pulled her tight against him, growling her name. The Fates had deemed him worthy of being Ana's mate, and he made a promise in that moment to do everything he had to do, to convince her that they were right.

Chapter Six

"What did Jasper mean when he said Ezra had decreed you were his?" Demon asked in the darkened bedroom.

Ana sighed. "I am wolf shifter, and Ezra is my Alpha. We were all made to pledge to him after he killed our Alpha. He now has that right."

The two of them were lying in the bed of the master suite, the thin t-shirt she wore the only barrier between them. Ana was amazed at how relaxed she felt. She would have thought she'd have been embarrassed by her actions in the kitchen, but Demon never gave her the opportunity. In true Alpha Razorback style, he decreed the moment to be "hot as fuck" and then carried her into the master bathroom. He'd stripped them both down, and led her into the huge shower. He had cared for her, soaping every inch of her, telling her how beautiful she was, and even took his time washing and conditioning her hair. Once he was sure she was clean, and more relaxed than she ever thought she would be standing naked with a dominant, he handed her the soap and demanded she learn his body.

Those were the exact words that he used, but she was starting to understand her razorback a little more now. He knew that she was a virgin, and by giving her free rein over his body with the soap, he was allowing her the opportunity to get familiar with his form. She had seen a lot of his body the night he had saved her, but she had been too busy being scared out of her mind to really pay attention. She had also discovered that when he demanded things of her in a tone that she had initially mistaken as anger, it meant he was feeling a little unsure as to what her reaction might be.

Determined to show him she, too, was willing to challenge her limitations in order to explore this bond between them, she took the soap from him and moved to his back. She'd seen glimpses of the substantial tattoo he had on his back, but it wasn't until this moment that she got to see it in all its glory. The tattoo was a large set of angel wings, each one starting from his shoulder blade, arching up and reaching slightly over his shoulders and then down his back, almost to the hard globes of his butt. They were a dark intricate ink, and they moved when his muscles flexed beneath her fingers. She took her time learning him, just as he asked.

A while later, and yet not long enough as far as Ana was concerned, he'd said he was clean enough. He'd leaped out to dry himself before pulling her out and gently dabbing her dry with a soft towel, and then pulled her back into the bedroom. He tugged a soft t-shirt over her head before using a hairdryer on her hair. He then put them both to bed. Ana had seen his cock, standing tall and erect, the head a dark painful-looking purple, but Demon didn't say anything about it, just settled her into the large bed and curled in behind her. She had been lying there floating on a sea of contentment when he asked his question.

"The right?" Demon asked.

"It is the right of the Alpha to grant the wish of any senior pack member, and I am just a dispensable lowly ranked submissive," Ana explained, patting Demon's arm until he quieted when he growled in displeasure at her words. "As Alpha, Ezra has the power to make decisions that affect others, and once he has spoken the words, they are law. If he decreed that I was to be Jasper's, then I would have to comply. I would be unable to defy his words and I would feel physical pain if I tried to."

"You gave yourself to me in the kitchen," Demon said, his hands stroking up and down her arm. "I know you did. Maybe not in the true physical sense of the word, but you did. Did it hurt you?"

"No." Ana rolled in his arms so that she lay facing him. "For the decree to stand, I have to hear him say the words. I never did."

"So maybe Jasper was lying?"

Ana shook her head sadly. "No, I don't think so. When Jasper said the words, they were truth." Wolf shifters could tell a lie among their own.

Demon scowled. "So can the fucker just tell you to die and you will?"

"No," Ana said smoothing the lines from his face, "he can't force us to stop breathing or anything like that. Our own self-preservation would kick in and refuse to comply."

"Can you be claimed?"

Ana sighed. "I can, but with the Alpha bond so strong within me, it would come with great pain. And even then, I would have two distinct bonds. Both of them strong, but the Alpha bond to Ezra would remain."

"How is this Alpha bond broken?" Demon asked in a calculating tone.

"His death, or mine," Ana answered solemnly.

"Okay then, so once I kill him, then we're good," Demon said calmly.

"Just like that? Ezra is a killer, Demon. He took our last Alpha out in a battle so fierce and so quick it was over before it had even begun."

Demon nodded. "He's gonna come at me anyway because I killed his brother in a not so nice way. Freeing you from this pack bond will just be a fucking fantastic benefit. He'll be coming for me any time now. Hell, I left him an engraved fucking invitation before I left your pack lands."

Ana frowned. "What does that mean?"

"I left him a message and some directions on the wall of that cell he had you locked into. I had heard about the new Alpha and Beta of the Eastlands pack, so figured whoever the Alpha was, he wouldn't take his brother being killed like he was lightly. I would guess he'll be heading this way in the next few hours."

Ana tried to sit up, but Demon held her still. "Ezra's coming here? We have to run. He'll hurt you. He won't just kill you, Demon, he will play with you first. I have seen him do it to the strongest in our pack. He is a killer, a true monster."

"A monster will fall at the feet of a Demon anytime, Ana."

He had such confidence. She envied him that strength, but feared for him nonetheless. The only time he had shown any type of hesitation was when they had spoken of his parents.

"So, am I allowed to ask you a question now?" Ana asked.

Demon huffed a sound that might have been a laugh. "You just did, but because I am in a good mood, I'll let you ask another one."

"What did your parents do that made you believe that you were meant to be the angel of death?"

Demon froze and Ana thought perhaps she had overstepped her place.

"If we are to be what the Fates believe we can be, then you have to open yourself to me, as I do to you."

Demon was quiet for a long while and Ana began to wonder if he would just let the question go.

"My parents were paired because of their levels of dominance," Demon said in a flat tone that had her wolf pressing forward, wanting to comfort her mate. "Both of them were Alphas. They were paired by a woman who many in our clan believed to be a seer. She told them their son would be born a warrior and would lead the clan, meeting any and all challenges. The razorbacks had been hunted for so long there aren't that many clans of us left. They thought I would be some fucking second coming or some shit like that."

Ana reached up to trace her thumb over his brow, trying to ease the tension there. "I have heard the stories, Demon, you don't need to finish the story if you don't wish to."

Demon tightened his hold, pulling her closer until their foreheads touched. "You probably heard that I killed my clan, including my parents. I wish I could tell you that wasn't true, but I can't."

Ana heard the self-loathing in his tone and leaned in to press a soft kiss to his lips. "I was trained to kill from a young age. Hell, it seemed like from birth, to be fair. My parents were always trying to push me to be faster, bigger, stronger, fucking meaner than any other male in our clan. To test that theory, they would have me challenge them. I would win. They were always to the death. My one saving grace is that I never took the dishonorable kill. I never drained their life's blood. That was something I refused to do. I figured I was damned as it was, I didn't need more stains on my soul."

If a shifter took a life in their animal form by draining their victim of their life's blood, consuming it until they died, then they took on that animal's strength. The repercussions for that were believed to be eternal damnation. Only the truly desperate or fundamentally evil would ever consider doing such a thing.

Demon continued talking in that flat tone that bothered her wolf so much. "My father, in particular, was so damn determined to have bred the world's most dominant razorback, he never saw the deaths of the others in the clan as anything but acceptable collateral damage. Not even when he had my mother challenge me."

Ana pressed as tight as she could to him, wrapping her left leg up and over his thigh, tugging his body into full contact with her own. "I cannot believe anyone would ever do that to another human being, let alone their own son. I am so sorry they did that to you."

Demon gave a slight shake of his head. "I am not telling you this for you to feel sorry for me. You asked me to be open with you. You need to know what you are getting yourself into, Ana. I wear these words"—he pressed a hand to his own chest—"and the wings on my back as a sign of who and what I am. I am Demon by name and Demon by nature, Ana. I did kill the males of my clan. I killed my mother when she challenged me, and despite trying to not hurt her, I had to kill her in order to survive. I challenged my father straight after that because he fucking deserved it."

"I get that, Demon, I do. If I had been with you then, even as submissive as I am, I would have been cheering you on from the sidelines. But I have a different theory to offer you." She reached up her hand to touch the tattoo on his chest. "Perhaps you wear these words as a reminder of what you have had to do to survive, and you had the wings done to represent what you were living for, but never knew what that was."

"Explain."

Ana smiled at his gruff tone. Her razorback was uncertain again.

"My mother was a New Zealander. She was human, and when she met my father, the mating bond snapped into place for them almost immediately. Because she was human, having me was difficult and not without risk. She died of complications from the birth less than twenty-four hours after having me." Tears formed as she spoke, and this time it was Demon reaching up to stroke her face in an attempt to ease her pain.

"As it is with true mates, my father passed into the arms of his ancestors soon after that, but not before he honored my mother's last request and named me Anahera. She was part Maori, and Anahera in English is Angel."

Demon stared at her for a long while, his frown clearing, and Ana was struck once more by how gorgeous he was. "You know what I like most about that theory?" Demon asked after a while.

Ana shook her head slowly.

"It would mean that you were always mine. Mine above and before all others. Mine to keep, mine to cherish, and mine to love."

Ana's heart began to thud. "Love?"

Demon smiled and the earth seemed to grind to a stop. "Yeah. You're my mate, Ana. My mate in truth. I've been falling for you from the moment you warned me in that goddamn ring. You are the only person who has ever looked out for me."

"You're my mate, Demon," Ana said emphatically. "I will forever look at that beautiful tattoo on your back and know it is there for me. I started falling for you when you came for me. Not just on to pack lands to break me free, but out to the carpark. You came for *me*."

Demon cupped her cheek in his hands and Ana melted. Despite the fact his hands were calloused, she had never felt so cherished and safe. "I always will, angel."

"Then make me yours in truth, Demon," Ana said breathlessly. "Please."

Demon's face morphed right before her eyes. The

awe that had filled his expression just moments before slid away to be replaced with a need and heat that had her heart pounding.

She had no idea what happened next, but she needn't have worried. Demon took her mouth with his. He completely took her over, using his tongue to sweep into her mouth and adding just the right amount of pressure to have her arousal spiraling out of control within her.

Ana didn't protest when he reached down and gripped the bottom of her t-shirt, and then lifted off her for a moment, breaking the kiss so that he could pull her t-shirt up and off. Ana had no time to even think about the fact she was laying naked in bed with a man for the first time in her life. Demon lowered his body to lay against hers and went back to kissing the awareness out of her.

Over and over he licked into her mouth. When he pulled back to bite seductively into her bottom lip, Ana felt her body's response. Soon the room filled with the scent of her arousal, and she could feel the strength of Demon's arousal against her lower abdomen. Demon broke the kiss and left both of them breathing heavily.

"Fuck, Ana." His growl was so sexy it had her shivering. "Your mouth is fucking addictive, but I wanna know what my mate tastes like."

Ana was desperately trying to comprehend what that might mean when he began to kiss his way down her body. He stopped at her breasts, and Ana cried out and arched her back when he drew the sensitive peak into his mouth. Again, he used his extremely talented tongue to great advantage and had her writhing beneath him on the mattress.

Ana felt hot, and restless, and so damn close to exploding into a million tiny little pieces she could do nothing more than moan. Demon traveled even further down her body, and Ana lifted up onto her elbows to watch his descent. There was a fever in his eyes that told her he loved her body. When he nestled between her thighs, he pressed until her legs spread wide, making a place for him between them and she caught her bottom lip between her teeth.

"Beautiful," he whispered in a voice that was the perfect mixture of need and reverence. "I love the fact that you are bare for my viewing pleasure."

"I get waxed," Ana blurted out.

Demon looked up and grinned at her. "I love that you do. But you are mine, which means this beautifully bare pussy is mine to take care of, too. If it's okay with you, I want to learn how to do it for you."

Ana swallowed at the thought, but nodded. Hell, the way she felt in this moment, she wouldn't deny him anything. She inhaled sharply when Demon looked back at her body, laid out as it was for him. Then when he leaned in and placed his mouth on her, she cried out. The sensation of his tongue sliding up and over her sensitive pussy was almost too much to bear.

Unable to tear her gaze away, she watched as Demon pleasured her with his mouth. The slide of his tongue up and over her swollen clit had her body shivering in reaction. When he placed his mouth almost completely over her and sucked, the sensation was so pleasurable she couldn't stop from shouting out. And when he took her clit into his mouth and bit down gently on it, she couldn't hold back anymore. Arching her back and inhaling deeply, she screamed Demon's name to the world at large.

Chapter Seven

The sound of his mate screaming his name had Demon's release pulsing close to the surface. He stayed with her, taking every drop of sweet cream her body released, not leaving her until the shudders of her release eased and she fell back against the mattress. When he had control of his own body again, he crawled up and over her.

"That was fucking beautiful," he said as he lay over her, holding his weight on his arms. "The way you submit to me and give everything you have is fucking phenomenal." He settled his hips between hers, reaching down to tug her leg up and over his hip, praying that this would give him more control over the pace and depth of his possession. "I'm going to try to take you gently, angel. Don't be scared."

Ana surprised the hell out of him when she wrapped both her legs around his waist and placed her hand on his chest. "I'm not afraid. The Fates believe I am the mate of the Razorback Demon, and I believe that, too. That must mean that I can take everything you have to give. And that has to mean in the bedroom as well. So, show me, my mate. Show me what it is to be mated to you."

Demon wanted to slam home into her, pound himself into his mate until he didn't know where he ended and his mate began. But his beast called for restraint. And didn't that fucking beat all. His beast, the animal that drove him to fight in order to fulfill this need for power, pain, and violence within him, demanded he be patient with their mate. He insisted Demon show her he could be what she needed.

Breathing deeply, he placed the head of his cock

at the hot, wet entrance to her body. Tensing every muscle in his body, he pressed forward. He groaned at the tight fit of her body, and when he came to the barrier he knew to be her innocence, he broke through it in a single steady thrust. Ana tensed beneath him, but never made a sound. *Brave mate.* He held still within her, allowing her time to grow accustomed to his presence within her body. When he felt her relax against him, he began to move.

Ana jerked at first, and when Demon froze, thinking that perhaps she was still in pain, she surprised him by sliding her hands to his ass and pressing down. "Don't stop." She groaned against his neck, grazing her teeth against the sensitive skin. "Move in me, take me, own me."

Demon growled as he leaned up and began to thrust into her, reveling in the way she moved her hips to meet his thrusts. He maintained a steady, firm rhythm, driving them both toward the edge of their release in a quick yet controlled manner. He knew he wouldn't be able to hold that tempo for long. His control shattered when Ana gasped and arched beneath him, and he felt the flutter of her pussy around his cock, a sure sign that her release was close.

Dropping his weight down on her, and reaching under her to cup her ass, he began to pound into her. "You are mine, angel. I own you, body and soul, but you own me, too. You fucking own me. Now, come for me, come for me hard."

Ana's body rippled around him and she screamed out his name for the second time. Unable to resist the erotic pull of her orgasm, Demon roared her name as loud as he could as he slammed home once more and gave himself over to his own release. He thrust a second time as his body jerked, giving her everything he had to give. On the third thrust, he slumped onto her, drawing in great gulps of air.

He pressed a kiss to her neck, nuzzling against her. "When I can claim you without causing you pain, I will. Here, this is where I am going to claim you. Once this fucking bond to that fucker Ezra is gone, I will claim you here."

Demon's beast grunted in pleasure at that thought, and he knew he had never been happier. But that moment was made even better when his mate bit gently on the side of his own neck.

"And I will bite you here," she whispered breathlessly. "Then all the world will know that you belong to me."

Demon felt the last part of his black heart, stained with the blood of so many sins, surrender itself to the light that was his mate.

****

Ana woke with a start, wrapped in the arms of her mate. She had no idea what brought her out of the deep sleep she was in, so she lay completely still, listening. Then she heard it. The muted scrape of nails against the wood panels of the deck. Inhaling, she caught the scent that had her filling with fear. The Alpha of the pack had come for her.

She tensed to move to warn her mate, but froze when he tightened his hold on her. He moved silently to press his mouth to her ear. "Took you long enough to wake up." His voice was calm. "Your fucking Alpha has been walking around outside for the past few minutes, disarming some of my perimeter defenses. Little does the cocky son of a bitch know I disarmed most of more difficult ones yesterday."

"Why would you do that?"

"Because I wanted him to actually get to the house. If I had left them armed, he would have been hurt before he got here and then I would have had to go out and hunt the fucker, and I can't be fucked. Stay here."

Demon slipped from the bed, and Ana sat up, pulling her hair behind her before grabbing the hair tie on her bedside table and pulling the long strands up into a bun. She stopped when she saw Demon frozen in the act of pulling on a pair of running shorts, his gaze locked to her.

"What?"

Demon grinned. "You have no idea how fucking hot you are. When you arch your back to put your truly amazing hair up, your breasts are thrust forward, and it is all I can do not to fucking jump you right here and now."

Ana smiled despite the heat she could feel rising in her face. "Save that thought for later. If Ezra is here, he didn't come alone."

Demon shrugged as he finished pulling up his shorts. "Don't fucking care. I want this done. I want you claimed. You're mine, and he is just one flea-infested, walking-dead wolf shifter standing in my way."

Ana slipped from the bed and pulled on her discarded t-shirt. "Well, if you are going to face that man, then I am going with you."

For the first time, Demon looked concerned and he turned to frown at her. "You will stay here."

Ana felt a surge of strength within her, and she knew she was finding her way to being the more dominant female match to her razorback. She knew she would never become an Alpha, but she felt her confidence building the more time she spent with her Demon.

"Nope." She pulled on a pair of Demon's running shorts, but had to roll the waistband a few times in order to keep them on. She was prepared to face the man who had aided in her torment since arriving in her pack, but she sure as hell wasn't about to do it with her hoo-hoo on display.

"Dammit, Ana." Demon growled. "I told you to stay here, and you will fucking stay here."

Translation: I have to protect you, I need you to be safe. I don't want to scare you.

Ana stepped up to her mate and wrapped her arms around his neck, pressing her body against his tense frame. "Demon, I told you before. You are my mate. I want everything you have to give, and that includes your boar. You are my razorback and I will stand with you." She thought about what it was he was about to face and frowned. "Well, how about not quite beside you, but slightly behind you. I know that I am getting a little more confidence, but Ezra scares the shit out of me."

Demon growled and his eyes shimmered red. Her boar did not like that at all. He grabbed her hand, and pulled her out to the living area. Ezra's scent intensified.

"Razorback," Ezra called from outside, his voice filled with rage and contempt. "I accept your challenge. Come out and face me and bring my little pack whore with you!"

Demon grunted a low feral sound, his body tensing before her eyes as his boar pushed forward. Ana pressed her hand against his back to calm him. She stood quietly while he took a deep breath and then moved with him when he opened the door to his house and stepped out onto the verandah.

Ana stayed behind him, but could see Ezra standing in the middle of the clearing in front of the house. He stood naked beneath the full moon, and her wolf whimpered at the dominance that seemed to be rolling off him. It felt stronger than anything she had ever felt from him before.

Demon scented the air, and grunted a disgusted

sound. "You have taken lives in your animal form, have you not? You must fear your death at my hand even more than I thought you did, dog."

Ana's stomach turned at what that meant. Ezra had to have challenged the more dominant males in the pack in order to have gained as much strength and dominance she could feel from him. He'd killed in his animal form, and he'd taken of their life's blood until death. He was damned eternally and Ana was shocked he would have taken such a drastic step.

"Come to me, Ana," Ezra said, dominance dripping from each syllable.

Ana whimpered as her wolf leaped to do as her Alpha demanded. She took a step forward, but was pulled back against her mate. Despite her immediate relief at begin held back, her body strained to follow the verbal directions of her Alpha.

"She is mine, pig. There is no bond stronger than that of a submissive wolf to her pack Alpha."

Ana felt Demon's growl of rage against her back.

"Fuck that, dog. Ana is mine. My woman. My wolf. My mate. And I will be damned if I allow you to put her between you and me and use her as you have the rest of your pack."

Demon tensed behind her and she sensed a change wash over him. His body turned rigid, and she felt the harsh hair of his boar forming along his chest, and she knew what he was about to do.

"Do it," she whispered, tilting her head to the side to make it easier and kept her eyes locked to Ezra's as Demon leaned in and bit her. She felt the bond between them snap into place, and she rejoiced in the rage that formed on Ezra's face even as he roared it to the world. She had that brief moment of celebration before the white hot shaft of pain ripped through her. She screamed with the intensity of it.

Vaguely she was aware of Demon's horror and regret that echoed down their newly formed bond. She gripped his arm where it wrapped around her and anchored herself to her mate as she rode out the pain. It was like nothing she had ever felt before. It felt as if acid traveled through her bloodstream and there was nothing she could do but weather it. She tasted blood in her mouth, and realized that she had bitten her tongue in an attempt to hold back her screams of pain.

The pain ebbed after what felt like a lifetime, but would have only been a few moments. She was slumped against her mate, breathing heavily, and bleeding from her mouth and her neck, but no longer compelled to get to Ezra.

Demon's continuous growl of anger vibrated through her entire body. "I'm okay, Demon," she whispered as she pushed to stand on legs that shook. "It's okay, my love. It's over." Demon pressed a kiss to the wound on her neck, and Ana felt the love he had for her shimmer brightly along their connection. "I love that I am bound to you, my razorback. But I find myself sickened by the atrocity that is the Alpha bond that links me to that asshole. Kill him for me."

Demon grunted, a sound she knew was part man, part boar, and she couldn't stop the bloodthirsty grin sweeping across her face. Her gaze hadn't moved from Ezra and she saw the frown that appeared on the Alpha's face.

Ana pushed herself away from her mate, and moved to stand at the top of the stairs. "I denounce you as my Alpha, and stand by my mate for all time."

Ezra snarled at her, and cursed incoherently. Ana frowned. Perhaps this was his punishment for what he had done. The quick yet inevitable fall into insanity.

Demon gently pushed her back a little and then leaped down the stairs to the ground. "I can sense that there are a few shifters standing in the edge of the forest. No doubt brought here by your pitiful Alpha to assist in my death if need be. Know this. I am about to end this disgrace of an Alpha you have all pledged to. I am the Razorback Demon and will burn this fucker to the ground before this night is through, but I will not follow his lead and take of his life's blood. I will send him into the arms of the devil with my own two hands. I will not take Alpha of this pack. You will be rogue."

Ana knew what that would mean for many of the men from her pack. They would have the freedom to go and do as they please. Something many of them had longed for, but had been unable to achieve under Ezra's rule. Her mate was smart. He had made his intentions clear to everyone in that clearing and no doubt they were all firmly in his corner.

Chapter Eight

Demon heard the excited murmurs of the shifters within the trees, but he never took his gaze from Ezra. He had no idea how many of his own pack he had drained in order to come at Demon all hyped up and uber dominant like he was, but it had Demon's stomach turning and his rage building at the thought.

"You killed my brother." Ezra's voice was barely recognizable as human.

"I did," Demon agreed with a nod, "and I enjoyed every fucking minute of it. My boar particularly enjoyed gouging a gaping hole in his stomach."

That was all it took to drive Ezra to the edge. He roared with rage and then leaped in Demon's direction, shifting within the blink of an eye mid stride. Demon allowed his boar to rise within him, but held him caged. He allowed Ezra to think he had Demon at a disadvantage, and drew him closer before he embraced the change and allowed his beast full rein.

The giant boar met the oncoming wolf with a grunt, and the two of them began to fight. Demon swung his giant head at the faster shifter, attempting to get to the soft belly of the wolf with one of his massive tusks, but the prick jumped out of range. The wolf leaped around him until he was able to use his speed to get past Demon's tusks and leap onto his back, biting deep into the flesh and muscle across the back of his neck, no doubt attempting to sever his spinal column.

This was a battle tactic many wolves used on animals, but he should have done his fucking homework. Razorbacks had a large amount of muscle and fat between their skin and their vertebrae around the neck.

There was no way in hell Ezra could reach it, despite his strength. Oh, the bite hurt like a bitch, but it wasn't deadly. Demon bunched the muscles in his neck and then threw his head from side to side as violently as he could, absorbing the pain and throwing the wolf from him. As soon as he was free, he stalked his prey.

The two of them fought back and forth, each of them scoring a few bloody hits against the other. Demon favored his right back leg, his left mangled and bleeding heavily, and there were more than a few long deep gashes along his sides where the wolf had achieved a direct hit against him. Although he hated to admit it, Demon knew he was facing a skilled fighter made even deadlier by the additional strength he had absorbed, but Ezra's determination and motivation were nowhere near as powerful as Demon's.

Demon was a patient fighter, he always had been, and Ezra was fighting on pure rage and emotion. A lethal mix that would only make him more prone to making a mistake, and then Demon would capitalize. He wanted this over with as quickly as possible. Demon had hurt his mate and the need to apologize and take care of her was riding him almost as hard as the desire to see this prick bleed out before him.

He watched as Ezra moved to the left, but from the way his muscles tensed, Demon knew he was going to leap right and come at him. A split second after Ezra committed to jumping in from the right, Demon swung his head with a growl of triumph. There was nowhere for the wolf to go. Only death and the giant tusk of an enraged razorback waiting for him. Ezra slammed onto his right tusk and Demon moved his head, making sure to gouge deep and true, ensuring the blow was lethal.

Ezra yelped in pain, the sound of a wolf that knew the end was near, and the cry morphed half way through to that of a man who faced his death. Demon waited, still in his animal form as Ezra bled out fast before his eyes. The two men's gazes remained locked together, and Demon read the fear shining in Ezra's eyes. Demon had heard his mate's approach so didn't even flinch when she stepped up beside him, her hand reaching out to press against his heaving side.

"There's my Demon," she crooned as she soothed the beast, touching him for the first time. "I pledge to you my Alpha."

Demon jolted as a second bond slammed into place between him and his angel. He grunted and Ana smiled at him. "Yeah, I know, you had the whole go rogue speech down, but I make up my own mind now. I am yours. Completely."

Demon grunted again when his mate moved to stand closer to the dying wolf, and moved with her so that if by some miracle Ezra could strike out at her, he was there to stop it, but he needn't have worried. Ezra had already slipped into death. The two of them stood there for a moment and Demon sensed the other shifters in the woods moving away.

It was over. The Eastlands Alpha was dead, his mate was bound to him in all ways, and the Razorback Demon finally had a future to look forward to. Perhaps the Fates weren't as clueless as he had originally thought.
****

"You know I never wanted to be your Alpha." Demon growled against her neck, making her shiver. "I'm your mate."

Ana reached up to wrap her arms around his shoulders with a sigh. "I know, my love, but I'm yours, and I want you to be mine in all ways possible."

Demon growled and held her tighter. He pulled back, thrust steadily into her, and the pleasure built within her with every stroke. "I like the sound of that. Does that mean I can give you orders and you have to comply?"

Ana laughed breathlessly. "No, my mate. Orders will never work on the mate of an Alpha."

Demon pulled back to lean on his elbows, resting his forehead on hers. "What if I asked you nicely and promised to behave?"

Ana giggled, undulating her hips and reveling in his groan of appreciation. "I wouldn't believe you. Demon by name and Demon by nature, remember?"

Demon laughed, a sound she was coming to crave. "Too true, my mate. Then how about I promise to fuck you the way you like it for the rest of our lives?" Demon began to piston his hips in a rhythm designed to drive her to the edge of sanity in an embarrassingly short amount of time, and she cried out his name. He lifted her legs to wrap them around his hips and she squeezed her internal muscles reflexively, wanting to hold him inside her.

"Fuck! Ana!" Demon roared as his rhythm faltered and he began to pound into her, deep furious thrusts that had her sobbing mindlessly as her orgasm built. Just when she thought she might shatter with the anticipation of what was building, her release rushed over. She screamed Demon's name as her body began to convulse beneath the waves of pleasure. Before she completely lost her mind to the bliss, she leaned up and bit deep into her mate's neck, cementing their bond, and completing her claim. She heard Demon's answering curse as her release and no doubt her claiming bite triggered his own.

Ana gripped onto her mate as the world spun uncontrollably around her. Demon would hold her safe, and be her anchor in whatever storm came their way, just as she would be the same for him. How could it be any other way? She was the fated mate of the Razorback Demon, after all.

The End

RUNNING HOME

Michelle Graham

Demon Dogs MC, prequel

Copyright © 2017

Chapter One

Michigan, 1988

Erica stood in the corner, trying her best not to cower, but as Tank advanced on her, she squeezed her eyes shut and turned her face away. It didn't stop the stinging blow across her cheek which smacked her head against the wall and resulted in an explosion of pain within her skull. With a whimper, she slid to the floor.

"That's it, bitch. On your knees where you belong."

Though her ears rang, Erica clearly heard the rasp of his zipper. Knowing resistance would only earn her more pain, she withdrew into herself until he'd finished with her and left her crying on the floor.

"I'll be back with Bones, and if you know what's good for you, you'll do what he asks the first time. Stupid cunt." The door slammed behind Tank.

The thought of Tank's Sergeant-At-Arms made it difficult to breathe. He was cruel whether she obeyed him or not, and though her wolf blood ensured she healed quickly, after Tank's beating she didn't think she could bear any more.

"Mommy?"

Erica looked up to see Ryder standing in the doorway. Oh, God. What had he seen? Struggling to her feet and wiping her eyes, she made her way over to him, wincing with each breath. "Go back to bed, sweetie."

"Why was Daddy hurting you?" The young boy's wide eyes shone with fear.

Erica clenched her fists. It was bad enough Tank knocked her around and raped her in their bedroom, but here in the living room where their sons could see? Never again.

"Come on, baby, we're going to go somewhere. We have to hurry."

Ignoring the pain and Ryder's endless questions, she hurried him upstairs. She woke Harley and instructed the boys to put as many of their clothes into a suitcase as they could while she ran to her room and did the same. She opened one of the drawers on Tank's dresser and tossed the clothing onto the floor before lifting the false bottom. From underneath, she withdrew a handgun, ammo, and several stacks of cash. Tossing the cash and ammo on top of her clothing, she tucked the gun into the waistband of her jeans.

The boys had dawdled and argued about what to put into their suitcase as each tried to fill it with toys. Erica glanced at the clock. There wasn't enough time. "Just leave it, boys. Mommy will buy you lots of new toys and clothes."

She hustled them out of the house and into the car, buckling them into their car seats before she lifted the suitcase into the trunk. The telltale rumble of motorcycle engines echoed in the distance, growing closer. Heart thudding, she slammed the trunk shut, looked down the road, and spotted headlights at the end of the street. Terror gripped her. She had to leave before Tank made it back. She jumped into the driver's seat, started the car, and had just thrown it into reverse when two motorcycles pulled up behind her blocking her path.

"Fuck!"

She watched in the rearview mirror as Tank slipped off his bike. Maybe she still had a chance if she could get them into the house before they noticed the boys. Hopping out of the car, she met Tank by the trunk of the car, her skin crawling when he stepped right in front of her.

"Where are you going?" When Tank yelled, it was bad, but when his voice went quiet, with just a hint of a growl, as it did now, Erica knew she was fucked.

"I'm just going to the, um, drug store. For some Tylenol."

Tank narrowed his eyes. Damn his wolf sense of smell. He knew she was lying.

"I'll be back soon."

She gasped when Tank wrapped his hand around her throat. "Don't fucking lie to me. Where. Are. You. Going?"

Erica closed her eyes and tried to think. She could still reach the gun, but the bullet wouldn't do much damage to an Alpha Wolf, not enough for her to get back in the car and go. Plus with the bikes stopped behind it, and Bones there, eyes gleaming in anticipation, Erica knew she'd never make it out of the driveway. If she was lucky, Tank would kill her for her betrayal. She wouldn't be that lucky though. He'd beat her. Again. And rape her. Again. And let his friends take their turns. Again and again and again. There was only one thing she could do to give herself a chance of escape.

Run.

Even though it meant leaving her boys with their

monster of a father, she knew the only way to end her pain was to die or leave. Thankfully Tank had never mistreated the kids and as sons of the Alpha, they were adored as princes. But as a mere woman, she held no such value, and Tank would take great pleasure in making an example of her. She took a last glance at her boys, silently promising she'd return for them when she could. Taking a deep breath, she woke the wolf slumbering inside of her and willed it to take over.

As the change raced through her body, Tank couldn't maintain his grip and dropped her. The clothes she'd been wearing shredded around her and she hesitated only a moment to get her bearings before taking off into the woods.

Chapter Two

Toronto, six weeks later

The blinding lights of the city spread out below him as Caleb stared out the picture window of his friend's condo. He hated the city. Hated the crowds, the noises, the smells. Dear God, the smells. Body odour, car fumes, chemicals of all varieties, all left him feeling nauseated until he'd made it back to his refuge up north.

So why the hell was his wolf so eager to go out there?

He couldn't explain what had even brought him to the city in the first place. A sudden urge to visit Jake had taken over, and like an itch that wouldn't go away until scratched, he found himself following the urge right into downtown Toronto.

"What do you mean, you want to go for a walk? Are you insane?"

Caleb turned to face his childhood friend. "I don't know. My wolf just keeps telling me we have to go outside."

Jake rolled his eyes. "You and your frigging wolf. You make no sense."

"I know, but I still want to go."

"Have it your way, but don't go puking all over my condo if you get sick again."

Caleb winced at the reminder of previous visits gone awry. There was a good reason he didn't make it to the city more than a couple of times a year. But fighting his wolf was a losing battle, he'd learned, so when the wolf said, "Go to Toronto," Caleb went. As Jake grabbed his keys and gestured for the door, Caleb wondered what was guiding the animal within him.

Sounds and smells assaulted his senses the moment they stepped from the lobby to the sidewalk in front of the building. Caleb choked for a moment before getting his bearings. Jake shook his head, muttering about how crazy this was, and though Caleb agreed, he knew he had to get moving.

Without giving it any thought, he let the wolf take charge of directing them, finding it amusing to watch Jake struggle to keep up the rapid pace Caleb set. Humans. They wandered the streets, his wolf clearly searching for something, but the sensory overload of the city made it difficult to find, especially when Caleb didn't really know what the wolf wanted. Within an hour, Jake was complaining about the cold, and though Caleb didn't feel it as keenly as his friend, he was growing frustrated.

He was just about to suggest turning back when he caught a scent among the stink of the city. Stopping in the middle of the sidewalk, Caleb closed his eyes and inhaled. Loam. Pine. And something tantalizing he couldn't name.

It smelled like home.

He set out to follow the scent, the wolf growing more eager as the scent grew stronger, and at last they stopped in front of an old building with a Chinese restaurant on the ground level. People hurried by on the sidewalk. Cars whizzed along the street. A homeless person huddled in the doorway of the neighbouring building.

"Chinese? You just wanted fucking Chinese food?" Jake panted beside Caleb. "We could have ordered take-out."

Ignoring his friend, Caleb closed his eyes and zeroed in on the scent. When he opened his eyes, he was staring at the homeless person. A woman, he realized. Her hair hung in dirty strings around her face, and she was dressed in a ragged coat, with no hat or gloves, despite the sub-zero temperatures. A tattered box containing a few coins sat in front of her. As Caleb made his way toward her, he recognized the telltale scent of a wolf.

What the hell was a wolf doing begging on the streets of Toronto?

He stopped in front of her, not saying anything, but watching closely. For a moment, she stared down at her hands, but then her spine stiffened, and she turned her face up to look at Caleb, eyes wide. The scent of fear poured off of her and she tensed. She was getting ready to run.

"I won't hurt you."

Her gaze darted around and Caleb had no doubt she was analyzing her options. So he sat down on the ground beside her. She glanced at him out of the corner of her eye, and then looked down again, settling a bit. When Caleb was sure she wasn't going to run, he spoke again. "I'm Caleb." She said nothing. Caleb glanced at Jake who motioned he was going into the restaurant. "What are you doing out here on the street? Where's your pack?"

He knew she heard him. Her hands gripped her coat a little tighter at the mention of a pack, but she didn't seem to want to speak. His wolf nudged him, anxious to make contact with the woman, but Caleb couldn't figure out why.

Mate.

Caleb sucked in a sudden breath, causing the woman to look at him. As he studied her deep brown eyes, he knew it was true. According to wolf lore, every wolf had a soul mate, though it was rare to actually meet them. Fewer than a quarter of the wolves in his pack were fated mates, and those who found their other half were considered blessed. The other wolves just fell in and out of love like everyone else.

He'd found his mate. But why was she begging on the city streets? Where had she come from? So many questions. One thing he knew for sure, he'd have to get her back to Jacob's soon.

"I don't know why you're here, or where you came from, but I want to help." He figured it was a bit too soon to spring the idea of being mated on her yet, though her wolf must have recognized him by now.

"You can leave me alone." Her voice was so quiet only a wolf could hear, but the determination in it was clear. "I don't need help."

"If you don't need help, why are you begging on the streets? Do you even have a place to sleep?"

She glared at him. "It's none of your fucking business. Get away from me."

At last she showed some spirit. "No. I'm not leaving until you come with me. My friend's condo isn't far—"

The woman recoiled and jumped to her feet. Grabbing the box with its meager collection, she bolted.

"For fuck's sake!" In spite of his wolf urging him to pursue the woman, Caleb stayed where he was. The humans wouldn't take too kindly to a man chasing a woman through the streets. He punched a brick in frustration, wincing slightly at the scraped knuckles. As he stared at his hand, the minor wound knitted itself back together until his hand looked good as new.

He went to find Jacob. He'd been beaten tonight, but now that he'd scented his mate, his wolf could find her anywhere.

Chapter Three

The following day, the temperature plunged even further, with news networks everywhere broadcasting an extreme cold weather alert. Caleb pulled his toque down over his ears, picked up his backpack with two thermal containers of soup, a bag of sandwiches, an extra hat, gloves, and a blanket, and headed for the door.

"You're nuts," Jacob called from the couch. "If you're so desperate for pussy, wait until tonight and come clubbing with me."

Caleb shook his head. Jacob didn't buy the idea of fated mates and had told Caleb, repeatedly, how crazy it was to go off pursuing a homeless woman because of some stupid wolf legend. "See you later, bro. Don't wait up."

Leaving his friend muttering to no one, Caleb headed back out into the city. His wolf easily pinpointed his mate's scent, and within half an hour he'd found her. He watched her from the window of a coffee shop down the street for a while before buying two extra-large coffees and heading out to talk to her.

He was still half a block away when she stiffened and turned in his direction. Caleb stood still and held the coffee up. She eyed him, and then relaxed against the wall again. Taking it as a good sign, Caleb made his way over.

"This isn't drugged, is it?" She lifted the lid and sniffed.

He settled beside her and passed her the bag with cream and sugar. "If I wanted to drug you, I'd have to use so much you'd be able to smell it a mile away. It's just coffee."

She nodded and he watched as she dumped four

packets of sugar into the cup. So she had a sweet tooth. He filed away the knowledge. She took a sip and let out a small moan. Inappropriate as it was, Caleb wondered what kind of moan she'd make while he fucked her.

"You men. All pigs." She must have scented his arousal.

"Don't make those sounds and I won't get turned on."

She arched an eyebrow at him and he shrugged. "Okay, it probably doesn't matter what you do. I'm a pig."

"I'm grateful for the coffee, but feel free to leave at any time."

Digging in his backpack, Caleb took out the extra hat and gloves and passed them to her. "I'm not going anywhere until you go with me." He leaned back against the wall and sipped his coffee.

They sat without speaking for hours. Caleb's wolf pranced around, demanding Caleb pick up their mate and carry her off to their den, or at least the nearest alley, to claim her. But his mate was skittish, and doing something like that would only drive her away. No, Caleb could wait her out.

Twice she got up, took some change, and disappeared into the coffee shop to use the bathroom. Caleb watched until she returned each time. She left her things with him, so he was pretty sure she wouldn't run again, but he needed to keep an eye on her.

As dusk fell, Caleb knew she was getting antsy. Though their wolf blood meant they didn't feel the cold as keenly, they still weren't meant to sit in freezing temperatures all day. They needed to get inside, out of the cold. He had to convince her somehow.

"Listen," he began. "I know you don't trust me, and I can't blame you, but I really do want to help. Let me get you a hotel room so you can shower and have a warm place to sleep tonight."

"Are you saying I smell?"

Caleb was smart enough not to answer. She shifted a little closer to him. "It is pretty cold out here." He swallowed as she leaned into him, her face only inches away, and one hand on his knee. "A hot shower would feel so good on my skin." She moved her hand higher up his leg and the vision of her, naked in the shower, combined with the pressure of her touch made him hard as a rock. "And then there'd be a big, warm bed. I could show you how grateful I am."

She was so close now her breath whispered across his neck, sending erotic shivers throughout him. He closed his eyes, waiting for her to cross the remaining space between them, when she pulled back, laughing.

Caleb glared at her. "I'm trying to help. You don't have to be a bitch about it."

Hurt and fear flashed across her face before she gritted her teeth and started gathering her things. Shit. He'd blown it again. His wolf panicked at the thought of losing her again, and he reached out and grabbed her arm.

She froze, flicking her eyes downward to where his hand gripped her. "Let. Me. Go."

Though she spoke softly, the anger was palpable. Caleb released her. "I'm sorry. I just—" He clenched his fists and looked down. "I really want to help. Please. I know you don't want it, but I'll follow you until you let me. I need to."

Chapter Four

Erica stared at the man, Caleb, and debated her options. The power in his voice was clear, and she'd be surprised if he wasn't at least a Beta wolf. But experience had taught her powerful wolves were dangerous. Did she want to run away? Fight him?

Or fuck him?

God help her, she really wanted to fuck him. How that was possible, she didn't know, but there was no denying the pleasant tingling low in her belly that had started the first time she saw him. And now? Her wolf wouldn't let her run. Her wolf also thought fighting might be good foreplay. Even though she tried to reason with it, the wolf was winning. The memory of Tank and what he'd done wasn't enough to dissuade the wolf, who insisted Caleb was someone who could be trusted.

In the end, the thought of a shower and a warm bed for the night made the decision for her. "Where are we going?"

Caleb's warm, brown eyes lit up. "There's a hotel not far from here with suites with a kitchen and separate bedrooms. Let's head there."

He helped her gather her few belongings and then led her to a spot a few blocks away, and a hotel swankier than any she'd stayed at before. The dirty looks she got from the hotel staff and other patrons held her back.

"I don't belong here," she said.

Slipping an arm around her shoulders, Caleb gave her a gentle squeeze. "Don't be ridiculous. Of course you belong."

They walked up to the reception desk and the clerk gave them a once over. "I'm afraid we don't participate in the shelter programs," she said. "You'll have to go somewhere else."

Erica held back, but Caleb tugged her forward. He opened his wallet and withdrew two cards, his driver's licence and an Amex Gold card. "We need a suite for the week."

The clerk scrutinised the picture on the licence and checked Caleb over. "We'll have to pre-authorize the whole amount, plus take a $500 deposit."

"Go ahead."

While the clerk processed the card and Caleb's information, Erica glanced around the hotel lobby. A family in the corner caught her eye. A mother, father, and two small children, all laughing together at something. The mother held one child on her hip and the father had the other one sitting on his shoulders. They looked so happy, and Erica's heart ached for her own boys. Leaving them had been the hardest thing she'd ever done, and it was the only part about her previous life she missed. She hoped they were doing okay.

"Okay, we're all set." Caleb gestured toward the bank of elevators on the far side of the lobby and set off. Tearing her gaze away from the family, Erica followed Caleb, not wanting to lose him in the crowd. When they reached the room, she was stunned by the interior. It was almost as nice as the penthouses at Tank's hotel.

"Wow."

"You take the master bedroom and en suite." Caleb pointed her in the right direction. "I'll use the main bathroom and smaller bedroom.

Still a bit shocked from the developments, Erica entered the master bedroom and closed the door behind her. She hesitated a minute before turning the lock. It wouldn't be a match for Caleb's strength if he really wanted to break the door down, but at least it sent a message and would give her a minute to prepare if he came in uninvited.

Erica dropped her small backpack beside the bed and headed into the bathroom. A large soaker tub took up one corner and she groaned. It had been weeks since she'd had a proper shower, let alone a soak in a luxurious tub. She started the water and stripped, avoiding the mirror. No way did she want to see what kind of mess she was in.

She wished she could brush her hair, but she didn't have a brush and there wasn't one in the room. She gathered the travel-size bottles of shampoo, conditioner, and body wash, and took a quick shower to get rid of the worst of the grime before she sat in the tub. When she finally lowered herself into the steaming water, she sighed, letting herself sink down.

The bath relaxed her so much she drifted in and out of consciousness, before finally becoming aware of a banging sound. Someone was pounding on the bedroom door. Shit. Caleb was probably wondering what had happened to her. Climbing quickly out of the tub, she grabbed the bathrobe from the counter and pulled it on as she headed to the bathroom door.

"Just a second!" She cinched the belt of the robe and then unlocked the bedroom door to find a relieved-looking Caleb.

"I was worried something happened," he said. "If I'd had to wait much longer I would have broken the door down and I really didn't want to give that clerk the satisfaction of not refunding the security deposit."

Erica tucked her hair behind her ears and glanced down at her feet. "I fell asleep in the tub."

"You should be more careful. You could have drowned." God, he sounded angry.

"Give me a fucking break. My first bath in weeks and I fell asleep. So what? And it's not like anyone would care if I drowned anyway."

He gripped her chin and tilted her head so she couldn't avoid his eyes. "I would care."

They stood for a minute, gazing into each other's eyes, before Caleb released her.

"So what was so important you tried to break down the door?"

"I wanted to know if you'd like to go for dinner."

"Oh. That would be nice, but I don't have anything to change into." Erica tightened the robe around her. "I don't really want to go out in the cold again."

"Right. Okay, I'll order room service." He started to turn away, but before Erica could close the door, he stopped. "I can ask my friend's girlfriend to bring some clothes for you. We still don't have to go out, but at least then you're not..." His voice trailed off as he allowed his gaze to wander over her.

Heat spread through Erica's cheeks as she scented his arousal. She realized he probably smelled her, too. Clothes would be a definite bonus. "That would be great. And if it's not too much trouble, I could use a hair brush and some proper conditioner. And a toothbrush."

He grinned at her. "I'll call Jake and then room service."

After he disappeared into the main room, Erica closed the door and flopped down on the bed. Coffee, food, a place to stay, and soon clothes. He was being so kind, but she questioned his motives. Sure there wasn't a huge werewolf population in a major city like this, which had drawn her here in the first place. So it would be odd enough for him to find a lone wolf, but there was no reason for him to go out of his way to be so good to her.

It was obvious he wanted her. Even grubby and half frozen, his arousal had been evident. While contemplating the motives of her rescuer, Erica drifted off to sleep.

Chapter Five

A feminine voice encouraged Erica to wake up. Disoriented, she blinked a few times before a pretty young woman came into view.

"Where am I?"

"Glad you're finally awake. I'm Carly. Jake's girlfriend. Caleb asked me to bring you some things."

"Right." Erica pushed herself up to a seated position. "Thanks for helping."

"No problem. Come have a seat over at the table and I'll help you with your hair."

Erica followed the girl to the little table in the corner and seated herself in the chair. Carly dumped the contents of a shopping bag on the table and selected a few items. "I brought some detangler because I figured you'd need some. I know how awful the knots get when you haven't been able to brush."

Embarrassed, Erica couldn't think of anything to say, but Carly seemed more than happy to fill the silence with constant babble as she worked away on Erica's hair. From her scent, Erica knew the girl was human, and she gathered from the way Carly talked she didn't realize her boyfriend's friend was a werewolf. It was probably better for her that way. Erica did learn that Caleb lived in Muskoka, and though she wasn't familiar with Canadian geography, she thought it was somewhere north of the city. It made sense. Carly also told Erica that Caleb was thirty-four, single, and quite well-off. Really, Erica had deduced all but the age already, but she liked the sound of Carly's voice. She sounded so happy. Had Erica ever been that content with life? Maybe when she spent time with her kids, but certainly not when Tank was around.

When Erica's hair had finally been freed of all

tangles, Carly laid out the clothes she'd bought for Erica. Leggings, jeans, panties, sports bras, t-shirts, and a sweater.

"You didn't have to do this for me." Running her hand over the soft fabric of the sweater, Erica blinked back tears.

Carly threw her arms around Erica and squeezed her tightly. "Oh, sweetie, everyone has rough times, and we all need help sometimes. There's no shame in that. Besides, any girl who's gotten Caleb's attention is so worth it. I've been trying to set that boy up for years with no luck."

Erica blushed. "I don't know about that."

"I'll head out to the living room to make sure the boys haven't caused too much trouble. Hopefully everything fits. And I'd be happy to take you shopping for more if you want."

Swallowing a lump in her throat, Erica nodded and then closed the door behind Carly. When dressed, she finally looked into the mirror. She'd lost so much weight the clothes hung off of her. But her hair looked healthy at least. At last, she took a deep breath and headed out to the main room, following the musical sound of Carly's voice.

As she came around the corner, Caleb caught sight of her and stood. Another man about his age stood beside him, and Carly squealed and ran to give her a hug.

"They're a bit big," Carly said as she gave Erica a once over.

Pulling at the sweater, Erica nodded. "I've lost more weight than I thought. I don't always—" She snapped her mouth shut and looked around.

They invited her to sit and Erica picked a single chair. She watched the three friends talking and laughing, and couldn't help thinking about everything she'd lost. Really, she hadn't had any close friends since high school, and Tank had knocked her up at eighteen so she really didn't have much of a life after that.

When the food came, they ate quietly, and Jake and Carly took off soon after, leaving Erica alone with Caleb again. He shifted down to sit on the end of the couch closest to Erica. Before he could say anything, she jumped up and started cleaning up the garbage from their take-out. He followed along and they worked in silence. What would happen next? What was he expecting? He didn't give her any cues, but awareness of him made her body tingle.

Once Erica had placed the last of the garbage in the bin, she could sense Caleb behind her and knew she couldn't get out of the kitchen without going past him. So she stood facing the wall, hands braced on the counter, willing him to leave so she could escape to her room.

She could feel the air stirring as he moved toward her, and she held her breath when he stood right behind her. He placed one hand on her shoulder and the other one over her hand. Erica closed her eyes and swallowed. Though only his hands touched her, she could feel the heat from his body and fought the urge to lean back against him.

"Are you going to tell me your name?" His voice was soft, warm breath sliding over her neck. Her body trembled with a horrid combination of fear and desire.

"Erica," she whispered.

"Erica. Nice to meet you." He lifted his hands off her, but her relief was short-lived when he spoke in his Alpha voice. "Turn around."

Unable to resist the power of his voice, she turned. He placed his hands on her hips and moved in closer, pressing his lower body to hers, and showed how much he wanted her. Unable to stop the small whimper from escaping her, she turned her head to the side. She hadn't meant it to be an invitation, but for wolves, baring the neck was an act of submission, and he took advantage of it.

He pressed his lips against her neck, eliciting a gasp. Desire flared to life inside her as he kissed her neck and nipped at her ear. She slid her hands up his arms and gripped his shoulders, overcome by lust. When he finally settled his lips against hers, she opened to him, allowing their tongues to tangle together.

With a growl, Caleb gripped her ass and hoisted her up to the counter, pulling her legs around his waist. She wiggled against him as he ground his erection against her, his kisses leaving a fiery trail across her neck and jaw. She needed his touch. Needed to feel his skin against hers. She slid her hands under the hem of his shirt, tracing her fingers over the hard lines of his stomach.

Caleb pulled away for a moment and whipped his shirt off over his head, and then grabbed hers and did the same, before coming back in for another kiss. The heat of his body seared into her flesh and fanned the flames of passion even more. Her pussy throbbed and clenched as her body lubed itself, preparing to welcome his steely length. And they weren't even completely naked. She couldn't remember the last time she'd been this turned on. Tank had never—

With a cry, Erica yanked her head away from Caleb and whacked it on the cupboard door behind her. "Fuck!"

She reached up to rub the back of her head, groaning at the sensitive lump that had arisen. Werewolves healed fast, but it didn't mean they didn't feel the pain of an injury. And it certainly helped to douse the lust which had taken over her body.

"Are you okay? What happened there?"

Erica looked down and shook her head. "I can't

do this."

"But, Erica—"

"No. Let me down, please."

Caleb lifted a hand and Erica cringed back, waiting for the blow to come. Instead, he growled and gripped her chin, and then turned her head toward his. "Tell me you feel nothing."

She squeezed her eyes shut and tried to shake her head, but he refused to let go. Her stomach tightened, her chest hurt, and she could only manage a whisper. "Of course I feel something. But I can't do this right now. Please." At last she opened her eyes to find his inches away, boring into her.

As the moment stretched on, Erica braced herself for his outburst. She winced when he tightened his arms around her and lifted her off the counter, but to her surprise, he set her down and released her. Erica let out a shuddering sigh and moved to go around him. He caught her hand as he went by and she glanced up at him again.

"Someone's hurt you. I can see that and respect your space. For now. But you will be mine."

Erica yanked her hand from his and stalked off toward her room, slamming and locking the door behind her. She threw herself down on the bed and took deep breaths as she tried to relax her body. Every muscle had coiled tight. Maybe another bath was in order.

And then she heard his voice outside the door. "Sleep well, Erica. In the morning, I'm taking you home."

Chapter Six

Home? What the fuck did that mean? He couldn't know who she was or where she came from. Did the Canadian packs have any ties to the ones in the States? Erica doubted it as she'd never heard any of the Demon Dogs mention it. So Caleb must mean he was taking her to his home.

No fucking way.

She'd never allow another man, especially an Alpha, to control her again. With Tank, she'd been young and moronic, with fanciful expectations of a fairy-tale ending. He'd quickly proved there were no happily ever afters. Caleb might think he could take her away, but she wouldn't let him. She had to do what it had taken her years to do the last time.

Run.

For a few moments, Erica considered leaving the clothing Carly'd brought her, but she didn't know when she'd be able to get new ones. It wasn't like she hadn't stolen when she'd first shifted back to human, weeks after leaving Michigan. But if she started packing, Caleb was sure to hear and come investigate. What to do?

At last she decided maybe another bath would work. She turned on the water and left the bathroom door open. The sound of the water should mask her activities. Then, as quietly as possible, she tiptoed around the room, gathering her things together and shoving them in her backpack. She dragged it into the bathroom to do the zipper, and then she waited.

Finally, hoping enough time had passed for him to fall asleep, she padded to the bedroom door, unlocked it, and then listened for any movement from Caleb. The TV had been on earlier, but she didn't hear it now. She closed her eyes and strained her ears, attempting to use werewolf senses she'd spent months trying to smother. Was that music? Yes. Coming from Caleb's room. It sounded as though he'd left a clock radio on. After a few minutes of listening, she figured he was out cold. She tiptoed down the hall but her gaze snagged on a dark object protruding from the bathroom.

She picked it up and a brief investigation showed it was Caleb's jeans, obviously kicked off and left lying on the floor. What was it with guys? The pants seemed heavier than they should, though. Erica patted the pockets and realized he'd left his wallet. Without overthinking it, she pulled the wallet out and opened it. Inside she found a wad of cash. She took it all and slipped it into her pocket before slipping out of the room.

****

Caleb awoke with a start. He glanced around the hotel room for what had woken him, but nothing seemed out of place. A slim beam of bright sunlight shone between the curtains. He'd overslept. Jumping out of bed, he grabbed his boxers off the floor in case Erica happened to see him on the way to the bathroom. Or maybe he should just leave them off, show her what she'd missed out on last night.

He gave a slight chuckle as he tugged the boxers on, trying to arrange his erection so it didn't jut out of the hole. He walked across the hall. Erica's bedroom door was still closed. Kicking his pants out of the way, he closed the door to the bathroom.

While in the shower, he couldn't help thinking of the encounter in the kitchen last night. Erica might claim to not want him, but her actions said otherwise. She'd responded to him like no woman before and his balls had ached with need after she'd stormed off. When she'd gone into the tub, he'd used the opportunity to jerk off while picturing her pouty lips around his cock.

Mate.

Caleb stilled the hand that had been idly stroking his dick and concentrated. His wolf was agitated.

Mate!

Shit. Caleb bolted from the shower and raced, dripping wet and naked, to Erica's door. He tried the handle and it turned easily. Not locked. Not a good sign. He burst through the door to find the room empty. A quick look proved the bathroom was deserted, too. There was no sign of her in the living room or kitchen, either.

"Fuck!"

Caleb hurried back to the bathroom and grabbed his jeans, pausing when his wallet tumbled to the floor. He picked it up and he smelled Erica all over it, and when he opened it, he discovered the missing cash.

"Fuck!" He drove his fist into the door. Right through the door. But fuck the security deposit. His mate was missing and with the cash he'd had on him, she could have easily bought a ticket far away from the city. His wolf longed to break free and give chase, but he knew he had to think with his head if he was going to find her.

Back in his room, he picked up the phone and called Jake.

****

"You're not serious."

Caleb twirled the dog collar around a finger. "I'm very serious. I have to track her and in a city like this I won't be able to do it as a human. Remember how long it took us the other day?"

"People are going to know you're not a dog."

"Werewolves don't exist, remember? People will see what they want to see, and if there's a leash, they'll see a dog."

Jake shook his head. "I'm already regretting this."

"Come on. I'd help you in a second."

"You misunderstand. I'm regretting that I don't have a camera to document this moment."

In a flash, Caleb had allowed his wolf to take over and transform him. Baring his teeth, he growled at Jake.

"Take it easy. I'm just kidding." Jake kneeled to fasten the collar and leash around Caleb's neck, muttering, "Moody fucking werewolves."

Caleb licked the side of Jake's face, earning a groan, but immediately he picked up on Erica's scent and started pulling Jake to the door. They made their way to the elevator and down, earning some surprised looks from other guests. In the lobby, Caleb found Erica's scent again and took off out the door and onto the street.

"Slow down, buddy. Heel!"

If Caleb could have rolled his eyes, he would have. But he slowed to a quick walk so his human could keep up, and followed Erica's trail along the city streets. It took them a while, but at last they came to the Greyhound bus terminal and Caleb's heart sank. She could have boarded a bus to anywhere. He sat on his haunches and looked up at Jake.

Crouching down beside him, Jake leaned in close. "What now?"

Caleb didn't know what to do and didn't know how to communicate with Jake. And he couldn't very well turn back into a human right in the middle of the day on the sidewalk. He searched around and spotted an alley down the street. He took off and dragged Jake behind him. The alley had a dumpster and Caleb ducked behind it before shifting back to human and yelling at Jake to toss him some clothes from the backpack he'd brought.

Once dressed, he headed back to the bus station and ducked inside.

Chapter Seven

Erica sat on the bench, legs crossed, one foot swaying lightly to the beat of the music. It wouldn't be too much longer before her bus left and then she'd be free of Caleb and whatever he planned to do with her. She'd paced back and forth in front of the departures board for a long time before deciding Ottawa would be a better place for her to go. Farther from Michigan, in case Tank was trying to find her, and closer to the wilderness so it would be easy to change. She hadn't been able to shift in a couple of weeks and her wolf was itching to be set free. And with the money she'd taken from Caleb, she'd have enough to put down first and last month's rent on a small place while she looked for a job.

She felt a little guilty for robbing Caleb. He'd been kind to her and cared about her in a way nobody had for a long time. And he'd ignited a spark in her that had been dormant for so long. In truth, she didn't think she'd ever had a man make her feel the way Caleb did last night, like she was the most precious thing in the world. And that made him dangerous. She couldn't afford to make another mistake.

A scent wafted past her and she closed her eyes. It reminded her of Caleb, all woodsy and sweet pine. When she opened her eyes again, the man stood right in front of her, arms crossed and glaring. Of course. She should have known better than to walk here. She darted a quick glance around and realized she had nowhere to run. There were too many people and no easy way to get to the exit.

Caleb squatted down in front of her. "Where are you going?" His eyes flashed with emotion. Was he angry? After stealing from him, she really couldn't blame him. At least they were in a public place. He wouldn't risk making a scene. Would he? But there was something besides anger in his gaze. Worry? Fear? Why would she frighten him?

"I needed to get away." Erica took a deep breath and tried to look anywhere but at Caleb. "I really appreciate everything you did, but…"

He placed a hand on her knee. "I want to talk to you. Please come back to the hotel with me."

Erica crossed her arms over her chest and resisted the urge to pout. "You can talk here."

"Erica, come on."

"No. We talk here, or we don't talk, but I'm not leaving."

She got a bit of satisfaction from the growl he let out along with a curse. He took the seat beside her on the bench. "I don't know how you ended up here, but I know you can't be happy living on the streets in the middle of a huge city. We need to be out in the open where we can run, where the air is clean, and where there's a pack who cares about us."

Her wolf salivated at his words, longing for the picture he painted, but she shook her head. "I don't need any of that. I'll be fine."

"Please. Come with me to my home and let me show you how good it can be." He'd started running his fingers along her leg, the touch leaving no doubt what would be good. Everything about him drew her in, his masculine scent, the heat of his body, the light touch of his hands. Even his wolf called to hers. Never had the wolf been so eager to be around a man.

"Bus number eighty-seven for Ottawa now boarding on platform three." The tinny voice of the announcement cut into her thoughts. Her bus. If she wanted freedom, she had to go now.

She looked into Caleb's warm eyes. He held the

power of an Alpha, there was no doubt about it, but right now instead of commanding her, he was a man asking for a chance. And for the first time, she realized she held power over him, too. Maybe this could work out after all.
****

Caleb nearly leaped for joy when Erica stood up and agreed to go back to the hotel with him. He took her hand, and though she hesitated at first, she wrapped her fingers around his. He didn't know what he would have done if she'd refused. Sure, as an Alpha he could command her to go with him, but that would only make her resent him. She'd obviously been burned in the past and he'd have to work to prove to her he could be the kind of partner she deserved.

At the door to the hotel, Jake said good-bye and headed for his place while Caleb and Erica went back to their suite.

"Did you want to leave now or stay here for another night?" he asked her.

She'd ditched her coat and shoes and sat on the couch with her legs tucked up under her. "Where do you want to take me?"

"I guess I didn't explain that part, did I?" Caleb ran his hands through his hair. "Okay, well, I live in the Muskokas, northwest of the city. There are lots of trees and wilderness. My family owns a big property and we rent cottages, but it's still got plenty of privacy."

"Is your pack big?"

"I guess. Our territory is large, most of the southern part of the province up to North Bay, but we mostly keep to the main pack lands. We have about a hundred wolves, though some are just passing through."

Her eyes widened. "A hundred? Wow."

"How big was your pack?" And where was your pack? Why did you run away from them? Though he longed to ask the questions, he didn't want to press her.

A strand of her hair had come loose from her ponytail and when she glanced down, it swung in front of her eyes. He brushed it back behind her ear, earning a small smile. "We have about thirty guys. I have no idea how many women because they come and go so frequently and I'm never sure who's human and who's not."

Caleb frowned. "There are humans in your pack? I mean we have humans living in the town, and some of them know about us, but we don't consider them part of the pack."

The hair came loose again, but she tucked it back before he could. What would it feel like to thread his fingers through the silky lengths? Did she like having it pulled during sex? He shifted in his seat as his cock started to thicken. God, she was speaking to him and he was imagining her in bed. *Way to show her you're a good guy.* "I'm sorry, what was that?"

She frowned and gave a light shake of her head. "Nothing. Well, my pack did a lot of mixing around. Not that they're my pack anymore." She stood and walked to the window. "Would your pack accept me?"

He went to stand behind her, resting a hand on her shoulder. Their faces reflected back at them in the dark glass while the lights of the city spread out below. "They have to accept their Alpha's m—" He stopped short. He didn't want to freak her out.

She stiffened. "Their Alpha's what?"

Caleb didn't know what to say. Erica turned around to face him, eyes dark, challenging him. Though he stared back, she wouldn't look away. He couldn't back down. So much for not upsetting her. Straightening up, he allowed a bit of his power to seep into his words. "The Alpha's mate."

She sucked in a breath and pressed her lips into a fine line, finally breaking eye contact. His wolf approved. Until she stepped around him and ran for the bedroom. Though she caught him off guard, he managed to get his hand through the door before she could close it.

"Move your hand!" She leaned against the door, squeezing his arm between the door and the frame.

"No. I told you we'd talk about it, so let's talk. We need to work this out."

"There's nothing to work out. I'm not your mate. I'm not anyone's fucking mate."

Caleb's wolf wanted to charge in, throw her on the bed, and show her once and for all who was the dominant one in this relationship. But the man refused to give in. If he had to resort to force, then he didn't deserve to be Alpha. He braced one hand against the doorframe and pressed his forehead to the door. "Tell me you don't feel it, too."

He waited, but she said nothing. "I know it's crazy," he continued. "To think we could be mates without knowing each other is ridiculous, but if you can tell me you don't feel it, too, I'll leave you alone, and drive you wherever you want to go tomorrow. No more questions, no more pressure." He took a deep breath. "Do you feel it?"

The silence stretched on. One heartbeat. Five. Twenty.

"I don't."

Chapter Eight

When Caleb finally took his hand out of the doorway, he eased the door shut, and Erica slid to the floor behind it. She drew her knees up to her chest and put her head down. Her wolf whimpered and urged her to go after him.

Mate.

No matter what she said to Caleb, deep down she knew what he was. She'd struggled to identify the strange connection she felt with him, but when he found her at the bus station today, her wolf had proclaimed it quite clearly. And though it scared the shit out of her, she found herself here at the hotel with him again. She'd been fine until he said it out loud and then she panicked. After everything she'd been through, why would the fates match her with another Alpha?

So what options did she have? She got up, locked the door, and curled up in the bed to think about it.

Option one: She could sneak out again now and hope their strange bond wasn't strong enough for him to track her. She still had all his money in her backpack. But he'd backed off like he said he would, so maybe he was serious about driving her somewhere tomorrow. Of course, once he had her in the car, he could drive her wherever he wanted.

Option two: She could go back with him, but refuse to be his mate, and they'd go their separate ways. In the same territory. While their wolves did their best to bring the couple together. Or where she'd have to see him with whomever he ended up choosing, because the Alpha had to have a mate and heirs. That would be a different kind of torment she wasn't prepared to deal with.

Option three: she could accept him as her mate

and go back with him to obey his every command.

And invite all his buddies to have a go at her, too.

I guess I'm fucked no matter what.

On that note, she drifted off to sleep.

****

After waking up from a nightmare about Tank for the third time, Erica gave up on sleep. She wondered, not for the first time since she'd arrived in the city, if Tank was looking for her. She didn't think it was possible. He might have tried to track her, but he would have had to leave the Demon Dogs for a while to do it, and illegal enterprises didn't run themselves. Still, every so often she had the sensation someone was watching her.

Restless energy flowed through her, looking for an outlet. She needed to change and to go for a long run. Maybe not as long as the one from Michigan, but long enough to ease the tension in her muscles. She settled for getting up to get a glass of water. Or maybe a mug of hot cocoa would be better.

She cracked the door open and listened for Caleb. When she heard his soft, even breathing, she slipped out to the kitchen. She made herself a drink and sipped it as she looked out the window over the city. When she started to yawn again, she set the drink down and headed back to the bedroom. She'd just passed Caleb's door when it opened.

"Are you okay?"

Erica glanced over her shoulder to answer and then did a double take. He stood in the door, hair tousled, in nothing but a form-fitting pair of boxer briefs. It did nothing to help her resolve. "I just needed a drink. I'm having trouble sleeping."

"Me, too."

Neither of them moved. Or they didn't move apart, at any rate. Erica found herself leaning towards him, the heat and scent of him drawing her in. A tingling sensation started low in her belly, spreading outward as she got closer, until she had to take a step or lose her balance. He stepped forward at the same time and now they were within touching distance. Erica studied the line of his collarbone, trying hard not to look higher. Or lower. She smelled his arousal, the scent growing stronger by the second and mixing with hers to make a heady combination.

They each took another step closer. The pounding of her heart matched the throbbing between her legs, and she started to feel light-headed. Her wolf urged her on, and Erica knew there was only one way to satisfy the wolf and her body.

She tilted her head up and met his eyes. They'd started to glow a bit, a sure sign his wolf was near the surface. No doubt hers were the same. A few moments passed, stretching on between them until Erica lifted a hand and placed it on his chest.

Caleb didn't need any more invitation. With a growl, he tugged her into his arms and brought his lips crashing down against hers. Their tongues struggled against one another, each trying to gain access to the other's mouth, until Erica finally relented and allowed him to plunge inside. Waves of desire pounded through her with each stroke of his tongue, and she whimpered as he cupped her ass and pressed her against him.

Leaving her mouth, Caleb nipped his way along her jaw and down the side of her neck, each bite drawing a small cry from her. She couldn't control herself. She couldn't think straight. Couldn't think of anything beyond him. This was how it was supposed to be.

She needed him. Needed to feel his skin against hers. Needed him to fill her.

"Caleb," she gasped. "Please."

He growled again and pulled away long enough to strip her shirt off before her breasts crushed against his chest, the delicious friction making her nipples hard as rock. He hoisted her into his arms and carried her to the bed. It only took a moment for him to toss her onto it, rip off her panties, and cover her body with his.

His lips captured one rock-hard nipple and bit down gently. The sensation zinged straight to her clit and she moaned, especially when his fingers found the sensitive nub a moment later and increased the stimulation. The tension wound tighter in her belly. How was it possible for her to be this close to orgasm already? But she was, and it only took another nip of his teeth on her breast to set her off. Erica shuddered and jerked under him, the spasms of pleasure rocking her entire body.

"God, you're gorgeous when you come." Caleb kissed her again, his fingers still working furiously between her legs.

She couldn't stand it anymore. She had to have him inside her when she came again. "Fuck me. Please. I need you to fill me."

With a groan, he got up off the bed and she cried out. She was so close and he left her hanging? A quick glance showed him stripping off his underwear and rummaging in the pocket of his jeans. A moment later he was back, tearing open a foil packet and rolling a condom down his shaft. Fuck. She'd been so eager she hadn't even thought about protection. They couldn't catch diseases, but getting pregnant was the last thing she needed.

He climbed on top of her and she spread her legs more willingly than she ever had. As he gathered her in his arms, he slid the entire length of his cock into her tight pussy.

"Oh, fuck, you feel so good."

Erica had to agree as he pressed his lips to hers, the rhythm of his tongue matched to the rhythm of his cock. She'd been incomplete before, but he filled more than just her pussy. It was as though his soul had entered hers. Her pleasure built quickly. With each stroke, he managed to hit something deep inside, and their bodies were so close it created the perfect pressure on her clit.

He buried his head against her neck, teeth grazing the skin. Her wolf pushed her to bare her throat, allow him to mark her, and claim her as his.

Erica tensed and Caleb immediately lifted his head. "What's wrong?"

"Don't claim me. Please. I'm not ready for that."

"You want me to stop?" His brow furrowed and his shoulders tensed as though he was in pain, and Erica had no doubt they both would be if they didn't finish this.

"I need to come on your cock," she whispered. "But don't claim me."

"Oh, thank God." He resumed thrusting into her, the pace frantic now.

It didn't take long and Erica exploded around him, her pussy clamping down on his cock, gripping him as he stilled. Caleb threw back his head and groaned as he reached his own orgasm. Time seemed to still as she lay cocooned in his arms, the aftershocks of her orgasm lulling her into a bit of a daze. Was sex always this good with a soul mate, or was Caleb just that good? Either way, she couldn't help but feel cheated at not having met him sooner.

Chapter Nine

Not claiming Erica at the moment of his climax took every shred of willpower within him. He fought against the wolf, who desperately wanted him to sink his teeth into her neck, leaving the mark that would seal their bond and signal to everyone who saw her she was taken. Only soul mates could claim each other in that manner, and he needed to do it soon. But after she took the chance on him tonight, he wouldn't push it. Yet.

Once they'd both recovered a bit, he kissed her, and stood up. "I'll be back in a second. Don't go anywhere." He ran across the hall to the bathroom, disposed of the condom, and cleaned up. When he returned, Erica had crawled under the covers and closed her eyes. He climbed in behind her and pulled her against him. She sighed and wiggled her bottom a little as she adjusted.

"Keep that up and we won't get any sleep."

She murmured something unintelligible and he realized she'd already fallen asleep. He kissed the top of her head and drifted off as well.

****

In the morning, Caleb woke to an empty bed. He jumped up and bolted to the door. "Erica?" After the explosive sex they'd had, he didn't think she'd run away again, but she didn't respond. He went into her bedroom and heard water running in the bathroom. Relieved, he went to the door and knocked, entering after she called for him to come in. He found her lounging in the huge tub with a smile on her face. That was a good sign.

"Want to join me?"

She didn't need to ask twice. Caleb slid into the tub and she leaned back against him. He ran his fingers over her shoulder and arm. "How are you feeling?"

She sighed. "Better than I want to."

What the hell did that mean? Caleb stilled his hand and looked down at her. "I'm not sure I follow."

Erica turned to her side and snuggled against him, her head tucked against his shoulder and under his chin. "I didn't want to give in to you. My experience with men … well, it hasn't been great." When she paused, Caleb didn't speak, though he wanted to know more. The way she'd acted, running away, resisting him even when he knew she was attracted to him, told him she'd been hurt. And hell, the fact she'd been living on the streets in the city rather than with a pack spoke volumes. But he wouldn't press. She had to tell him in her own time.

"I was with the Alpha in my old pack," she said at last. "And he made it clear I was his property, and what I wanted didn't matter at all. I was only seventeen when he first came to me, and I was so thrilled to be with him I ignored the warning signs and made excuses for his behavior."

"How old was he?"

"Thirty."

Caleb clenched his jaw. A thirteen-year age difference didn't matter all that much if the girl was in her twenties or beyond, but when she was seventeen? The fucker should have known better. "And your parents were okay with this?"

"My dad was already dead and my mom had her own issues. She was just glad someone took me off her hands." Erica traced small circles on his chest. For a moment, she debated telling Caleb about her sons, but then decided this wasn't the right time. "Anyway, I'm just really scared. I didn't want anyone else, but it's so fucking good with you."

He chuckled. "I'll say."

She gave him a light smack. "Not just the sex.

Everything just feels so … right. So I'll go with you, to your home. If that's all right."

He kissed the top of her head. "Of course it is."

"I'm just not ready to be claimed yet. I need to get my head in the right place."

"Our wolves aren't going to like that."

She chuckled. "I know. And I know eventually the instinct will take over, but if we can hold off, even for a little while, that would be good."

"We should probably hit the road soon, then. I hate the city."

She got up on her knees in front of him, a sly expression on her face. "Let's make sure we're really clean first."

With a groan, Caleb drew her close for a kiss.

****

The drive home went by quickly. Caleb and Erica chatted easily, though they avoided any heavy topics. There'd be time for that later. When they arrived in the little town Caleb called home, the first stop he made was at a little grocery store. He took Erica's hand as he led her inside. Her stomach tightened. What were the other people in this town like? The other members of the pack? How would they feel about their Alpha bringing someone home?

An older man stood behind the counter and his eyes lit up when he saw Caleb. He came around, shuffling his feet as fast as he could to embrace the younger man. "You're back! We've missed you."

Caleb returned the hug. "I've been gone less than a week."

"That's long enough. Your place is here." He pulled away and peered through his glasses at Erica. "And who's this lovely young lady?"

Caleb put his arm around Erica's shoulders and

pulled her close. "This is Erica. Erica, this is George, one of our pack elders." Caleb planted a gentle kiss on her temple. "She's going to be joining our pack."

George looked between the two of them, a knowing grin on his face. "I'll bet she is. So you're wanting to call a meeting then?"

Meeting? Erica's gut clenched. Why did they need to meet? As Alpha, surely Caleb could just order them to accept her. While Caleb and George made the arrangements, Erica peered around the store. There were only two other people: an elderly woman, and a man in his forties. Erica looked twice at the man. There was something familiar about him, but she couldn't figure out what it was. He wasn't a member of the Demon Dogs. Maybe she'd seen him in Toronto? While she thought about it, the man looked up and saw her. A slight frown creased his brow.

"Let's head out to my place." Caleb took Erica's hand and started leading her out of the store. Erica took one last quick look at the man as they left.

Caleb took Erica back out to the truck. She got in and stared toward the floor, not really seeing anything, and flicked the zipper tab on her coat as she thought about meeting the rest of Caleb's pack. As he got in, he looked over at her. "Hey, what's wrong?"

"What's this meeting about?"

"Whenever there's someone who wants to join the pack, we call a meeting of the senior pack members, and that person is presented. Then a month-long waiting period starts where the new person lives here and participates as a pack member. At the end of it, we vote on whether to grant full membership."

"Oh." Erica glanced out the window while she rubbed at her upper thigh. Maybe the man would be there and she'd figure out where she knew him from.

Caleb placed his hand over hers and she turned back to look at him. "You'll be fine. It's just a formality."

"Won't they want to know about me, though? I can't—"

"Don't worry about it. You don't have to share anything you don't want to. Besides, you've got the Alpha vouching for you, and I hate to brag, but they usually go along with what I want."

She managed a small smile. Caleb leaned over and kissed her, and then set off again. Erica tried to concentrate on the gorgeous scenery and not the anxiety over being presented to his pack. The land was full of dense forest, all covered with a pristine blanket of snow winking in the sunlight. There were wide, smooth swaths devoid of trees and Erica guessed there were small lakes and rivers under the snow. Aside from the little town where the grocery store stood, there weren't many houses, and those they did pass were usually set back quite a distance from the road, barely discernible through the trees. At last Caleb turned off the main road and into a driveway with a sign out front.

"Wolf's Lodge?"

Caleb grinned. "Subtle, isn't it? This is where I live. The property has been in my family for generations and my grandfather was the one who decided to turn it into a business. We've got a big lake with ten small cottages around it people can rent out, mostly from spring to fall, but they're all winterized so we get some visitors this time of year, too."

Erica admired the big house in front of them, loving how it was surrounded by forest. She could make out a vast patch of undisturbed snow behind it and guessed that must be the lake. It would have been a great place for her kids. Her stomach ached with a pang of sadness that she'd never get to share this with them.

"Where are the cottages?"

"They're spread out and there's a road around the whole place to join them. The main house here is where my parents still live."

Startled, Erica looked back at him. "Your father's alive? But how did you become Alpha then?"

Caleb shrugged. "He retired. He had to petition the elders and the senior members and then when they agreed, there was a ceremony to transfer power, and that was it."

"Wow. In my pack the only way to get rid of an Alpha is death."

Caleb squeezed her knee. "I'm glad you're not with them anymore. It sounds like it wasn't a great pack." Erica remained silent as Caleb parked the truck in front of the house. He led her through the front door.

"Mom? Dad?" Caleb called as they entered the house.

A moment later, a woman who looked just like an older, more feminine Caleb, came rushing down the hall. She threw her arms around him. "I'm glad you made it back okay."

"Why wouldn't I?"

"You know she hates it when you go to the city." Erica turned to see a large, handsome man in his fifties standing in a doorway. He had to be Caleb's father.

Caleb pulled Erica to him. "Guys, this is Erica. Erica, my mom, Janet, and my dad, Malcolm."

"George already called us, dear." His mom had a twinkle in her eye. "Erica, we're so happy to have you here. Our home is yours and you're welcome any time."

Erica swallowed a lump in her throat. "Thank you."

"You should get her to your house to get settled," Malcolm said. "Come back for supper and we'll go to the meeting together."

They said goodbye to Caleb's parents and got back in the truck. "Where's your house?"

They started down a narrow, snow-covered road through the forest. "On the other side of the lake. I built it five years ago."

As they drove, Erica noticed several of the little rental cottages, each with a driveway and a pier into the lake. There was enough space between them she couldn't see one from the other. Finally, they pulled up in front of a huge timber house which sat right on the water's edge.

Caleb grabbed their bags from the back and then led her inside. The main floor consisted of one large space, with a kitchen and island along one wall, and a huge fireplace along the other. In between was a dining table and living room set, facing out to a wall of glass which overlooked the lake.

"It's incredible!"

Caleb led her up the stairs and into the master bedroom which featured another fireplace, and another huge window. Erica gazed out across the lake, just able to make out the backs of the other cottages. For the first time in a very long time, she felt at home.
****

Dinner and the meeting went off without a problem, and the community welcomed Erica eagerly, as Caleb knew they would. He put her to work helping him and his parents around the resort. It wasn't a busy time of year, though they'd had a couple of guests during the three weeks Erica had been there.

One evening, he and Erica were returning from a run into town and they saw a silver BMW with Michigan plates parked in front of his parents' house. He'd become so attuned to Erica he sensed her tension even before he smelled her fear. "What's wrong?"

"It's him," she whispered before turning terrified eyes toward him. "Tank. The Alpha. Caleb, you can't let him find me!"

Caleb clenched his jaw. *How dare that bastard show up here.* "Don't worry, sweetheart. He won't." Caleb didn't slow down but drove the truck down the road to his house. "Get in, lock the door, and stay in there. I'll go find out what's going on, and then I'll come for you."

Erica bolted from the truck to the house and Caleb took off as fast as he could for his parents'. When he stormed through the front door, he heard voices coming from the living room. He found his parents chatting with a big man in a leather motorcycle jacket, tattoos visible on the skin of his neck and his hands.

"Who's this?"

"This is Tank. He's the Alpha of Erica's pack." His mother raised her eyebrows at Caleb as she introduced the man.

Tank stood up and held out his hand to Caleb, but Caleb refused to shake it. "What are you doing here?"

"I got a call from an acquaintance that my old lady had shacked up with some wolf up here."

Old lady? Erica never said they'd been married. And who was the acquaintance who'd sold them out? "Which acquaintance?"

"Guy goes by the name Ripper."

Caleb knew right away who Tank was talking about. Ripper was a wolf who'd moved into the territory a few years back, but hadn't formally joined the pack. Caleb had been fine with letting him hang around because he hadn't caused any trouble. Until now.

"So why did you come here?"

"I came to bring my old lady home. I can't let another man take what's mine." Tank took a step closer, glaring at Caleb.

"You treated her like shit, so she left. And she's my mate. You have no claim on her." Caleb stepped closer. He and Tank were pretty evenly matched in size, and neither one seemed willing to back down.

"How about our sons? Doesn't that give me a claim?"

Caleb blinked. She'd never said anything about kids, either.

Tank smirked. "She didn't tell you, I guess. She got up and ran off in the middle of the night one night with no explanation. Left me and the boys behind. She just couldn't take the pressure. You should let me take her off your hands before she does the same to you."

Caleb clenched his fists. The fear Erica had of this man was clear. If she'd left children behind, there had to be a good reason. "She's mine now. You need to get the hell out of my territory."

"I'm challenging you. Tonight. I'll fight for what's mine. Just make sure she's here when I get back."

Tank stormed out the door, slamming it behind him. Caleb moved to watch out the front window until he'd left the property. When the silver car had disappeared down the road, he went back to his parents.

"Erica is terrified of that man," he told them. "If she left, she had a good reason. Dad, call the elders and gather everyone together. If he wants a challenge, that's what he'll get. When he gets back, bring him to the gathering circle. We'll meet you there."

Without waiting, Caleb took off back to his house. He found Erica crouched on the floor in the master bedroom looking across the lake toward his parents' house. He went to her and pulled her into his arms.

"What happened? How did he find me?"

"Ripper. He moved here a couple of years ago and

never formally asked to join the pack. But he kept to himself and didn't cause trouble. I don't know how he knows Tank, but he recognized you and called him."

She shook her head. "The man in the store the first day. I knew I'd seen him somewhere before. He was a hang around with the Demon Dogs for a while. Fuck! So what's going to happen now?"

"Tank challenged me for you. I have to fight him."

"What? No!" Erica pulled back to look at him with wide eyes. "He'll kill you!"

Caleb shook his head. "No. He won't. There's no way in hell I'm going to lose you. I love you."

Her eyes shone. "I love you, too."

A tear spilled onto her cheek and Caleb reached out to brush it away. "I'm never going to let you go. You know that. But I need you to tell me everything. He said you had kids. Were you married?"

She pulled away from him and went to stare out the window, arms around her waist. "He couldn't bother with marrying me. It was enough for him to call me his old lady. Tank first knocked me up when I was eighteen and I had Harley. A year later, Ryder came along. They're like little princes, revered by the others. But I was just a piece of property. Tank has a wicked temper and he'd hit me. Force me to fuck him." She turned to face Caleb. "I made excuses. By then my mother was dead and I didn't have anyone. He started sharing me with the other club members and some of them were pretty rough, but he didn't care. He made it worse if I didn't cooperate.

"One night, he'd finished beating me and forcing me to suck his cock, and had gone out to get one of his buddies for more fun. My youngest saw it and I knew I had to go. I packed the boys in the car, stole some money and a gun from Tank's stash, and tried to leave, but he got home before I could go." The tears streamed freely down her cheeks now, and Caleb fought the urge to comfort her. She needed space to finish.

"I couldn't go back to him. I knew he'd beat me senseless for trying to leave, so I changed, and I ran, even though it meant leaving my babies behind. He'd always been good to them. It took me weeks to make it to Toronto as a wolf. I managed to steal a few clothes and some money, but I had nothing. Until you came along."

She ran back to Caleb and threw her arms around him. He squeezed her and held her as she cried. After hearing her story, there was no way Caleb would let that asshole take her away. He kissed Erica, their tongues tangling together desperately.

"Caleb," Erica said when he moved his lips down her neck. "I want you to claim me. Right now."

Chapter Ten

Erica knew it was the right thing to do. Every time they'd made love the past few weeks, it got harder to avoid, and with Tank here now, she had to make sure she and Caleb were bonded. There was no way anyone would question them.

"Are you sure?" he asked her.

"More sure than I've ever been."

He groaned and kissed her again. Erica let her wolf close to the surface and opened herself to Caleb, body and mind. He growled and she felt his wolf meet hers in a connection that transcended the physical. Her body throbbed with need for him and she pulled him down to the floor with her, not even bothering with the bed a few feet away.

They ripped at each other's clothes, nipped at each other's skin. When they were both naked, Caleb pushed her onto her back and dove between her legs. She was so wet already she didn't need it, but when his tongue circled her clit, she gripped his hair and ground her pussy against his face. He growled against her, the vibrations sending her into her first orgasm.

Caleb flipped her over and tugged her ass up, entering her in one swift, smooth thrust. He pounded her at a furious pace and it wasn't long before she felt another orgasm approaching.

"I'm going to come! Caleb, do it now."

He leaned over her back and sank his teeth into the side of her neck, just as he exploded inside of her. The heat from his cum triggered her orgasm, and as they came together, their wolves united. Still buried inside of her, Caleb rolled onto his side, holding her tightly against him.

"I love you," he said.

"I love you, too."

"Now let's get ready to deal with this ex of yours."

****

Erica and Caleb made it to the meeting area before the others. They curled up together in their wolf forms as they waited. Soon, other pack members began to join them, forming a circle around them. It wasn't long before a huge number of wolves had assembled, all sitting quietly and waiting. Finally, a distant howl signalled the impending arrival of the elders with Tank. Erica's stomach hurt and she hoped this was resolved quickly. Now that they'd joined their souls, she couldn't bear it if something happened to her mate.

The wolves parted to let a group through and Erica recognized the hulking form of Tank among them. When he and the elders shifted to human, the rest of the pack shifted, too, with Caleb and Erica the last to do so.

The mating mark throbbed on the side of her neck, more obvious in this form, and she heard a murmur spread through the crowd as the others noticed it.

"I've come to challenge you for the right to take Erica back to her pack where she belongs." Tank's voice echoed through the clearing.

Caleb stepped forward. "She is my mate. My soul mate. We are a bonded pair and you cannot break that."

Tank laughed. "I can if I kill you."

"Then she'll die, too. Either way, you lose."

Unseen hands pulled Erica back to the edge of the clearing as Caleb and Tank began to circle each other. She chewed her lip as she waited. When Tank lunged at Caleb, she gasped, but her mate easily side-stepped and landed a blow to Tank's face. He grunted and fell back, the circling continuing.

They continued in this manner, exchanging blows, and while Caleb proved to be a skilled fighter, he couldn't avoid every hit. After one particularly powerful blow, Caleb went down, his blood staining the snow beneath them, but just as Tank went in for another, Caleb grabbed his leg and yanked the other man to the ground. He jumped on his back and wrapped his hands around Tank's throat. Tank bucked and tried to throw Caleb off, but he couldn't. Tank's movements slowed as his oxygen supply dwindled. His face became red and puffed as he struggled to get air.

Tank met Erica's gaze, and in spite of the situation, he smirked at her. She frowned, and then her eyes widened when she realized Tank was shifting. It was against the rules of fair engagement, but Tank had proved many times he didn't really care much for rules.

Fearing for her mate, Erica shifted and leaped into the circle between Tank and Caleb, but Tank surprised her when he turned and ran. Erica tore after him, but he had a head start and he'd always been faster. Within moments though, several wolves from Caleb's pack, including Caleb, sped past her. They pursued Tank as far as Caleb's parents' house, but they were too late. He'd made it into his car before they got there and managed to peel out of the driveway and down the road.

Caleb and his enforcers shifted back to human and stood watching. Erica caught up a moment later and went to stand beside her mate.

"Should we try to chase him?" Caleb asked.

Erica would have loved to say yes, but at this rate they'd never catch up. "Let him go. He'll have to live with himself and his cowardice." She slipped her arms around him and squeezed. "I'm so glad you're okay."

He kissed her forehead. "I had something worth fighting for. There was no way I was going to lose."

"He's already taken so much from me, I couldn't help but worry." She buried her face against his neck, inhaling his scent to reassure herself.

"I was thinking," Caleb said. "Maybe we should go down and get your sons. Bring them back here."

Her breath caught. "Are you serious? Even though they're not yours?"

He stroked her cheek and she leaned into his touch. "If they're part of you, they're part of me. I know how hard it must have been for you to leave them."

Hope filled Erica. "I love you, Caleb."

"I love you, too."

As they made their way back to their house, Erica felt like maybe she'd get to have her happy little family after all.

The End

ALPHA'S SUNSHINE

Moon Point, 1

Elyzabeth M. VaLey

Copyright © 2017

Chapter One

Sisu wiped the counter with the worn rag. He made a mental note to check the inventory for some new ones, for although Moon Point was not the best bar in the city, it still belonged to him.

He took in the rowdy environment. A group of men played darts in the corner. Others debated enthusiastically with a mug of mediocre beer in their hands and a tray of greasy, half-eaten food on the table. Scattered in dark, secluded corners, couples made out. Red Hot Chili Pepper's *California* started to play and drunken voices joined in singing the chorus.

Sisu took a deep breath. Alcohol. Fritters. Heavy perfume. Sweat. Smoke. Wet dog. The place stunk. Yet, even though he only came once a month, it still smelled like home. He owned three other businesses now, all of them of better quality, but Moon Point would always be his favorite joint. His roots were here, in this place, within this gritty neighborhood.

"Get me another, will you?"

Lee, his friend and Moon Point's manager, waved an empty mug in front of his face. Sisu took the glass and refilled it.

"I should charge you, you know?" Sisu said.

Lee cocked his head and gave him his standard Hollywood smile. Batting lashes included. Sisu rolled his eyes. The list of men who had fallen for that face was endless.

"Consider it part of payment," Lee said.

Sisu raised his eyebrows.

"Are you sure?" he asked.

Lee laughed. "Never mind, it'd cost you too much."

"Indeed it would." Sisu tended to another customer and then returned to Lee's side. "What I don't understand is what you're doing here on your day off."

"I could ask you the same question. When was the last time you relaxed?" Lee said.

Sisu shrugged.

"See? Besides, this is a great place to be. Free drinks, free food, and entertainment. What more does a man need?"

"I wouldn't mind me some pussy," Sisu said.

"Make it some cock, and I'll agree." Lee smirked. He waggled his eyebrows suggestively. "Wanna have some fun?"

Sisu opened his mouth to retort when a cool draft brushed the hairs on the back of his neck. He glanced toward the entrance and froze.

A couple walked into the room. The man was tall, scrawny, and reeked of human, but the woman was something different. His mouth watered. Even within the hundreds of smells permeating Moon Point, he could pick out her scent. Sweet, like ripe strawberries. Tempting, like fresh mango fruit. He sniffed the air. There was something else. Musky. Piquant. Delicious.

The wolf within him surged, slamming against his

chest. Sisu gasped. What the hell? He shook his head and took in a measured breath. The woman's fragrance wrapped around him. His insides burned as his beast fought for release. Shifting was prohibited in the bar. He clenched his teeth and grabbed the countertop. A single word popped into his mind.

Mine.

Sisu snarled. The rhythm of his heart changed into a frantic beat. His nails dug into the wood.

My mate.

Desire pumped through him. His cock hardened. Every cell in his body screamed for her. She was his. Regardless of her name, her precedence, her past, or her present.

Mine.

"Sisu," Lee whispered. "What's wrong?"

"Her." He ground out the words, unable to tear his gaze from the pair. The man tugged the woman by the hand. She walked a step behind him, twisting the strap of her purse and keeping her head bowed.

Fear.

It rolled off in waves from her. His woman.

Sisu growled. He would kill the man who harmed her. His teeth pricked his bottom lip as they transformed. The wolf within him howled in victory.

"Sisu." Lee grasped his forearm in a punishing grip. "I don't know what the fuck is happening, but I can imagine. Look at me." The puma shifter gripped his chin, forcing him to obey. "You need to calm down, now. People are looking at you. Besides, you'll just scare her if you go over like a caveman." Urgency danced within his green irises. "Close your eyes. Inhale through your nose, exhale through your mouth."

Sisu swallowed. At the back of his mind, he knew Lee was right.

"Embrace the knowledge of finding your mate, but don't let the animal control you. You're not a pup anymore. You are stronger than that." Lee spoke in soft undertones. "Corner him. Bury him deep within your soul. You don't know anything about the girl. She doesn't smell like a shifter. You need to let the human part of you do the work."

Sisu followed Lee's orders. Gradually, the wolf receded. He took one last shaky breath and opened his eyes. Lee smiled at him.

"Welcome back."

"Thanks," Sisu said. The corner of his lips lifted.

Lee chuckled. "You look like an idiot in love."

Sisu scowled. He ran his fingers through his hair. "Damn it, Lee. What do I do?"

Lee raised his hands in a sign of defeat. "Hell am I supposed to know?"

Chapter Two

From behind the bar, Sisu observed as Kara, the waitress, approached the table where his mate and her companion sat. The man gestured widely and spoke in a loud voice while ordering. His woman didn't move. When Kara spoke to her, she barely replied with a shake of her head.

Sisu frowned. Why was she so afraid? Did her friend, or whatever he was, scare her? The atmosphere in the building? Something else? He had to find out.

"Lee, take over the bar, will you?"

His friend's eyebrows shot to his hairline. "What are you going to do?"

"Relax. Nothing crazy. I'm just going to take a closer look," Sisu said, grinning mischievously.

Lee scratched his neck and pursed his lips. Finally, he nodded. "But you're going to have to pay me extra for this."

"Yeah, yeah."

Sisu waved him off and followed Kara into the kitchen. He tapped her on the shoulder. She turned around to face him. Sisu blinked. No matter how many times he spoke to the owl shifter, the intensity in her large azure eyes always threw him off.

"Mr. Virtanen, how are you?" she said.

"I'm okay, Kara. However, if you don't mind, I'll deliver the order to that table you were just seeing to."

"Um, sure." Kara shrugged.

"Don't worry, if they leave any tips, I'll pass them on to you."

She flashed her pearly whites. "Thank you, sir."

"Table Four," someone called from within the kitchen.

359

"That's yours," Kara said. "I'll bring them their drinks."

Sisu picked up the order of spicy wings, nachos, and onion rings. He straightened his spine and carefully balanced the tray on his hand. He hadn't done this in years, however, it appeared waitressing was like bike riding: one never forgot how to do it.

He approached the table, sweat trickling down his back. His mouth dried and his pulse quickened. If she hadn't noticed him earlier, she'd definitely see him now. What thoughts would run through her mind? Would she find him as appealing as he found her?

He sniffed the air. He still couldn't figure out what she was. She didn't smell completely human. Something was off, different. Goosebumps broke over his flesh. His wolf whimpered. Whatever it was, it drove him insane. He had to have her.

"Yes, we're here. Yes. I've ordered some food for all of us. Hope you guys like chicken." The man spoke loudly into the phone. Sisu cocked his head. The conversation continued. "Do you have what I need? Yes, yes, I know. Yes, of course May is here, too."

May.

That was her name. Spring, life, blossoms, fresh rain showers. Everything he loved. He looked toward her. Their gazes locked. His heart somersaulted.

"About time. I'm starving."

The man's voice broke the spell. May turned away. Sisu fought to breathe. She was delectable. He could picture himself drowning in her gaze, watching the sparks in her eyes flicker while he contemplated her with a love which would know no boundaries.

The man took a sip of his beer and banged the mug against the tabletop. Sisu's growl stuck in the back of his throat.

Easy now.

Hands shaking, he managed to place everything on the wooden surface without spilling. Now what? He didn't want to go back to the bar. He wanted to speak to his mate. To hold her. Take her home with him.

He glanced at May. Her cheeks flushed a delightful rose. She appeared flustered and he realized perhaps she had been staring at him too. Elation pumped through his veins. He took a step in her direction. She gasped and jumped in her seat, accidentally knocking over her drink in the process.

Her date started to shout expletives, but Sisu ignored him, focusing on May. She had stood up and was frantically digging into her purse, while repeatedly apologizing.

Her long hair covered her face, but the sound of her voice traveled straight to his cock. It reminded him of a summer breeze caressing his fur, of the sunshine warming his flesh.

"It's all right." He touched her elbow, hoping to ease her worry. Instead, she scampered backward as if he'd burned her.

"Sorry. Here," she whispered. Visibly trembling, she offered him a pack of tissues.

Sisu reached for it. Their fingers brushed, but this time she didn't run from it. He rubbed his thumb across her satiny skin. His pulse skipped. Adrenaline whizzed through his system. He never wanted to stop touching her.

"Thank you," he said.

"Cory, no," May said, pulling away from him.

Sisu whirled around. The petty human lifted his hands in a peaceful gesture, but hatred showed openly on his face.

"I wasn't going to do anything, May, just ask this

waiter to finish cleaning up this mess."

"Of course," Sisu snapped. The tissues crumpled in his fist. "Her drinks are on the house. I'll get someone to take care of this."

Sisu strode back to the bar. He asked Kara to take care of the mess, grabbed a bottle of tequila and a shot glass, and poured himself some. He downed it in one go. He was about to go for another round when Lee stopped him.

"She's looking at you, you know?"

"What?" Sisu glanced over his head. "No, she's not."

Lee burst out laughing.

"What the fuck are you laughing about?"

"You. You should have seen your face. I swear, for an instant you glowed." Lee chuckled.

"Lee, one day, you'll be in my position and I will be the one laughing."

"I don't think so, because unlike you, I can flirt. Damn, what you did back there was a disgrace to humanity."

"Lee," Sisu warned.

The shifter grinned and released the bottle of alcohol.

"Maybe drinking will help you loosen up, or ruin everything."

Damn cat was always right. Sisu capped the bottle and returned it to the shelf. Out of the corner of his eye, he noticed movement. People were coming inside. His eyes widened.

"Lee, we've got company."

Chapter Three

Sisu stared at the three shifters entering the bar. Two of them he knew: Alkaline and Kade, the brothers.

The former was the leader of the Claw Gang, a pack of feline shifters involved in shady business practices. He and Alkaline had tried establishing a partnership a few years ago, but it hadn't worked out. The six-foot-five brute with a golden-red mane had believed he could submit Sisu to his will. He'd quickly learned he'd barked up the wrong tree.

"Claws," Lee whispered. "What do you think they're doing here?"

"I have no idea."

The Claws rarely came into this particular neighborhood. Moon's Point welcomed all shifters, but cats were not at the top of the list of their frequent customers. Most of the sleek beasts preferred to keep other company.

"I think—"

Sisu cut him off by raising his hand. He watched the scene before him unfold in slow motion, his blood turning cold at the sight. May's date welcomed the lions warmly, a sickeningly fake smile on his face. Then, May greeted them. Kade and the other guy shook her hand, but Alkaline bowed and brushed his lips over the back of her palm.

Sisu's vision blurred, and red spots danced before him.

Mine.

He would destroy the shifter. Alkaline would never see the light of day. How dare he kiss what belonged to him?

"Damn lion," Lee murmured. "She doesn't look

too happy to see them, though, right, Sisu? Sisu?"

Sisu ignored his friend. He jumped over the counter and strode toward the group. He could feel his jaw snap as his canines sprung forth. His nostrils flared. May's scent intensified. The wolf clawed at him. He rolled his neck. His bones cracked. His paws hit the floor and he set off at a run.

The sounds around him transformed, becoming more acute. Someone screamed. Chairs scraped against the floor. Glass crashed into a million pieces.

Sisu planted himself in front of the group, growling. The cats hissed but didn't retract.

"Get out," he said. His voice came out guttural, unnatural.

"Or what?" Alkaline asked.

Sisu's hackles rose. He took a menacing step toward them.

"I'll kill you," he snarled.

"Bring it on, dog."

Sisu barked. He licked his jowls. He could already taste his enemy's blood. He would destroy the lion and claim his woman. He glanced in her direction. May stood behind the group, eyes closed, clutching her bag to her chest like a shield. The scent of terror hung in the air like a thick cloud full of rain. No. He didn't want that.

He stepped in her direction just as a body hurled into him. He skidded across the floor knocking over a table. Large, yellow paws pressed down on him, pinning him to the ground.

"You're scaring her off."

Sisu recognized Lee's voice behind the emerald puma eyes.

"Is that what you want?" he insisted. "She's human, Sisu. You're destroying your chances at happiness. Control the animal."

Sisu's gaze darted toward his mate. He whimpered. Lee was right. What the hell was he doing? He was an alpha. Always in control. Leader of a pack. Quiet. Thoughtful. Deadly. Having his enemy touch May had caused the animal to break loose. It was taking over him.

"Shift back to your human form and I'll fix this fucking mess."

Lee stepped off him. Sisu rolled to his feet and watched the puma shifter saunter to the group and bow, offering his neck. Sisu swallowed the bile. Lee was an alpha like him, and he was debasing himself. By exposing his most vulnerable point, he was communicating to the Claws that they were above him and they could do with him whatever they pleased.

Sisu turned away. Somehow, he'd repay Lee, but he couldn't continue watching. He rushed to the back of the bar into Lee's office. Shifting back to his human form, he rummaged through the room, desperately searching for some clothes. He had to go back out there, help Lee and see to May.

"Fuck," he swore and dug his fingers into his scalp, tugging hard.

Lee didn't have a single item he could use and he sure as hell couldn't go out there naked. He'd already created enough of a commotion.

May.

Her beautiful face flashed before his mind. The wolf within him stirred, causing his chest to constrict painfully. Shame made his ears burn. His primal recklessness could have ruined everything.

Sisu sunk into one of the chairs in front of Lee's Ikea-model desk and buried his head in his hands. What was he going to do?

The door creaked loudly and he spun around. Lee

peeked from the opening. Apparently satisfied at what he saw within, the puma shifter entered.

"Here, put this on. You busted the button on your jeans, but I think you can still use them. The t-shirt is from an old uniform we had in storage, but I think it'll fit you." He threw the folded garments at him.

"Thanks," Sisu said. "Where is she? Is she okay?" he asked, while tugging on the black t-shirt with the bar's logo.

"Kara is speaking to her and giving her some cool water. Alkaline and the rest have left."

"Her companion, too?"

"Yes. I think he ran as soon as you took shape." Lee chuckled.

"Coward," Sisu muttered.

"Agreed." Lee sighed. "In any case, you're going to have to talk to her. I suggest doing it in here. She'll feel safer than if you whisk her away to your Neanderthal cave."

Sisu frowned. There was little humor in his friend's tone.

"Wait, Lee. Come on, if you had been in my position wouldn't you have done the same? Alkaline had his hands on her."

Lee spun around.

"No," he shouted. Lee gesticulated widely. "I wouldn't have. I'd have acted human. I would have waited to see what was happening and I wouldn't have jumped on them like a rabid animal."

Sisu's jaw dropped. He'd known Lee for most of his life and the puma had never shouted at him.

"Lee, what's wrong? What happened out there? Why did the Claws leave without a fight? I saw you bowing to them, I know the sacrifice you must have made, but—"

Lee's shoulders sagged.

"You have no idea, Sisu, but it's not important."

"It is to me," Sisu said.

"No, you have other priorities now. You have a girl out there, basically held hostage, waiting for an explanation. Deal with it."

"Lee—"

"It's not important, Sisu. It's done. I'll go get May," Lee said.

"Lee."

But the other man didn't turn back.

Chapter Four

May sipped at the glass of water they'd given her. The cool liquid traveled down her throat, but it did little to ease the tightening in her gut. Her fingers trembled as she set down the cup.

Kara, the waitress, had attempted to explain what had happened earlier, but May didn't need an explanation. She knew about shifting. She understood how it worked. What she needed was someone to tell her why every time she glanced at the man with ice-blue eyes and dark, silver-streaked hair, her knees went weak and her chest hurt with a keening ache that urged her to get closer.

She tugged the strap of her purse to confirm it was still in place. She couldn't afford to lose its contents.

"May?"

She turned to face the man who'd introduced himself as Lee. Though equally as handsome as the wolf shifter, the puma didn't spark any reaction in her.

"Have you found my brother?" she asked.

"I'm afraid not. He fled when the fray started. I'm sorry," Lee said.

May blinked back tears. Dammit. She should have known that would happen. She never could count on Cory.

Lee sat across from her at the table. He gave her a sympathetic smile.

"Listen, Sisu wants to speak to you, he'd like to apologize. I think Kara told you he's the owner of the business, right?"

Sisu. Kara had told him that was his name, but she'd never heard anything like it. May chewed on her bottom lip, the urge to whisper his name making her mouth tingle.

"Why does he only want to apologize to me? Why not the rest of the customers?" she said, instead.

Lee's eyes filled with undisguised amusement. May stiffened.

"I can't explain. You must speak to him." Lee offered her his hand. "Come on. As big as he is, he's harmless. I promise."

May pressed her lips together. The throbbing within her grew, mingling with her erratic heartbeat.

"Okay," she said.

She followed him to a closed office. Every step made her quiver until her teeth practically chattered. Lee knocked and a gruff voice invited them to enter. Her mouth dried and her stomach rolled even as her feet propelled her forward and into the tiny room.

Lee said something, but she couldn't make out the words from the rushing in her ears. Warmth radiated through her body. She couldn't rip her gaze from the man before her. The intensity in his blue eyes caused a shiver to race down her spine. She forced herself to look away. It wasn't a good idea.

Her mouth dried as she took in his body. He wore a black t-shirt with the bar's logo, but it was too tight on him and stretched over his thick muscles, leaving little to the imagination. She dipped lower. Heat infused her cheeks. He wore the same jeans he'd been sporting earlier, except, they were open at the top, giving her a glimpse of dark curls which arrowed downwards. Her pussy tingled with awareness and her nipples tightened into peaks.

"Why don't you sit down, May?"

He spoke her name as if he'd said it a thousand times, as if they were lovers.

May forced herself to move. She took the chair he

offered, only flinching slightly when he sat across from her and their knees bumped.

"I'm sorry."

She studied his face, taking in the details, from the long dark lashes to the scar on his nose and the freckle on his chin. She stared at his lips. What would they feel like? Soft? Demanding? Would he mind if she nibbled on his bottom bow?

"Are you scared?"

His voice startled her. Husky, deep, it reverberated within her and spread, zeroing in on her pussy. She pressed her legs together and shook her head.

"I'm not scared, I'm terrified," she admitted.

His lips curved into a smile. It oozed sexiness, but also reassurance. He touched her knee. Heat filled her. Her stomach fluttered.

"Most shifters are harmless and respect humans. However, Alkaline and his pack are not exactly friendly. Why were you with them?"

His harsh tone had May drawing her gaze back to his eyes. They flashed with unmasked anger. She blinked. What was wrong with her? A stranger grinned and she swooned? Was this some kind of shifter magic?

"May, I need to know."

May rolled her lips inward. Even though he sexually attracted her, she didn't know anything about this man except his name and the fact he was a shifter. Through life, she'd learned two things: don't trust anyone, but especially don't trust shifters. Even if his demeanor compelled her to spill her secrets and confide with him, she couldn't.

"I want to help you," he persisted.

His sincerity overwhelmed her.

"My brother owed them money. They had a game of cards scheduled and I merely accompanied him," she said.

There, that was partially true. He didn't need to know the finer details.

"Your brother," Sisu repeated.

"Yes. My brother."

"Not your boyfriend?" he insisted.

"No, Cory is my step-brother. Why are you smiling?"

May stared at Sisu. His eyes glittered and a predatory grin spread over his face. He leaned toward her, and set his arms on either side of her chair. He scooted closer. His legs opened, trapping hers in between his powerful thighs. Heat emanated from him, making her blood boil in response. Her panties dampened. She lifted her hands, desperate to stave him off, but Sisu closed the distance. Her open palms collided against his muscled pecs. A gasp tore through her.

"Do you believe in soulmates, May?"

Her jaw dropped. "No," she cried out.

"Why?" he rumbled.

"What does this have to do with anything?"

"We are soulmates, May. You are my mate," Sisu stated.

"That's ridiculous. You don't know me. I don't know you. I'm human." She practically screamed the words.

"It doesn't matter, sunshine." Sisu took one of her hands in his. Her mouth became moist. Her nerve endings stirred, a pleasurable shiver coursing down her spine. The pounding in her chest expanded.

"We are drawn to each other like moths to flames. From the moment I saw you walk in tonight, my wolf recognized you. All night long, I've been searching for ways to get close to you. All I've been thinking about is how to make you mine, May." Sisu brought her hand to his lips, kissing the back of it. He lowered his voice. "I want to consume you, mark you, claim you as mine, forever."

"No," she whimpered.

"Yes. I know you feel it, too. I can sense your heartbeat here." He touched her wrist. "It's wild, May, just like mine. And your gaze, it keeps drifting to my lips. You're dying to kiss me." Sisu took in a deep breath. His nostrils flared and his pupils dilated. "I can smell your arousal, sunshine." A growl-like sound came from him. "You want my body pressed to yours, naked, sweaty. My cock within your pussy, pumping hard and bringing you to the highest heights of ecstasy possible."

"You're insane."

The words sounded hollow and meaningless. She was lying and she had no doubt he knew it.

"Only for you, sunshine."

Sisu's fingertips grazed her chin, his touch more gentle than the caress of a feather. She closed her eyes, not daring to look at him. Sounds faded until all she could hear was her own heavy breathing and the rustle of his clothes as he came closer.

The first touch of his lips was like a rain drop on an early spring day. A phantom drop. The kind which made one wonder if it would soon start raining. The type which caused thirsty plants to stretch their stalks toward the sky.

Her body swayed forward.

Sisu groaned deeply, his mouth pressing to hers, hot and unyielding.

Thoughts scattered. The world tilted. May reached for him. His hand clasped hers. The pressure of his lips intensified. She whimpered. Her heart hammered, and the knot within her transformed, rolling and spreading like hot lava, chanting for more.

She twisted away from him.

"No, I can't," she said. "Soulmates don't exist."

May stared at their entwined fingers. They fit together like matching puzzle pieces. She glimpsed at Sisu, who regarded her quietly. The blue in his eyes nothing short of reassuring, comforting. Loving.

No. This wasn't right. It was madness. She swallowed drily, trying to push back down the fear which climbed up her throat. She needed to leave. Now. She pulled at her arm, but Sisu held on tight.

The ache within her turned violent, like claws digging into her tender skin. Cool sweat rolled down her back.

"Hey, it's all right, sunshine." Sisu rubbed his thumb over her wrist in soothing circles. The pain decreased. "You don't need to be scared. We'll take it one step at a time, okay? Do you have a way to get home?"

May shook her head. Sisu smiled.

"It's all right. I'll take you home. After all this craziness, you must be exhausted."

Chapter Five

Sisu helped May to her feet and led her through the bar, her hand firmly in his grasp. He wasn't about to let her out of his sight again. Never. He didn't know what it would take, but he'd convince her soulmates did exist and she belonged to him.

The beast within him squirmed with anguish. The animal wanted everything now. He didn't know how to wait. Sisu breathed slowly through his nose.

Easy now.

She would succumb to him. Already, she felt something, even if she didn't realize it. And there was definitely sexual attraction. He hadn't been lying when he told her he smelled her arousal. His cock throbbed at the memory of the thick musky scent. He glanced at May. He inhaled slowly. She intoxicated him, but he had to give her time to adjust. For the moment, he'd have to content himself with holding her near.

They walked past the bar and he caught Lee's eye. His friend gave him the thumbs up.

"Should you be staying and helping? Lee said the business belonged to you," May said.

"It's not necessary. Lee's got it under control."

At least he hoped so. He hadn't really found out what had transpired in his absence. May was his priority tonight, but he vowed to call Lee as soon as he sorted everything out with her.

He opened the door for her and took her to the alleyway at the back. The streetlight gave off a yellow glow that threw long shadows across every corner. He shuddered. He could feel eyes on him. The fact he still didn't know why May and her brother had been hanging out with the Claws nagged at him.

"Did your brother owe the Claws a lot of money?" he asked.

"I'm-I'm not sure."

Sisu grimaced. Her tone didn't back up her words. He suspected she lied. Why? He took her in. Though she hadn't released his hand, her nerves were apparent from her stiff posture and the constant plucking at her purse strap. He considered asking her about what she carried in there, but thought better of it. Maybe later, when they were somewhere safe. The alley was not the best place to hold a conversation.

"All right, sunshine. Here is my horse-drawn carriage." He pointed at his Harley.

"That's not a car."

Sisu chuckled. "Very observant." He pulled her closer and grasped his helmet. "You're going to wear this. If I can't protect you, this will help."

He helped her into the protection gear, running his fingertips across her jaw. She shivered and closed her eyes. Sisu bit his lip. If it weren't because he'd promised her he'd take it slow, he would ravage her mouth.

"I'm a good driver, and I promise I'll go slowly, okay? All you need to do is hang on tight and mimic my motions, as in, lean with me when necessary."

"I'm not sure this is a good idea, Sisu. Maybe I should take a cab."

Sisu stared at her. *Sisu.* His name on her lips sounded decadent. What would it sound like when they made love? When he brought her to orgasm again and again and she pleaded for him to stop?

"Say it again," he said.

"What?"

"Say my name again, May. I need to hear it."

"Sisu?" she whispered.

He took in a shaky breath and leaned in to kiss

her, but she turned away. Sisu ran his fingers through his hair. Patience. That was what he needed.

"Hey, it's okay. I said I'd give you time. But, I'm taking you home yes or yes. I won't let anything happen to you. Trust me."

She shrank from him. Her uncertainty easy to read.

"I promise, May," he said.

She chewed on her bottom lip for a few seconds, her gaze darting from the motorcycle to him and back. Finally, she nodded. Sisu smiled.

"Give me your address."

She dictated the street and number and he typed it into the GPS attached to the handles.

"We'll be there in no time."

He climbed onto the bike and twisted to help her get on. The rear suspension dipped and she squealed.

"That's normal, just hold on to me."

Her arms immediately wrapped around him, squeezing. She pressed herself hard against him, her body heat traveling straight to his groin. Sisu bit back a groan. He vowed that one day, he'd fuck her over his bike.

He started the engine and rolled out into the main street. He sped up gradually, enjoying the freedom of riding his Harley with his woman at his back. She might have never ridden a bike before, but every time he dipped, she moved with him, every time he braked, her legs squeezed around him. They were dancing intimately at almost ninety miles per hour.

Finally, after almost forty minutes, the navigator announced they'd arrived to their destination. He slowed down.

"Is this it?" he shouted.

"Yes."

Sisu parked in front of a modest one-story house

with a lovely wooden porch, illuminated by moonlight and a lamp fixed on the wall. He jumped off the bike and hurried to help May.

"You okay?"

She struggled to undo the strap of the helmet. He placed his palms over hers. They shook.

"Allow me."

She dropped her hands to her side. Gently, Sisu undid the strap and helped her out of it. A warm summer breeze blew her hair into her face. Unable to stop himself, Sisu brushed it back, tucking it behind her ears. The confusion in her eyes drew him in. Brown like autumn leaves flecked with sunshine, they pierced into his soul.

"May," he muttered.

Her lips parted. He trailed his fingertips across her jaw, his thumb over her bottom bow. A tremble coursed through her and a small gasp escaped her lips. She stepped back.

"Thank you for driving me home, Sisu. Good night."

Chapter Six

May bolted. Sisu probably thought she was incredibly rude, but she couldn't care less.

She wasn't sure what had driven her to accept his offer to take her home in the first place. She should have declined. The man scared her in a way that had her knees shaking and her heart skipping beats.

One moment, he was the big bad wolf, probing her for questions she couldn't answer, and the next he was piercing her with a gaze which made heat flood her core.

She couldn't deny he aroused her. Everything from the possessive twinkle in his eyes to his muscled frame made her body respond in a way she'd never experienced before.

It was unnatural, just like his talk about them being soulmates.

Soulmates.

The single word thrown into their conversation so casually echoed in her head like church bells calling for mass.

Soulmates.

She didn't believe in that type of thing. She never had. Her father had used it as an excuse to abandon them. Her mother had toiled through life, throwing her trust into men and relationships which never lasted.

You are my mate.

Impossible.

Sisu called out her name, but she ignored him. Couldn't the guy take a hint? Nausea hit her, accompanied by a sharp, stabbing in the heart, and she tripped on the steps to her porch. She would have fallen, except Sisu materialized out of nowhere, grabbed her arm and pulled her up, steadying her.

"Are you okay?" he asked.

"How did you get here so fast?"

She placed her open palm over her breast, hoping to calm her racing heartbeat.

"Shifters can run a little faster than humans."

His eyes sparkled, and his firm, sculpted lips lifted into a smile. She gaped at them. The memory of their kiss was still fresh in her mind. Her panties moistened. The unpleasant sensations of moments before receded.

Sisu cleared his voice. Heat crept up her face, but she forced herself to look upward.

Her breath caught at the smoldering heat in his gaze. He tugged her arm and brought her flush against him. With his other hand, he grasped her chin and cocked her head back.

"You can't stare at me like that, sunshine, and expect me to act like a gentleman."

May opened her mouth to defend herself, but words wouldn't come out. Sisu's grin turned devilish. She swallowed. She didn't want this.

He slid his thumb across her cheek. Her eyes drifted shut.

Who was she kidding? She wanted this more than the air she needed to live. "Please."

The plea coming from her startled her for a split second before his lips pressed against hers, sweet at first, then more insistent. He touched her bottom lip with his tongue and she opened to him willingly, exploring him as eagerly as he did her. She held onto him, bringing herself closer. Her pussy throbbed insistently.

More.

The voice in her head barked loud and clear. The ache within her returned, squeezing and expanding, flitting through every one of her nerves.

"No," she cried out.

Sisu immediately released her.

"It's okay, May."

"No, I can't, Sisu."

Her voice sounded shrill. Sweat beaded at her temples. What was happening to her?

"Why are you so scared, sunshine?" Sisu whispered. "Is it me?"

"No. I don't know what it is. All I know is every time you touch me, it hurts."

The words tumbled out and she slapped her hand over her mouth in shock. Sisu gaped at her. Embarrassed, May fumbled in her purse for her keychain.

"May, look at me."

She didn't acknowledge him, concentrating instead on unlocking her home. She quivered so badly she couldn't fit the lock. Gently, Sisu plucked them from her and opened the door.

May hurried past him, hoping to close the door before he could say anything else, but he followed her, blocking the entrance and allowing only a sliver of moonlight to filter inside.

"Sisu, please go."

"What do you mean it hurts every time I touch you?" he insisted.

"Sisu—"

"May, this is important. Tell me," he demanded. "I don't want to hurt you," he said, softening his tone.

May searched his face. Maybe if she told him the truth, he'd go away. She sighed.

"Here." She pointed to the center of her chest. "Every time you come close, touch me, kiss me, it aches."

"Describe it."

She shrugged. "I can't."

"Try."

She chewed on her bottom lip, thoughtful. "Sometimes it's like a vise squeezing me, and other times like claws digging into my flesh from within."

"Do you feel warm? Uncomfortable? As if your body was crawling out of your skin?" He pelted her with questions.

"I-I'm not sure. Please leave. I want to be alone."

Sisu regarded her quietly, but didn't budge. His eyes narrowed into slits, the blue within shifting into a sharper hue, his pupils growing larger and reminding her of what he truly was: an animal. A wolf.

Someone she couldn't trust.

"Go away," she whispered.

"I'm not going anywhere, May." Sisu stepped further into the room and shut the door. "Where's the light switch?"

"It's to your left," she said softly.

Light flooded into the room, throwing his features into sharp contrast. Rugged and untamed, he commanded the small space. His jaw was set, his mouth firmed into a determined line. May met his gaze.

"You can't stay here," she said.

"I must, if only for two reasons. One, I think I know what might be causing your pain and how to stop it, so we need to talk. Two, you said your step-brother owed the Claws money. Have you thought that when they don't find him, they could come for you?"

"That's not possible."

He took a step forward. She backed up away from him.

"The Claws won't just forgive a bet. I've dealt with them before, May."

May clenched her purse tightly. He was wrong.

He didn't know. He couldn't.

"But—"

Sisu came closer. Her back hit the wall.

"No excuses, May. If you don't let me stay indoors, I'll camp outside until you let me in."

May gawked at him. "Sisu, this is insane. My brother has been dealing with the Claws for some time and they've never come here. As for the other thing, I really don't think it's necessary to solve the issue. If you go away, it will evaporate. After all, you're the source. It didn't exist until I met you."

"I'm not leaving you." He growled. "You're my mate."

His mouth crashed against hers, hot and savage. Her body burst alive whilst her mind blanked. She heard the dull thud of her purse tumbling to the floor when his tongue pushed past her lips, entwining with hers. She wrapped her arms around his neck, taking in his taste, seeking more. Sisu threaded her hair between his fingers and pulled her head back. His teeth scraped her jaw. Liquid passion traveled to her core. A low moan racked her body.

"Does it hurt?" he demanded, his voice husky, like warm honey.

"No," she admitted.

"Good," he said, before smashing his mouth against hers once more. Grasping her hands with one of his, he held them above her head. The fierce pang began anew, compressing her from within.

"Now?"

She nodded.

"Work with it," he said "Don't be afraid. Ignore it and concentrate on me, sunshine."

May's head swam. The pain demanded her attention.

"I can't," she choked.

Sisu pressed closer. His arousal was evident against her hip. His grip on her wrists tightened. He nibbled her earlobe, eliciting a gasp from her.

"Don't think about it. Feel instead. The heat of my body. My touch. My hard cock pressing against you."

Sisu nipped her neck and then suckled the spot. Goosebumps sprouted across her flesh. He stroked her breasts over her t-shirt. Her nipples pebbled into painful tips.

"I need to taste these," Sisu said, hoarsely.

Darts of desire traveled to her pussy at his words. The crush within her became dull. Lustful fire burned in her veins. She wanted Sisu. Her body yearned for him like it'd never done for any man.

"Taste me," she whispered.

Sisu didn't waste any time. He tore her t-shirt from her and unclasped her bra. Her breasts spilled onto his waiting hands. He grasped each nipple with his thumb and forefinger and twisted. May arched into his touch. Her pussy convulsed. She wanted more.

"Sisu."

He stroked them and pinched them again, keeping his gaze on her face. Then, he lowered he head and sucked one of her nubs into his mouth. May held onto his shoulders. The gnawing throb returned, accompanied by the voice which resonated deep within her soul.

More.

May struggled, frightened at the sudden intensity. Sisu grasped her hands again, firmly keeping her in place.

"May." He growled. "Ignore it."

She melted against him. He snapped open the buttons of her jeans and snaked his hard palm underneath the fabric of her panties. She gasped.

"So fucking wet for me."

He pushed his fingers inside of her. May mewled and rocked her hips in response.

"Have you ever been this wet for anyone?" Sisu asked.

"No," she moaned.

Sisu pumped his fingers in and out of her slowly.

"Nor will you ever be, sunshine." He thumbed her clit in maddening circles, driving her closer to the edge. "Do you know why?"

May bit her lip. Sweat rolled down her back. She wanted more than this. She wanted Sisu.

"Do you know why, May?" Sisu repeated.

"No."

"Because you belong to me. My mate."

Sisu plunged his fingers into her and pressed down on her clit at the same time.

My mate.

A cry tore through her at both his words and the fierce orgasm crashing through her.

Chapter Seven

Sisu lay awake in May's bed. He'd dozed off for a bit, but he couldn't sleep. His mind returned to the woman in his arms.

After she'd found her release, he'd picked her up and carried her to the bedroom. His wolf urged him to claim her immediately, but the look in May's eyes warned him to slow down, so he waited.

Apparently dazed, May took off her jeans and put on an oversized t-shirt. She slid under the duvet and turned to him.

"Please, don't go."

Sisu didn't need to be asked twice. Fully clothed, he kicked off his shoes and climbed into bed next to her. May pressed her back to him, so they were spooning. She tightly clutched his hand and drifted off to sleep.

Something had changed within his mate. He couldn't say exactly what it was, but the fact that she appeared not to be struggling against their destiny encouraged him.

Sisu brushed his lips over her temple. May stirred, snuggling closer to him. His wolf thumped within his chest. The beast was content, but not satisfied. It wouldn't be until it officially claimed her. For that to happen, however, he knew he'd have to throw down May's walls and inhibitions.

The pain she talked about was familiar to him. He'd experienced something similar as a pup, before his wolf had first come out. It was the awakening of a trapped animal, one which yearned for freedom.

"What are you?" he whispered, inhaling deeply.

May's fragrance was human, but there was something else in her which he recognized. It was primal, animal like.

There was no way around it. They'd have to talk in the morning. He had to know things about her and her past so he could put the puzzle pieces together and create a picture. It was either that, or fucking until something changed again.

His cock twitched at the prospect. Sisu bit back a frustrated groan. His cock was at half mast, May's proximity inspiring it to stay forever firm. He closed his eyes. He hadn't even had a proper look at her pussy, but he could still taste her juices on his lips from when he'd licked his fingers. His erection grew. *Fuck.* Sisu considered going to the bathroom to take care of himself. He didn't want to leave May alone, but he was starting to become very uncomfortable. Besides, come morning, how was he going to talk when all he wanted to do was ravage her?

Carefully, he tried to disengage himself from her embrace. She held on harder.

"Sisu?" she whispered, sleepily.

"Yes, sunshine? Sorry to have woken you. I needed to go to the bathroom," he blurted.

"Is that your cock digging into my ass?"

"Yes," he admitted.

May turned in his arms and placed her leg over his, bringing him closer. Welcoming warmth radiated from her. Sisu scrutinized her face. Her eyes were wide and luminous under the moonlight filtering through the partially opened windows.

"I'm so horny," she whispered. "I've never felt anything like this."

May placed her hand on his abdomen. Sisu held his breath.

"I want to touch your skin," she said.

Sisu threw off his t-shirt.

"Everything."

May kneeled on the bed and cupped his cock through his jeans. Sisu groaned. He had to be dreaming. Like an anxious teenager, he jumped out of bed and slipped off his jeans. His cock jutted out proudly, pre-cum leaking from the tip. May reached over and wrapped her hand around his girth.

"May," he choked out her name. "Are you sure about this?"

"Yes."

She started stroking him, top to bottom, bottom to top and repeat. The pressure and speed increased. Sisu's breath hitched.

Abruptly, she released him.

"Get on the bed," she said.

He did as she bid, propping his head against some pillows. May leaned over him, running her fingers through his chest hair, teasing his nipples and dipping lower.

"Is this some kind of shifter magic, Sisu? Am I under a spell?" she asked.

Sisu swallowed drily.

"I don't understand what's happening," she continued, "but I do know I want this, now."

Grasping his cock, May swept her tongue across his weeping crown. Sisu groaned. Flattening her tongue, she slid it across his length, before taking him deep. Sisu swore. The feeling was unlike anything he'd experienced before, and he'd gotten his fair share of head. She cupped his balls, toying with them.

She swirled her tongue across the bulbous head and gave him such a lustful look it made him harder. Inch by tortuous inch, she began her descent over his cock once more. Unable to take her maddening pace, Sisu sunk his fingers into her hair and pushed down. May swallowed convulsively, giving him room to reach the back of her throat.

"That's it baby, just like that." He gasped.

His hips jerked. Her lips and mouth continued to work him. His balls tightened. He rocked his hips faster. May took him to the root. The reverberations of her moans shot straight into his groin, triggering his release. He howled. His canines pricked his teeth and he sucked in air. He clamped his mouth shut.

Fuck.

If she saw that, she'd run. He forced himself to breathe through his nose. Slowly, he opened his eyes. May, sat in front of him, licking her lips like a hungry cat.

Sisu pulled her into his arms and kissed her deep. She melded against him, returning his affection.

Sisu's heart beat like a wild drum. He wanted to tell May he loved her. That he was proud she was his mate, but he remained silent. Although she'd just given him the best blowjob in his life, he could tell she was still unsure of what was happening. He would have to content himself with keeping her close for the night. Tomorrow they'd talk. Tomorrow they'd sort things out. He yawned. Tomorrow.

****

Sisu jumped at the sound of the loud pop music coming from down the hall.

"There's someone out there," he said.

"My phone," May mumbled. "Leave it."

Sisu lay still for about one minute before the thing started blaring again. He got out of bed, slipped on his jeans, and went in search of the damn machine. If May didn't want to answer it, he'd at least switch it off. He found the source of the noise in the entrance where she'd dropped her purse. Sisu's eyes widened. How much money did she carry in that thing? He shook his head.

They needed to talk. Grabbing her phone, he started to head back to the bedroom when the name flashing on the screen caught his eye.

Alkaline.

He blinked. He had to be seeing wrong. This had to be another Alkaline. But how many men had the same name? Fury mingled with jealousy built within him. He strode into the room.

"What is the meaning of this? Is this Alkaline? Lion shifter, Alkaline?"

"What?"

May sat up in bed, blinking like an owl under too much light. Her hair curled in messy waves around her flushed face. A pang struck Sisu's heart. She appeared vulnerable, innocent. Delicious in every way. He pushed the feelings aside. The wolf didn't understand the complications of real life. The animal had to wait.

"You lied to me, May. You told me you hardly knew the Claws. You said you were just accompanying your brother and yet Alkaline's phone number is flashing before me. Why?"

Sisu held out the vibrating gadget. She took it from him.

Sisu raked his fingers through his hair and took a deep breath. His mind reeled. He sat on the edge of the bed and took one of May's hands in his.

"May, Alkaline and I have never gotten along. He does dirty business. The kind of practices I don't like. He deals with drugs, prostitutes, gambling rings. I don't. If you're involved with them, I need to know."

Chapter Eight

May stared at their entwined hands. Sisu's was large, tanned, warm, comforting. She could visualize herself holding it every day. Yielding to his strength, his confidence, his trust in this crazy thing about soulmates.

Every time she glanced his way, something inside her stirred. She wanted to get closer. She yearned for him. His touch. His scent. His proximity.

She hadn't told him, but after the mind-blowing orgasm he'd given her in the entrance to her home, the ache had faded. When he was at her side, it subsided, changed into something malleable, something which whispered in her ear and urged her for more, enticing her to believe. Only when she thought of asking him to leave, did it violently rekindle.

She looked Sisu in the eye. There was no anger or fear in his gaze, only patience and understanding.

Tell him.

Her instinct spoke loud and clear. She had nothing to lose.

"You're right, Sisu. I didn't tell you the truth. But can you blame me? I hardly know you. Even though we share this." She waved her arms in the air, struggling to find the appropriate words. "This connection. I know nothing about you and I grew up in a world where soulmates and insta-love doesn't exist. That's a myth left for romance novels."

"It exists for us, sunshine."

"Maybe, but I was brought up to believe soulmates was a term loosely used by men as a ruse to trick women into their beds."

May sighed. It was time to come clean.

"My father was a shifter."

Sisu's eyes widened. He licked his lips.

"Go on," he said.

"My parents had an off-and-on relationship for a year before my mother became pregnant. According to my mother, Killian, my father, didn't really believe I was his child and, though he stayed until I was seven, their relationship was rocky to say the least."

May swallowed the lump that formed in her throat every time she thought of her mother and father.

"When I was seven, my father left for good. I distinctly remember the day."

May wiped at her eyes.

"He sat me down and told me he'd met someone, his soulmate." She smiled through her tears. "He explained he wouldn't be living with us anymore, but he'd keep in touch."

"I never heard from him again."

"Bastard." Sisu growled. "Now I see your reluctance to believe in love."

"There is more. My mother never recovered from my father's abandonment. She slipped in and out of relationships. Every time one of them failed, she'd come to me. I spent all my life hearing stories about unworthy men who treated my mother like shit."

Sisu tensed.

"That wasn't everything. My mother didn't hide the fact that Killian had been a shifter. Occasionally, she'd throw comments at me."

"What do you mean?"

"Things like, thank goodness you're not one of them, I'm glad you aren't a freak. Those shifters are animals, dirty, dangerous beasts."

"Between your mother and father, I can now see why you're so averse to shifters," Sisu said. His eyes blazed and the nerve in his jaw ticked.

Her phone started ringing again.

Sisu snarled. He sucked in his cheeks. "But all this still doesn't explain—why were you hanging out with Alkaline?"

"Three years ago my mother became terminally ill. I cared for her until the end. The day before she died, she revealed she'd been lying to me all my life."

May laughed derisively. "It's taken me two years of ongoing therapy to get over that alone."

Sisu stroked her forearm, giving her the necessary courage to continue.

"She admitted to having tricked my father into having a child. He'd been truthful to her from the start, but she'd ignored his warnings and had hoped to tie him down. She didn't understand shifters would spend their lives searching for their one and only. Regardless of that, my father did love me. She confessed he had tried to keep in touch with me, see me, take me out, but she hadn't let him. She destroyed any letters he sent me and eventually moved us away. In her delusion, she thought he'd find us, but he never did."

"I'm sorry."

Sisu tucked a lock of her hair behind her ear. The feather-light touch made her shiver.

"This is where Alkaline and my step-brother come in. For months, I pondered on whether or not I should try to find my father. I only had his name and an old picture to go by. I did some research on the Internet, but the results were overwhelming."

"So what did you do?"

"I knew my brother had been gambling with shifters, so I contacted him to ask for his help. I figured shifters would know other shifters, and it'd be easier that way. He put me in touch with Alkaline. He said they'd help narrow down my search and find him. I was supposed to give them the information I had the night we met."

"Shit, I'm sorry, May. I fucked things up for you." Sisu's face fell. He passed a hand across his face.

"It's okay, Sisu. I guess it's why he's calling me.
"

"Is that why you were holding on to your purse all night? Because you had the picture and the information in there?" Sisu paused. "And money? I saw the bills when I grabbed your phone."

May nodded.

"Yes, a thousand grand. It was the agreed-on price. Alkaline wasn't going to help me out for free."

"Shit." Sisu pulled her into his lap. She wrapped her arms around his neck, surprised at how natural the gesture felt.

"Now everything makes sense." Sisu rubbed soothing circles across her back. "Including your pain."

"My pain?" she repeated.

Sisu's gaze didn't waver.

"May, I think you might have shifter genes."

May pulled back. "What? That's impossible. I'm human. I've never changed into anything else."

"Easy, sunshine. You might have never shifted because you didn't know you could, or maybe you only have some shifter traits. After all, your mom was human, but the ache you tell me about, that's what I felt when I first transformed. And even now, it's a constant presence within me. It's the beast in my soul, driving me onward. It has a voice of its own, which only I can understand and interpret. It's wild and wonderful at the same time."

Sisu cupped her cheek. "It's nothing to be afraid of."

May stared at the man in front of her. The thing within her swirled, squeezed her heart tightly, making itself known. What if he were right? What if she were a shifter? What would that imply to them? It'd explain her feelings, her sudden compulsion to be with this man. To hold him, kiss him, make love to him. Keep him as hers, forever. May swallowed.

Then, the phone rang.

Chapter Nine

May stared at the gadget vibrating atop her bed, Alkaline's name clearly flashing against the backdrop. She froze.

"Pick it up," Sisu coaxed.

"I'm scared."

"I'm here for you, but you need to hear whatever he has to say. He'll only keep calling if you don't."

May took in a deep breath. She knew Sisu was right. This was Alkaline's third or fourth missed call. She didn't quite understand why he was so desperate to speak to her, but she knew she couldn't postpone it any longer. She grabbed the machine and slid her index across the screen. Sisu's hand on her waist tightened, and she was glad for his solid strength beneath her.

"Hello," she said.

Alkaline spoke quickly, his tone harsh and businesslike. Disappointment wormed its way into her gut at his words. She thanked him for his help and hung up, biting her lip to keep the swell of tears away.

"What happened?" Sisu asked, running his fingers through her hair.

"Alkaline said the deal is off."

"Why?"

"He simply said that after the incident last night, he can't in good faith help me anymore or take my money."

"In good faith? The incident last night?" Sisu snarled. "What the hell is that supposed to mean?"

May shrugged. A tear crawled out of the corner of her eye.

"He wouldn't explain."

"Goddamn bastard," Sisu barked. "I'll rip him to

pieces."

May jumped, alarmed. "No, don't. It's probably best this way. It's better not to know."

Sisu tugged her back into his lap and cradled her cheek. "Don't cry, sunshine. I can help you, too."

"How?"

"Alkaline is no longer the only shifter, you know, and I've got my sources, too, love, but there's also a way for us to confirm if you're a shifter or not, right now."

"There is?"

"Yes, although, you might not like it." Sisu looked sheepish, increasing her curiosity.

"Tell me."

He cleared his voice. His piercing gaze found hers. Her breath hitched.

"I mark you."

May's brow furrowed. Her heart beat wildly against her rib cage.

"What does that mean exactly?"

"It's easy, love. We have wild sex and I give you a tiny bite on the shoulder, right about here." He brushed his fingertips slightly over her collarbone. She shivered.

"It'd be like a hickey," he said.

"Will it go away?"

"No, but it will fade into something akin to a sexy birthmark. Humans won't know what it is, and shifters will know you belong to me."

"Oh."

"If you're a shifter," Sisu continued, "something within you will change and you will bite me back, claiming me as yours. If you're human, nothing will happen."

"Nothing?" May winced at the whine in her voice. She didn't like the idea of Sisu not bearing her mark. "But how will other women know you're mine if nothing happens?"

Sisu's blue eyes twinkled and his grin grew devilish until he was beaming. May's cheeks burned.

"You don't need to look so pleased. It was just a question," she mumbled.

His deep rumbling laughter resounded within her, giving her a strange sense of homecoming.

"Sunshine, human or shifter or both, we belong together. You are my mate. I want no other woman, and don't sweat it, they'll be perfectly aware that all I want is you," Sisu said, lightly kissing her cheek.

May leaned into him. His hand curled around her back, holding her close.

"When we're together I'll only ever have eyes for you, May."

May shivered. The depth of his feelings showed through the blazing intensity in his gaze. This was more than lust. This connection ran deeper than blood. Sisu didn't need to speak for her to see it. It radiated from him.

"When we're apart, I'll only be thinking about you. Your taste," he continued, brushing his lips over hers. She gasped when he nipped her bottom bow, tugging. Pent-up arousal shot through her system.

"Your fragrance." Sisu buried his face in her hair. A low moan of approval came from him, ricocheting straight to her core.

He twisted and pushed her back against the mattress. Looming over her, he slid his palm down the side of her breast, over the curve of her waist and hips, and rested there. Her legs parted of their own volition and his lips curved into a sinful smile.

"When I'm not at your side, I'll be remembering the passion in your eyes and the heat between your legs."

He cupped her sex, one of his digits worming its way beneath the elastic of her underwear.

"The way your body responds to me and only to me," he rumbled, entering her with two fingers.

"Sisu," May whispered.

He took possession of her mouth, pressing his tongue and demanding for more like a persistent sledgehammer. May curled her hands over his biceps. Her mind swam with emotions and thoughts, but her body responded to Sisu like a fine-tuned instrument waiting to be played. They broke apart, gasping for air.

"Do you have any idea how hard you make me? How desperate?" he whispered in her ear. "You bring out the wolf in me, May. I've yearned to make you mine from the moment I saw you. All I need is your consent."

May gasped. Sisu's eyes had shifted. The blue in them deeper, wider, almost taking over the white. She turned her head to the side, aghast at the surge of emotions swirling within her.

You are his.

The words rang in her head, threading with the curling pain which had taken permanent residence in her chest.

"Deny it," Sisu dared. "Look me in the eye and tell me you don't want me."

May licked her lips. She gazed up at him. The nerve in his jaw ticked.

"I want you," she said.

Sisu grinned, and for the first time, she glimpsed his sharp canines. May swallowed. She expected the throbbing to increase, but instead, it changed again, rolling over her like a wave in the ocean on a hot summer's day. It had the sting of the salt, but the pleasure of the coolness.

"You are mine," Sisu declared.

Yes.

Chapter Ten

Sisu ripped May's t-shirt to shreds. Her cry of surprise echoed in the room, mingling with his heavy breathing and the rushing in his ears.

She wanted him. She'd finally said it aloud and he wouldn't give her a chance to change her mind. He'd claim her. Mark her. Show her how well they fit together, forever.

He tore her panties and she rewarded him with another gasp.

"Mine. My sunshine," he said.

His voice sounded deeper, huskier. His wolf lingered at the edge of his consciousness, eager to come out and play. To stake its claim. He couldn't allow it. Not yet, but soon.

Sisu nudged May's knees apart and stood between them. He took her in. Her pussy glistened with her juices, her lips red and puffy, beckoning to him. Her stomach rose and fell with each one of her breaths. Her breasts, the chocolate areolas and tight nipples, jiggled. Her bee-stung mouth parted and her eyes shone with lust and concern.

He wouldn't allow that last emotion to develop.

"Do you have any idea how hot you look? Naked, flushed, eagerly waiting for my touch. I'm so hard it's almost painful."

A whimper escaped her.

"And those noises, fucking hell, every single one of your tiny noises has me staining my jeans like a teenager."

"Please, Sisu."

He kneeled before her and pressed his face to her cunt, inhaling deeply. Her musky, feminine fragrance entered his system like a drug. He ran his tongue across her slit. She yelped and pulled his hair.

Sisu chuckled.

"Easy now."

Placing his hand on her lower abdomen to keep her from squirming, he licked her again from bottom to top. Her body bowed. He left open-mouthed kisses on her outer lips. Then, he lightly touched the hood of her clit before dipping his tongue into her weeping hole. May moaned and bucked. Her fists clenched and unclenched on his hair, urging him on. Sisu replaced his tongue with his fingers and moved to her clit. He pressed the flat of his tongue against it. May cried out. Pumping his digits in and out of her, he sucked her clit hard. She screamed her climax.

Leisurely, Sisu lapped at her juices until the tremors in her legs ceased. Sisu got to his feet.

"Now, it's my turn." He grunted.

Grabbing a condom from his back pocket, he rid himself of his pants. He kept his gaze on May. She leaned back on her elbows and watched him with undisguised hunger.

"You're desperate for this, aren't you?" He palmed his cock, spreading the pre-cum at the top. "You want it inside of you, pushing, and shoving, filling you to the brim."

"Yes," she said, hoarsely.

"You're going to get it, sunshine."

He ripped open the wrapper and rolled on the latex. Grasping May's legs, he pulled her to the edge of the bed, lifted her legs to his shoulders and sunk into her welcoming heat. May cried out, digging her nails into his biceps. Sisu held still. He shut his eyes. The wolf within him jumped within its confines, eagerly chanting for more.

Fast.

Now.

Claim her.

Sisu breathed slowly through his nose. A snarl escaped him. The wolf had never challenged his restraint as much as it had done since he'd met May.

"Fuck me, Sisu," May said.

She rolled her hips against him. Sisu reopened his eyes. May's brown orbs were changing. The flecks of gold he'd seen earlier were spreading, taking over the white. With a roar, he pulled back and slammed into her. A low and needy sound erupted from May. Grasping the back of his head, she pulled him down and kissed him deeply. He pumped into her, gaining speed with every thrust.

"Tell me you're mine," he said.

"Yes, yes," she panted.

"Look at me and tell me."

Their gazes locked. Her eyes glowed like liquid amber.

"I'm yours, Sisu" she stated.

Sisu howled victoriously and bit her shoulder. Her pussy clenched around him, wave after wave of her orgasm drawing him closer to his own release.

Pinpricks of pleasure traveled through every one of his nerve cells. His vision swam. The wolf ran wild in his chest, battling for freedom. The tangy smell of sex, sweat, and May's fruity fragrance filled his nostrils. The sound of her panting turned louder, mingling with his own harsh breaths. Sisu struggled to breathe.

Mine.

"You're mine too," May whispered in his ear.

Suddenly, May turned her head. Her teeth sunk

into him. Sisu threw back his head, gasping. He ejaculated, his seed spewing forth and filling the condom.

Sisu collapsed over May, breathing hard. He licked the mark on her shoulder, sealing it. A low, sensual moan came from her.

He pulled out, and set the used condom aside to discard later. Throwing himself on the bed at her side, he rolled her so she lay on top of him. May squealed and giggled. She rested her cheek on his breast, drawing lazy circles over his heart.

"I can hear something inside you," she said softly, "different to your heart beat."

"My wolf," Sisu said.

"Yes."

"Look at me," Sisu said.

She moved so her chin rested on his chest and she could gaze at him. The color of her eyes had returned to their normal hue, but the flecks of gold he'd seen earlier were brighter than before. He inhaled deeply. May still smelled differently. Not entirely human, but not like any shifter he'd known.

"You're wolf, too," he said. "You've claimed me. Your eyes shifted and your teeth did too. You bit hard."

A slow smile spread over her face. Her eyes twinkled.

"I guess I have." Her lips pursed. "But this hasn't answered any of my questions. I'm still not sure of what I am. I didn't shift completely. I don't know if I can. I—"

Sisu interrupted her by pulling her up and kissing her until they broke apart due to lack of air. She rested her forehead against his.

"We'll find out more, I promise, but I can tell you exactly what you are," he said.

She glanced down at him quizzically.

"You are my mate. My soulmate. You're my

sunshine."

The End

CHECKMATE

Wren Michaels

Copyright © 2017

Chapter One

Seven days. Seven days he'd stalked her like prey from the shadows. Moonlight soaked her flaxen hair as it beamed down through the glass-paneled roof. The soft red lighting of the bar shadowed her face, yet those bright blue eyes were like beacons in the dark. With painted-on jeans and a skin-tight t-shirt, she played the crowd for suckers at The Howler, hustling pool and drinking her way into every man's wet dreams.

Jordan recognized her scent the minute she crossed the threshold each night, rich and seductive human blood masked by an array of amber and musk. Yet, there was something unique about her that he couldn't quite put his finger on. Rather, he'd like to sink his teeth into. She had an allure he'd never encountered before, one that raked his skin with an itch he couldn't scratch, dried his throat to cotton at the sight of her, and launched his heart into an erratic dizzying beat.

She was a mystery, showing up out of nowhere, coming into his bar the last seven nights in a row. No one knew much about her, and her story was much the same to any who would ask—she was visiting family. The only information anyone had on her was the name the regulars called her by, Trix, for she refused to reveal her real name. She always paid in cash, on the few occasions she had to.

Jordan tipped back his bottle of beer, letting the cold liquid quench his throat.

"It's been a week, Jordan," Zeke said, sliding next to him in the dark corner booth.

"For being my intel man, you aren't giving me much to go on." Jordan stared his second-in-command down. As Alpha of Eden's Bayou, Jordan needed to know of any possible threat to his pack. And Zeke was damned good at his job, until now.

"She's like a ghost, man. I searched everywhere for the last week. No one in a hundred-mile radius has heard of her or even seen her around. She said she's here visiting family. She very well could be."

Jordan shook his head, though his stare never left her as she bent over the pool table for a shot. "Not likely, since she seems to spend more time visiting my bar than any family. And she's always alone."

"She ain't wolf, Jordan. I don't think she's even a shifter. Don't smell like one I've ever been around, anyway. Her scent is pretty human to me."

"There's something about her though." His lips curled to the left as he watched her shirt creep up her back each time she leaned in for another shot across the table. "Somethin' ain't right."

Jordan twisted in his seat, his jeans tightening around him as she caressed the pool stick like an intimate lover. She raised her head, pressing her cheek against the wood and locked onto his gaze. A fiery tingle struck his heart and sweat slicked his skin from head to toe. He raced to unbutton the flannel shirt now threatening to choke him as heat sweltered his flesh.

"Dude, you okay? You look like you've got a fever." Zeke raised a brow.

Jordan tugged open the top three buttons and tossed him a nod. "It's just hot in here. Humidity rising in the bayou."

Zeke folded his arms. "Dude, it's February and fifty degrees."

Jordan eyed the woman as she stretched the length of the table for a trick shot, swaying her hips in a rhythm that ensnared his attention like a moth to a flame. His tongue darted out, licking his lips in anticipation. Her cue stick connected with the balls, slapping them around the table and sinking her shot. It snapped his attention back from her hips that almost called out to him to grab her from behind and claim her.

"Jordan?" Zeke slammed a hand on the table. "Did you hear me?"

Jordan shook his head. "Sorry, what?" He cleared his throat and slammed back his beer in hopes it would douse the heat raging through him.

"I said, Bayou Vista is on the move. Since you had me on this wild goose chase about this chick, I had to rely on sources to keep tabs on the surrounding packs. We need to have a plan in place if they try to attack again." Zeke huffed. "You reckon she could be a spy for them?"

"Unlikely. If she knows exactly what we are, she would have taken off long ago. Roark doesn't normally send humans to do his dirty work." Jordan continued studying the mysterious girl as she claimed her victory shot at the bar, scamming another unsuspecting customer out of money and dignity.

"Something feels off, man. My skin's crawling, like there's an electricity in the air," Zeke said with a shake of his head.

Jordan felt it, too. Only he thought it came from the woman who'd consumed his thoughts for the last week. She drew him to her. When daylight came and she disappeared, his soul hollowed with an emptiness he'd never known. But at night, when she walked through that door, his body thrummed, as if coming alive again after a dead sleep.

He'd never experienced that feeling, that sensation. He'd often heard others talk about similar experiences, but that was with their mates. A desire drawing them to their soulmate, a hunger to claim them and become one.

Jordan had yet to find his mate, but it certainly wouldn't be with a human. Yet every moment they remained in the same room, his every thought was of her: shredding her clothing, burying himself in her, and making her his.

He refused to let any other members of the pack know her effect on him, hoping she'd eventually head back to wherever it was she came from. Because every moment she stayed, his concentration on the needs of his pack waned and focused on her.

"Let's put a couple extra guys on watch around the bar tonight and back at the homestead. Just in case," Jordan said, running a hand over his stubbled chin. It'd been days since he'd even shaved.

"I'm on it," Zeke said, pushing his way out from the booth.

Jordan inched his way around to the edge of the booth as well, but stopped as Trix darted from the bar directly in front of Zeke. Her bright-red fingertips inched their way up his chest as her lips curled into a coy smile. Jordan's heart seized as he watched her flirt.

Arching her fingertips around his heart, she dug the tips of her nails into his skin. Jordan stood helpless, unable to move. His feet refused to lift from the floor, as if he was frozen in place.

"Zeke," Jordan yelled out, panic hitting his gut as he realized it was no longer flirting but an outright attack.

Zeke's rigid body stood like a statue. The woman's eyes darkened to shined onyx. Her lips chanted some language Jordan couldn't understand, and a gust of wind blasted the doors off their hinges. Windows shattered around them, blowing through the room in a rainstorm of glass.

Something pulled Jordan's body, dislodging him from the floor without his control. He flew backward, as though someone had punched him in the gut. Bodies all around him shot through the air, like a vortex sucked them from the bar.

Jordan's back crashed into a tree outside the bar and the air whooshed out of his lungs upon impact. His limp arms and legs collapsed beneath him and his face kissed the dirt. Fangs protruding, he heaved himself up from the ground and leaped into the air toward the bar, only to bounce off an invisible wall.

"Zeke," Jordan yelled out from the doorway. Some kind of ward prevented him from getting back into his own damned bar. "Zeke!"

But he didn't answer. Zeke's body swayed like a pendulum, caught in the woman's hypnotic trance. Fuck, he should have followed his gut instinct days ago, instead he fell prey to his dick and salivated over the bitch. Probably all part of her plan. She must be a witch. She had him under some spell, just like Zeke now. That would certainly explain his sudden lust at the very sight of her. All part of a detailed game of distraction she'd been laying for days.

"You bitch! Let me the fuck in there and I might just let you live." Jordan slammed his palms against the door frame. But the force of the wards blew him back once more, and his spine cracked as it broke the tree.

A howl gurgled in his throat as he fought for breath. Searing pain leached up his back as the bones fused themselves back together. As the last vertebrae snapped in place, he leaped from the ground and made toward the bar again. Thanks to the ancient blood in his veins, he healed quicker than any of the others.

But something in the air stopped him cold. That scent.

Wolves. Bayou Vista wolves.

Fuck.

"Let me in. You have no idea what kind of danger you're in!" Jordan cried out. "For fuck's sake, Zeke, wake the hell up!"

Panic rode the waves of nausea tumbling in Jordan's stomach. Fear for his brother and fear for his pack.

Several sets of yellow eyes surrounded the perimeter of the bar, peeking out from between the trees. The rival pack outnumbered them, but Jordan refused to give up his pack to a bunch of thugs and lowlifes. His pack was his family, the last of a generation of pure-bloods, the ancients. And the Bayou Vista pack wanted to infuse them with their hybrid-tainted blood—part vampire, part wolf, part fae. They didn't like the power the ancients held over them, having the strongest bloodline.

Jordan could easily dispose of three of them on his own. But as the number of eyes increased in the darkness, so did his odds of losing. He needed his brother. He needed the rest of his pack, who were currently back at the homestead five miles away. The only other wolf working tonight had been Benny, the bartender.

Jordan closed his eyes and channeled his Alpha side, burrowing into Benny's psyche. *Benny, you need to run back to the homestead and get help. Roark and the Vista pack are here. Run!*

Benny darted into the darkness, shredding his clothes as he leaped into the air mid-change.

If Jordan could just get inside and wake Zeke the fuck up, they could at least hold them off until reinforcements arrived.

The yellow eyes disappeared from the trees, replaced by a dozen men walking from the edge of the forest perimeter toward the bar.

"Listen to me, Trix," Jordan pleaded. "You have no idea what you're about to be up against. There's a pack of asshole wolves headed your way. Let my brother go and we can help you."

The woman glanced over her shoulder at him, then to the figures walking toward the bar as the moonlight uncovered them.

"They can't get past my wards. I have unfinished business with your brother," Trix said, and she turned her attention back on Zeke.

"Dammit, Trix. You're about to get killed, and so is Zeke. Fucking use your head, woman!" Jordan slammed a hand against the door frame, sending him sailing back through the air. Fuck, he was going to make her pay for that.

"What's the matter, Jordan? Can't get a drink in your own bar?" Roark laughed as he leaned against the opposite blown-out door. "Pity, she's a pretty li'l thing."

"Get the hell out of here, Roark. You have no business here."

"I have plenty of business. We're all about done being held under the thumb of the Eden's Bayou pack. Vista's time is here and now. You so-called pure-bloods think you're so high and mighty. But you're just a bunch of sanctimonious assholes trying to rule over the rest of us. So fuck you, your pack, your bitch here, and your brother. It's all ours now." Roark ran a hand under his nose and smirked as he wiggled his fingers through the doorway. The wards had no effect on him.

Jordan's eyes widened. "Zeke, fucking wake up."

Trix dropped her hand from Zeke's chest. Blood stained a circle around his heart where her fingertips had been. She turned in a circle, staring at the men entering the bar from all ends.

"Yeah, I guess you didn't think about other wolves showing up to your little party, did you? If you want to live, Trix, let me the fuck in here. I promise you'll survive. Just fucking drop the wards. Now!" Jordan clenched his hands into fists, snarling through his teeth.

"Fine," Trix said, waving her hand as she dropped the magical wards blocking him entrance. "I have your word I am to stay alive?"

"Absolutely," Jordan said, crouching, ready to strike.

As the wards dropped, he leaped into the air. One arm swatted the bitch away from his brother and she flew backward over the bar and dropped to the floor.

He never said she wouldn't leave unscathed.

Chapter Two

Nyah's eyes fluttered open and she attempted to wake up. Darkness shrouded her, except for the moonlight streaming in from the window behind her. She rolled over and a wave of pain crashed her head, forcing a moan from her throat.

"What happened?" she choked out as her fingertips caressed a lump at the back of her head.

A low growl hummed through the air in response. Her heart raced at the sound and she shot up from the bed. Before she could grasp her surroundings, a hand clutched her throat and slammed her against a wall.

Arms and legs flailing, she dangled in the air, gasping for breath.

"Who the hell are you?" a gruff voice said. If she hadn't been fighting to get air into her lungs, that voice would have melted her insides to a puddle. Sexy and animalistic, it still sent a wave of heat through her.

She clasped her hands to his and tried to pry his fingers from her throat. Fine, if he wanted to play that way, she would, too. Pressing her hand to his chest, she mumbled an incantation and her hand blazed with fire.

The man dropped her from his grasp. "What the ever-loving fuck?" He stripped out of his shirt and threw it to the floor, stomping out the flames engulfing it.

"Don't choke me, and I won't have to do that again." Nyah rubbed her neck, attempting to swallow back her fear mixed with excitement.

The stranger stepped back and moonlight shimmered against his light-brown skin. Muscles flinched as he curled his hands to fists. For a wolf, the man was as smooth as porcelain. Not a hair on his head or his chest, save the dark stubble that dotted his stark jawline clenched as tight as his hands.

She'd watched him for a week, studied him. Though the coven told her the target was his brother, Zeke, the one they called Jordan had stolen her focus, and it cost her. Damn him. Something about him intrigued her. Maybe it was his quiet, broody nature sitting in that back booth every night just taking in the surroundings. Maybe it was how his gaze stalked her from across the room, undressing her within the depths of his dark-brown eyes. Maybe it was his protectiveness over his pack, because when he wasn't watching her, he was watching everything else going on in that bar, from the patrons to the workers, the ones who'd nicknamed her Trix.

She fell prey to whatever charms he used on her, and she kicked her own ass for it. Nyah should have been back to her sister's coven by now with the heart of her killer still pumping in her hands. Instead, she stood eye to eye with a wolf.

"You tried to kill my brother. While I said I would let you live, I didn't say you wouldn't be punished for it." Jordan closed the space between them, releasing that low growl again from his chest.

"What happened after you knocked me out?" Nyah folded her arms, holding her ground. The wolf didn't scare her. She'd been up against their kind before.

Jordan backed her against the wall and slammed his hands above her head. Blood trickled the length of three claw marks on his upper arm. Nyah fought the instinct to touch them, heal them, remembering her enemy towered over her. Heavy, weighted breaths huffed from his mouth against her ear, sending a ripple of exhilaration to her core. As much as she didn't want it to, it turned her on. His nearness, his growls, his ferocity with her.

"I won, if that's what you're asking." He leaned

in and sniffed along her neck before pulling back. "Who are you, Trix? Obviously, you're a witch. But what I can't figure out is, which coven has a beef with my pack? We haven't had any trouble with witches in centuries."

"The name's Nyah. They only call me Trix because the bastards in your bar don't know how to play pool."

He gripped the hair at the back of her head and yanked her face toward him. "I don't care about your pool hustling, I care about why you tried to rip Zeke's heart out. Now tell me, before I rip yours out with my teeth."

He wouldn't hurt her, of that Nyah was sure. The evidence of that pressed against her belly. He was just as turned on as she was, and she'd use that to her advantage. She'd get close to him to get close to Zeke and then avenge her sister's death. Maybe she'd kill both of them, send a message to the wolves that when they kill a witch, they should know who they're dealing with. They may have taken her sister, but Nyah was the stronger of the twins. Even more now since Norah's death fused their powers back together in her veins.

She didn't care about the coven her sister joined years ago when she ran away from their abusive father. She did care about losing her only remaining family. Nyah was now the last of the Winston Witches, descendants from Salem. Norah would never know what Nyah had done for her, killing their dad, making him confess with his last breath that he had indeed killed their mother. And she would have made damn sure he wouldn't do it to her sister.

But instead, Norah lost her life at the hands of a wolf. This Zeke person. All the evidence given to her from the coven pointed to it. And she had lain in wait for him to show up at the bar to exact her revenge.

"Does it matter? If you're going to kill me, just get it over with." Nyah pressed into him, allowing her belly to twist and rub against the bulge threatening to rip open his jeans.

Another low growl emanated from his throat. "Obviously you're not working for Roark since he tried to kill you tonight. So who wants my brother dead?"

Nyah dragged a nail along the edge of his jeans, scraping the skin. "I do."

Jordan gripped her wrist, and in a move so fast it blurred her vision, he slammed her back into the wall, pressing his other hand against her cheek, forcing the side of her face to scrape the rough finish. "Do not toy with me, bitch. You have no idea who you're dealing with."

"Nor do you," she choked out, punctuating it with a laugh.

She closed her eyes, and as another incantation left her lips, her body disappeared from his grip. He slammed into the wall before spinning around in a fury. Nyah reappeared on the other side of the room, a smirk twitching on her lips.

Before her body took on full form, Jordan crossed the room in a blur and tossed her onto the bed with such force the air whooshed from her lungs as she hit the mattress. He launched himself on top of her, pinning her with his hands and legs.

"This is your last chance, Nyah, or I swear my teeth will rip a hole in your throat and I'll leave you to bleed out." Jordan panted above her. "Why do you want my brother dead?"

Nyah tried to suck in a breath, but the weight of Jordan above her crushed her lungs to the point she couldn't even move. "He … killed … Norah."

Jordan tilted his head and jerked back. "Who the fuck is Norah?"

Nyah coughed as he eased his chest from hers, allowing air to return to her lungs. "My twin sister."

Jordan shook his head and pushed himself off her, though still pinning her with his hips as he sat above her. "Impossible."

"The fuck it is. I know who killed my sister. And I *will* have his heart for it and return it to the coven so another wolf can never again terrorize a witch." Nyah spat at him.

Jordan's lips pulled into a seductive grin that Nyah wanted to punch off his face. Asshole.

"Wouldn't you think he'd recognize you then, if you were a twin?" Jordan crossed his arms. "He had no idea who you were. I even sent him on recon to find out. If he already knew you or your sister, he would have told me." Jordan leaned back down, clasping his fingers around her throat. "So let's try the truth this time."

The heat of his touch ignited her body, and it pissed her off. How could she even be turned on by this smug asshole? "That *is* the truth, you arrogant bastard."

Nyah gripped his fingers closing in on her windpipe, preventing her from getting out another incantation. She kicked her leg up and kneed him in the balls, and he toppled off the bed. Nyah rolled to her knees and Jordan slung an arm around her waist while clasping his hand around her mouth.

"Zeke," Jordan yelled over his shoulder.

Zeke whipped open the door, slamming it into the wall, almost off its hinges.

"She says you killed her sister," Jordan said. "What was her name again, darlin'?"

"Norah," Nyah mumbled against his fingers before she bit down on his hand. "Norah Winston, you asshole."

Jordan clenched his jaw through the pain, and his

left eye twitched as Nyah looked up at him, still in his hold. "Do you know a Norah Winston?"

Zeke shook his head. "Never heard of her."

"She's supposedly Trix's twin. I said highly unlikely that you killed her then, because you should have recognized Trix , too." Jordan leaned in and pressed his lips to Nyah's ear. "So tell us how you came to the conclusion my brother killed your sister. You've got one chance, or I let Zeke here avenge his almost death. Speak fast."

Jordan released his grip and thrust Nyah onto the bed. She glanced at his still-hard cock pressing against his tight jeans. He got his kicks from this shit. Probably lived for rough sex and beating women, just like her father. The fucker.

"I told you, my name isn't Trix. It's Nyah." She sprung up from the bed and launched a fist into his chin, knocking him backward to the floor. Nyah darted across the room to Zeke, her last chance to take him out. Go big or go home.

She slammed her hand against his chest, digging her nails into his flesh. Zeke gasped, as his arms that almost pushed her back fell limp to his sides. But something gripped her from behind and flung her to the ground.

Zeke dropped next to her, blood trickling from his chest. "I … didn't … kill … her."

Nyah's heart seized at the dying man's words. He sucked in another gasp, blood gurgling to his lips.

Jordan dropped to his brother's side and gripped his face in his hands. "Don't you leave me, Zeke. Fight it."

"You swear you didn't kill my sister?" Nyah rolled over and looked into the dying man's eyes. The eyes never lied.

Zeke nodded and coughed up a river of blood.

Nyah held her hands over his chest and whispered a spell as a bright white light glowed under her fingertips. The same fingertips that could bring death, also brought life. Her blessing and her curse.

Zeke sucked in a gasp of air before coughing it back out, rolling to his knees. "Crazy-ass bitch."

"You're fucking welcome, asshole." Ungrateful dick, like the rest of them.

"Oh, I'm the asshole? You're the one who fucking tried to kill me. Twice!" Zeke rubbed his chest and glared at her.

Minor details. *If this Zeke guy didn't kill Norah, who the hell did?*

"Looks to me like you owe my brother an apology," Jordan said, sitting on the floor with one arm draped over his raised knee. A sexy smirk twitched on his lips.

She ached to kiss it off his mouth and knee him in the balls again at the same time. He infuriated her, yet she ached to have his body press against hers again.

Don't fall for it, Nyah. You have no time to lose. You have to find Norah's killer.

"I saved his life. That should take care of it," Norah said, pushing herself to her feet.

Nyah brushed past Jordan, slamming into his shoulder. His hand gripped her by the elbow and spun her around, thrusting her back onto the bed.

"What the fuck? We're done here. You can let me go." Anger thrummed in her veins, just shy of the excitement welling beneath it.

Jordan nodded his head toward his brother. "Zeke, go have a rest. I'll catch up with you later."

"Thanks, bro." Zeke turned and gave Nyah the finger as he closed the door behind him.

"As for you," Jordan said, crossing his arms as he made his way to the bed. "I'm not through with you yet."

"What do you want with me?" Nyah inched her way up the pillows, ready to strike back at him.

"I haven't figured that out just yet." He ran a hand along his face, rubbing his chin. "But until then, we need to figure out who actually killed your sister."

Nyah swallowed hard. For the first time since she arrived in Eden's Bayou, it hit her. Norah was truly gone. Dead. All she had to survive on was her anger. Her determination to find her killer and make him suffer. Now, she had nothing. All her clues had led her to a dead end. The emotions balled up in her throat and wedged themselves there. She forced back a pool of tears welling in her eyes.

No tears. Don't let him see you cry.

"Why? What's in it for you?" Nyah choked out.

Jordan paused, staring at her with dark eyes. "Because someone obviously fed you false information. They wanted you to kill my brother. Which means we both need to get to the bottom of it. And, I'm sure you want closure for your sister. You healed my brother. I'll help you find your sister's killer."

She didn't need his help. Didn't want it. The longer she stayed in his presence, the more he seduced her with his eyes and his large, protective body. He could have ripped her to shreds a number of times tonight, but he hadn't. He fought with her. Fought for the truth and let her live. She almost needlessly killed a man tonight in blind rage with only hearsay to go on. It struck her heart she could have had a hell of a lot more blood on her hands tonight if it weren't for him. Yet he sat there and offered to help her.

Nyah was in over her head.

Chapter Three

Jordan's heart raced as he stared into Nyah's glassy eyes. She could have easily torched him again, or performed some kind of freakish spell. But she sat there, vulnerable. She needed help.

The intensity in her eyes told him he was going to be in trouble. His heart quivered, melting at her pain.

Fuck, what was wrong with him? He wasn't some fucking sap.

Just moments ago they wrestled and fought, yet the entire time all he could think about was ripping her clothes to shreds and claiming her body for his own. The way her long blonde hair fell through his fingers like silk ribbons. He ached to grab her again, this time in the throes of passion while he drove himself into her.

His gaze raked her body, falling on two pebbled nipples stretching against her shirt. It took everything in him not to palm them and free them from their covering. The fire in her blue eyes now glassed over like ice.

She was obviously in pain at the loss of her sister. And something told him it was probably the first time she'd let herself grieve. But she was a strong, very powerful witch, and Jordan had to watch himself. She could have taken him down. But she hadn't. Jordan could have killed her as well, many times over tonight. But he hadn't.

Why?

He ran a hand down his face, trying to wipe away the thoughts filling his head. "You should rest. Tomorrow we'll work on finding out who's behind all this."

"How can I trust you? What if you try and kill me?" Nyah stared him down.

Jordan arched a brow. "Oh, like you tried to kill

me and my brother tonight?"

She pointed a finger that brushed the tip of his nose. "Hey, I never tried to kill *you!*"

"Oh right, like starting my shirt on fire was just some ploy to get me to strip for you?" Jordan crossed his arms with a smirk.

Nyah's lips curled to a pout. "Maybe."

Jordan's dick twitched at the sight of her plump lips in that adorable pout. He'd love to slide himself right between them.

Shit, he had to stop thinking of her that way. Just as he talked himself down, her heartbeat sped in his ears and he zeroed in on her chest. Her fast pulse hummed like an electric current in the air.

Maybe she was feeling it, too. That undeniable draw. An insatiable lust his brain couldn't shut off. His own heart sped at the thought, and he forced down a growl making its way up from his depths at the thought of pushing her back on the bed and fucking her until his name left her lips in a primal cry.

Nyah nodded and rolled over, inching her way to the edge of the bed.

"Where are you going?" Jordan clutched her by the elbow.

Nyah glanced over her shoulder to his hand, and then to his face. "Back to my motel room?"

"No, you're not. You're staying here. Where I can keep an eye on you."

"You gonna cuff me to your bed, handsome?" Her tongue darted over her lips.

"I'll do you one better." Jordan winked and reached for the drawer in the bedside table. He pulled out the syringe, bit off the cap, and stuck it in her arm. "Sleep tight, darlin'."

"What?" Nyah gasped and glanced down at her

arm. "You're fucking … drugging … me?"

A limp arm hung over the bed as she collapsed onto the pillows.

"Sweet dreams."

He always had tranquilizers handy, should one of the young wolves get unruly during their first couple of full moon cycles until they learned to shift of their own accord. He never thought he'd need to use it on a human. But, this one was a witch, and he couldn't let her run off in the middle of the night and attempt to kill them again.

Though, in his heart, he knew she wouldn't do it. She had plenty of chances tonight. He saw her strength, her abilities, but he also saw her weakness. She wasn't a killer. A killer didn't hesitate. Someone who'd never taken a life had that moment of regret, that moment of guilt and remorse before ever even laying a hand.

Drugging her was more for her own safety than his or Zeke's. If the rest of the pack knew there was a witch on the homestead, he didn't have time or energy to explain the situation.

Jordan stared at the beauty sleeping soundly on his bed. Closing his eyes, he inhaled her scent mixed with amber and musk. He forced himself off the bed and released the deep breath. Nothing had ever smelled so good to him in his life. This desire welling up in him, almost an ache for this creature he hardly knew, had him bewildered.

He needed air.

He rushed out of the room and ran into Zeke in the common area of the large three-story estate.

"Awful quiet in there. Did you fuck her or drug her?" Zeke asked.

"Really?" Jordan shook his head and rolled his eyes.

"Well, the noises that came from the room earlier

sounded a helluva lot like foreplay. Just sayin'." Zeke smirked. "Not to mention you haven't been able to stop talking about her or take your eyes off her since she got here."

Jordan fanned his arm toward his bedroom. "That insane woman tried to kill you about ten minutes ago, or did you already block that from your memory?"

"Wasn't the first time someone tried to kill me today. And, she was fighting to avenge her sister. I get it. If someone killed you, I'd do the same. Only I wouldn't hesitate." Zeke shrugged.

"You caught that, too?"

"If she had really wanted us dead, we wouldn't be standing here. She's a witch, a damn powerful one. She said Winston. The same witches who ran our ancestors out of the colonies and into the south."

Jordan sighed and nodded, collapsing into a recliner. "I know. I know."

"What's wrong?" Zeke quirked a brow.

"I wish I knew. There's just something about her, I can't fucking explain it. I can't stop thinking about her. I go near her and everything inside me feels like an all-consuming fire raging through my blood. Her scent, it's like a drug and it takes all my power not to throw her against the damn wall and fuck her until I can't see straight." Jordan glanced at his hands. The ones that were around her throat, holding her down on the bed. The ones that tingled as they connected with her skin. "I think she put a fucking spell on me."

"Or, she could be your mate," Zeke said, a smirk twitching at the corners of his mouth.

Jordan shook his head. "You're fucking high. There's no way she's my mate. She's human. And a witch! No. Not in our bloodline. We've never mated outside of a wolf. Another pack, maybe. But not with a human. It can't be so. She's got me under some spell. I swear it to you. The moment she got here, I knew something was up."

"If she had you under a spell to throw you off, then how come you still feel this way when she's knocked out of her gourd right now in the other room?" Zeke pointed to the other room. "What you just described was exactly how it was for me with Gina. I think you've found your mate."

A tremor ripped through Jordan's heart. That couldn't be true. He refused to believe it. Why? Why her?

"No. I'm the fucking Alpha of this pack, a pure bloodline wolf pack. Why would the powers that be mate me to a witch?" Jordan laughed at the words coming out of his mouth.

The idea was complete insanity. He would have to claim her, bite her, turn her, and make her part of the pack. She would never do it, nor would the pack ever accept her.

"I have no idea. But you can't change the fact if it's true. If you ignore it, should you even have the willpower to, you'll never again find your mate. You have one shot at it. And you absolutely know when it hits you."

"I *don't* know. It can't possibly be her. I wouldn't be this confused, right?" Jordan fought the panic in his heart.

The more he thought about it, the more the idea took residence in his mind. It would explain everything, his feelings, his lust, his carnal desire to claim her. He'd been attracted to humans before, even had sex with them. But he'd never experienced this need, this ache that overwhelmed his entire being the moment he even thought about her, let alone stood in the same room with her.

"You're confused because you're trying to fight it."

Jordan looked at his younger brother, wise beyond his twenty-six years. "She would never be accepted by the pack. I ... I couldn't bring her in to the homestead. A place she would be shunned. I would never be taken seriously as Alpha again. This just can't be, Zeke. It can't."

"You're Alpha. What you say, goes. They don't have a choice."

Jordan snorted. "Easy for you to say, you're mated to Gina. Fucking gorgeous, smart, a wolf, and the best tracker we have in Eden's Bayou."

"They don't have to like it, but they have to accept it."

"She fucking tried to kill you!" Jordan shot out of his chair and paced the room.

Zeke folded his arms, leaning against the hallway door frame. "She also healed me. She didn't have to. If I can get over that fact, maybe you should try."

"I can't destroy our bloodline. Maybe this is a test. Maybe I'm not meant to have a mate, to keep us ancients, we have to suffer. I don't know." Jordan ran a hand over his smooth, bald head. "I do this and we're no better than the Bayou Vista pack."

"Maybe it's time to stop thinking we're better. And start evolving." Zeke shrugged. "She's the last of her kind. We're the last of ours."

Jordan's shoulders slumped, and he glanced at the bedroom door.

"You want her, yes?" Zeke asked.

"More than anything I've ever wanted in my life." The words flew off his tongue before he could stop them. He realized what his brother had done. Fuck.

"You have your answer. She's your mate." Zeke

pushed off the wall and headed toward the kitchen.

Jordan forced down a snarl climbing the back of his throat. "I will not yield to it."

"Bro, you're not gonna have a choice." Zeke disappeared down the hallway.

Jordan marched to the bedroom, kicked the door open, and lunged at the bed where the woman … his possible mate still slept. He gripped the wrought-iron headboard and hovered over her before lowering his face to the nape of her neck, inhaling a long, slow breath, taking in her scent.

Tremors rocketed through his hands and arms as his heart raced in his chest, thumping loud and hard against his ribcage. Moonlight lit the side of her pale face like a sleeping angel, her golden hair like a halo. To say she was stunning would be a falsehood, for there were no words he could think of to describe her beauty. He'd never laid eyes on such a creature as her.

Maybe there was indeed a reason he was to be mated to her. She was the last of a powerful line of witches. He, the last of the ancient pure-bred wolves. Their new bloodline would be invincible. Maybe Zeke was right.

He swallowed hard as he inhaled her scent once more. But he wouldn't take her while she slept. He wanted to look into her eyes as he claimed her, hear her shout his name as he thrust into her, giving her pleasure unknown.

Tomorrow, he would claim his mate.

Chapter Four

Nyah blinked herself out of her sleep. The pink and orange skyline out the window signaled dawn was upon her.

Dawn! What the hell happened?

She shot out of bed and glanced around. The fog cleared her head and she thought back to last night, when that asshole wolf tranq'd her.

A loud snore from the corner of the room startled her, and she whipped around. Jordan lay passed out in a corner chair in the room, arms draped at his sides and head slung back.

She inched her way over to him. His tight gray t-shirt lifted a couple inches with each deep inhale of breath, revealing that ridged torso she caught a glimpse of last night after she set his shirt on fire. Veins bulged in his arms as he twitched and flinched in his sleep, as if running in his dreams. *Figured, just like a dog.*

Yet she couldn't fight back the urge to run her tongue over every inch of his mocha-colored skin. He was decadent, like a dessert ... an indulgence she wanted to dive into. Their heated exchange last night left her body aching, and not just from the fight, but from longing for his touch. For his hands to rake her body in passion instead of anger and frustration.

She had to get away. Nyah didn't understand these impulses, these feelings welling up in her for a damned dog. She was a witch. She would never let herself get seduced by a wolf.

Yet, his offer to help her find her sister's killer came out of left field. True that he was curious, only because he said it had to do with finding out who would want his brother killed. But the look in his eyes said far more. That underneath that asshole persona might just be a good person. There was concern there, the same concern that fixated in his eyes when he spoke of his brother.

Did that mean there were feelings between her and Jordan? They hadn't even spoken to each other until last night. But they did share a week's worth of wordless conversations … glances, glares, stares, shredding of clothing with a gaze. Those said more than anything.

She'd caused enough damage here. She had to get away and find her sister's real killer. Nothing good would come of staying here. Nyah would only lose her focus.

She tip-toed to the door and creaked it open, checking the layout for an escape route. But a hand came from behind her over her head and slammed the door shut. Her heart leaped to her throat.

"Going somewhere, Nyah?" Jordan whispered into her ear, launching a shudder down her spine.

"You planning on holding me hostage?" She closed her eyes and sucked in a deep breath full of his orgasm-inducing cologne and a manly scent that warmed her belly.

"I thought we were going to work together." His warm breath tickled the back of her neck.

She spun around to face him, her lips inches from his. "Was that before or after you drugged me?"

"Just like I knew you would, you tried to escape. You see why I did it?" Jordan tilted his head until his lips hovered over hers, spiking a flood of excitement through her veins.

Her hands shook at her sides and she forced them to remain there, struggling against the overwhelming urge to grab his face and kiss that smug smile right off his mouth.

"Let me go, Jordan. We're done here." She forced

the words she knew she had to say, yet didn't feel.

He shook his head. "We're far from done, darlin'."

She closed her eyes and launched a punch into his rock-hard abs. That was going to hurt later. He hunched over and squinted his eyes, and Nyah took the chance and ran for the window. But his hands gripped her by the waist and swung her around until her back hit the wall, knocking the breath from her lungs in a whoosh.

He slammed her hands above her head and pinned her with his hips. His stiff cock pressed against her abdomen, telling her he was just as turned on as she was. Her insides melted like hot lava as he ground against her, pressing his hands against hers, gripping them tight as if trying to hold on.

"What do you want from me, Jordan?" The words barely made it off her tongue in a whisper before he crushed his mouth to hers.

A low growl rumbled in his chest as he slanted his lips and swept his tongue over hers, making love to her mouth. Nothing had tasted so good to her in her life. Warm and hot, his mouth melded with hers, making her forget who she was, who he was. The only thing that mattered were his kisses, and she didn't want them to end.

A moan bubbled up from her throat and woke her from her temporary state of insanity. What the fuck was she doing? She pulled back and yanked her hand free of his grip and slapped him across the cheek.

"What the fuck was that?" He jerked back.

Nyah narrowed her eyes. She couldn't give in. She had to hold her ground. "I could ask you the same thing."

His large hand gripped her by the waist as his other hand gripped the back of her head by the hair and yanked her neck taut. "I thought you were enjoying the kiss. Do I need to convince you again?"

His soft, warm tongue ran the length of her neck up to her ear. Heat pooled between her legs and her knees buckled. The hand that gripped her waist, slid around to her back and he yanked her tight to his body, catching her fall.

"I know you want this as much as I do, Nyah. I can hear your heart beat faster each time I touch you. I tasted your rising pulse with my kiss. I can smell your arousal, so sweet and delicious it makes me want to come just holding you, knowing I'm making you wet. You can't fool me. I'm a wolf."

"Doesn't matter. We can't do this. We shouldn't do this." A whimper laced her words. But everything inside her told her to grab him and never let go. Her body physically ached for him, only relieved by his touch, his kiss. She'd never felt more whole than when his lips were on hers.

He pressed his lips to her ear and the heat of his breath forced her eyes shut, welling goosebumps on her flesh. "Release yourself to me, Nyah. Give in. Let me feast upon your body and I will bring you pleasure like you've never known. I will worship it with my lips and tongue."

He kissed his way down her neck to her chin and stared into her eyes. Nyah swallowed hard over the ball of emotions in her throat. He didn't just look at her. He stared into her soul.

"You're my mate, Nyah. You know it. I know it. You felt it in my kiss. I know you did, because we're connected. We're missing pieces of a puzzle. I felt it the first time you walked into the bar. Everyone else disappeared and there was only you. I thought maybe you'd put a spell on me, but your pulse"—he paused and pressed his tongue against her neck, closing his lips down around it to massage the flesh before pulling back—"tells me you feel it."

Words left her and she only responded in a moan.

He traced a finger along her jeans, unbuttoning them with one hand before slipping his hand into her panties. "Your scent is like a drug for me. The wetter you get, the hotter I burn for you."

Two fingers slid between her lower lips and slipped in her arousal, ripping a gasp from her chest. The sensation darting through her body set her on fire, and only he could quench it.

He pressed his lips to hers, vibrating as he uttered his command. "You're mine. And I will claim you."
****

Jordan's heart thundered to the point it made him dizzy. His fingers danced inside her, so warm and wet for him. He knew she wanted it. Zeke had been right. She was his mate. Her scent drove him to the brink of insanity, and if he didn't get his cock inside her soon, he'd rip through his jeans.

She rocked her hips against his hand and the most beautiful moan whisked across her lips. He had her. She would be his.

He pulled his hand from her panties, gripped her by the shoulders, and pinned her back against the wall. "Tell me you want it."

Her eyes widened in surprise. "Yes," she whispered.

With lightning-fast speed, he yanked her jeans to her ankles and palmed her mound before slipping his fingers between her lower lips once more. An aching moan burst from her lips as he massaged her swollen clit until her knees buckled and her orgasm ravished her body.

He threw her over his shoulder and tossed her to the bed, ripping off his shirt and barely getting his jeans off before he lunged at her. Jordan all but shred the rest of her clothing, slinging it across the room.

Two glorious teardrop breasts stared up at him, topped with perfect hardened nipples. He ran a finger along them before diving at one and sucking it into his mouth. A warm hand wrapped around his cock, and the shock made him drop the breast from his lips and let out a moan.

He stared down at her … his woman. His mate. It suddenly didn't matter, human, witch, or wolf. What mattered was being inside her, becoming one with her, sealing their connection. Something brought them together. The universe wanted their worlds to collide.

He pressed himself at her entrance and slammed his hands down on either side of her head, gripping tight to her hair. With one long thrust, he entered her, and she bucked beneath him, letting out a moan as he filled her channel. Her thick arousal glided him in and out of her in a rhythmic dance as he stared into her eyes.

Fire burned hot in his veins, shooting flames through his body as he worked himself harder, faster, deeper inside her. He dove at her neck and sunk his teeth into her flesh. Sharp nails dug into his back as she held on, releasing his name on a scream as he came inside her.

He threw his head back and a loud growl bellowed from deep inside him. He'd never had a release so hard, so wrought with desire and passion that it exhausted him and he collapsed on top of her.

She traced her nails along his back, cradling him in her arms. Peace settled in his soul like he'd never known, a wholeness. He believed it now, that one knew when he'd found his mate. Her scent filled his nostrils and it calmed him, the scent of their sex mixed with arousal and her body. It was like home.

He nuzzled himself into her neck and kissed along her skin.

A giggle slipped from her lips and she ran a finger along her neck where his lips had been, then jerked back. "Did you … did you actually bite me?" Her eyes grew wide.

"It's part of the mating process. I couldn't help it. My wolf took over and just followed instinct. When we find our mates, we bite them and make them ours. That's how it works."

"Oh, hell no. It's bad enough I had sex with a dog, tell me … tell me I'm not about to become one." She pushed him off her and wiggled her way to the edge of the bed.

Jordan hitched a shoulder. What the hell happened? Just moments ago they were riding waves of bliss. "Hey, I told you, you were my mate. We don't have a say in it. Nature takes its course."

She jumped off the bed and gathered up her clothes. "The fuck it does. Not when you turn me into a fucking wolf without telling me!"

"We're going to be the most powerful bloodline now. You, the last Salem witch. Me, the last Alpha of the ancient pure-blood wolves."

The anger in her eyes blazed, darkening them from their normal rich blue to almost black. "That's what this was about? Mixing bloodlines? Forming a power bond? The fuck? I thought you were being metaphorical with all that mate shit. Poetic. Romancing me. You're a sick bastard."

Jordan hopped off the bed and stomped over to her. "I was telling you the truth. You and I cannot be undone. We're mated. We're meant to be. Nothing is going to change that. I had a hard time accepting that myself until Zeke pointed it out to me. I couldn't understand why I was so drawn to you. Why my body ached to be near you. Why you clouded every single thought in my head for the last week. I didn't want to believe I was fated to a witch. I gave up my pure-blood for you. Don't take this lightly."

"Excuse me?" She pressed a hand to his chest and launched him backward onto the bed. "You gave up for *me*? You just stole my humanity! Took away the last thing I had that was my own identity. You stole my witch blood, and I'm just supposed to roll with it?"

Jordan shook his head. "It doesn't work that way. You'll still be a witch, just half-wolf. Not a pure-blood, so you'll only change on the full-moon. Unfortunately, you won't be able to change at will off cycle. But you'll retain your witch powers."

She stared at him like he had two heads. "Do you hear yourself, Jordan? Do you even realize the insane things coming out of your mouth? Do you not comprehend what you just did to me?"

"Hey, you were just as into it as I was. I confessed to you that you are my mate. I even gave you the fucking choice and told you to tell me what you want."

What the fuck did she want from him? He couldn't take it back. Eventually she'd have to come to terms with it. Jordan stared into her eyes and the look she gave back punched in him the heart. He felt her pain, her fear, her resentment. It sucked the air from his lungs, like a fist to the gut.

Being mated, he now was a part of her, and she a part of him.

"Look, I'm sorry," he said, taking a step toward her. But she inched away from him. He held out a hand to her.

She eyed his hand and then glanced back to his

face. "If you say sorry to a smashed plate, will it suddenly become whole again?"

Jordan closed his eyes and sighed before reopening them. "Nyah, let's talk about this. Please. I honestly did not mean to hurt you or to take anything away from you. How do I explain this … when you're mated, you become a part of everything. I'm yours, you are mine. Do you understand what that means?"

A tear slipped over her cheek and caressed her trembling lips. Jordan stepped toward her and brushed it away with his thumb.

"You're still you. You're still a Winston witch. You're just also a part of me now, too. You have my heart, my soul, my protection. I will work to fix this between us. I'll work to make sure you will always have a place in this world, in this pack. You're under Eden Bayou's protection now. You have a whole family."

She shook her head. "I'm a witch just mated into their pure-bloodline. You really think now that I'm a mix-breed that they'll accept me?"

"I'm Alpha, they have to."

"Don't you see, Jordan? I don't want that. I don't want someone to be forced into accepting me. I don't want someone to pledge their allegiance to my face, but stab me in the back with their words. I didn't ask for any of this."

"Then why did the powers that be make us mates, but to make a difference in this world. Two souls through space and time separated, finding each other. We're meant to be. I know in my heart you feel it and understand those words."

Nyah took a visible hard swallow. "I don't know what this is. Yes. Fine. I'm incredibly attracted to you. I can't begin to explain it. I don't understand how I want to beat you upside the head, but at the same time have you

435

wrap your arms around me. How you can bring me to my knees with a touch, with a kiss, and melt me from the inside out. I have never needed anyone in my life. I've always been the fighter, but with you … I feel safe. I like it, and I hate it."

Her words hit his heart. He cupped her face and strummed his thumb along her cheek. "This is new for both of us. Together we can figure a way to work things out. I promise you."

She turned her face into his hand and closed her eyes. Sliding his hand through her hair, he pulled her to him and captured her lips with his mouth. A soft moan broke through the kiss and he tightened his arms around her.

"I don't even know you. Yet this feeling in my heart says to trust you." She shook her head. "You do me wrong, and I'll make sure you wear your spleen on the outside of your body. Got it?"

Jordan smirked, but she quirked a brow and his smile flat-lined. "Duly noted."

She pushed him onto the bed and straddled him. "I have this insatiable need to ride my wolf."

And hell if his cock didn't respond, already at her command.

Chapter Five

Nyah waited for the rise and fall of his chest to even out, signaling Jordan had fallen asleep. They'd spent the better part of the day making love, filling the aching need in their souls to be joined, and she hoped she'd worn him out enough that he'd be out for a while. There were only a few hours of daylight left and she didn't want him following her. But for good measure, she whispered a few words and his snores reverberated off the walls. A little sleeping spell wouldn't hurt for a little insurance.

She needed time to think … alone. The idea of being part wolf now scared the piss out of her. Not to mention being mated to Jordan. What the hell did that even mean? She knew of the lore, the fated mate thing of the animals, but had no idea it actually existed. Or that she'd end up a victim of it.

Maybe victim was a strong word, since she clearly was a willing participant. Yes, she had feelings for Jordan. Overwhelming lust-filled, body-aching, all-consuming feelings. But was it enough to forge a life over? To give up her humanity and try and live life as some mixed breed, like a science experiment?

These "powers that be" that he spoke of must have had a ridiculous sense of humor. And she would have a thing or two to say to Gaia about this herself. Because what the actual fuck?

She changed into her clothes and opened the door. The minute she crossed the threshold, her heart sunk.

Guilt? Regret?

No … it was emptiness. Like her soul had just been hollowed out.

She clutched her hand to her chest. Seriously? What, now she couldn't function without the man? Absolutely absurd. She needed no man. But the ache in her heart at leaving him just about swallowed her.

She had to get out. Now.

Nyah bolted for the door and took off down the path through the woods. Late-day sunlight filtered through the barren trees, clasping together like praying fingers above her. Even with the sun's warmth, the Louisiana winter still had a bite in the air. She had no idea what happened to her leather jacket last night.

Didn't matter, she had to get back to her sister's coven in Baton Rouge and figure out what the hell was going on. Had she been set up?

She also had to see if there was some kind of spell or incantation she could do to solve this wolf issue, because tonight was the last night of the three-day full moon cycle. Which meant, if what Jordan said was true, she could be in real danger.

Her car still sat in the parking lot of the bar, only now she had a lot less windows. And so did the bar. Events from last night blurred in her mind, but the place looked like a tornado tore through it. Glass littered the parking lot, shrouding it in a rainbow of colors as sunlight hit the fragments. She walked through what used to be one of the doors that blew off when her spell took hold.

Her nose twitched as she picked up a scent … blood. A lot of it. But two distinct smells hit her, Zeke's and Jordan's. The blood she spilled attempting to take the life of an innocent. And Jordan's, spilled defending it. Guilt ransacked her soul, and she collapsed to her knees as the emotions overtook her.

"I almost needlessly took a life here last night." She dropped her head to her hands and succumbed to the tears. "Norah, please help me. Help me find your real killer so you can rest in peace."

"Nyah," a soft voice called out her name from behind her.

Nyah shot to her feet and whipped around. The panic in her heart calmed when she came face to face with Angela, the high priestess of her sister's coven.

"Angela, what are you doing here?"

"We came to make sure the wolf was dead." Angela and six others from the coven entered the bar. "Tell me he's dead, Nyah."

Nyah shook her head. "No. He didn't kill Norah. We're chasing the wrong lead."

Angela rushed her and her icy fingers wrapped around her wrist. "It has to be done. This is our only chance. Tonight is the last night of the full-moon cycle."

"Did you not just hear what I said? We have the wrong guy. Zeke didn't kill Norah."

"Sam, you must get the Bayou Vista pack here tonight. They must attack at the exact moment Nyah takes the heart," Angela said.

"As you wish, ma'am." Sam nodded and ran out of the building.

"What are you talking about?" Nyah shook from Angela's grip, who still clung to her hand.

"Do you not want to avenge your sister's death?" Angela glared at her. The fire in her eyes struck Nyah to her core. It wasn't concern, or revenge, it was lust. A hunger.

"I told you, Zeke didn't kill Norah. There's no need to kill the wolf."

"There's always a need to kill a wolf. But this one in particular is of the ancient pure-blood line that we need for the spell. And only you are strong enough to perform it."

Nyah's heart beat sped until it thrummed in her ears. "What are you talking about?"

"I'm talking about taking back what's rightfully ours. Our coven's land, power, ancestry!"

Nyah shook her head. Nothing made sense. But a dangerous electricity filled the air, and Nyah knew nothing good could come of it. The hairs on her neck stood at attention and as she turned around she realized why. The rest of the coven had encircled her in crystals, making a barrier, a magical cage to bar her from using her powers.

"What are you doing? This doesn't make any sense! We have to find Norah's killer, or we're all in danger. I don't understand," Nyah pleaded.

Angela leaned in. "You just need to do your job and kill the wolf if you want what's best for the coven. You want us to survive, we're family, we're all daughters of Gaia. But you, the last of the Salem witches, a descendant of the Winston bloodline can help us stay alive for centuries with your power."

"How will killing a wolf bring your coven power?"

"Oh, *it* won't. But it will clear this ancient land, the burial grounds of our sisters gone before us in this fight. Beneath us lay the ashes of those who fought the wolves, the packs that terrorized our ancestors for centuries. The heart of the Eden's Bayou Alpha under the full moon will release the souls of our departed. Then we send in the Bayou Vista clan and let them take each other out and cleanse this land as they rip themselves to shreds."

Shit. Nyah had gone after the wrong man. If she'd had been successful, she could have killed Jordan instead. Somehow she mixed Zeke and Jordan up. All she was told was that he was a light-brown male, bald, and brown eyes. They looked similar, but Zeke had no facial hair. Jordan had a constant five o'clock shadow.

Nyah looked down and clenched her hands to a fist to stop the tremors shaking them. That meant Jordan was in danger. If they found out Jordan was the true Alpha, they'd kill him.

Angela's shrill voice interrupted her thoughts. "And then, at the apex of the full-moon you, the last Salem witch, transfer your power to us in your most sacred act."

Nyah arched a brow. "What makes you think I'm going to transfer my power to you lunatics?"

A wicked smile slicked Angela's lips. "You won't have a choice, as upon your death your power will disburse into the aether, but our ancestors will be there to harbor it and bestow it back upon our coven in an ancient ritual. Your sister's sacrifice was the first step in this long-awaited ritual to bring back to our kind what was taken from us."

"You … you killed Norah? To distribute her power to get to me? You bitch!" Nyah lunged at her, but the minute her body nicked the edge of the circle of crystals, a shock rattled her, like that of a lightning bolt. Pain ripped through her body as if she were being torn from all sides. Her legs collapsed and she dropped to the floor.

Angela kneeled beside the crystal circle, caging her in. "Sometimes in life, sacrifices have to be made for the greater good. My coven sisters and I thank you for your sacrifice, and you will be rewarded to know that your blood will allow many future generations of witches to survive."

Angela lifted one of the crystals and reached into the circle and gripped Nyah's wrist, taking a quick swipe at it with an athame. Warm blood seeped from her wound, running the length of her hand to her fingertips. It trailed a line along the wooden floor toward a chalk circle

Angela had drawn in the middle of the bar.

Angela threw her arms up. "Awake, my sisters. Feed and thrive!"

****

Jordan's eyes flung open and he shot out of the bed, only to collapse on the floor. Pain riddled his body, as if someone just Tazered him. He shook his head and forced himself to his knees as he fought off the blackness threatening to take him down.

What the actual fuck?

"Nyah," he choked out.

He glanced around the room, but there was no sign of her. Air fought its way back into his lungs as he sucked in a heavy breath over his racing heart.

"Zeke," Jordan cried out as he stumbled his way to the bed and threw on some clothes.

Zeke's loud stomps stopped as he hit the door. "What's wrong?"

"Nyah, she's in trouble." Jordan wiped the sweat from his brow and choked down the fear rising in his gut.

"Where is she? How do you know?"

"I felt it. Someone's hurting her. I don't know what's going on, but summon the pack. I have to find her."

"She's going to be a constant pain in our ass, isn't she?" Zeke shook his head.

"Probably. But she's my pain in the ass. And she needs our help. Go!"

"Where should we go?"

"Meet at the bar. I'm betting she went there to get her car. I can still smell her scent in the air." Jordan burst out the door and shifted mid-air, covering the ground faster in his wolf form. Just as he'd thought, he tracked her scent straight in a beeline to the bar. Only as he approached, he picked up far more than just her scent.

A myriad of smells hit him, from people to herbs, and gasoline.

Witches.

Fucking patchouli and sage, they were cleansing the bar for some kind of ritual probably. Which meant Nyah was in the middle of it.

Jordan kicked up speed as adrenaline fed his legs. He had no idea what he'd find when he got there, and he prayed his brother and the rest of the pack wouldn't be far behind.

As he neared the bar, he shifted back to human form and inched his way along the outside wall trying to get an idea of what was going on inside. His nose narrowed in on Nyah immediately, and fear spiked her heart rate so loud it thumped in Jordan's ears.

The coppery scent of blood hit him like a punch, and it belonged to Nyah. Shit. Jordan counted at least six witches inside, and who knew if there were more in the parking lot. Nyah lay on the floor, bleeding out while the women danced around her, chanting like a bunch of doped-up hippies.

He hated witches. All except Nyah.

Darkness pulled the sun below the horizon. The full moon rose in the sky, heading toward its apex.

"Come on, Nyah. Come on," Jordan grunted. He closed his eyes and tried to channel her through his Alpha link, hoping her change had started and she could hear him in her mind. He needed her to drop the wards the witches had in place, once again blocking him from entering his own damned bar for the second time.

A loud groan echoed through the room as Nyah rolled over, eyeing Jordan at the door.

That's it, darlin', hear me. I need you to get these wards down so I can get in there and help you. It hurts, I know that. I can feel it. Channel me, take my strength from our bond. Use it, use me to help break you free.

Nyah slapped a hand to the floor, trying to crawl her way toward Jordan.

No, save your physical strength. I'll come get you. Just close your eyes, think of me. Think of me helping you, giving you my hand, my heart, my strength. Lower the wards, baby. I know you can do it.

He prayed, even though they'd just mated, that their bond would be strong enough to pull it off. She was a Winston witch and he the last of the ancient Alphas. Surely they could tap into each other.

It was a long shot, but it was all he had at the moment.

Nyah stretched a hand toward him and closed her eyes.

"Wolf!" someone screamed from inside the bar.

Fuck, they spotted him.

"Nyah, now!" Jordan shouted.

A blast of white light shot from Nyah's fingertips and a shockwave rattled the walls of the building. Jordan hoped that was it as he took a running leap and shifted mid-air. Nothing between him and the witches but air, and he tore through the screaming lot, not caring who or what got caught in the crossfire.

Nyah pulled herself to her knees. "Jordan," she screamed. "Help me. What's happening?"

Jordan ripped the head off two of the witches and tossed them to the floor as a group of them fled out toward the parking lot.

Don't fight it, Nyah. Let it happen. You're going through your first change. Your body will heal itself during the process. If you fight it, you'll only make it last longer and it'll hurt you more. You can do this. I'm right here.

Shrieks and blood-curdling screams wailed from

the parking lot. Jordan hoped that meant the rest of the pack had arrived and were making short work of the rest of the witches.

"Jordan, trap…" Nyah said, reaching her hand to him.

"What are you talking about?" Jordan said just as something pierced him from the back.

Jordan sprang up as an old hag of a witch attempted another strike, this time at his chest. He swatted at her with his paw, scraping his claws across her face. Her scream was drowned out by his growl as he pounced on top of her. But she jammed the athame into his chest, ripping a whimper from his lung as he rolled over to the floor. Pain leached his body, as if his spirit were being snuffed out.

"Jordan, no!" Nyah screamed.

His last thought was of Nyah, and he prayed she'd survive the change and run. Run fast and furious to the homestead and be safe. He knew his brother, who would become the new alpha, would take care of her. He just prayed the rest of the pack would accept her as their own as well.

His eyes snapped shut as the blackness claimed him.

Chapter Six

Nyah's heart sank as she watched her mate die before her eyes, and there was nothing she could do about it. The full moon rose high in the sky, and it pulled at her, yanking something inside of her outward. Fear sliced at her as the crunch of bones snapping, realigning, changing, and shifting filled her ears, knowing they were her own. She dropped to her hands and knees, tucking her chin to her chest as she heaved heavy, labored breaths through the pain.

Jordan told her to let it happen. Not fight it. But how the fuck did she not fight something this unnatural … this preternatural thing happening to her? It wasn't supposed to be like this.

The slice on her wrist sealed, as if it had never happened. Just as hair sprouted along her arms, and her nails grew into long claws.

Nyah released a guttural scream that changed to a growl as the rest of her body followed, elongating, raising up, filling out, forming the body of a wolf. Dark blonde fur covered her face along her snout where her nose used to be.

Suddenly everything in the room became sharper, clearer, more defined. The sound of a cricket miles away stood out among the crunching and cracking and snapping of body parts from the parking lot. A mosquito buzzed in the moonlight outside the bar, only to be swallowed by a bat that swooped down from the dark of night.

Blood, coppery and acrid, filled her nostrils and immediately she knew it belonged to Jordan. His scent filled her, slicing her heart in two.

She padded over to him, bleeding out next to Angela on the floor, covered in even more blood. A cough rocked her body as she choked on blood dripping along her lips.

"Abom … ination," she choked out. "Die."

"You first, bitch." Nyah lunged at her and ripped her throat straight from her neck.

Another wolf padded into the room with a scent she recognized from the other night, when Jordan saved her from the rival pack attack, the one he called Roark.

Roark shifted to human form and leaned against the door. "Well, aren't you a pretty little she-wolf. A baby freshly turned."

A slow, intermittent thump hit her ears and she whipped around. Jordan was still alive. She had to change back and heal him. She couldn't do it from her wolf form. It had to be from her witch side.

Norah, please help me…

Nyah closed her eyes and concentrated on her human form, her witch form. Like channeling her power during an incantation, she let her spirit take over, guide her, fill her.

She dropped to the floor, and a shiver claimed her naked body. But she was human. Pain radiated through every inch of her, but the drive to save her mate was stronger. Her long fingernails dug into the floor and she dragged herself to his side.

"Don't you leave me now. You got me into this shit. Hell if I'm living through it alone." A hazy white light shone through her fingertips as she laid her hands along his blood-soaked chest. His fur thinned beneath her hands as it turned back into skin. The warmth that once radiated off his flesh was now cold and lifeless, graying as it died before her eyes.

"No," Nyah shouted. "I won't let you slip away."

Nyah fought, channeling everything she had left inside her. A hand touched her shoulder and she looked up into the smiling face of her dead sister, Norah. Her spirit form merged with Nyah, thrusting her head back as the force took over her body. A flash of light burst from her fingertips and struck Jordan's chest.

He bolted up like he'd just been shocked back to life, coughing as he rolled over.

Nyah swallowed hard and clutched a hand to her chest, feeling her sister's life force coursing inside her. "Thank you," she whispered.

Jordan scrambled up from the floor and lunged at Nyah, wrapping his arms around her as he crashed against her lips. But it wasn't a thank you for healing him. Each sweep of his tongue told her how thankful he was *she* was still alive. The concern and tenderness in his movements were for her, not for him.

He gave his life for her. And she gave it back to him.

****

Jordan pulled back from the kiss and stared into the eyes of his mate, his love, his future. "You did it darlin'. You did it."

Nyah slid a warm hand along his bare chest. Her simple touch lit a fire along his skin. "My sister helped me. She gave me her strength and her power to help save you."

A smile lit his lips. "No, baby, not me. I'm talking about you. You survived your first shift. And you changed back at will. That is an incredible feat for a hybrid, let alone a newly turned. You are simply amazing, and I'm so damn proud of you."

He needed to taste her lips once more, soak himself in her essence, her strength and beauty. She embodied what it meant to be a wolf, strong and wild, yet somehow she'd managed to retain her witch half and control it. Now he knew why the powers that be mated him to her.

"Never thought I'd live to see this day." Roark laughed from across the room. "An ancient sucking face with a witch. And then you went and made her a wolf. Maybe there's hope for the Eden's Bayou pack yet."

Jordan brushed a hair from Nyah's face as he pulled back from the kiss. He stared at Roark, unsure of what to say to him. For so long he considered him an enemy, a power-hungry leader of the rival pack. But it was his pack that took care of the witches in the parking lot. Not Jordan's, as he spied Zeke and the pack walking in unscathed, while Roark's pack was covered in blood and worse for wear. Bayou Vista made it there first.

"She's my mate." Jordan finally spoke up. "And I'm damn proud of it."

Roark tossed him a wink. "You remember that."

Jordan stood and offered a hand. "Sometimes we ancients have to learn shit the hard way."

Roark smirked and shook his head. "Oh, don't think I'm going to forget the ass-whooping I owe you from the other night. Don't mistake my respect for your newly acquired mate for respect for you. But maybe we can work out some kind of deal for our packs' future well-being."

Jordan nodded. "Fair enough. We'll talk."

"We may even come help repair the bar if we get allowed entrance to it. What do you say?" Roark asked, tossing a wink to Nyah.

"Baby steps, Roark. We'll talk. But not tonight. Tonight I'm taking my mate home and having my way with her." Jordan gripped her by the waist and tugged her close to his body.

"What he means is, I'll be having my way with

my wolf," Nyah said, clasping her hand to his as she dragged him out of the bar in a run and shifted.

The End

FROZEN HEART

Beth D. Carter

Copyright © 2017

Chapter One

Gabrielle Thorpe ignored the crash of the downstairs door as she focused on the latest series of photos on her laptop. She'd been back in the States a total of thirty-six hours from Bhutan, sixteen of which had been devoted to sleep, and she still felt like death warmed over. What she desperately needed was a hot meal and a carafe of coffee, but she was too eager to study the photos to concentrate on anything else.

"Kenny is here," Mark said casually. He sat at the other desk, labeling all the photos once she was done inspecting them.

"Mmm," she said, not really caring.

"You think he finally changed clothes?"

The question distracted her enough to blink at him confusingly. "What?"

"Remember? Before we left for Bhutan, he'd worn the same clothes two days straight."

Footsteps echoed up through the stairway, gaining in volume with each floor passed. Gabrielle and Mark looked at the door expectantly, and a second later, it smashed open as Kenny bounded through. His stringy hair touched his shoulders and the sporadic growth on his face needed a trim.

Mark wrinkled his nose. "Nope."

"Dudes!" Kenny cried. "I've got a fantastic hypothesis!"

Gabrielle raised an eyebrow. "Does it include showering somewhere between here and your parents' basement?"

"Huh?" Kenny looked down at himself. "What're you talking about? I wiped myself down."

"*Wiped*?" Mark asked, aghast.

"Yeah," Kenny said. "With those disposable cloths. You know, the baby ones."

"Oh my God," Gabrielle muttered.

Kenny waved his hand dismissively. "Never mind that. Let me ask you … what if the Yeti was actually located in the Arctic?"

He clapped his hands and then drew them apart as if he'd just performed a magic trick. He looked back and forth between Gabrielle and Mark, apparently waiting for their reaction. It was obvious, by the expectation on his face, that he waited for her to be as amazed as he seemed to be.

Instead, she began ticking off her fingers. "One, shut the door behind you. Two, you will properly bathe tonight because there's no telling what type of infestation you're growing. Three, the Yeti is somewhere in the Himalayas, hence my recent expedition into Bhutan."

Kenny kicked the door shut with his foot and then hurried over to her desk. He pulled out his laptop from his backpack.

"Yeah, I know, but I think I found something," he said, so rushed his words strung together. "No, no, no, I'm *positive* I found something. Yeti or Big Foot, I'm not sure but the damn thing is too big not to be investigated, Gabs."

He fired up the laptop and turned it around so she

could see what he was rambling about. Gabrielle watched as he scrolled through his blog site until he landed on a photo where something big and blurry was framed by the white backdrop of trees, snow, and ice. She pulled the laptop closer and stared through her glasses at the large, upright creature captured in the photo.

"I've never seen this photo before," she said. As a cryptozoologist, she'd seen and studied every single photograph taken of the legendary Yeti and his supposed footprints. "Where'd it come from?"

"Got emailed to me from someone who visited my blog."

Gabrielle frowned. Kenny ran a site devoted to their study of cryptids, and he was always getting emails and photos from people who swore they found one of the many undocumented creatures she was searching for, although the majority of the pictures were fake.

She scrolled a little further down, searching for more photos, but paused as she came across a picture of herself several years ago, being given permission to hold a sacred pelt belonging to a nomadic tribe in the Himalayas. It had been when she, Mark, and Kenny had broken off from their expedition to follow a story of a skinned Yeti, only to be included and embraced by the leader. He had said her hair color resembled the holy relic so she must be a divine messenger. His blessing had given her access to take a sample of the fur.

"Tuaq, Alaska," Kenny said, bringing her out of her memories. "That's where the photo was taken. It's the northernmost edge of the Gates of the Arctic National Park, right under the Boreal-Arctic transition zone where vegetation begins to thin out. What if the Yeti is actually located there? Oh, wait! Or better yet, what if he migrated there?"

Gabrielle scrolled back up to the photo in question

as Mark came over to stand behind her.

"Oh wow," he said. "It's up on two legs. And white. You think it could be the Yeti, Gabs?"

"No," she said, shaking her head. "I'm positive the Yeti is somewhere in the Himalayas. This is … I don't rightly know what this is. I wish it wasn't so blurry."

"That's the kicker, though," Mark said. "Photos are always blurry. Or obscure. Just once I'd like a clear picture. Maybe with a big sign that says, 'Yes, I'm a cryptid.'"

"Did you do any tests on this?" Gabrielle asked, ignoring Mark. "Photoshopping? Man in a costume?"

"I would need to see the original to rule out any photoshopping," Kenny admitted, "but I did do a little research. Seems like the man who took the photo went out illegally to hunt moose, since hunting season was over at the end of September. It was near twilight and he saw this creature running through the woods, going fast. He brought up his camera and took as many pictures as possible. This was the best one of the bunch."

"It would be interesting to see the rest of the photos," Mark said.

"I'll have him send them to me," Kenny said. "There's a place in Tuaq called the Frosset Lodge located just north of the town, and it's the closest building to where these photos were taken. And low and behold, they have rooms available since it's now off season."

"I just got back from a trip, Kenny," Gabrielle said with a sigh. "There's still a lot of data Mark and I have to sift through, not to mention the college will want a report of our trip—"

"I believe in this photo, Gabs," Kenny said, interrupting her. "We need to check this out. I feel it in my gut. This could be the Yeti we've been searching for, or at least the missing link."

She pursed her lips as she stared at the photo. She couldn't help but be extremely curious about it. "And I'm positive this isn't a Yeti. This creature has a snout. And it's white."

"So it's the Abominable Snowman?" Mark asked.

She scowled at him. "No such thing."

"Well, Gabs, most people think there's no such things as cryptids," he pointed out. "And although our grant is about hunting for the Yeti, maybe this creature is part of that legend."

"Maybe," she hedged. "But we can't be rushing off to check out every picture that turns up blurry images of humanoid creatures walking upright. That's unrealistic, not to mention impossible."

"Aren't you the least bit curious, Gabs?" Kenny asked.

Gabrielle studied the photo again. Of course she was, though she wouldn't admit it out loud. She took off her glasses and rubbed her eyes, taking the moment to think. The trip to Bhutan had been exhausting and time-consuming, and so far, yielded no definite proof of the Yeti. Just some random tracks and unusual scat, which would have to be sent to the college lab for analysis. Perhaps it *was* time to consider outside-the-box thinking.

"Okay, listen," she said. "First, we have to examine the rest of those photos, and if they seem in order, we'll go." When the two men high-fived each other, she held up a hand. "But only for a few days. We'll interview Kenny's source and search the area for any proof of this creature. If we come up with nothing, then we'll come back home and I'll present our findings to the college board and hope they give us more money to keep going."

"Thanks, Gabs," Kenny said.

"Don't thank me. We've got to find something proof positive, Kenny. Otherwise we're out of money."

"Don't worry," he said. "I have a good feeling."

Chapter Two

Jaeger walked through his lodge, eyeballing the place to make sure everything was in order. Hunting season was finally over and he was able to breathe a little easier. Even though he had three guests booked, scheduled to arrive later in the afternoon, it would be a relief the tourists wouldn't be traipsing through the forest with rifles.

"You need to be more careful," Agathe said from the doorway of the kitchen. She spoke in her native tongue, a mixture of Greenlandic and Danish.

"I'm always careful," he replied in the same language.

She raised a wrinkly finger and pointed at him. "You were out running the other night. You risk yourself when it isn't a full moon."

"Stop, you worry too much."

Agathe threw her arms up in the air, making the two gray braids of her hair bob around her head. "Well, who am I to warn you? I'm only your den mother. Raised you, took care of you and your brothers. Protected you when you wanted to run through the night and had warm milk waiting for you when you came home."

Jaeger placed his hands on her shoulders. "You're right, Agathe. You are the mother of my heart, but you worry too much."

She sighed and patted said heart. Since the top of her head only came to the center of his chest, it was about as high as she could reach.

"You are all that's left of the *Frosne Hjerte* pack," she said. "Your brothers have joined other packs for their mates. You must now give me little pups to supervise and to carry on your ancient name."

He rolled his eyes and walked away. "We have guests coming today, Agathe."

She placed her hands on her rounded hips. "You are avoiding the conversation."

"Yes, I am," he admitted, heading toward the grand staircase that swept from the foyer to the second floor.

"Hunting season is done. Why are they coming?"

He shrugged. "I haven't a clue, but while they're here, behave yourself."

She snorted. "And you better be careful when you go out running at night."

He bounded up the stairs to do one last inspection of the rooms. "I'm always careful, *den mor.*"

Her harrumph could be heard through the whole lodge.

A little after one that afternoon, a truck arrived with his guests. Jaeger watched for a moment at his office window, observing the two men who got out of the back and the woman who emerged from the driver's seat, bundled up for the cool Alaskan temperature. October rarely got warmer than twenty-five degrees Fahrenheit during the day, and with the sunlight hours growing steadily shorter, warmth was hard pressed to be found. Most inhabitants of Tauq, Alaska, stayed indoors around fire stoves, swapping stories and drinking coffee.

The smaller man unloaded some black equipment bags that looked like they held cameras. It made sense to wait until after hunting season to take nature photos. Alaska was breathtaking this time of year. Jaeger left his office and hurried outside to greet his guests.

A slight breeze was blowing, bringing with it a touch of frost. Snow had already fallen, giving about a foot where the drifts lay the highest. More snow was coming. Winters were hard in the Arctic and only the strong survived. His ancestors had adapted long ago to not only survive, but thrive. As Jaeger stepped out from the warmth of the lodge, the woman turned. She had a plastic smile on her face, one he recognized because he had the same bland greeting gracing his own mouth. He quickly identified she had strawberry-red hair, hazel eyes, and a spattering of freckles over her face before the breeze shifted and her scent drifted by, teasing his nostrils. Suddenly, every nerve in his body came alive, as if he'd touched a live wire, and for the first time in his life, the wolf deep in his soul stirred awake while he was in his human form.

Jaeger narrowed his eyes as every molecule in his body focused on her. She stopped in her tracks as their eyes met, gazes locked. He plummeted into the depths of her eyes and saw the future. What could be, or maybe what *should* be, visions of them traveling through the clouds and soaring through the heavens. His wolf locked onto her scent and pawed, wanting free. His incisors grew and he had to clamp his lips shut to keep them hidden until he was able to will them to settle.

"Hello!"

One of the men called out a greeting, shaking Jaeger out of the unexpected lust he found himself in. The woman blinked her big eyes, and it was enough to pull his attention from her and salvage what little sanity he had left.

"Hello," he responded. "Welcome to Frosset Lodge."

He forced himself to glance at the others, the two men traveling with her, but like a magnet, his gaze kept being pulled back to her.

"I'm Jaeger Larsen," he said. He meant it to everyone, but he only had eyes for her. He waited for her name.

She smiled and walked toward him with her hand out. "I'm Gabrielle Thorpe. This is my team, Kenny Smith and Mark Pope."

He took her outstretched hand, and electricity tingled up the nerves. It struck him hard, the awareness it brought, and along with it a new problem, because his dick went hard as stone. She must have felt the spark between them, too, because her lips parted and her heartbeat skittered out of control. He could hear it, hell, he could *feel* it beating wildly. For him. For them. Through his head rolled one word.

Mate.

****

As soon as they had landed at the small Nome Airport, Gabrielle considered staying on the small plane until it took her back to civilization. She'd just come back from trekking through the Himalayas in Bhutan, where the thin air stole most of her energy and the cold settled in her bones. Alaska wasn't as cold as twenty-three thousand feet, but it was still too soon. Her bones hadn't yet thawed.

At least the chartered plane from Nome to the small runway just outside of Tauq was quick. Gabrielle watched the landscape scroll by, mesmerized by the beauty. The Himalayas were majestic, breathtaking, and to most people Alaska couldn't compare. However, she realized she preferred the more simplistic vastness on display below.

As she stepped from the rental Jeep that had brought them from the airstrip to the lodge, Gabrielle took a deep breath. The air was cold and hit her lungs hard, momentarily freezing her breath. The lodge was beautiful, the quintessential rustic cabin, except this one was two stories tall and must have had about four thousand square feet of real estate. A verandah wrapped around the whole house with a stone chimney rising through the roof, and she could just imagine sitting on rocking chairs and watching the sun set on the vast Alaska horizon.

The door opened and she turned, and her gaze locked onto the most handsome man she'd ever seen in her life. Her belly did a strange little jiggle that radiated out to every nerve ending and pushed her heart to beat double time. She had this overwhelming urge to rush up to him, grab him, and kiss him until they both needed oxygen. Big, handsome, pale-blond hair and dark, dark eyes, she tried very hard not to stare but couldn't pull her gaze off him.

Words went on around her. Hellos and greetings, pleasantries that had her focusing on the man's lips. Jaeger Larsen. She held out her hand, wanting … no, needing, to feel his skin on hers. When he finally touched her, it was like coming home. One word blasted through her mind.

Fate.

"I'm Gabrielle Thorpe. This is my team, Kenny Smith and Mark Pope."

He squeezed her hand. "Welcome."

She smiled. "Your lodge is absolutely beautiful."

"Thank you." He leaned in closer to her. "Please feel free to explore it. You are the only guest here at this time."

His words meant one thing, but the promise in his eyes meant something else. He looked over her shoulder, straightened, and nodded toward the men behind her.

"Of course, I meant all of you."

Gabrielle grew a little warm and knew she had to be blushing. She hoped it would just look like a little wind burn from the cold breeze. Jaeger picked up her suitcase resting next to her leg and gestured for her to enter the lodge.

Once inside, the warmth wrapped around her and helped chase the chill away. A large staircase wound up the center of the room, its mahogany banister polished to a shine. A bank of windows rose from the ground, stretching up to the second floor. On the deck outside, a round fire pit, now empty, was waiting for someone to come out and utilize it. The décor could have easily sunk into antler chandeliers and taxidermy hell, but Jaeger Larsen seemed to have abandoned that stereotype. Instead, bookshelves lined one wall, filled with all types of tomes. Plaid furniture in rich warm colors complemented the bold rug patterns lying on the floor. Paintings of the Alaskan wilderness, with and without snow, hung on the walls.

Kenny and Mark crowded in behind her, sounding more like bulls barging into a china shop, and she was thankful there wasn't anything to smash. They dumped their various bags on the floor and hurried over to the fire roaring in the large fireplace. Gabrielle took off her coat and draped it over her arm.

An old woman came bustling from what looked like the kitchen area, carrying a tray loaded with mugs. Jaeger hurried to help her and took it from her to set upon a side table.

"This is Agathe," Jaeger introduced her. "She runs the kitchen, so if you need anything don't let her stoic demeanor scare you."

Agathe gave him the stink eye, huffed, and returned to the kitchen. Jaeger looked at Gabrielle and winked.

"Tea, if you wish," he said.

"Thank you," Gabrielle murmured. "I think I'd like to freshen up some. My team and I have an interview to conduct in about an hour."

He raised an eyebrow. "You're a reporter?"

"Oh, no," she said. "I'm a cryptozoologist. I'm here to investigate a photo that was sent to us about a creature that might or might not be related to the Yeti."

Chapter Three

Everything inside Jaeger turned to ice. He must have said the right thing because Gabrielle pulled out a tablet and showed him a set of photos, ones he knew very well because he was staring at himself. They had to have been taken the night he'd decided to stretch his legs and let his wolf run free, safe from the knowledge he wouldn't accidentally be struck by a hunter's bullet.

Along with the realization that someone had caught him with a camera was the fact that his mate was there to oust his wolf. She was a cryptozoologist? How could he ever tell her about the legends of his people or the fact he could shift into wolf form? To her, he was the stuff of mythology. A werewolf, for lack of a better term.

Or a monster.

And it was her job to expose him.

He would have to think about how to proceed because now that his wolf knew her scent, it wanted her.

"You seem to have accepted my profession well," she observed.

"I'm not sure if the word 'accepted' is what I'd use," he said. "I think I'm more curious and a bit confused. I believe cryptozoology is considered a pseudoscience at best."

Her shoulders went back and her pert little nose rose just a little, as if she were preparing for battle. Perhaps she was. After all, her chosen profession wasn't exactly normal.

"Many modern-day accepted beliefs were once considered pseudoscience," she said, a bit stiffly. "Like the earth being round. Or us circling the sun instead of vice versa. Less than a hundred years ago people were still dying from infection."

"Granted," he replied. "But creatures of mythology? Like Loch Ness … or, say, a werewolf?"

"Werewolf? Um, no. That's not a cryptid, that's folklore."

"I'm surprised you distinguish between the two."

"Is belief in a cryptid so hard to fathom?" she asked. "Every year new species are being discovered, on land and in the sea. One day I plan to be the one to present evidence of one."

"And you're currently on the hunt of the Yeti. Aren't they in the Himalayas? Why come to Alaska?"

"The pictures, of course."

"I would've said that creature in the pictures is more related to Big Foot."

Instantly, he could tell it was the wrong thing to say. Her face smoothed out and went blank. She put her tablet back into her shoulder bag and then wrapped her arms around herself, as if protecting herself.

"I know cryptids aren't the norm for most people," she said. A definite chill had settled in her tone. "I often get the eye roll or snort of derision. I can see the disbelief in their eyes along with the thoughts that I might be crazy. Even my own parents think this is just a little side hobby, not real. Certainly not real science. But I don't need, nor do I ask, for acceptance. I've paid for three rooms, so if you don't mind, I'd like to head to them now."

"If I've offended you, I am sorry," he murmured. "Let me make it up to you. Would you like to explore where those pictures were taken?"

Cautionary hope flittered through her eyes. "Did you recognize the area?"

"Yes, I did," he said. "We can go explore it tomorrow if you'd like. I own two snowmobiles."

Excitement lit up her features, making her shine.

He had to fight the urge to grab her and drag her upstairs like a damn Neanderthal. He glanced over at her companions, who had partaken of the tea, and decided it really wouldn't be a good idea to act on his more basic desires.

"Thank you," she replied. The chill in her words had thawed a bit. "I would like that."

"Then it's settled," he said. He gestured to the staircase. "If you will follow me?"

She nodded. Kenny and Mark put down their cups to grab their gear, and moments later Jaeger led them upstairs. Jaeger wasn't that concerned about her profession. After all, she was hunting him, and as long as he didn't shift, there was no way she would ever suspect the creature she wanted to find was the very person who soon planned to share her bed.

****

"What was that all about?" Mark asked as soon as they all climbed back into the rented Jeep.

"What was what all about?" Gabrielle hedged. She knew exactly what he was asking but was trying hard not to analyze her reaction to Jaeger Larsen.

"Don't play coy," Kenny said from the backseat. "It wasn't like we're deaf and didn't hear the exchange between you and Mr. Universe."

The description momentarily distracted her. "Mr. Universe?"

"Yeah, he's like six-foot-five, all rippling muscles, and buns of steel," Kenny said. "I'm not gay, but even I can appreciate a fine piece of the male species when I come across one."

Gabrielle chuckled. "I'm thinking you may need to reevaluate which side you bat for."

Kenny flipped her off.

"Some serious hormones were bouncing off both

of you," Mark said.

The humor fled, leaving Gabrielle feeling a bit defensive. "So what, he's a good-looking guy. Can't I appreciate that for a change? Most of the time eye candy isn't readily handy."

"Is she talking about us?" Kenny asked Mark.

"Yeah, I think she just called us ugly," Mark replied.

"Stop it," Gabrielle said with a wave of her hand. "Kenny, directions to your photographer, please."

As she followed Kenny's instructions, her mind drifted back to Jaeger. She'd never felt such an immediate and complete attraction to anyone, and it disturbed her equilibrium. As much fun as it might be, she simply didn't have the time or the energy to devote to an affair, and that was all she could give to him or to herself.

Fate, my ass.

They were meeting the man who took the photos in a small restaurant located off Main Street. The roads had been plowed, but Gabrielle was thankful for the chains on the tires. She parked the Jeep and all three of them hurried into the small restaurant. Once inside, they looked around and a man held up a hand, waving them over. He was clearly Inuit, with the broad forehead and flat nose of his ancestors.

"Hello," he said, greeting them. "I'm Qannik."

"Gabrielle," she said. "This is Mark, and I believe you know Kenny."

They shook hands and then sat down. Immediately, Kenny pulled out the series of photographs he had printed out. Some had the creature blown up, but the larger image only disintegrated more from the pixilation.

"First, I want to say thank you so much for

contacting me," Kenny told Qannik. "We've never seen anything like this creature before."

"Neither have I," Qannik said. "There are stories, though. Ones I never believed in until I saw this thing with my own eyes."

Gabrielle nodded. "I've read the accounts, but those beasts are usually black or brown haired. Mistaken bear sightings. The main difference between those stories and this creature, though, is the snout. This isn't a bear."

"No, it was not a bear," Qannik said.

"Tell us what it looked like," Mark urged.

Qannik took the photos that Kenny had and began pointing. "It was strong and it walked on two legs, although the legs were more disjointed. Like … like a dog, you know, how the joint kicks out."

"Yeah, I see it here," Kenny murmured, looking over Qannik's shoulder. "If it was on four legs, it would look exactly like a wolf."

"A wolf," Gabrielle said softly as she stared at one of the photos. "A werewolf."

Jaeger had brought up the folklore creature in the first place, and now they seemed to be looking at one. Was it possible he knew something and wasn't sharing? If so, why would he keep such a secret? Gabrielle had been half skeptical about the photo yielding any significant clues, especially anything having to do with the Yeti, but all her instincts suddenly jumped alive. No, it wasn't a Yeti, but maybe she had just found something else. Something that could erase the wounds of the past.

When they returned to the lodge, dusk was beginning to fall and the temperature was dropping. Another vehicle was parked in her spot. She stopped next to it and they all piled out of the Jeep.

"I thought we were the only visitors," she said.

The door to the lodge opened and a man stepped

out. He wasn't very tall, but was very fit for his age. Hair cut so short it made him almost appear to be bald. He wore a ribbed turtleneck, jeans, and hiking boots, and he saluted her with his mug of tea.

"Hello, Gabs," he said. "Funny meeting you here."

"Dendy," she muttered. "What the hell are you doing here, you bastard?"

Chapter Four

"How did you know I was here in Alaska?" she demanded.

"What?" He opened his arms. "No hug hello?"

"Why are you here?" She folded her arms across her chest. She wasn't about to give an inch.

"Why are *you* here?" he countered.

She rolled her eyes and marched up the porch steps to push past him. Kenny and Mark were close behind her. As soon as she stepped inside, she saw Dendy had brought his assistant, Ernrider. The two men were as slimy as slugs and about as useful.

"Funny to see you here, Kid," Ernrider said.

She flipped him off and headed for the stairs. Jaeger came from the kitchen and their gazes met. He narrowed his eyes and did a quick sweep from her and Dendy and back again.

"We're checking out," she informed him.

"Gabs!" Kenny exclaimed as he rushed up to her. "We can't leave just yet. There's the thing, and the other thing, and maybe that new thing."

He held up a hand to shield his face and mouthed the word *werewolf*, like she didn't know how to translate Kenny speech.

Jaeger came forward and took her elbow. "Come to my office."

He was dragging her even before she realized what was happening. A second later, he pulled her into a spacious room and closed the door behind them. A large desk dominated one side of the room, with two leather chairs resting by another fireplace.

"Let me go," she said, pulling her arm free.

"You aren't leaving."

She narrowed her eyes and stuck a hand on one hip. "Last time I looked I'm a paying guest and can terminate my reservation at any time."

"Because of that man?" he asked, pointing at the closed door.

"That *man* is an asshole. I can't believe you rented a room to him!"

"I haven't."

That took the wind out of her sails. Her mouth opened and then closed on an awkward huff.

"Oh, um," she mumbled. "But I thought…"

"He was here inquiring about rooms. As I was gathering material together, you parked the Jeep, and he went out to greet you."

"Greet is a strong verb. I would use the phrase 'make my skin crawl.'"

He walked over to her, and with each step, butterflies in her belly woke up and started flittering. Everything else died away. Dendy, her job … thoughts about a possible werewolf existing. He touched her hair, rubbing the light-red strands between his fingers.

"Do you feel this between us?" he asked softly.

She opened her mouth to answer, but his lips settled on hers and all coherent thoughts fled. At first it was just a chaste kiss, a mere dusting of mouths. But then he leaned firmly into her, and his tongue grazed the seam, seeking entrance to the dark caverns of her mouth. She allowed him access, and the kiss changed from barely there to red hot in an instant.

He swept in, plundering swiftly, seeking her tongue to dip and twirl with his. He went deep and then pulled back, only to plunge back in, teasing her, drawing forth a moan of desire. She wanted more, so much more. She wanted to melt into him, give him everything, forget about the world around them.

And that scared the shit out of her.

She pulled back and blinked at him. Her lips tingled at the loss of his, and she licked them in hopes of easing the sting. He reached for her, but she evaded him, moving back.

"Gabrielle?"

"No," she said, holding up a hand as if warding him away. She drew in a great gulp of air in hopes of steadying her nerves. "I can't."

"Can't?" he asked, the word so thick it came out like a growl. He ignored her outstretched arm and took hold of her shoulders. She placed her hands on his chest and stared up at him. "You can't deny this power between us."

"No," she whispered. "But that doesn't mean I'm going to give into it."

"Why the hell not?"

"Because I'm leaving in a few days. And I don't really do affairs."

He opened his mouth, as if to argue, but then abruptly closed it. A frown settled between his eyes, creasing the area between them.

"I've had one affair in my life," she said. She took a deep breath. "And he betrayed me. Took my research. Made me look like a fool. I spent years trying to get over it, to forget that he made me believe and then made me question everything I had come to value."

"Dendy," he muttered.

She nodded. "I know this situation is nothing like that one, but I vowed to myself long ago to stay focused on my work. And that's why I'm here. To work. So you see why I can't?"

"No," he said. "I can understand your reluctance but know this, Gabrielle. You are different. In my life I've never felt like this around anyone. Can you say the same?"

"We just met," she replied, a bit breathless because that was what he did to her. "It's hormonal. Attraction based on our aesthetics, enhanced by psychological factors of possessing traits and desires in which—"

He shut her up by kissing her again. This time she didn't bother pushing him away, instead she wrapped her arms around his neck and sank into the kiss. Being with him like this, it was hard to remember why she *should* push him away. All her arguments fell flat. Would it be so bad to give into the attraction? What would it hurt to share his bed for the time they had together?

A knock sounded on the door and he raised his head. The sudden intrusion shocked her back to reality and she hastily pulled away from him, far enough this time so he couldn't touch her again.

"No," she said. Although she wanted to go right back into his arms, she forced herself to walk away. "I need to stay focused on my work."

"You're a stubborn woman, Gabrielle. You know it's only a matter of time."

She narrowed her eyes and raised her chin. "You have business to conduct, and so do I."

With that, she turned and headed for the door. When she opened it, Dendy stood there, hand raised and ready to knock again.

"How *did* you know I was here?"

He did a one-shoulder shrug. "Let's say a little bird might've told me. Did you miss me, Gabs?"

She pushed him out of her way and strode determinedly through the lodge and up the stairs. Once in her room, she let out her breath and sagged onto the bed. Resisting Jaeger while dealing with Dendy was too much for her to handle.

****

Jaeger studied Dendy as he watched her walk away. Now that he knew some of Gabrielle's story, he wanted nothing to do with the man. Just knowing at some point he had touched his mate made Jaeger want to rip the smaller man's arms off.

"I don't think we'll be able to conduct business after all," he said.

Dendy's eyebrows arched high on his forehead. "After one private moment with Gabs? I must admit, she's good."

Jaeger's wolf prowled inside him, wanting free so he could rip apart the man who he now saw as his rival.

"You say one more derogatory thing about her and I'll punch you so hard you'll forget why you're in Alaska," he said softly. The words were a vow.

Dendy lost his smugness. "Yes, I see now we can't rent rooms here. Then let me say good day."

"You better hurry to the hotel in town," Jaeger replied. "Night is falling. And it can get very dangerous out there."

"You're threatening me? Over *her*? She has no business being in this business, a two-bit hack who couldn't even finish school, calling herself a cryptozoologist."

Jaeger moved fast, so fast that Dendy hardly blinked from one moment to the next as he grabbed the front of his sweater and brought him up on his tip toes. The three men watching behind them all yelled, and the next instant, Dendy's friend was there trying to pull him out of Jaeger's grasp.

"I would leave now if I were you." Jaeger let him go and both stumbled back.

"We'll go," his friend, Ernrider, insisted.

Jaeger, Kenny, and Mark watched both men flee

the lodge. The door slammed shut behind them.

"Wow," Kenny said, sounding impressed. "I think the jerk peed himself."

"No," Jaeger muttered. "But he was close."

"She had found a great piece of evidence," Mark told him. "A tribe in the Himalayas who had a pelt of what they said was the Yeti. She was able to obtain a skin sample, but Dendy stole it from her and claimed it as his own. Turned out to be a new species, a hybrid bear that brought him national recognition and brand-new funding. Kicked her to the curb."

Jaeger's protective nature rose to the surface, and he had a new perspective on her chosen career.

"Thank you for letting me know," he said. "Agathe has finished dinner if you'd like to eat."

"What about Gabs?" Kenny asked.

"I'll bring her a plate," Jaeger said. "I need to talk to her."

"Sure," Mark said. He grabbed Kenny and pulled him along toward the kitchen. "We'll just, you know, eat. You go take care of Gabs."

Kenny gave him a thumbs up.

Chapter Five

Gabrielle stared at her laptop screen and wanted to scream. The webpage she stared at recorded everything about why she was in Alaska, a blog of day-to-day activities and the hunt that something might be wandering in the Arctic Circle.

Little bird, my ass.

Memories surged, every single one of them ugly. The blog almost felt like another betrayal, although she didn't think that was Kenny's intention. And maybe she was just over-reacting. After all, she'd been such a young, idealistic girl when Burt Dendy had sunk his hooks into her, spinning tales of the Yeti and making the hunt seem romantic and glamorous. She'd changed her life around for him, began to miss school, and after she'd spent the entire semester allowance following him to the Himalayas, her parents had yanked their support which forced her to drop out of college.

A knock sounded on the door, bringing her out of her thoughts. She wiped her cheeks, surprised to find she'd been crying. "Come in."

The door opened and Jaeger stood there, holding a tray in one hand. A covered plate and a can of beer was his offering. He came into the room and shut the door with his heel. "Dinner," he said, setting the tray upon the dresser near the door. "Agathe's mixture of her homeland and Alaska. Braised caribou, prepared like *Mørbradbøf*, with onions and cabbage."

She raised the lid off the plate and inhaled. Her mouth watered.

"Thank you, it smells amazing." She cut a piece of the meat and with a fork, lifted it eye level to inspect the meat. "I've been to Tibet and Bhutan, and I've eaten many odd things, but this will be the first time for caribou."

He shrugged. "A little tougher than pork. I will warn you that it does not taste like chicken."

She smiled and ate the morsel on her fork. The flavor burst across her taste buds, slightly salty, very savory, and a little chewy.

"She's a very good cook," she said once she swallowed. "Is Agathe from the Netherlands?"

"No, we're both from Greenland, by way of the Vikings," he replied. "I came here about ten years ago to set up this lodge."

"Vikings?"

"Yes, both our families are direct descendants, and Agathe's family has served my own for many generations."

Gabrielle raised an eyebrow. "Is that still common? I mean, I've studied tribes in various parts of the world where family traditions are handed down like that, but that's a practice not readily found in more modern civilization."

"Agathe is a traditionalist," he said with a shrug. "I have two younger brothers she could've gone with, but she decided to stay with me. And I'm thankful to have her. She is a den mother here at the lodge."

"I can see why," Gabrielle murmured around a mouthful of food. "This is really wonderful. Does the lodge's name mean anything?"

"Frosset means frozen in Danish," he said. "My family's moto is *Frosne Hjerte*. It means frozen heart. Frosset seemed like a fitting name."

They lapsed into silence while she ate and she was surprised it wasn't uncomfortable to be around him and not talk. His presence was actually more soothing, even though her senses still danced at his nearness. When she finished, she laid her utensils on the plate and wiped her mouth.

"Thank you for bringing this to me," she said. "Do you always provide personal service like this to your guests?"

"No," he said. He sat down on the bed and patted the space next to him.

She hesitated for a moment, weighing the pros and cons of being near him. She had an inkling of where he wanted the evening to end, but she still wasn't quite sure if it would be a wise move.

"Will you be up for snowmobiling tomorrow?"

"Yes." She wrapped her arms around herself. That seemed to help stifle the urge to sit next to him. "Although I know it's a long shot that any evidence or proof will still be out there."

He frowned. "What is more important to you? The proof that cryptids may exist or proving to yourself you made the right career choice?"

"Ouch," she muttered, narrowing her eyes. "You don't hold back your punches, do you?"

"We may not have known each other very long, but I feel a connection with you, Gabrielle."

She blew out a puff of pent-up frustration that startled her bangs. She didn't want to admit that she felt it, too. "I don't trust easily anymore, especially when it comes to my work."

"Mark told me about your history with Dendy."

She reached over to her laptop and turned it around.

"That's how Dendy knew I was here," she said, pointing. "Kenny wrote a blog and tweeted about it. So I guess a little bird did tell him."

"Does he do this often? Pop up wherever you are, uninvited?"

Gabrielle shook her head. "This is the first time since our partnership dissolved, and I don't know why now."

He studied her for a moment. "Why the Yeti?"

She hesitated for a moment, trying to find the words she never voiced aloud before. "I've always felt like there was more to this world than what our eyes can see or our hands can touch. I became an anthropology major but was seduced by the dark side, per se. In this case, legends of the Yeti. And the search can be addicting."

He cocked his head. "So you do this because you believe in the supernatural?"

"I don't classify it as supernatural."

"Many people would. Many people probably think you're crazy."

She snorted. "Yeah, well, there's a few who don't. I have funding through a local college interested in the Yeti legends. It's through their history department that Mark, Kenny, and I were able to explore for so long. And for us to come here. I'm on the last bit of our grant so I'm hoping to find something positive to bring home to them. Can I ask you a question?"

"Of course," he replied. "You can ask me anything, Gabrielle."

"Why did you use the word 'werewolf'?"

He didn't answer right away. Instead he patted the bed again, and this time, she sat down. Her heart beat accelerated as her pulse jumped from simply being near him. There it was again, that electric arc that seemed to wrap around them like gossamer strings. Was it really just physical attraction that would die away as soon as it was satisfied? An itch to scratch? After all, she'd only been with one man and that relationship had ended in betrayal.

Maybe it was time to take a new model for a test drive. Erase the old with a new memory, something to look back at fondly whenever Dendy showed his face again.

"Maybe, like you, I, too, believe in things our eyes cannot see or our hands cannot touch," he murmured. Their gazes met, locked. He leaned closer until his warm breath fanned across her face. Her heart thumped with anticipation and her panties grew damp. The time for denial fled. She wanted this. Wanted him.

Jaeger possessed her mouth, curling one hand around her head to hold her in place while he kissed her. This was different than before. This kiss had a touch of possession in it. He plundered her mouth and she let him as her mind went blank. It was only him and her, and the presence of a bed beckoning her to lay back. Jaeger left her mouth and made his way to her ear where he sucked lightly on the sensitive area behind the shell.

"Oh, wow," she breathed. "That feels so good. *You* feel good. M-maybe we should, um, stop."

"One more kiss," he whispered.

Jaeger kissed her cheek as he slowly moved his hands down until he cupped her breasts. She gasped as he teased the nipples with a fingertip.

"One more?" he asked before he pressed his lips against hers again. A light, feathery brush of their mouths as he continued to tease the turgid peak under her bra.

"O-okay. One more," she agreed, stuttering a little from the desire wracking her body.

One hand left her breast and he slid it down her side, over her hip and across her thighs until it nestled between them. Instinct, or maybe reflex, had her legs opening. Hoping, yearning, he'd touch her further.

Taking the invitation, he moved suddenly. Not releasing her, but only shifting until he kneeled between her spread thighs. Determination seemed to shimmer in his movements as he placed a hand on her chest and pushed her until she lay flat on her back. He then unsnapped her jeans and tugged on them. Gabrielle lifted her hips so he could slide them down. The momentary break in the sensual haze he'd wrapped around her made her wonder if she should call a halt to this, but her body didn't want to stop. So she gave into the demands of what she really craved.

One more kiss.

Jaeger pulled her jeans off, dragging her panties along with them. He slid his hands under her bare ass and lifted as he bent over her. Okay, so one more kiss was placed on her pussy mound, but that only led to another and another, until fingers slid along her slit and opened her up to his loving.

"Oh!" She gasped. "Lick my pussy!"

Jaeger obeyed, starting from the bottom of her pussy and licking up, until he drew her clit into his mouth. Gabrielle panted, bucking her hips against his mouth, wanting more. He gave it, sliding his tongue up and down, sucking and licking until Gabrielle was in heaven, her mind in a daze as she gave herself up to the unbelievable pleasure.

"I'm going to come," she cried. She thrust her fingers into his hair. "Please oh, please don't stop."

Gabrielle's legs twitched and she lifted her pelvis off the bed, wrapping her thighs around Jaeger's head. The tension built, coiling higher, until it suddenly snapped and threw her off the plateau. Gabrielle gave a breathless little scream as light burst behind her closed eyes.

She fell back limp, her limbs wet noodles she couldn't move. Jaeger left the area between her legs and lay beside her. Not caring that his face was wet with her release, she leaned forward and kissed him, tasting herself upon his lips. It was sexy as hell.

He brushed her hair off her forehead. "Gabrielle," he murmured, his voice soft and endearing.

"What about you?"

He smiled. "Not about me, love. This is all for you."

She closed her eyes, content. Wow. A man who gave pleasure without expectation? She might have found her mythological creature after all.

Chapter Six

Gabrielle was nervous as she descended the stairs for breakfast. She had passed out last night after the mind-blowing pleasure Jaeger had given her, but now in the light of day, she wasn't sure how to handle it. Would he ignore her? Would he mock her? Or worse, would he pretend last night never happened?

Dendy had insisted their relationship remain a secret. For years she had dealt with that and she could do it again, remain quiet about what had happened in her room. But when she approached the kitchen, Jaeger came out from his office and smiled at her. His smile relieved a lot of lingering tension and she relaxed. She smiled back and Jaeger put his arms around her in a hug.

"Good morning," he murmured.

"Morning," she replied.

"I've already pulled the snowmobiles out from the shed, so right after breakfast we can head out."

"Okay."

"You have warm clothing?"

She nodded. "I never really unpacked from my trip to Bhutan. I have my Himalayan gear in my suitcase."

He smiled, took her hand, and led her into the kitchen where Agathe was dishing up plates of eggs, biscuits, and bacon for everyone. A carafe of coffee was on the table where Kenny and Mark were already shoveling food into their mouths.

"Right after breakfast, we're heading out on snowmobiles to the area where the picture was taken," she told them.

Kenny took a gulp of black coffee in an effort to talk. "We are?"

He jumped up and began to shovel more food from his plate into his mouth, until his cheeks puffed out.

"Not you, Kenny," Gabrielle said quickly. "Slow down."

His mouth dropped open in shock, and the look on his face was as if she had just kicked his puppy. Some of the food fell out of his overstuffed mouth back onto the plate.

"I only own two snowmobiles," Jaeger said, sounding regretful. "The company I usually rent from has shut down for the season."

"You and Mark can explore after us," Gabrielle replied quickly. She reached over and closed Kenny's mouth.

He sat down, looking a little dejected.

After breakfast, she went upstairs and changed into her snow clothes. Jaeger waited for her out back, and she climbed onto the one next to him. A moment later, Jaeger took off, heading south toward the wilderness, and she throttled after him.

The trip was refreshing. The cold air cleared her head, brought a sense of rawness to the moment. She felt exhilarated, alive. A sense of wonder, and hope. The exact opposite of what she had felt in Bhutan. Perhaps it was time to move on from searching for the Yeti, to get out of the search all together. She was tired of remembering Dendy in everything she did. Perhaps she should go back to school and finish her original life plans.

They entered the forest and it wasn't long until Jaeger pulled over and signaled to a grove of aspen trees. Their yellow leaves were already frozen, and some had begun to fall to the ground, but it was no mistake they were the trees that had been in the photo.

She turned off the snowmobile and dismounted to

walk to the trees. From her pocket, she took out the photos, and holding them up, she compared each one until she found the right angle from where the picture had been taken. Walking forward, she looked back to confirm she was in the right spot. Jaeger watched her, arms folded as he waited on his own machine.

Just as she thought, any prints that might have been left had already been swept away from the wind. Walking in the direction the creature must have taken, she examined all around, looking for any type of evidence. Something white was stuck to the bark of a tree and she hurried forward. At first, she thought it was just a bit of snow, but as she got closer, it swayed a little in the breeze. Excitement gripped her. Once closer, she realized it was fur. Thick, white fur.

"Oh my God," she whispered. Taking off her backpack she pulled off her gloves to grab a plastic evidence bag and tweezers. Carefully extracting the small patch of fur from the bark, Gabrielle put it in the bag.

"It's probably just bear fur," Jaeger said from behind her.

She jumped a little. "Ah! You scared me. Uh, no, I don't think so. A polar bear has hair. This looks to be fur, and it's too high up on the bark to be an animal on four legs."

"Like a wolf, you mean?"

She narrowed her eyes. "Yeah. Perhaps it's my werewolf."

"Perhaps."

There was something very closed off about him as he stared at the fur in the bag. Shaking off the odd feeling, she placed the bag of evidence into her backpack. They headed back toward the hotel, and this time she was leading the way. As soon as they arrived, Kenny and Mark came bounding down the porch steps.

"Our turn!" Kenny cried. He was bundled up head to toe and waddled slightly. She decided to hold off telling them about the fur until after their exploration.

She went up to her room and took off her snow clothes, laying them on the luggage rack that every hotel room in the world seemed to have. Sitting on the bed, she dug the package of fur out of the backpack and held it up to the light. Something told her it wasn't ordinary wolf fur. The same thrill that had gripped her when she'd seen the so-called Yeti pelt now zinged through her blood. Placing the plastic bag back into her backpack, Gabrielle walked into the bathroom to take a shower.

As she dried off, she heard a noise and opened the bathroom door. Jaeger stood in the doorway with a bottle of wine and two glasses. Although it was the middle of the day, the sunlight had started to fall, casting the room in shadow. Gabrielle's heart pounded with anticipation, and she knew now was the time to either give in to the desire between them or deny it, and she really didn't want to say no.

"Close the door," she whispered.

He stepped into the room and used his heel to shut the door. She dropped the towel and stood naked before him. Jaeger put the bottle of wine and glasses on the dresser and made a beeline toward her.

Their lips met and she immediately felt the change between them. There wasn't any hesitation, no coy reserve left at all. He wanted her and she wanted him, so Gabrielle opened for him. He nibbled and devoured until they were both breathless.

He swept her up in his arms, his muscles bulging as he held her, and she wrapped her legs around his waist as he carried her to the bed. He didn't stop until they were at the bed and he tumbled her onto the mattress, coming down on top of her. Gabrielle needed to feel his skin against hers, needed to feel her own softness pressed against his softness. She tugged his shirt up and over his head, tossing it aside. He kicked off his pants. The man was beautiful. Hard muscles, an ass that made her want to take a bite out of it. His cock was big and thick, and it jutted out proudly. He leaned over and trailed his lips down her neck, his fingertips traveling upward until they reached her breasts. She hissed and arched her back, thrusting more into his hands as his thumb flicked over her nipples.

"Jaeger, please!"

His mouth engulfed her right breast while he played with the other, rolling the taut nipple around. Gabrielle threw her head back as he sucked and teased her. And then he moved down her body and pried her legs apart, his fingers sliding up her thighs to find her dripping pussy. One finger pushed through her slit, into her core, and her hips undulated. He used her natural lubricant to tease her, pumping in and out between her plump pussy lips and making sure to bump against her clit. He leaned forward to lap up her juices, first off her thighs and then following the trail up. While his finger continued to tease, he sucked her sensitive clit into his mouth. She cried out and her fingers curled into his hair as she began to thrust against his face, in time with his fingers that fucked her. She felt herself begin to splinter apart and then she screamed his name as her orgasm swept over her. He lapped it up, licking her until she gave a little shudder and went limp.

"Oh, my God," she said a bit breathlessly. Jaeger kissed his way back up her body until he found her mouth again.

"Ditto," he murmured. "You're so beautiful."

He reached for his jeans and pulled out a condom. Turning over onto his back, he donned the rubber. Then he took hold of one of her thighs and pulled it over until she straddled him.

"You're mine," he said in a deep, guttural voice. Taking hold of his dick, she raised up and sat down on him.

"Yes. Yes!" she cried as he filled her up. He rolled them until she was on her back and he was nestled between her legs. And as he pressed forward, she suddenly knew her entire world had changed.

****

As soon as he entered her wet depths, something meaningful singed through his blood. His wolf howled inside him and his incisors elongated. He wanted to bite her, mark her, make her his forever. His one true mate. As their bodies merged, he felt their souls joining, becoming one.

"Fuck!" He groaned when he bottomed out all the way inside her. His balls rested snugly against her. "I don't think I can last long, Gabrielle. Your pussy is so tight."

"I need you so badly, Jaeger. Please!"

Her plea drove him wild, and he pounded into her harder, deeper. Her tight little pussy was sucking him in, turning his brain to mush. He was fast losing control and he so wanted this moment to never end. She felt so damn good wrapped around him, skin to skin.

"Christ, Gabrielle," he ground out. "Are you close, sweetheart?"

"Yes!" she cried. "Yes! Jaeger!"

He reached down between their bodies and touched her clit, and that was all she needed to fly apart. He felt her pussy spasm around his cock and her incoherent cries of pleasure pushed him over the top and he came with a loud shout.

His wolf wanted to bite, to sink his fangs into her

skin and taste her blood. Cement them together and complete the bond. But he didn't allow it. He couldn't because she wasn't ready to know the full truth of who and what he was.

****

Something woke her up. The tiniest bit of noise roused her from the relaxing slumber she'd fallen into after the mind-blowing sex. The room was dark except for the moonlight streaming in the window. She reached over and clicked on the lamp resting on the nightstand. Jaeger, wearing his jeans, was bent over her items resting on the luggage stand.

"What are you doing?" she demanded.

He turned, with her bag in one hand and the bag of fur in the other. Ignoring her nakedness, she jumped out of bed and marched over to him. She snatched the items away from him and glared at him.

"Were you trying to steal them?" she asked. Fury had her shaking. "*Steal* from me? Why do all the men in my life want to hurt me? Get out!"

"Gabrielle—"

"No! Get out!"

They stared at one another, and a myriad of emotions crossed over his face. She didn't care. In an instant he had hurt her, more than she thought possible for someone she'd just met, and far deeper than someone who was just supposed to be a fling. He bent and picked up his shirt, and then turned and left her room. The door closed softly behind him.

Chapter Seven

Trying hard not to cry, Gabrielle blindly stared out her bedroom window, replaying everything that had happened between her and Jaeger. It wasn't fair that she could fall for someone so fast and have him hurt her just like Dendy had. The same exact way. And the question *why* zinged through her head. He wasn't in the scientific world. He wasn't even in the cryptid community. So why would he steal her fur?

Was he working with Dendy? Was that why the asshole was here in Alaska?

The thought made her sick to her stomach. A movement outside caught her attention, a form heading away from the lodge. The low visibility made it hard, if not impossible, to identify who it was, but she didn't think it was Jaeger. The person was too short. Was it Dendy? If so, why was he there?

Spying on her?

Making up her mind, she grabbed her coat from the foot of the bed and hurried out of her bedroom. The lodge was dark except for a fire burning in the fireplace. She hurried to the front door and left, running down the porch and out into the snow before logical thoughts could settle. It was dark and cold, but she was determined to get to the bottom of why Dendy was following her and if Jaeger was helping him.

She soon entered a spattering of dense forest trees. Once in the treeline, all light ceased reaching her. Gabrielle halted and looked around. She saw something move off to her right and she took off running, trying to catch up, but once she reached the spot, there was nothing. More movement, this time off to her left, and once again she chased after it. A moment later, she came to a dead stop and looked around. The slow realization that she had no idea where she was hit her, and fear spread through her already very cold body.

Then laughter came trickling from behind her. Gabrielle spun and saw Burt Dendy, watching her with a nasty little smile on his face. She wanted to rush up to him and hit with all the pent-up fury she still held, but the rifle hanging by his side made her hesitate.

"Why are you here?" she demanded. "Why are you doing this to me?"

"Because your fucking assistant posted those pictures of you in that tribe!" he yelled. "It shows *you* getting that pelt. You! Not me! And now there's an investigation into my claims of discovery."

The admission stunned her. For a moment, she didn't know what to say, and then all the rage that she'd bottled up for years came pouring out.

"It was *my* discovery, you bastard!" She thumped herself on her chest. "You stole my research and took all the accolades for your own."

"*I* gave you this career. *I* showed you the thrill of hunting the Yeti. And yet *you* find a new species of bear? I don't think so! This was under my watch. *My* fucking expedition!"

She stared at him for a moment because his words were so incredulous they bordered on stupidity. In fact, she was a little flabbergasted.

"You never even wanted to hunt down that nomadic tribe," she said. "It was *my* decision and you told me to go. Your exact words were if I wanted to waste my time then go. So I did. You had nothing to do with it."

"I can still break you, little girl," he muttered

"You can't hurt me, Dendy," she said, and was suddenly surprised to realize that it was true. He had hurt her, but he had not broken her heart. She had never loved him. Perhaps all she needed, after all, was to confront not just him, but her own emotions. With that knowledge, the anger ebbed, leaving her feeling light and free.

"When that idiot friend of yours posted you were coming here and that picture, I knew I had to get the jump on any evidence you might find," he said.

That was when Gabrielle realized Jaeger had nothing to do with Dendy. She rethought the scene she saw earlier, with him holding the pack of fur and wondered if perhaps he was simply looking at it. He lived in this frozen world, so maybe he was helping her try to identify it. Relief surged through her heart.

"So you followed me to steal more of my work?"

"Steal? You should *thank* me for giving you direction. A purpose. If it wasn't for me, you'd still be floundering in academics, moldering behind a desk and kissing the asses of your parents."

"You're so delusional," she said. "And karma is a bitch. Good luck with your future reputation, because I'm pretty sure you're going to need it."

A growl floated across the wind and Dendy spun around, bringing his rifle up. Another noise came and Dendy took off running.

"Wait!" she cried, trying to run after him. But the snow drifts were high and her limbs were uncoordinated from the cold. In seconds, she was alone in the woods with no knowledge of where to go or where to turn.

It dawned on her that she had made a very bad decision. Perhaps if she just followed her own footprints back… Gabrielle turned and followed the tracks the way she'd come. With each step, however, she grew colder and colder until she couldn't really feel her feet. She stumbled and fell, and it was difficult to get back up. Her teeth chattered from the force of her body shaking, but the next time she stumbled, she couldn't move. Gabrielle lay in the snow until her body stopped shaking. Suddenly, she began to get warmer.

She knew that was a big problem.

"J … J-Jaeger," she called out, knowing that it was impossible for him to hear her. It was impossible for *anyone* to hear her. It flashed through her mind that she was going to die in the cold, because of Dendy. That really pissed her off. Too bad she couldn't move a muscle to kick the shit out of him.

Gabrielle closed her eyes. She didn't want to die of exposure, but she'd been in the Himalayas enough to know the drill. In the next moment, however, two strong arms picked her up and cradled her against a warm body. She opened her eyes and stared at a long snout, white fur, and pointed ears. Had she died? Was she now in cryptid heaven?

The creature held her tightly, and soon the ice within her thawed. Pins and needles tingled all over her arms and legs, especially in her feet. But with warmth came clarity, and she blinked a few times to make sure she wasn't seeing things. Fear blossomed through her first, then shock, and finally a mixture of wonderment and disbelief. She slapped a hand over her mouth in an effort to stifle a scream, because in all her travels, in the years she searched for the Yeti, never once did she ever think she'd be in the arms of one. The last thing she wanted to do was frighten the beast and have him attack her. Was he taking her to his den? Was he going to eat her?

Then the lodge was there, and the creature set her on her feet on the first porch step. Her first instinct was to scramble away from him, and that was exactly what she did. She backed up until her heel hit the next step and down she sat heavily upon her bottom. That left the

493

creature staring at her with huge, dark eyes. Gabrielle didn't blink, didn't breathe. She simply stared at the … the … thing … she didn't even know what to call it.

It cocked its head and waited. For her? What did it want? Why did it bring her to the lodge? Was it intelligent?

Her fear began to drain away as curiosity took over. Slowly, she stood back up. The creature didn't move. Its eyes were wide, intense. Slowly, she extended a hand, palm up, holding it out for him to sniff. It was what she'd do to any dog, and being this close to the animal, she saw the wolf traits shining through. The creature dipped its head low since it stood as least six feet tall, and stretched toward her hand. She touched the fur. Soft, but with an underling bristly coat, and pure white in color. It was the same as the fur she'd found on the tree bark.

She ran her hand down the side of his face, toward his ear. It tilted its head toward her caress, so she petted him again. The fur was too thick for any gender identity, but something told her it was male.

Then he took a step back, and before her eyes, it mutated. Or shrunk. Or something, because bones cracked and popped and he fell onto four legs. It transformed from a humanoid cryptid to an ordinary arctic wolf. Then it whimpered and sat on its haunches, and Gabrielle suddenly understood that was how it hid in plain sight. She smiled and held out her hand, and the wolf came right up to her to let her pet it. Knowing it wouldn't hurt her, she wrapped her arms around the neck and hugged the animal.

"Finally," came a nasty whisper from the darkness. "It's mine."

Gabrielle spun around and saw Dendy, rifle raised and aimed at the wolf.

"No!" she cried and jumped forward to protect the

wolf just as the rifle exploded. All she heard was a menacing growl as pain engulfed her.

Chapter Eight

Jaeger sat in his office, in front of the fireplace, staring into the flames. His mind wasn't on them, however, he was thinking about Gabrielle. He had wanted to make sure the fur was his, and thus had pulled it out of her bag to check. Now he had a dilemma, lie to cover up why he was interested in that piece of fur, or tell Gabrielle the truth. A woman who was a cryptozoologist … her career was certainly an interesting aspect of his mate.

He heard footsteps run down the stairs and a second later, the front door opened and closed. Jaeger rose and looked out the window to see Gabrielle hurry away from the lodge toward the woods. Concern sluiced through him. It was dark and she didn't know the layout of the land, as well as wearing only a coat in the freezing temperatures. He turned to leave, intent on following after her, and Agathe stood in the doorway.

"Are you going after her?" Agathe asked.

"Yes. Get a warm bath ready and some blankets. She'll be frozen in moments."

"All right."

Agathe hurried off, moving fast for someone her age. Jaeger headed outside and stared at the way Gabrielle took, the tracks a direct path. He had no clue why she'd go out at night, but he was going to give her a stern lecture as soon as possible. Right now, it was more important to bring her back.

He didn't bother with a coat. His wolf would keep him warm enough, but as he followed after her, it soon became apparent why she had run off into the night. A second pair of footprints emerged, and across the breeze a harsh and bitter scent wafted. Dendy. Jaeger paused and listened. He heard faint voices, although he couldn't pinpoint where they were coming from. Frustration gripped him, so he began to strip, removing his shirt, pants, and shoes before he allowed the change to take over. Heat and pain engulfed him as his bones shifted, elongated, popping and cracking as he turned from man into a hybrid type of wolf. Like many of his kind, he was able to walk upright or on all fours, and now he chose to protect his mate. He let out a roar and zeroed in on where the voices were coming from.

"J-Jaeger!"

His ears shifted forward as he heard his name, uttered desperately. Off he ran, hurrying, knowing it was only a matter of time before Gabrielle's body began to shut down from the freezing temperature. He found her lying down, curled in a fetal position, and he gently picked her up to share his body heat with her. Then he ran back to the lodge, back to Agathe who waited to help his mate.

As he sat her on her feet at the lodge, however, he saw the fear overtake her. Fear of him, and it broke his heart. He couldn't talk to her and ease her concern, that he trusted her enough to reveal who and what he really was. Then she touched him, stroked his fur, and he loved how her courage took over. Her fear seemed to melt away, so he decided to go for broke and reveal his species' truest secret. He finished the transformation into the wolf.

Here was the elusive secret she'd been searching years for. Concrete proof that the creature she'd been hunting was able to hide in plain sight. And although he'd never encountered one, her hybrid bear had probably been the Yeti, killed in its half-transformed state. Would she understand? Most cryptids were, in fact, shifters.

With his attention focused entirely on her, he

failed to identify the threat until it was too late. Dendy had shown up, rifle raised, and then Gabrielle was shielding him with her body. A shot fired, and the acrid smell of blood and gunpowder filled his nostrils.

He growled and attacked, jumping on Dendy who stared wide-eyed first at Gabrielle's supine body and then into his eyes. Jaeger's instinct was to go for the jugular, to rip it out and end the miserable man's life, but Kenny was there, stopping him.

"We got him, Jaeger!" Kenny yelled at him. In one hand was a phone. "Mark and I filmed him shooting her. We got you transforming, too, but we'll edit that part out. Please ... we'll keep your secret but, please, help Gabrielle."

He backed off, stepping off the man he wanted to kill. Kenny and Mark took hold of Dendy as Agathe picked up the rifle and pointed it at the stunned, scared man. He turned to his mate. He could hear her heart beating, although it was faint. A dark-red stain spread out from her body onto the snow, and he knew she was bleeding out. If he didn't do something, she would die.

Please forgive me!

There was no time to debate whether or not she'd want the mating connection. If he didn't initiate it, she'd die. And if she died, he might as well curl up and die as well. He bent his head and sniffed at the area between her head and shoulder. His fangs rested on the soft skin, and then he bit.

****

Gabrielle was cold. She wandered the dark, lost, and then a ray of sunlight appeared. She put her hand up to shield her eyes from the powerful rays. The warmth drew her and she walked toward it, moving from the lonely darkness into a warm paradise. A green valley stretched out before her with tall trees and blossoming flowers, and she smiled, more than content. A wolf emerged, walking toward her. It was big, its fur white as snow. His dark eyes stared at her, but she wasn't afraid. She held out a hand to it, and as it walked toward her, it transformed into a creature, her rescuer, before completing the change into man.

Jaeger.

He had shared his deepest secret with her and saved her life. Happiness and love filled her.

I saved your life by biting you.

His voice echoed around her. His lips didn't move, but she could hear him, and it was the most natural thing in the world.

You aren't like me, he continued. *You won't change. But you will have a long life, like me. Heal faster. We are mates. We are one.*

Gabrielle smiled.

And woke up.

Jaeger held her hand, eyes closed, head bowed. She lay in her bed at the lodge, nice and warm. She touched the top of his head and he opened his eyes. They looked at one another.

"Yes," she whispered. "Mates."

The End

WOLF HUNTER

Elena Kincaid

Copyright © 2017

Chapter One

Logan sat with his feet propped up on his desk in his office. His chair squeaked as he swiveled in it. "I need a new fucking chair!"

"I've been telling you that for months," Hannah called out from the front office.

"I wasn't talking to you," he grumbled. "Damn nosy shifter hearing."

"I heard that!"

He hadn't meant to say that last part aloud, but couldn't bring it upon himself to give a crap at the moment. He was bored. Very fucking bored. The last few cases he took on were way too easy and now he just wanted to get his hands a bit dirty and meet a challenge. He flung the copy of *Men's Magazine* he had been holding onto his messy, mahogany desk and smiled wickedly at the small photo on the lower right hand side of the front page. "Asshole thought he could hide from me, did he?" Then again, perhaps the *asshole* in question was just messing with him and wanted to be found. There was his next challenge, he thought. It had, after all been three years since he had lain eyes on the rat bastard.

He heard the front door open. His nostrils flared as he sniffed the air, detecting a human male. He smelled faintly of expensive cigar smoke and peppermint, mixed in with a bergamot-scented aftershave. The man introduced himself to Hannah, Logan's annoying but indispensable secretary, and though he would never admit this to her, she was someone he considered a friend.

He heard Hannah lift the receiver. "Your two o'clock is here, Mr. Munro," she said into the phone, though it was only for show. The intercom went nowhere considering the fact that he had smashed his landline several years ago. He hadn't bothered to replace it yet and wondered if the human would notice the absence of a phone on his desk.

Logan had actually forgotten he had an appointment today, and humans tended to be boring clients, however, he had nothing better to do. "Send him in," he said quietly, knowing that only Hannah's ears could hear.

"Go on in, Mr. Petridis."

Logan stood after his potential client opened the door to his office and entered. He extended his hand for the man to shake when he reached his desk. "Have a seat, Mr. Petridis, and tell me what I can do for you."

"Call me Constantine, please," he replied with a moderately pronounced Greek accent as he sat down. The human, despite being a good six inches shorter than Logan's six-foot-three, gave the impression of being a formidable man—or he would to other humans, at least. He had a head full of thick salt and pepper hair mixed in with black, he wore a serious expression, his face was sparingly lined with age, and his eyes were a bright bottled green, shrewd, assessing, and the brows above them were now furrowed in confusion as he stared at Logan's desk.

Yep, he notices there is no phone.

"Ah," the man said, though he did not elaborate

on whatever revelation he had just had. After a beat, he added, "My girls are missing. I need you to find them and bring them home safely."

"How long have they been missing?" Logan asked. "And wouldn't this be more of a matter for the police?"

"One has been missing for three days now, and the other went after her yesterday," Constantine replied. "I do not think it would be a good idea for law enforcement to get involved."

Logan leaned back in his chair, mentally cursing the annoying squeak it made, and exhaled loudly. This was all he needed right now! It was true he usually got hired by independent contractors rather than bondsmen—wealthier clients who wanted to deal with their wayward family members their way, and most of whom were shifters like him—but he didn't deal with family drama or love-struck teen runaways, that was for sure. "So let me get this straight, Constantine. Your daughter runs off and then your other one decides to chase after her and you want me to find them and drag their asses back here? With all due respect, sir, do I look like a *private dick* to you?"

The middle-aged man in front of him arched his brow at him sardonically.

Touché, Mr. Petridis. Logan would be the first to admit that he could definitely be a dick sometimes. Regardless. "I'm a bounty hunter, Constan—"

Before Logan even had time to finish his sentence, Constantine took out a stack of cash from his inner coat pocket and threw it down on the table. The hundred dollar bills were neatly wrapped in a currency strap into what Logan assessed amounted to ten grand.

"There's your bounty," Constantine said matter-of-factly. "You'll get another ten thousand for each of my daughters once you return them safely to me." He paused for a moment before adding, "She didn't run off, Mr. Munro. She was taken."

Taken! Now that sounded more up his alley. "Call me Logan." Ten k was ten k, Logan thought as he leaned forward and folded his hands on top of his desk. Thirty grand in total would be even sweeter. "Start from the beginning," Logan prompted. He saw the man visibly relax and that made him feel sorry for the guy. Logan wasn't a father, but he understood the bonds of family, even when on the outs with one of his. Pack life had become considered antiquated, even cult-like amongst most shifters, and pretty much non-existent as of about a century ago, so it was family, including extended and close friends that were at the forefront for shifters. Someone had messed with Constantine's family and due to his calmness and assuredness, and his lack of wanting to go to the police, this kidnapping was personal.

"I know what you are," Constantine suddenly blurted, shocking the hell out of Logan. Wolves may live amongst humans, seamlessly blending in, but for the most part, their existence was kept secret.

"And what am I?" Logan asked.

"Twenty-three years ago," Constantine began, "when my wife Maria and I still lived in Greece, I came outside to find a wolf cub in my backyard. My heart nearly stopped. That was because the wolf was playing with my then four-year-old daughter Theodora. Just as I was about to approach, prepared to take my daughter to safety, I heard my little Thea giggling as she cuddled the cub, and I saw that the little wolf meant her no harm. It was scared of me though, trembling when I approached. The clouds were looming on top of us, about to let loose a storm, so I decided to offer the cub shelter and food for the night.

"Imagine my surprise when I brought the wolf inside and it transformed into a ten-year-old girl before my very eyes. The child, Teresa, she told us about your world and about the rare True Alphas among them, like you are, born even stronger and faster than even most of your own kind. She told us that her parents were murdered by a teenaged alpha's family when they refused to give up their daughter to them. The family claimed that since she was the mate of their alpha, then by all rights she belonged with them."

"Whose rights exactly?" Logan snorted with disgust. These wolves definitely sounded like the cultists he detested, the ones who thought themselves superior with the desire to rule in packs once again and subjugate humans.

"I didn't presume to know your ways then, nor do I now," Constantine said. "She was only a scared little girl and we all fell in love with her. We left Greece and claimed Teresa as ours when we came to America, and now they have found us."

Now Logan understood why this man needed *his* help. Constantine must have heard about him—his track record after all, was impeccable, whether he was hunting a wolf or a human. He smiled, feeling the blood lust from his inner wolf. This day had definitely gotten more interesting, he thought. "I'll get both your daughters back. Teresa may be a lone wolf, but her senses are sharp, and I'll intercept her before she tries to take on the pack on her own. And don't worry, Theodora will be kept alive since they are more than likely using her as bait…" Constantine suddenly furrowing his brows caused Logan to pause mid-sentence.

"You are mistaken, Logan. It is my Teresa who has been taken. My Thea has gone after her."

Constantine reached into his pocket and produced

a photograph of his daughters. It was a close up, what appeared to be a possible selfie. The sisters were smiling brightly, and though they were not blood related, and bore no resemblance to each other, it was still easy to spot something familial about them. Logan felt his cock jump to immediate attention when closely examining the features of the one Constantine pointed out to be Thea. She very much resembled her father with her bottle-green eyes, heart-shaped face, and long, wavy, jet-black hair. Her nose was small and a little upturned, her lips full, and the dimples in both cheeks only added to her somewhat exotic-looking beauty. He couldn't recall ever having such an immediate visceral reaction to a woman, let alone from just a photograph.

Definitely a lot more interesting!

Chapter Two

Time was of the essence. Logan knew that. Which was precisely why he was currently flooring his Harley on I 287. As soon as Mr. Petridis left his office, he began his research. Constantine told him what he knew of the wolves from Greece as relayed to him by his shifter daughter, and it didn't take long for Logan to trace the Kostastakis wolves from Greece to New Jersey. Through his contacts, he also discovered they had several properties scattered throughout Northern Jersey as well as some in upstate New York. What he hadn't yet figured out was in which one of them Teresa was being held and how much of this information Theodora had pertaining to these locations.

His reaction to the photograph notwithstanding, the human girl would have to be his first acquisition. She was the one in more immediate danger. "What the fuck was she thinking?" he muttered into his helmet not for the first time since learning of her brazen act. A human girl going after a pack of shifters, and one of them an alpha no less, was on a suicide mission.

He managed to re-trace her steps to one of the houses in New Jersey and when he finally arrived there, leaving his bike out of sight, what he saw puzzled him. A few wolf-shifter men lay twitching on the ground. He then heard a piercing scream coming from inside of the cabin, making his hackles stand, and his inner wolf furious.

He rushed inside. Thea was on her knees with her hands restrained behind her. The man in front of her had his hand poised to slap her … again, by the looks of the red mark on her cheek. He saw one more twitching shifter in his peripheral vision but paid no mind to him for the moment. The fact these men dared to lay hands on a woman had already signed their death warrants, but as he sniffed the air, inhaling the intoxicating scent of Thea, he immediately resolved to make their deaths that much more excruciating.

"Mate," he said aloud. There was no mistaking it. Her earthy feminine musk permeated his senses, along with a distinct ambrosia underlining it that would call only to his wolf. His body shook with need and fury. He growled loudly as his canines dropped and his nails elongated into sharp claws. The two men instantly turned in his direction and then he smiled wickedly at their identical fearful expressions as they must have realized an alpha had just stepped into their presence. He could see their legs shaking, and the pair of them fighting to keep upright instead of falling to their knees in submission.

Logan's almost maniacal bloodlust and the need to protect his mate prevented him from doing anything calculated like he would have wanted. Before the two wolves even understood what was happening, they fell dead to the floor, their throats ripped out. He turned to Thea, who was shaking on the ground in undisguised fear—of him. He wondered if she actually thought he'd hurt her, but then again, he had just single-handedly dispatched two men in front of her without so much as a scratch on himself.

He smiled at her, trying to reassure her that she was safe and extended his hand to her after wiping off his blood-stained hand on his shirt. "Come with me if you want to live," he joked, in a poor imitation of Arnold Schwarzenegger's Austrian accent.

Instead of taking his proffered hand, Thea just stared at him, her eyes unblinking, and then she reached for a pink object beside her and lunged forward with it, making contact with his thigh.

"Ow! Fuck!" He growled as shockwaves ran up and down his leg.

He saw Thea's eyes widen. "You didn't … you didn't fall."

"Was I supposed to?" he asked, his voice rising an octave. The pain in his leg was starting to subside, but it still fucking hurt.

He then glanced over at the still-twitching figure on the floor and recalled the men outside in the same state. When he looked back at Thea, she had just managed to stand. He reached for her when she swayed a little, but she swatted him away.

"Don't you touch me," she spat at him. He could see that she was still afraid of him, but she squared her shoulders determinedly and lifted her chin. "And stop looking at me like that!"

"Like—"

"Like you own me. Like I'm your *mate*." She emphasized the last word as if it was something dirty. "I heard you call me that, and I am telling you right now, that ain't happening. No one owns me!"

Logan shook his head. It wasn't hard for him to come to the conclusion she could only associate the word to mean something negative, given what had happened to her sister, what had been happening to Teresa since she was just a small child, but he had no time right now to go into detail with her on what being mated truly meant. Instead, he was just about to tell her they needed to get the hell out of Dodge before the twitching figures stopped twitching—not that he'd have too much trouble dispatching them as well, but he didn't want the unnecessary bloodshed or for her to be more afraid of him than she already was—when she bolted.

****

Thea wasn't surprised when the psycho wolf

easily caught up to her. What did surprise her, however, was that the tall, and extremely handsome, she begrudgingly admitted to herself, brute swiped her feet from under her and ran the rest of the way cradling her in his arms. He then gently deposited her on the back of a motorcycle.

She immediately brought her leg around and hopped off. "You can't just kidnap me," she squeaked.

"I'm not kidnapping you, Theodora. I'm rescuing you." He huffed in frustration. "Your father hired me." He reached for a helmet. "Now let's get this thing on you and get out of here."

She was about to protest again about not getting the answers she came here for, when her supposed savior interjected. "I'm going to get Teresa back, too. I promise."

Thea could sense the sincerity of his words and she also didn't put it past her father to hire someone, especially given how frantic he sounded on the phone when she last spoke to him, but there was also the small matter of this lunatic thinking that he owned her. She realized, though, that she'd have to deal with that *after* he helped rescue her sister, especially since she now knew her weapons would not work on *all* wolves.

"My car," she stated. "It's a rental, but they'll be able to trace it to back to me."

"I am going to assume the men twitching on the ground will recover eventually—I'll have questions for you about that later," he said. "They won't need a rental car to identify you. They've seen your face, and no doubt knew who you were the minute you stepped foot here." He shook his head at her again. "What the hell were you thinking? Never mind. No time for that now." He practically shoved the helmet into her arms. "Put this on," he ordered.

Everything in her wanted to defy him, just as further proof he had no claim on her, but protecting her head won over. She dutifully put on the helmet.

"Tell me where the car is and I'll have someone come get it."

"Don't you need a helmet?" she asked petulantly.

He gave her a sly smile. "I only wear one for show … and to avoid getting a ticket." He knocked on his head and said, "Hard head. Let's go."

She put her hand out, palm facing forward, to stop him from lifting her. She was perfectly capable of getting on a motorcycle on her own. He held up his own hands in acquiescence, but she could see that he was warring with himself not to throw her onto his bike. Once again, she had to begrudgingly admit how incredibly hot he looked as he straddled his Harley. She had to clear her throat before speaking, and then she told him the location of her car, which was about a half mile away, before climbing on behind him.

"Hold on," she heard him say before they sped off.

Chapter Three

It had been far too long since Thea rode on the back of someone's motorcycle. Her high school boyfriend of two years had had one, and it made her dad go ballistic every time she was even five minutes late coming home. To say that her father was ecstatic when they broke up would be an understatement.

She envied the man in front of her for being able to feel the wind blowing through his tousled dirty-blond locks as they zipped along the highway. He was right, of course, from what she knew about shifter physiology, about her head being a lot more fragile than his.

He leaned back into her as she hugged him tighter, his hard muscular back pressing up against her front. She cursed her own traitorous body for its reaction to him, and she couldn't help the shivers coursing through her at his nearness. Not only did he smell amazing with his clean, fresh scent, mixed in with a little woodsy spice, but when she closed her eyes, all she could see was the penetrating gaze of his soft baby-blue eyes. The man was gorgeous, boyish and yet rugged looking, and he definitely gave off the vibe that he was not to be messed with. He was very tall, muscular, and his presence quite imposing.

She was afraid of him back at the cabin when he tore those men apart like they were nothing more than ragdolls, even more so when her advanced Taser had very little effect on him when it had easily dropped the other shifters. She had learned to move with her weapons like they were a part of her, infusing her training from her kickboxing classes, and the men, unsuspecting of the damage a mere human could do to them, were taken completely off guard.

None of her earlier fears, however, compared to

the one she was having now—falling for the man who claimed ownership over her.

They arrived in Brooklyn—Park Slope—about an hour later and parked in front of a brownstone with a small, well-looked-after garden in the front. "Why are we here?" Thea asked.

"I live here," he replied as he gently prodded her on the small of her back to walk in front of him. "I promised your father I'd deliver you safely to him, but they'll be looking for you now. You'll be safe here while I go search for Teresa."

Thea whirled around on him. "She's my sister." Her voice broke on the last word and then she felt her ire stir. "If you think for one second that I am going to stay here like a good little girl and wait—"

He placed a finger gently over her lips, the move shocking her into silence. *How dare he!*

"I get it," he said. "You're going to be a complete pain in my ass until we find your sister and make me chase after you again unless I take you with me." He stepped in closer, invading her space. She could feel his breath on her face as he next spoke. "And I find good little girls to be extremely boring, Thea. Now let's go inside so you can tell me all about your little pink toy."

She gulped loudly, making him chuckle, cursing herself again for her visceral reaction to him. She had never had this reaction to another man before, probably why she always easily walked away from her past relationships.

He led her inside. A large name plate on an apartment door on the first floor made her stop in her tracks. "Logan Munro," she read aloud.

"That's me ... my office," Logan replied. "I live upstairs."

"So my dad was the highest bidder, I take it?" She

folded her arms, waiting for a response.

"What the hell are you talking about?" he asked, appearing confused.

Thea wasn't buying it, though. Instead, she kicked him in the shin, instantly regretting it as the pain shot up from her toes to her leg while her blow literally had zero effect on him.

"What the hell are you doing?" he snapped.

"Ow, ow," was all she could muster in response at first as she began hopping on her uninjured foot. Finally, through gritted teeth she replied, "I was trying to kick you." She felt like such a ninnyhammer.

"Are you always this violent?" He growled his displeasure.

She snorted. "Are you the pot or the kettle?"

Logan pursed his lips. With a roll of his eyes, followed by an exasperated sigh, he threw her over his shoulder and carried her upstairs, and deposited her, not so gently this time, on his couch after they entered his apartment. He left her alone for a minute and returned with an ice pack before sitting himself down in front of her on his coffee table. He handed her the ice pack. "For your cheek." Thea heard him add in a mumble, "Fucker's lucky he's dead."

He shocked the hell out of her, by lifting her injured foot, removing her four-inch heeled boot, and then gently rubbing her toes. "Nothing's broken."

She let out a long slow breath. "I'm sorry," she finally said. He was being incredibly generous, given the fact her second injury was incurred trying to do *him* bodily harm. "I shouldn't have kicked you."

"No, you shouldn't have," he said matter-of-factly as he continued to massage her toes. "For starters, you could have really hurt yourself had you put just a little more pressure into your kick. And second of all, it wasn't very nice. What the hell did you mean by your father being the highest bidder? For what exactly?"

"We knew that Leon had located Teresa a few weeks ago," Thea began. "So we started digging into what he and his followers were up to."

"Leon Kostastakis, you mean?" Logan asked.

"Yes," she said, figuring that her dad must have already filled him in on the history between Leon's pack and her sister. "Teresa and I came across your name in our findings. He was going to hire you to … retrieve us," she concluded on a distasteful note.

Logan stopped his attentions to her foot, but he still kept hold of it on his thigh. "Let's get two things straight right off the bat." He looked angry, making her flinch. "Make that three. One, I would never hurt you, so stop being afraid of me." He took her hand, the one she was holding the ice pack with, and gently placed it over her bruised cheek. He let his hand linger there for a moment before continuing. "Two, I would never deliver innocent women to a bunch of cultist criminals. And lastly, I take cases on a first come, first serve basis, and those I deem worthy of my time. I don't drop a client because someone else offers me more money. It's not how I operate, not to mention the fact it would ruin my reputation."

Once again, she saw the sincerity of his words on his face, heard it in the tone of his voice. Her gut told her he meant every word. Teresa had told her once that not all shifters were bad, which wasn't hard for Thea to believe since her sister was one of the kindest people she had ever met. Teresa had also spoken of her family many times, all of whom were nothing like Leon and *his* family. But Leon was an alpha, and so was Logan, based on not only the abilities he had displayed earlier in the cabin, but also from what she had read about him in

Leon's files. Alphas were uncommon, and extremely dominant.

Teresa had not been able to sense Leon as her mate from that young of an age, but he, being a teenager at the time, had sensed her. His family had groomed him for leadership, to take what he wanted, and now he would stop at nothing in order to keep Teresa, like she was nothing more than his possession. Her sister had felt the threat of this looming over her since the murder of her parents, never allowing herself to find someone of her choosing to be happy with. She was terrified of what Leon might do to a man she became involved with. Now Thea had her own reason to be terrified.

She cast her eyes down and whispered, "I told you before that I won't be owned by anyone."

And then Logan was on the couch next to her. She felt his fingers under her chin, gently prodding her to look over at him. "I *do* want to own you," he said, his voice raspy. "I want to own you body and soul, as you will own me, but I want you to give yourself to me freely. Mates are a beautiful gift to be cherished and protected, Thea."

She couldn't help the shiver of excitement that ran through her body at his words. She had to press her legs together when she felt that same rush reach into her core. "And if I refuse?" she asked, her voice breathy.

"I won't take you against your will, if that's what you're asking me," he said firmly. And then she saw a sly smile forming at the corner of his lips. "But that doesn't mean I'll stop trying to convince you. I see how your body is reacting to me, Thea. You want me, but you're trying to convince yourself you don't. I can see how you are pressing your legs together and I can smell your desire. You may not be able to sense a mate like wolves do, but you can still recognize me as yours."

"You're arrogant, aren't you?" she asked, but her voice quivered, losing its bite.

He only smiled wider at her words. "Confident, not arrogant. We were made for each other, you and me." He stood up. "I need to make some phone calls to my outsourced contractors. I'm going to put some detail on all of Leon's properties tonight, get some of their routines down." He took out his phone and sent a text. "Your rental car will be taken care of shortly."

"Thank you, Logan," she said, "for everything."

"You're welcome." His smile was breathtaking, revealing perfectly straight white teeth and making his eyes sparkle. "Thea…"

"Mmm?"

"A wolf always catches his prey."

Thea got the feeling he wasn't just referring to Leon and his demon pack.

Chapter Four

"Tell me about those Tasers," Logan prompted Thea after they finished eating. He had quickly whipped up a bowl of spaghetti with sauce from a bottle when he had heard Thea's stomach growl, to her utter embarrassment. She told him she hadn't eaten since early that morning, and even then it was just a granola bar and coffee. He'd see about taking her out for a proper dinner date once her sister was rescued and Leon, along with his goons, were taken care of.

Thea walked over to the couch to grab her handbag and brought it over to the dining table. She took out the pink Taser and placed it on the table before reaching back into her bag and producing another one in black. She pressed her lips together, and then dug into her bag again. This time she produced what looked like a lipstick, followed by a perfume bottle, and several pens.

"These are all Tasers?" he asked incredulously.

She nodded.

"What, you don't have any disguised as tampons?"

"Nope," she said. "The tampon is just a tampon, I'm afraid."

Logan was still shocked at what he had seen at the cabin earlier. "I've never heard of a Taser having any kind of effect on a shifter, let alone incapacitating them for quite a lengthy time."

She took a seat opposite him. "That's because it's something Teresa and I have been developing together for years. We discovered that even after the twitching stops, the body feels weak from the extreme disruption of the dual nervous system … man and beast, if you will." She paused, as if gauging his reaction. He nodded for her to continue. "My sister is an engineer. She works for a company that develops mechanical prostheses. I'm her research assistant and this"—she gestured toward her weapons on the table—"is our little side project." She pointed to the pink Taser. "This one delivers the most power." Pointing to the black one, she continued, "This one here is almost as strong as the pink one, but you can shoot it from up to fifteen feet away from your opponent."

She then went on to explain that the lipstick Taser, which was also as powerful as the pink one, had to be used at close range, while the perfume-bottled one could be used at a distance. The benefit of them both was their discreetness. If she had been captured and searched, and the lipstick were in her pocket, it could have easily been overlooked and remained in her possession.

Fucking brilliant. "And the pens?"

"They mostly just stun. Come in handy if you need to question someone."

Logan was thoughtful for a moment. "This kind of power … I'm guessing it can obliterate a human."

"We'd never use it on one," she said defensively.

"I know," he said, holding up his hand in placation. "I'm not accusing you of that. I'm simply saying that to be able to figure out the right amount of power to bring down a wolf shifter, you'd need to test it on one."

Logan could see that she understood what he was getting at. Thea bowed her head and bit her lip, clearly unhappy with how she and her sister had developed their technology. She finally met his eyes again, hers pooling with tears. "She was so scared all the time." She paused and took a deep breath. "Teresa always knew he'd find her. She didn't want them to take another family from her so she begged me to help her." She paused again and turned her head to the side, a tear rolling down her cheek.

Logan moved his chair closer to her and took her hand.

"The first few times after we started to get closer to the right strength were the worst," she continued. "She'd scream and her body would convulse. God, I even fucking passed out with her a few times." She closed her eyes, as if trying to blot out the painful memories.

Logan pulled her to him and wrapped his arms around her. "We're going to get her back," he whispered in her ear. "I promise you."

Her eyes were still watery when their gazes met and she stated, "The Taser wouldn't have worked on him."

"It fucking hurt, Thea, but no." His voice sounded raspy and tortured to his own ears when he added, "If you had found Leon before I found you, he would have killed you. I would have lost my destiny before even realizing I had one."

She gave him a shaky smile just as another thought occurred to him. "What were you and your sister planning on doing if your weapon did end up working on Leon like the others?"

Thea hesitated for a few beats before responding. "There's no way Teresa could win a fight against an alpha, but with him down, she was going to..."

Logan hugged her close. He didn't need for her to finish her sentence. Teresa was going to take him out. There was no other way. The rest of his cultist pack would disband without their alpha. "Once I take care of Leon, his pack will no longer be a threat," he told Thea. "Teresa was just a child when they killed her parents. She had no alpha in her corner, but I can assure you that she does now." He'd make damn sure the survivors of the Kostastakis family and pack members would know that he'd end them as well should they ever fuck with any member of the Petridis family again.

"You'll stay here with me tonight," he told her. "Tomorrow night, after my men gather enough information and they get Teresa's location, we'll go get her."

Surprisingly she didn't protest, especially after he told her that he had people watching her parents as well, making sure they were safe. He had heard the relief in her father's voice when she had spoken to him on the phone earlier and he pretty much commanded her to do as Logan ordered when she said she wasn't going to sit out. Logan suspected her father had plenty of experience with the stubbornness of his own daughter and it was easier to let her do her thing while keeping her safe than to try and stop her.

"Do you have more of these?" he asked inclining his head toward the assortment of Tasers.

She nodded. "We keep them locked up at work."

"Good to know in case we need more. In the meantime, you should go get some rest." He stood up and offered her his hand, pleased that this time she took it instead of swatting him away. He stood close to her, towering over her five-foot-four frame, and ran his knuckles gently over her non-bruised cheek. "You can sleep in my room," he said, pointing it out to her. "It's bigger and has its own bathroom. I'll take the guest room."

"I don't want to impose," she began, but he stopped her with a gentle kiss to her lips. It was chaste, and nothing like the way he actually wanted to kiss her, but once again he feared scaring her off.

He pulled back and saw that her eyes were still closed, and her expression conveyed that she had been just as lost in the kiss as he was despite their quick meeting of lips. He smiled at her when she finally opened her eyes. "You're not imposing, Thea. I like having you here." He'd like it even more if she moved in, but he wasn't going to tell her that … yet.

She cleared her throat and took a few steps back. "I'm just going to take a quick shower before I turn in."

"There are clean towels in the cabinet," he said, expecting her to turn and go, but she just stood there, staring at him.

Finally, after a few more moments, she cleared her throat again and said, "Good night," before heading for his room.

He was going to need a cold shower himself if he had any hopes of falling asleep tonight, especially since now his mind was conjuring up all kinds of delicious images of his naked mate in the shower.

"Oh, my God!"

He heard her squeal from his bedroom, quickly dousing out his erotic images of her. He ran to his room and threw open his bedroom door, ready to dismember whoever was threatening his mate, but he found her safe and sound, gawking at the guitar in a display case on the wall. "Was that really signed by Slash?"

"Jesus, fuck! You scared me." He didn't scare easily, but this woman could bring him to his knees, and without any enhanced fancy gadgetry. Once his heart rate returned to normal, he answered, "It was actually *his* guitar that he signed and gave me."

She turned to him, awestruck. "Wow! How'd you manage that?"

Logan shrugged. "Payment for my services. You're a Guns N' Roses fan?"

"Hell, yeah! My father loves them and it sort of spilled over onto Teresa and me." She turned back to the display case. "So … um … what did he hire you to do?"

"I can't tell you that," he replied.

She turned to face him again and rolled her eyes.

"Or you'll have to kill me?"

Logan barked out a laugh. "No, honey. Client confidentiality and all."

She smiled back at him. "Oh. Well, okay then."

As much as he wanted to stay and talk more with her, or even better, to rip all of her clothes away from her luscious body and devour every inch of her skin before sinking his cock deep inside of her, he turned to go. There was only so much torture he could endure and the sweet smell of her arousal was only adding to his inferno.

When he reached the door, he turned around and said, "By the way, Slash isn't human." He chuckled as her jaw dropped before turning to leave again.

"Well that explains his inhuman guitar-playing skills," he heard her say after he had already left the room.

Logan's pocket vibrated with a text from one of his contacts. He found Teresa in upstate New York and was sending him live feed of her location and would be sending periodic updates of the goings-on there. After he powered up his laptop, Logan studied the surveillance. His cold shower would have to wait for now, he decided, but he thought perhaps his favorite pastime would help him relax and get his mind off of a certain naked woman in his bathroom while he stared at the computer screen.

Chapter Five

The cool shower was a soothing balm to Thea's tired, bruised, and overheated body, but for the first time since her sister was taken while stepping out for her lunch break three days ago, Thea felt confident she would get her back. Her Tasers may have not been powered high enough to defeat Leon, but she had one sexy badass alpha on her side now. In truth, now she had an inkling of what kind of power would be needed to bring down an alpha with a Taser, she was thankful she and Teresa had not gotten that far. She shuddered to think what such voltage could have done to her sister.

When Thea stepped out of the shower and dried herself off, she boldly put on Logan's navy-blue t-shirt she had spotted draped over the hand towel bar. She couldn't help the gooseflesh that broke out over her skin from his scent. His fresh musky aroma made her entire body quiver with desire. She had to hold herself steady for a moment by pressing her back against one of the tiled walls. If just the thought and smell of him could unnerve her like this, she imagined he'd destroy her if he actually touched her right now.

When she finally regained her composure, she stepped back into the bedroom. She heard music coming from the living room—the soft notes of a song's finale played on an acoustic guitar, and then instantly transforming into another one she recognized. She heard the opening chords of "The Sound of Silence" being strummed, and then came the most beautiful male singing voice accompanying it.

He sang hello to darkness, his voice deep and soft. Thea put her hand to her chest, standing in awe of the sound, the actual depth of his tone surprising her.

It never ceased to amaze her how sometimes a

singing voice could be so different-sounding from a speaking one. Logan's voice was a little deep when he spoke, the sound almost like velvet, but as he sang and the melody grew in intensity, so did his dirty bass. She remembered seeing an acoustic guitar, as well as two electric with impressive amps around his living room, but she hadn't really taken the time to equate it with him playing the instruments with so much on her mind.

She dropped her wet towel on the bed and walked out of the room. He sat with his back to her on the couch, a laptop open in front of him, but he had his head slightly bowed toward his guitar. She saw his shoulders lift and stiffen, becoming aware of her presence.

"Don't stop," she whispered as she walked closer to him.

She found his eyes closed when she reached the couch. It was as if the guitar were an extension of him. And the words pouring out of him came not just from his voice, she observed, but seemingly from his very soul. She could see he felt every word he was singing, holding the long notes beautifully, seamlessly, some of them with raspy gravel. Every note he played was written on his fingers and transferred into his instrument. She wanted to see what he saw in the naked light.

Thea sat down beside him and stared at his face, marveling at the range of passionate emotions he displayed. His version of the Simon and Garfunkel song was louder, grittier, reverberating down to her own soul. She felt tears pooling in her eyes, but they stayed trapped there, much like she was currently trapped under his spell. She had never understood why women felt the need to throw bras and panties up on stage at a concert, but if she had been wearing any of those things right now, she'd definitely throw them at Logan.

Her breath hitched as he began the last verse

about people praying to neon gods. He sang even more intensely, carrying the same climactic depth throughout until the last line, holding a note with vibrato before ending just as softly as he began on the word "silence."

"That was so beautiful, Logan," she whispered, surprised she was even able to string a sentence together at the moment.

She watched him open his eyes slowly. When he turned to her, his gaze was penetrating, ensnaring her so completely she dared not turn away. His voice was gravelly when he told her, "My shirt looks really good on you." He tried and failed to give her a cocky smile. Instead, he produced a shaky one, making her sure that he was just as affected as she was.

While still staring at her, he began to strum a few chords, changing melodies until he was satisfied with the up-tempo rhythmic strum of the song he wanted to play—Ed Sheeren's "Shape of You." She felt her heart spike and short, panting breaths escaped through her lips, all the while he never broke eye contact with her.

He got as far as singing about bed sheets before putting his guitar aside and grabbing her by the back of her neck and pulling her to him. She felt like the magnet the song sang about, instantly drawn to him.

Their lips collided fiercely, his hands tangling in her hair and hers in his thick locks. She moved herself even closer to him to the point where she was almost sitting on his lap. He groaned in her mouth as she tugged on his hair and then he was standing, drawing her up on her feet, without breaking their kiss. He let his hands travel down her sides to her waist. Thea moaned when Logan grabbed her ass. He then lifted her to straddle his hips. She locked her ankles behind him as he carried her toward the bedroom, but they never made it that far. She bit down gently on his bottom lip as he carried her, causing him to actually let loose a growl, the sound of it sending a stab of desire to her core. He playfully nipped her back right before he pushed her up against the wall and then his hands were exploring everywhere he could reach while his hard body kept her securely pinned.

Logan kneaded her breasts through the shirt she was wearing at the same time she fumbled with pulling up his. She wanted it off, to feel his naked skin against hers. She managed to pull it up to his chest, forcing him to break their kiss so that he could pull it up and off the rest of the way himself. As soon as he was free of his shirt, their mouths collided again. He kissed her hard, their tongues warring, exploring, and finding a rhythm.

"Get this off," he breathed against her lips as his hand snaked under her shirt, "or I'll fucking rip it off."

Thea tried to comply, but with her back pressed firmly against the wall and Logan pressed against her front, she had very little room to maneuver. A tearing sound told her not to even bother. Pieces of her shirt began to fall away until she was completely bare, her body set on fire with how much she wanted him. He pulled back a little to gaze at her, and he grunted appreciatively. She stared at his mouth as he bit his lip and smiled slyly. She lost all sense when he licked his lips. Then she fisted his hair with one hand and grabbed the back of his neck with the other, pulling him back toward her for another impassioned frenzy of a kiss.

Her moans and his grunts sounded throughout the room continually as they devoured each other. He bit her top lip first, then her bottom, before moving to gently kiss her bruised cheek. With both hands, he cupped her ass firmly, leaving them there as he continued to trail quick open-mouthed kisses to her other cheek, down to her jaw, neck, and stopping at her breasts. He sucked one turgid peak hard into his mouth, making her moan loudly.

"Ah, fuck!" she groaned, when he slid one of his hands around to her front and thrust a finger into her wet, needy channel.

That seemed to be the last shred of patience for them both. She reached between them and began to undo his belt, and he withdrew his finger to help her along. His jeans fell around his ankles and Thea grabbed a firm hold around his impressive length. Pre-cum glistened on the thick mushroomed head, and this time it was she who licked her lips.

With a growl, Logan removed her hand from his cock and replaced it with his own, positioning it at her entrance. In one swift move, he impaled her to the hilt, stilling once fully inside. They stared at one another as he began to move, thrusting long and hard. She kissed him then, while her hands tangled in his hair.

"Oh, God," she said in between kisses. "I fucking"—kiss—"love"—kiss—"the way"—kiss—"you feel."

"Good," he said as he buried his face into the crook of her neck, "because I plan on fucking you all night. You feel amazing." He nipped her neck. "I fucking love your tight little pussy."

His words sounded dirty and lovely at the same time, inflaming her libido and need to come. She returned his bite to her neck with her own, never before having the desire to bite someone. She kissed and bit different spots, again and again as he pounded up into her, her back bumping the wall. "More, Logan. Harder." It was as if she couldn't get enough.

Their mouths collided again, teeth clashing. He fisted her hair at the base of her neck and the slight bite of pain felt amazing, making her moan into his mouth. And then she was coming, screaming his name, her orgasm hitting her with the force of a freight train.

Spasms rocked her body, making her shake in his arms. Through her haze of immense pleasure, she heard him calling out her name, filling her, grateful for being on the pill so that she could feel him spill inside of her.

He broke apart their kiss to look at her while he remained inside of her and she widened her eyes at the feral look she saw on his face. His blue eyes practically glowed, his canines were elongated, his nostrils flared, and deep, harsh breaths escaped him.

"Don't move," he ordered, his voice sounding garbled, barely human. "I want to…" He closed his eyes and shut his mouth, flinching as if the move caused him physical pain.

Afraid to move, Thea kept very still, but she became concerned when she saw blood trickle out of the corner of his mouth. "Logan," she breathed. "Are you okay?"

"You're mine," he declared, once again sounding more animal than himself.

"Yes," she whispered. She couldn't deny that anymore. He was right, that though she felt their connection differently, and not by scent as he did, she felt it, too, nonetheless.

His eyes were pleading. "I want to bite you. Mark and claim you." He closed his mouth and again she saw more blood trickle out of his mouth. "I'm trying … will wait until you let me."

She reached out slowly and placed her hand against his cheek. He was hurting himself so that he wouldn't lose control and bite her. "Do it, Logan," she said with a quiver in her voice. Then more assertively, she added, "I won't be able to walk away from you after tonight. I'm yours."

Without another word, he sunk his teeth into the fleshy part between her neck and shoulder. Thea tilted her head back and let out a sound that was a mixture of both pleasure and pain. She felt an invisible tether to him snapping into place as he sucked on her blood, binding her to him. She already knew she would not be able to transform into a wolf from his bite, but they would forever be connected now. She'd feel him even when they were not in the same room, sense him when he was near, and claiming bite or not, she'd never want any other but him.

When he was done, he licked her puncture marks to seal them and hugged her close, his body shaking slightly. "You own me, Thea," he said against her neck.

Chapter Six

Logan couldn't pinpoint how they got there. He was on the floor, his back against the couch, the coffee table pushed further out, enough for him to stretch out his long legs, and Thea was on top and in between his legs, her head resting on his chest. She must have fallen asleep again, he thought as he played with her hair. It had been hours since he claimed his mate, hours of making love to her over and over again, dozing off in between. He had tried to convince her to go to sleep in the bedroom where she would be more comfortable, but she refused to leave his side. He was selfish just enough to be grateful she decided to stay near him instead. He would have happily joined her in bed, but he was afraid that having his mate snuggled in his arms in his big comfy bed would have completely knocked him out when he needed to periodically keep watch on the surveillance.

Thea gazed up at him then with her sleepy eyes and a small goofy smile. "What time is it?"

"About four AM." He reached out and poked one of her dimples. "These are just way too cute. I'm going to have to find a name for each of them."

She buried her face into his chest and laughed. When their eyes met again, he saw a wicked gleam in her eyes right before she planted a sweet kiss on his chest, and then another, and another in a different spot. She lifted herself up on her knees as she kissed down to his stomach, arching her back just a little. He knew exactly where she was heading, but his little minx sure took her time getting there, teasing him as she kissed and licked a path down to his cock. She'd glance up at him every so often, watching him watching her. She looked so fucking hot, so much so that if he didn't want to feel her lips around his dick so badly, he'd flip her over right then and there and fuck her into oblivion.

"Ah! Shit." She had caught him unawares. Just when he had thought she would continue to tease, Thea popped him in her mouth and sucked him hard, hollowing out her cheeks. He let out a harsh breath when she grabbed him by the base and squeezed, meanwhile her tongue was doing circles around the head before sucking him again. She took him deeper, and then added a twist to the root of him as she went back up.

She played him masterfully slow, quickly becoming attuned to what drove him wild. He brought his legs up closer to him and spread them apart wider to give her more room. His balls grew tighter when she sucked him down again and moaned around his cock. Nothing about this, about them, was perfunctory. He could smell how turned on she was by giving him pleasure and he had to thank whatever fates deemed him worthy of having her as a mate, because they fit so perfectly together, so naturally.

"Oh, fuck, honey, I'm gonna come."

"Oh, yeah?" she asked, briefly popping him out, her voice all breathy. She put him right back in and moaned around him again, never breaking eye contact.

He groaned loudly and then called out her name along with some complimentary expletives about how good her lips looked around his cock, and then he came. He felt his orgasm everywhere, from the crown of his head to the tips of his toes. The tingling sensation ripped through him as she swallowed everything he gave her.

When he was done, he pulled her up to him and kissed her hard on the mouth, tasting her and himself. Despite being sated for the moment, he felt crazed, lustful for more of her, so he agilely flipped her on her back, spread her legs apart wide, and pulled her closer to him. He dove right into her center and devoured her pussy like a starving man. "You fucking taste like honey," he murmured against her lips. She smelled amazing, too, sweet, and a little musky from their joining.

Logan also learned quickly how to play *her*, licking her lips, then in between them, and in and around her center. He teased her clit with just the tip of his tongue, before laving it completely and then sucking on it. He found a rhythm that made her moan and pant heavily, hitting her sweet spots, and then breaking for the tease to prolong her pleasure. She moved her head from side to side, her hands squeezing her breasts, and seconds later, her hips bucked, her legs tightened, and she came in his mouth while screaming his name and moaning her release.

He lay down on top of her, his cock growing painfully hard again, and he plunged inside, slowly this time. He entwined his hands with hers, stretching them out over her head, staring into her eyes as he unhurriedly rocked back and forth.

Logan marveled at how different his life had become in just a day. His mundane existence now had more purpose in the form of a mate to love and cherish. Already he was quickly falling for her, and by the way she was gazing at him, flushed, wearing a lazy smile as they both took and gave their pleasure, he became sure the feeling was mutual.

They both came, in sync, not for the first time that night, a blinding intensity despite the slowness. He kissed her softly until their spasms had subsided and then he sat up leaning against the couch again, pulling her with him to straddle his lap.

They sat holding each other for a while before Thea pulled back and spoke. "Can you show me what you look like?" she asked. "I want to see your wolf."

Logan suddenly felt giddy that his mate wanted to

see his wolf. He could feel his animal giddy with anticipation, too. "You won't be afraid?"

She shook her head vehemently. "I'm not afraid of you. And I've seen my sister's wolf many times. She's beautiful."

Logan nodded and Thea sat back on her haunches just far enough away to give him room to transform. He cracked his neck from side to side, maneuvered his body to where he was on all fours, and let his bones and sinuous muscles grow, crack, and contort seamlessly into his sandy-colored wolf. She never flinched or looked away as he transformed.

"Wow," she breathed. Thea moved in closer to him. "You're gigantic!" She giggled.

He made a chuffing sound in lieu of laughter, quickly becoming accustomed to and loving her bluntness. Then she threw her arms around him. "My wolf," she said.

Only yours, he would have said to her now if he was in his human form.

His computer pinged, ending their moment. Logan quickly shifted into his human form and went over to his laptop. "Shit," he said.

"What's wrong?" Thea asked, panic rising in her voice.

"They're moving her tomorrow. We gotta go. Now!"

Chapter Seven

Logan found himself speeding down a highway again, with Thea securely behind him. His guy at the upstate site informed him that Leon was tipped off about Logan's involvement. The two wolves whose throats he had ripped out were probably a good convincing factor. Leon was running scared now and back to Greece from what Logan's contact had told him. Logan needed to intercept them before they left, and with such short notice, and some of his other men too far away at the other sites, he'd be facing fifteen men and an alpha, with Thea and her toys, his shifter contact already waiting at the site, and possibly Teresa if she wasn't badly injured.

He hated the thought of killing so many shifters, especially since they'd be virtually no threat once he took Leon out, but he'd do it if it came down to protecting his woman and her sister. He steeled himself for the possibility of not having a choice.

"What the fuck?" Logan said when he pulled up next to a familiar Ducati about a half mile away from the site. "Son of a bitch."

"What is it?" Thea asked.

He had no time to answer her since the *son of a bitch* in question came out of his hiding spot wearing a cocky expression as he walked toward them. "Now, now, Logan. If I'm a son of a bitch then so are you, and frankly, that's no way to talk about our mother."

"Your brother is your contact?"

"I'm Ian, beautiful," his little brother said, addressing Thea when he reached them. He took Thea's hand and brought it to his lips. Logan nearly choked on a laugh at her grimacing face.

"Charmed, I'm sure," she replied drily at his old-fashioned attempt at suaveness, before pulling her hand back. "Do you know where Teresa is?"

"Don't worry, beautiful. She's still inside. She appears to be unharmed and—"

"I'm going to ask you once, to explain what the fuck you are doing here and to tell me where the hell Scott is," Logan interrupted through gritted teeth. He hadn't seen his brother in three years, but he just decided to show up in the middle of a job, the most important one he'd ever had, no less.

"It's been me the whole time, big bro," he said. "Scott's been at location number two."

"I'll fucking deal with you later," Logan snapped, his patience wavering. He grabbed Thea's hand, an action that did not go unnoticed by his little brother, and began walking toward the house.

"Wait, she's human," Ian called behind him.

Thea whirled around. "And not someone you want to mess with."

Logan didn't bother turning around when he asked, "You heard her. Are you coming or not?" He may have been mad as fuck at Ian, but he trusted him to have his back in a fight. And since Ian was apparently well informed of the goings-on inside, he'd be an even bigger asset. Logan didn't wait for an answer. Instead, he tugged on Thea's hand and began walking again, impressed as hell with his little spitfire. He heard Ian's steps behind him.

"Three out back and two in front," Ian informed as they reached the location.

He would have preferred the cover of darkness under normal circumstances, but when it came to hunting wolves, their vision was as impeccable at night as during the day. The door opened, and the three of them moved downwind to avoid being detected just yet. Four men came out and walked over to the garage with bags in their hands.

"Back first," Ian suggested. "If we attack the front, they'll all swarm in at once."

"Agreed," Logan said. They might have a chance to take out three while the others are distracted outside and busy inside.

They stealthily went around back. Just as Logan was getting ready to pounce and Thea reached into her pocket, Ian held out his hand to stop him. "Seriously, Logan, I see the mark. I know what she is to you. You're going to let your mate walk into the line of fire like that?"

Logan was actually touched at his brother's concern. "I'll kill anyone who so much as breaks one of her nails."

"And his mate happens to be a badass," Thea interjected.

As proof of her bad-ass-ery, Thea stepped out into the line of sight of the three guards, and with a smile on her face, she walked toward them to their utter confusion. It was Logan who held his brother back this time. "We may avoid some bloodshed." He counted her steps and gauged how many feet she had left. "Sixteen … Fifteen."

She held out her black Taser and watched as the one in the middle began to shake. It looked like he was doing some kind of ritualistic dance at first, and then he fell, twitching and convulsing on the floor. The other two exchanged frightened looks right before they set their sights on Thea.

"What the hell?" Ian muttered beside him, but Logan ran out from behind the trees and extended his claws, his feral side taking over. He saw Thea retract the wires from the black Taser, her pink one already in her other hand, but she would not be able to hit another one with how fast they were running. She'd have to get one of the guys at close range, which would mean he would have to have his hands on her. Even the thought of that fueled Logan's rage. No matter, he'd get to her before either of those fuckers would.

He reached Thea and pulled her behind him just as one of the shifters reached them. He grabbed him by the throat and lifted him off the ground, cutting of his air supply. He heard dual growls coming from Ian and the shifter he was locked in battle with. He flung the guy he was holding to the side and went to aid his brother. Ian was a great fighter, but the asshole he was fighting was huge and just as skilled. Thea beat him to the punch with her Taser. She got him in the leg and it was almost comical how the big guy's eyes widened before he began the same ritualistic dance as the first one. He went down hard just as the back door opened.

"We gotta go now," Logan yelled. There was no time for the element of surprise. Leon could easily sneak out the front with Teresa while they were preoccupied with fighting his pack.

They ran, reaching the door in time so that Logan and Ian could push back two shifters inside. Once again, he pulled Thea behind him as soon as they were inside. Leon was there and he was holding Teresa, a pink object poised at her throat, and his twelve remaining wolves surrounding them.

"How many of these do you think I owe your sister after what you did to my men?" Leon asked, staring directly at Thea. "And after that, maybe one for every year I had to spend looking for her after your filthy human parents took her away. I'm not completely sure she'd get up again after two dozen or so hits in a row, do you?"

Several things happened at once. Thea went around him, yelling at Leon to release her sister along with a bunch of nasty expletives, and prepared herself to lunge at him, but Logan pulled her back and secured her in his arms. He cooed softly in her ear, trying to calm her. He wasn't going to let Leon go through with his threat. And then Ian, beside him, uttered the word "mate." Logan heard a growl escape his brother, watched his canines drop, and saw pure fury was written across his features. Logan turned to Teresa, to see her staring directly at Ian. She mouthed the word "mate" back to him.

"She's not even your fucking True Mate?" Logan spat at Leon. All this time and pain he had caused Teresa and her family, murdering her biological parents, and the fucker wasn't even her mate.

"Easy, Ian," he said to his brother. The last thing he needed was for Ian to challenge an alpha, a fight that would end with his brother dead, so he spoke up instead. "I, Logan Munro, challenge you, Leon Kostastakis, for position of Alpha."

He just spoke the antiquated words these cultists would understand. For Leon to refuse in front of his men, his family, his followers, it would make him lose all credibility as their leader. Logan didn't miss the twitch in Leon's left eye. Perhaps Leon had been expecting them to surrender, or leave quietly without Thea's sister, or maybe he even counted on all hell breaking loose with a battle while he quietly, like the fucking coward Logan now saw he was, slipped out with Teresa.

Logan smiled, his canines, longer than those of a regular wolf, dropped, making the twelve wolves step back reverently. He kissed Thea on the top of her head and pushed her toward his brother. He took off his leather jacket, not wanting to get any blood stains on his favorite new purchase, and handed it to his mate.

"Please be careful," she whispered to him, grabbing his hand.

He squeezed lightly. "Always." He turned to his brother. "Protect my mate and I swear to get you yours."

"With my life," his brother swore. He and his brother exchanged grateful looks. If things didn't work out in Logan's favor, he at least knew his brother would do everything he could to protect Thea in his stead.

Logan walked toward Leon as the other shifters moved back to give them room. "You need the girl as a shield?" Logan goaded, inclining his head toward Teresa. Leon still held onto her with a Taser at her throat. "Too chicken-shit to accept my challenge?"

Leon practically shoved Teresa toward one of his men. "Hold her," he said. "If she moves, use that thing on her."

Logan heard Thea whimper and Ian growl, but he tuned them out and focused on his prey. He'd never fought an alpha before, but he knew it wouldn't be as easy as simply going for the instant kill.

"I accept your challenge," Leon said. He gave a loud growl, his own canines dropping and his claws coming out. Logan could almost smell the bloodlust on his opponent as he charged him.

Logan met Leon half way, and their bodies collided. Pushing and pulling at each other, ducking the other's blows. Logan ducked again and then managed a swift upper cut to Leon's chin on the way up. His head snapped back, and Logan took advantage by delivering several hard blows to his stomach and ribs, followed by a swiping kick that left Leon writhing on the floor.

Vaguely, through his feral state, he heard Leon utter the command, "Do it." When Logan heard Teresa's scream, followed by Thea's, and then Ian's harsh growl, he understood. He saw Teresa, twitching in the arms of the wolf who held her, and too late he realized it was meant to be a distraction.

He felt the sharp pain of claws digging into his neck, a pain like no other he had ever felt before. He could feel the blood pouring down his neck, could hear Thea screaming his name in the distance. His head felt heavy, almost dazed, and then a blow was delivered to the right side of his head, dropping him to his knees and hands.

"I'll have both of them," Leon said into Logan's ear. "I'll use the human filth to entertain my men."

Logan yelled when he felt claws digging into his back, but it wasn't the excruciating sting that caused him to cry out, but the vision of his sweet feisty girl being passed around like she was nothing. He saw her face, devoid of the bright light that shone within her, and he no longer felt much of anything.

Swiftly, he sat up on his haunches, took another blow from Leon, who resembled every bit the predator kneeling beside him, just toying with his prey before he killed him, but Logan swung with his right hand, digging his claws in Leon's neck when he made contact. He left his claws fastened there, to Leon's horror. Now Leon's sole focus was on dislodging Logan's hand.

"I know that fucking hurts like a bitch, doesn't it?" Logan neither expected, nor waited for a response. He swung with his left hand and dug his claws on the other side of Leon's neck, curving his fingers. Leon's hands wrapped around Logan's wrists as he thrashed and yelled. Seconds later, Logan had him pinned on his back, writhing, his throat exposed. He retracted his claws from Leon's neck and went in for the kill, ripping out Leon's throat with his teeth.

He sat back on his haunches, momentarily spent as a scuffle ensued around him. He heard a few bodies fall, thudding on the floor, followed by the sound of tearing flesh, and then Thea was there, putting her arms around him. His brother was there next to him, too, cradling Teresa in his arms as she still twitched.

Thea cupped his face, lifting it so that he would look at her. "Logan, please tell me you're okay."

"I will be, honey." Already his wounds were closing. He felt the tightening and pulling of his ripped flesh as if it were sewing itself back together, but his wounds were delivered by an alpha and therefore taking longer to heal than normal. He'd probably feel a little bruised for a day or two.

He finally focused on his surroundings of the aftermath. The two wolves who had stood closest to Thea and Ian lay twitching on the ground. Another, who had stood in a direct path to Teresa, also lay twitching, while the one who had held her and later tased her lay dead with his throat ripped out. He looked over at his brother to see that Ian had blood around his mouth and chin as well as his shirt and hands.

The rest of the men stood assembled around him as if waiting for some kind of instruction. He decided he'd give it to them. He stood, wincing from the pain. Thea stood with him, supporting him. "As your new ruling alpha, I order you to all get a fucking life." He heard murmurs of confusion around the room as the men stupidly glanced between him and each other, so he decided to elaborate. "Go out into the world, get jobs, find your mates, build a house with a white-picket-fucking fence, or move back to Greece. I really don't give a shit what you do, but get with the twenty-first century already." He let out a breath as one of his cracked ribs repaired itself. "More importantly," he went on," if any of you fuckers ever come near my family, and that includes the members of the Petridis clan, I will end you. Spread the word to the twitching assholes on the floor and outside when they are able to absorb it, and the ones at all your other locations and such." He ended with another antiquated phrase these men would understand. "My word is law, and so it shall be done."

The shifters bowed in acceptance of his words. Logan knew that they had a long way to go before learning to stand on their own, if ever, but at least to them, he was now their alpha, and therefore his word to leave them in peace really was law. He wasn't about to babysit grown-ass men who were in dire need of learning how to fend for themselves.

Thirty minutes later, he and Thea, and Ian and Teresa, who had somewhat recovered, were on their way back to Brooklyn in Scott's van. A few of his other men were driving his and Ian's motorcycles back for them.

Thea and Teresa sat huddled together in the back on the bench seat across from him and Ian. "I'm so glad you're okay," Thea told her sister.

"Me?" Teresa shook her head. "That bastard told me he was holding you somewhere and that he'd order his men to kill you if I ran away."

"Actually, she was very damn impressive wielding those Tasers," Ian admitted. Then he said to Thea, "You were pretty *badass*!"

"She definitely is," Teresa said, beaming at her little sister. She then went on to explain she knew Leon wasn't her true mate the moment he grabbed her. She was too young back in Greece to have known he was lying, but the moment she was in his presence, it was unmistakable, just like she had known without a doubt that Ian *was* her mate when he stepped into the room.

Mr. and Mrs. Petridis had been practically crying with relief on the phone when speaking to their daughters and then Logan spoke with Constantine to let him know that he would be returning his ten grand. This particular job was definitely pro bono, what with the added bonus of finding his mate, and as he had stated earlier to the cultist shifters, the Petridis clan were now his family.

"Are you and I good, big bro?" Ian asked him.

"We would have been good three years ago if you hadn't run off," Logan stated.

"If it's any consolation, she and I broke up a month later."

"You think this was about Casey?" Logan asked, his voice rising.

"Kimberly," his brother corrected. "Her name was Kimberly."

"Whatever," Logan huffed. "This wasn't about some girl I was dating that my brother stole. They were all just temporary for me anyway." He turned to Thea and said, "All of them until I found the one I was waiting for."

Thea gave him a breathtaking smile, full of dimples at his declaration.

"For me, too," Ian quickly added, looking at Teresa.

Teresa waved it off. "None of us were born on the day we met."

"And yet I feel like I was," Logan said, still holding eye contact with Thea. Before he let his mind run wild with all the things he planned on doing to her once he got her back to his apartment, he turned to his brother. "You ran off instead of facing me. I would have punched you in the face and then moved on, but instead, you not only left me without my brother, but without a partner, and with a shit-load of extra clients, for a business you convinced me to start with you."

"I know," Ian said. "I'd get all these ideas in my head and attack them without thinking them through, and because of that, I would always chase the next thrill. You, man, you were always so sure of yourself. You were even sure of me with the bounty hunting business. I'm sorry, man."

"I'm not letting you come back as my partner," Logan said firmly, but business aside, he had already forgiven Ian when he entrusted him with Thea earlier.

"And you shouldn't," Ian said. "I'll be happy if you let me work in the field. I missed it. I missed you."

Logan punched Ian in the arm. "We're good, you little turd." He then mumbled, "I missed you, too."

Thea and Teresa sat giggling at their exchange. Who better than them to understand the bond of siblings, he thought.

"I'm actually surprised you never showed up on any of my doorsteps," Ian added. "I left you clues."

Logan rolled his eyes. "I saw your latest in *Men's Magazine*." Once again, he locked gazes with his beautiful mate, although he was speaking to Ian. "I was about to come find you, but then my day had taken a very interesting turn in the form of one very *electrifying* woman."

Thea gave him an impish grin. "And you always catch your prey."

Epilogue

Six months later

Thea walked out of the bathroom to find Logan awake. He lay naked, the covers thrown off, with one arm under his head and one leg slightly pulled up and bent, obscuring the view of his long, thick, and magnificent cock. He bit his lip as she walked toward him, wearing one of his button-down shirts. God, he looked so sexy, just lying there casually, and peering at her with undisguised desire.

She got on the bed and crawled up his body, planting a kiss on his lips when she reached his face. "Morning, sleepyhead." She buried her face into his neck, breathing him in, and sighed when his arms came around to hug her.

"How long have you been up?" he asked, his voice still thick with sleep.

"About an hour. Just wanted to finish typing some of my notes from the lab." She moved down a little to lay her head on his chest. "How come you never play that one?" she asked, referring to his electric guitar in the display case that *the* Slash had signed and given to him. Not once in the four months that she had been living with him, had she ever seen him play that guitar.

Four glorious months of living with the man she loved … her mate. She was even happier knowing her sister was finally happy and not living in constant fear. Teresa and Ian were living together as well, and Ian, according to Logan, was a changed man in the sense that he no longer felt the pull of running off again. He hadn't once asked for Logan to make him partner again and had said he was able to focus more out in the field without the weight of ownership hanging over him.

"Logan will never admit it," Ian had said to Thea, "but he was made for leadership. He leads unconsciously and most just follow."

"He's easy to look up to," she had said. "And he adores you, you know."

"I know. I won't let him down again," Ian had promised.

Snapping her out of her memory, Logan said, "I do play it." He gave Thea a swat on her ass, and rolled her over before getting out of bed and heading to the display case.

Thea couldn't help but admire his firm, glorious ass and his well-defined sculpted back as he moved.

He took out the guitar. "I play this one when I'm jamming with Slash."

She sat up. "You actually play with Slash?" she squeaked. "Oh, my God."

"You gotta hear this when this baby is plugged in," he said, fiddling around with some chords. "I'll take you with me next time."

"Yes," she squealed, pumping both hands in the air. "Although, as excited as I am about the prospect of that, it won't compare to the private concerts you give me or the VIP treatment I get afterward."

"Oh, yeah?" Logan asked, giving her a wink. He settled on "Paradise City," playing and singing to her, his voice drowning out the sounds of the non-amped electric guitar, and like the dutiful concert goer she was, Thea got up on the bed and began to jump around and dance.

He made it about half way through the song before returning his guitar to its display case and rejoining her on the bed. He tackled her and pinned her beneath him. "Do you have any idea what your little dance just did to me?"

She shook her head and was still out of breath when she answered, "Show me."

With a growl, he attacked her mouth, his tongue swiftly invading hers. He then ripped open her shirt, sending some of the buttons flying and pinging off the walls. She thought about how fortunate they both were that they made a good living with the amount of shirts, both his and hers, that had been ruined in the past six months. She'd never get enough of him.

"I'll never get enough of you," he echoed her sentiment right before getting back to devouring her mouth. He cupped a breast and massaged, rolling her nipple between his thumb and forefinger.

Thea locked her ankles around his hips and grabbed his ass. "I can't wait."

"Me, either," he said against her lips, and then he impaled her. They both stilled briefly, much like they always did when they first connected. She always wanted him so badly and usually in the moments leading up to their joining, her desire became even more heightened, so much so that when he would first enter her, she had to revel in that relief of finally having him inside of her.

She held on to him as he set a fast pace, thrusting in and out of her with long hard strokes. "Oh, God, Logan. I love you and I love how you fuck me."

"I fucking love you," he ground out. "I love you so much. You feel like my heaven." He kissed her again and moaned into her mouth. "Harder, baby?"

"Yeah."

"Mmm. I love your tight, sweet little pussy. It tastes like honey."

Thea moaned loudly at his words and the sexy huskiness of his voice. He knew how much she loved his complimentary dirty talk. She dug her nails into his back and elevated her hips slightly to give him room to go even deeper, and when his cock began to hit a particularly sweet spot inside of her repeatedly, her orgasm crashed over her, the build-up to it intense. A few more thrusts from Logan had him coming as well, calling out her name as he spilled inside of her.

They kissed again, passionately, not pulling apart until both of them had stopped shaking. Logan cupped her cheek. "How's that for a VIP treatment?"

Thea giggled. "I'd say I'm one lucky girl. Oh, and there's actually a present waiting for you downstairs."

"Really?" he asked, his eyes lighting up. She found it so endearing how he got all excited whenever she bought him something, like a kid on Christmas morning. "What did you get me?"

"You'll just have to wait until you go downstairs." She and Hannah had finally decided to get him a new chair for his office. Despite his constant grumblings over his squeaky chair, he never buckled down to get one. He did, however, manage to finally get a new phone to replace the one he had smashed when his brother ran off.

"I'm the lucky one, Thea," he said as he stared down at her adoringly. "I know for certain that with you in it, my days will never be boring again."

And neither would hers. She set out to rescue her sister, unaware that her future would forever change that day. She had spent so long holed up in a lab developing a weapon, living a passionless existence, until Logan came along and sparked new life into her heart and she let herself be willingly caught by her hunter.

The End

RETURNING TO THE COYOTE

Roberta Winchester

Shifter Brethren, 1

Copyright © 2017

Chapter One

Rafe

She's coming home.

The girl who never smiles.

At least, she rarely smiled, back when we were kids. She did sometimes.

But only for me.

I haven't seen her since she went away after college. It's been years.

Three years, four months, and sixteen days.

Not that I'm counting.

I loved her.

I love her still.

I thought she loved me, too. She never said it, though, hell—*I* never said it. Maybe if I had told her, she might've stayed. I don't blame her for leaving, not really. The house where she grew up, the one next to mine, well … it wasn't a happy place back then, thanks to her asshole father. I wouldn't have come back home all this time either.

He's gone now, and the house sits, dark and

empty.

Waiting for her.

Rumor around town has it that she'll be back soon, to take over her father's farm.

Next to me. With nothing to separate us but an empty field and a stretch of woods.

Every day I head into town to work, put in my day at the shop, and then hurry home to watch for her. My cabin is on a hill, and from my front porch I can see the gravel driveway leading up to her father's—to *her* house. I don't mean to stalk her, that creepy shit isn't me.

But God, I miss her.

It's quiet here. Too quiet.

It's my own fucking fault. I drove her away. It wasn't *just* because I was too chicken shit to tell her I love her. It wasn't just because of her father that she left, either.

No, the reason she left and didn't come back was because I told her the truth about what I am.

That I'm not entirely human.

****

Corina

I would've given anything to avoid returning to this house. I refuse to call it home. It was my father's home. Not mine. I cannot believe he left it to me in his will. I suppose there was simply no one else for him to leave it to. No other family. Certainly no friends.

I plan to clean the place out. Give away or sell anything I don't absolutely need. I'll keep anything I find that belonged to my mother. That is, if there's anything left my father didn't destroy when he was still alive. I'm surprised a heart attack killed him. I expected it would be liver failure, long before now.

I lift the latch on the battered aluminum screen door, hold it open with my elbow as I fumble with the key while trying not to drop my luggage. When I attempt to shove open the old wooden inner door, it sticks. The house is humid this time of year. I remember that. No air conditioning. Between the stifling temps, my father's ranting rages, long, sweltering days working in the fields, and the kitchen overheated from Mom's constant cooking, summers here were absolute hell.

I brace myself as the door eventually swings open.

"Holy God." I gasp. I can't help it.

There are beer cans and liquor bottles *everywhere*.

The kitchen table is coated in dust and spills, dark mildew spread across the peeling, laminate surface. Empty prescription pill bottles lay upended and scattered amid dozens of plates mounded with mold.

The floor—God, I can remember when it used to shine. Either Mom or I used to mop it every day. But now—now I have to choke back the bile rising in my throat at the sight of the impenetrable layer of filth covering the once beautiful hardwood.

A flash of movement passes through my peripheral vision and I look up just in time to see a mouse running across the cluttered countertops underneath the cupboards.

And this is just the kitchen. What does the rest of the house look like? A sharp stab of pain lances through my chest.

I expected a mess, but this. *This*. This is beyond the pale. Where do I even start?

How, *how* do I do this alone?

"Hey, Ina."

I freeze. Only one person in the world calls me by that nickname. I would be lying if I said I hadn't thought about him the second I'd found out I had to come back here. And for much of the twelve-hour drive. But I can't—not now—I'm not ready for him. Not yet. Not when I am reeling from what I've just walked into.

If I don't turn around, maybe he will go away. Damn it, why did I leave the stupid door open?

"Corina. It's me, sweetheart."

I still don't turn around. It's weird, I know, but the last time we saw each other—well, we had a pretty epic fight and I haven't even tried to contact him in more than three years. And the way I feel right now, exhausted and drained and kind of like I'm cracked and bleeding underneath my skin—I'm afraid seeing his face at this moment will break me. Hearing his voice is bad enough. I forgot how much I loved the sound of it, so smooth and deep and soothing, it's like sinking into a warm bath on a cold night.

"Ina." That smooth voice cracks a little, and I turn, unable to stop myself.

Rafe is standing in the doorway, the evening sun shining against him, illuminating him in gold. He's wearing well-fitting blue jeans and a thin white t-shirt that clings to his *very* healthy-looking torso. His hair is shorter than I remember, but still the same jet-black shot through with natural gray peppering. He has a beard now, closely trimmed, and his eyes, so familiar and exactly as I remember, a fascinating shade of hazel—gold, green, and warm brown, all at the same time. I cannot help but stare as my heart kicks within my chest.

"Ina," he repeats. "It's good to see you."

But, damn.

I open my mouth to speak, but I suddenly cannot breathe. The muscles contract in my throat and my eyes begin to burn, and I realize, with utter mortification, that I am going to start crying.

Damn it, I knew it. I *knew* seeing him would be a bad idea.

He steps closer to me, his eyes locked onto mine, like he's searching for something. The muscles around his eyes are pulled tight and his gaze is intense, all-consuming, as he stares at me, and I have to look away.

You left me, those piercing eyes say.

Well, yes. He was the only thing keeping me here, and when he dropped a bomb on me, I fled. Anyone would have. Even now, after three years, looking at him fills me with an apprehension I never had before he told me … before he told me…

That he's a shapeshifter.

I shudder at the memory, so near the surface as we stare each other down, yet again, as if the last three years haven't happened.

I decided, after leaving and some time passed, that Rafe, *my* Rafe, was either losing his mind or inventing a ridiculous story to chase me away. It made more sense to me to think he was suffering from mental illness or commitment issues than to believe my boyfriend was a magical, mythical creature.

My mom, she would have swallowed Rafe's story, hook and line, without question. She raised me on folklore and fairytales, and she used to tell me such stories were often rooted in reality. She was the most accepting, open-minded person I had ever known.

But she's dead, has been for ten years. There is no such thing as magic. There is no room in this world for such a fantastical, beautiful delusion.

"I'm glad you're back," he says, and I realize I still have not acknowledged him, not with a single word.

Shame heats my face. Regardless of the weird way we parted, this is Rafe. This is the man who made life worth something for me, the only person in the universe I cared about after Mom died. But then he had to go and tell me that stupid story about being a coyote shapeshifter. How am I supposed to live here now, with him so near?

Think of something, for God's sake. Anything.

"Um, yeah. Thanks."

Great job, Corina.

He narrows his eyes a little and then tears his gaze away from mine. I've hurt him again, with just a few words. Too few words, that's the problem. If he is still the same man I thought I knew before, he wants to have 'the big talk'. The one that broke us. But I simply cannot bring myself to mention the elephant in the room—or should I say, coyote? The very thought makes my stomach twist.

He steps inside the kitchen and lets out a low whistle as he takes in the disastrous interior.

"Holy shit, Corina."

I blink, his change in tone pulling me back, out of my head and into this hellhole that is my new reality.

"I knew your dad had it bad, but damn. I had no idea it was *this* bad."

I clear my throat. For some reason, that pesky lump in there refuses to go away. I need to get him out of here so I can deal with my shit head on, without any witnesses—even if I have to be rude, even if I have to make him think I want nothing to do with him.

"R-right." I choke a little, but keep going. It's got to be the stench in here that's affecting me so much. It smells like dead mice, mold, and booze. "Thanks for stopping by, Rafe. But you should go home. I need to get to work. We'll catch up later."

His gaze snaps back to mine, his eyes a flash of gold and green. "You're not staying here. Not when this place is like *this*."

"Of course I am." What the hell is he about?

"No."

He closes the distance between us, standing so close, his chest almost touching mine. He's still using the same soap. Mint and sandalwood. I resist the urge to lean into him, to fall against his chest. He's an oasis of clean relief in this catastrophe of a house, an island of good in the deluge of all the terrible memories this place is to me.

"Come back with me. Stay at my place." His voice is soft and hypnotic, and he brushes his fingertips against my cheek and then my forehead, sweeping aside a strand of my hair. I close my eyes, helpless to resist relishing his touch, his calming voice. "I'll help you with this, Ina. Let me help you with this."

God, I wish I could. He has no idea. I open my mouth to tell him to yes, yes, *please* get me the hell out of here.

But then, the voice of reason steps up and cuts through the fog of emotions clouding my better judgment. She's a bitch, my voice of reason, but she's kept me alive for all these years. *Stop. Remember. Remember what happened three years ago, she says. The man thinks he can turn into a coyote. And you cannot be in love with a crazy person. You've had enough crazy in your life to last an eternity.*

I force myself to pull away. "No." I find my voice, and it's a little stronger now. "I'm staying here."

"The hell you are," he grumbles, crossing his arms over his chest. "No one deserves this, Corina. Least of all you."

Ah. My heart gives a little skip. God, how I wish things had turned out differently between us. But I'm not going to let my feelings for him stand in the way of doing what I came here to do. "Rafe, I've got to take care of this place. This is what I came back for."

He takes a step backward, his jaw going rigid. Pain flares in his eyes. Then just as quickly as it comes, it goes, replaced by something else I'm not sure how to name.

Shit. "I'm sorry, Rafe. I didn't mean—"

"You're coming with me to my cabin." His gentle voice has hardened in a way I've never heard before. I'm not really sure what to do with it. Stubborn Rafe is something new.

Before I know what's happening, he's picking up my luggage and walking out the door.

What the hell? "Rafe!" I follow him, slamming the kitchen door behind me. "What are you *doing?*"

He doesn't stop. He keeps walking, fast, his long legs taking him and my luggage further away. This tall, broad-shouldered, hulking man is toting my pink suitcase in one hand and my rose-embroidered makeup bag over his shoulder, and if I wasn't so pissed and confused, I would laugh. As it is, a bubble of bizarre, irrational giddiness is unfurling in me, threatening to take over, making me want to blindly follow him for the sake of not having to make any more decisions right now with my overemotional, overtired, overtaxed mind. The idea of choosing—I can return to my father's house—or follow Rafe to his cabin—what kind of a choice is it, really?

"When did you get so bossy?" I shout after him, trying to catch up.

I don't think he hears me. But when we're halfway across the field, he abruptly stops and turns, his face ravaged with grief. Any more words I might've said die on my tongue. A gust of warm summer wind kicks up, tugging at my cotton skirt. Stalks of wheat whip against my bare legs.

"I got so bossy." His voice is rough and clipped and he pauses, inhaling a rasping breath. I blink, trying to clear my eyes, trying to see if this impassioned man is truly my sweet, soft-spoken Rafe. "I got so bossy," he repeats, "when I realized I let you go because I wasn't strong enough to chase after you and drag you back home. And now that you've come home, I'm not letting you go, not ever again."

His possessiveness takes my breath away. His stance is stiff, defensive, bracing for a fight. Even standing there with my girly luggage, he's looking kind of raw and edgy. Well, if a fight is what he wants, a fight is what he's getting. I'm not in the mood for this. I close the distance between us until I'm standing within reach of him.

I swallow, take a breath. "What do you mean, you *let* me go? I left because—"

"Because of me."

"*No*, Rafe. It was because—"

Because of my father. I'd completed my undergraduate degree at a local college so I could try to help him survive his alcoholism, but every single day was utter hell and absolutely nothing I did helped him. The only reason I didn't give up and leave this place forever was Rafe. And when Rafe ruined my trust in him, there was nothing else to keep me here.

So, yeah, I guess, it's fair to say Rafe was definitely the reason, but damn. Has he been stewing in guilt like this for the last three years? A pinching ache fills my chest. We're going to have it out, it's inevitable. I get it. I can see he's not going to let it go until we do.

"Okay, yes. Yes, it was because of you, Rafe." My blood is rushing hot through my veins, rising to the surface as long-simmering anger bubbles over. "You're a lying sonofabitch. I *trusted* you, trusted you like I have never trusted anyone before in my entire life and you betrayed me. You *lied* to me. And such a ridiculous lie. What the hell were you thinking? If you didn't want to be with me anymore, you should've simply *told* me."

"I wasn't lying, Ina." He drops my luggage and wraps his fingers around my arms, slowly rubbing his hands up and down my skin. "I'm sorry. Please forgive me, I know you think I'm crazy, but I can prove it to you. I would have three years ago, but the way you reacted—I was afraid if I showed you, I'd scare you and you'd never want to see me again. As it was, you ran away anyway. It's been *killing* me, Ina."

Oh, my God. He's serious. He thinks he can prove his lie to me. My anger fizzles, transforming into nervous fear.

My Rafe is insane. How did this happen? What if he's suffering some serious, abnormally early-onset dementia? What if it kicked in years ago and I was so knee-deep in my own problems I didn't notice?

Shit. I'll watch him closely, that's what I'll do. I'll pay more attention now, now I know what I'm looking for. He's had my back for all these years, now I'll have his.

"Take me to the cabin," I say, my eyes prickling with unshed tears I hope he cannot see. "I'll stay with you tonight. Once I'm rested, I can start working on my father's house."

He blinks, slowly, as if he's reining it in, collecting himself. His eyes soften. Almost immediately, he's back to the old Rafe. "I have tomorrow off, it's Saturday. I'll help you."

I nod, air leaving my lungs in a deep exhalation. I didn't realize I'd been holding my breath.

Rafe lets go of my arms and picks up my luggage. When he speaks again, his voice is so low I barely hear him. "And when you're ready," he says quietly, "when you're ready, I'll show you."

Chapter Two

Rafe

She thinks I'm bat-shit crazy, I know she does. She's silent as we make our way up the hill to my cabin. I've scared her, just as I feared I would, though not in the way I'd expected.

How the hell am I going to fix this?

Carefully. Slowly. I'll start by putting her up in my bedroom and I'll sleep on the couch. It's the right thing, I know, but it sucks.

I walk through my front door and set her stuff down next to the armchair by the fireplace. She follows me in, her arms crossed tightly in front of her chest. She looks a little wounded and vulnerable, and I hate myself for being the reason. She used to spend a *lot* of time here with me, lounging in front of the fire on cold nights, making out with me on the couch. And though I haven't changed a thing, her gaze is searching, roaming around the room like this is her first time here. When she sees the couch, her cheeks redden and I know she's remembering, but she doesn't move any closer to me.

"You're safe here, Ina." I approach her, my hand outstretched, a plea. "I'm *not* a lunatic and I'm not going to hurt you."

She doesn't seem to believe me. Her trust in me is gone. I'm afraid it's going to take some time to repair the damage between us. I just hope she doesn't give up on her father's farm—or on me—and skip town again before I can change her mind about me. My chest tightens at the thought.

But she takes my hand. Her slender fingers tighten around mine, squeezing. The sensation shoots straight to my heart. I can breathe again.

She even smiles at me. It's a tentative smile, but it's a smile, all the same. Looking at her, with her sweet smile and those tired, baby-blue eyes, I know I'm going to do everything I can to make her happy and keep her that way. Starting right now.

"You can sleep in the bedroom tonight. I'll take the couch," I tell her, clenching her hand, hoping she feels reassured.

A flicker of relief passes over her face and she nods. "Thanks, Rafe."

I try to ignore the pang of disappointment twisting within me. I don't know why I thought she'd respond any other way.

"Of course," I manage to say, all neutral and cool, like I honestly don't care. But I release her hand and turn away so she can't see my face.

"Are you hungry?" I ask, making for the tiny kitchen adjoining the living room.

"Ravenous."

"I'll make dinner."

"I do love a man in the kitchen," I can hear her smile in her voice. It's something she often said to me. Before. A spark of hope flares, deep inside me.

I divert my attention to the fridge, but I can hear her taking her luggage down the hall to my bedroom. I hope it's clean enough in there. I haven't had anyone in my bed in three years, four months, and sixteen days.

Not that I'm counting.

God. The thought of Corina in my bed again. Her soft, sweet scent of roses and vanilla. Her satin-smooth skin. Her thick, silky hair fisted in my hands.

Damn. I haven't thought this through. The beast in me wants out right now. Bad. I've gone too long without her.

Ina was my first. My one and only. Coyotes tend

to mate for life, but Ina doesn't know—she doesn't know she's the only girl for me, doesn't know what I am, doesn't know how sorry I am for fucking everything up between us. But I plan to help her understand, plan to show her everything. If she'll let me, if I can do what I've got to without scaring the shit out of her.

I intend to start tonight. That is, at least, if I don't shame myself in front of her first. Looking at her is enough to get my blood up, pumping all through my body and into certain places that are causing me some serious pain right now.

It doesn't help she's so damn beautiful, wearing that tight, blue t-shirt, the same color as her eyes, with a thin, gauzy little skirt. Her dark hair is longer than it used to be, swinging low down her back. She looks healthy and strong, and I can't help but think that being away from here has been good to her. But what if—

What if she's found a new guy?

No. Why didn't I consider this? What if she's totally over me? What if I pissed her off so badly three years ago, she decided to forget about me altogether?

Fuck.

My stomach clenches. I feel sick. I lean my forehead against the cool refrigerator door, my hands white-knuckled around the handle.

"Rafe, what's wrong? You're white as a sheet."

I nearly jump out of my skin. People don't usually sneak up on me. Animal instincts and all. But Corina, she's thrown me so off-kilter. I know I should give her more time, but fuck it, I can't help it. I *have* to know.

"You—are you—" I take a ragged breath and turn to her, liberating the refrigerator door from my death-grip. "Have you started dating someone else? Since me? I know it's been a long time, so I understand…"

I can't finish. I *don't* understand, not really. If she

says yes, I'm not sure I can take it.

She places a hand on my chest, her eyes wide and staring. I wish I could see inside her head. Since I can't, I lean into her touch instead, willing her to tell me what I want to hear, even if it's not the truth.

She shakes her head. "No. No, there's no one else."

My breath escapes me in a harsh exhalation. My eyelids slide closed as I savor the extreme relief washing over me.

"What about you?"

I open my eyes and try to read her expression. Curiosity? Concern? I want her to feel the same level of apprehension I did. I know it's selfish, but I can't help it. I remain silent for a minute, and another, watching the muscles in her jaw tighten, watching those soft pink lips of hers press firmly together.

I want to kiss her. I *need* to kiss her. If I don't, I am going to die, this very second. My inner beast trembles inside me, wanting out. Wanting her.

"No, Ina," I murmur, struggling to find my voice. "You know it's always you and me and nobody else."

The muscles in her face relax and I see a relief that mirrors my own. Before she can pull away, I bring my mouth down to hers, claiming those lips with my own. She doesn't draw back. Instead, she responds to my kiss, pushing up onto the balls of her feet to reach me better.

Yes, *yes*. The beast is prowling under my skin, finally coming awake after all this time. Gently, I deepen the kiss, probing my tongue against hers. She reciprocates. I groan, low and long, and she suddenly shoves her body, hard, against mine.

I can't stand it. I wrap my arms around her and push her up against the refrigerator, sliding my hands down, grasping her hips, pulling them against mine until I'm grinding against her.

"*Rafe*." She gasps my name as she tears her lips from mine.

But she doesn't tell me to stop.

I plunder her mouth with mine, thrusting into her pelvis, trying to ease the heat, the ache, the insatiable longing.

Her hands slide between us. She unzips my jeans.

Yes, yes, yes. Any and all logic in my brain has completely shut down. I think I'm dreaming. I must be. It's as if the last three-plus years haven't happened. I forget waiting, I forgot about giving her time. I forget our last fight, and I guess she does, too, because her hand is wrapped around my—is this really happening?

I thrust into her hands, her warm, slender fingers urging, kneading, gripping me.

My breathing is short, rough. "Ina," I pant. "Ina, I *need* you."

She lifts her skirt, bunching it in one hand while she slides her panties off with the other. I can hardly believe this is real. And I don't intend to give her a chance to change her mind. I *can't.*

I surge into her with one, savage thrust. The beast has taken over, refusing to allow me to be gentle, demanding more, *more*. I comply, urging myself deeper. Ina writhes against me. Her hands slide over my shoulders and then she's wrapping her legs around my waist, driving me impossibly deeper still.

Holy hell.

"Rafe." Her voice is high, breathless. I remember that sound. It's the one she makes a second before she starts to climax.

Her voice pushes me over the edge, stealing away the last of my willpower. This is going to end, too soon. I shove into her with one forceful thrust after another, my breath dissolving into low, rumbling grunts as she whimpers.

"Ina." I moan. "Ina, I'm going to—"

"*Rafe!*" she cries my name as she peaks over the edge. *My* name, because I'm still the one she wants. The thought finishes me.

I come, hard. I close my eyes, bracing myself. It's like an electric, white-hot eruption of power blasting through my entire body. A shout bursts from me and I'm trembling as my eyes slide open.

Holy. Shit. I can't believe I forgot how insanely incredible it is, being with Corina. I want to do this again and again, every night for the rest of my life.

"Ina." I gasp as my breath returns to me, as my vision slowly begins to refocus.

She's looking at my face, her eyes no longer filled with desire but instead with—with *shame*—I think, and regret.

No. I step away from her, watching as she scrambles to redress, her movements jerky and hurried. My throat tightens. "Ina," I choke out. "*Don't.* Don't regret it. Don't—"

She turns away from me and doesn't look back as she disappears down the hallway. I hear the bedroom door slam.

Fuck.

It takes me all of about three seconds to decide I'm not letting this go. But when I try to open the bedroom door, I can't get in. She's locked me out.

"Corina, let me in."

Silence. So it's like this, then.

"You wanted it. too, you know you did. Come *on*, Ina."

She still doesn't open the door. I pound on it,

open-handed, smacking the wood. I really want to break the damn thing. I want to hit it as hard as I can and punch my way through the wood. But, pissed off as I am, I don't want to scare her. That's not me. But hell, it's hard right now. Frustration rolls over me in waves.

"Open up. I want to talk to you."

The handle jiggles, and then the door opens, ever so slightly, revealing a fraction of her face. But it's enough that I can see her eyes are red and glistening.

"I'm sorry," she says, her voice barely more than a whisper. "But that was a mistake. I got caught up, remembering how we used to be—"

"It's how we should be, Ina, and you *know* it." My voice breaks. "There's *no* reason we can't go back, pretend the last three years didn't happen."

"That's impossible."

"It's not, I—"

And then it hits me, so hard I slump against the doorframe. I'm never going to get Ina back unless I completely give up trying to convince her that I'm a shifter. But it's who I am, what I am. Can I live the rest of my life keeping my true nature a secret from her?

I must. It's not a choice, not really.

I can't live the rest of my life without her.

"You're right, Ina."

She blinks, her hold on the door faltering. "What?"

"I'm sorry for—" For what? I can't tell her I lied to her when I told her I'm a shifter. What do I do now? Lie about lying? "I—I'm sorry for chasing you away. I'll not bring it up again. I'll not lie to you."

Her eyes flash, the delicate blue irises darkening with anger. I've said the wrong thing. Again.

"Goodnight, Rafe. Thanks for letting me stay here. I'll be out first thing in the morning."

And then she slams the door in my face.

Chapter Three

Corina

When I wake up a little after sunrise, he's gone.

I planned exactly what I was going to say to him, first thing, about how he said he'll 'not lie to me' and how that's utter bullshit and he knows it because that's what he did to create this whole mess between us in the first place. Last night showed me, after what he said about lying, that he's not crazy. He's a liar. So, yeah, we're done.

But when I open the bedroom door and step out into the hallway, I find nothing but silent emptiness waiting for me. At the sight of the vacant stillness, the absence of Rafe, a little twinge of something—guilt? Loneliness? —pinches in my chest and I suddenly feel weird about how I reacted last night. He was right about one thing, I *did* want it. Bad.

But it can't happen again. I closed the door on Rafe a long time ago. I need to get back to my father's house and bury myself in all the work that's waiting for me there. I'm determined to make this life work for me. I want that house. I want to make it like it was, long ago, long before my father ruined it. I'll do it for me and I'll do it for my mom. She would hate to see it like it is now.

I want a beautiful old house filled with pastel colors and lace curtains and a thriving little farm with bees and chickens and herbs and flowers.

And I'm going to get it. No drama with my ex-boyfriend is going to stand in my way.

Regardless of what happened last night.

Satisfied with my resolve, I shower and dress quickly, anxious as I am to leave. My stomach is throbbing with hunger when I gather up my bags. I should've let Rafe make me dinner before I did something stupid and ruined the evening.

It was the damned couch that did it, sitting there, reminding me of things I've tried to forget. And when Rafe told me he hasn't dated anyone else, that I was his last and his only—well, that did it for me. He sealed the deal with that *kiss*. How the hell was I supposed to resist that?

I'll stay away from him from now on. He's my neighbor, so it's not going to be easy, but I'll have more than enough on my plate now to keep me distracted and away from him.

I finish packing and I make a hasty exit out of Rafe's bedroom. The rest of the cabin is still empty. Good. This is good. No awkward tension to deal with at the moment.

I drop my luggage next to the door and prepare to lift the latch and get out before Rafe can show up and try to stop me, when something on the kitchen counter catches my eye.

A note. With my name. The shortened version, the one only Rafe uses. I can't help myself. I ought to walk away and forget it. But it's calling to me, a folded piece of creamy paper with his handwriting in black ink, resting innocently enough on the butcher-block countertop.

It will only take another second. Besides, he's not here. He probably went into town to put some hours in at his family's machine shop. He said he'd help me today, but I don't expect him to and I don't blame him for hiding from me, not after last night.

Damn it. Do it and get it over with.

I cross over into the kitchen and pick up the note.

Ina,

Breakfast is in the oven, iced tea in the fridge.
Love, R

Not what I expected. He made me breakfast? I open the oven door and sure enough, a stack of thick, fluffy, blueberry pancakes waits for me, the oven on a low setting to keep them warm. There's even a yellow pat of butter melting in the middle of the top one, trickling golden streams of happiness down the edges of every pancake.

Oh, Rafe. My favorite. No one else but my mom knew or cared that my favorite thing in this world was and still is blueberry pancakes and iced tea for breakfast.

Screw leaving. I'm not letting this go to waste.

I grab a plate and fork, pour some tea, and tuck in, allowing myself a few moments of unfettered, guilt-free, unbridled joy.

And then I look at Rafe's note again. It's sitting there, in front of me.

Love, R

Since when does he sign with '*love*'? In all the years I've known him, I've yet to hear the word from his lips. I gave up, long ago. I'd always meant to tell him myself, but a persistent, prideful part of myself always insisted on waiting until he said it first.

Honestly, I think it's one of the reasons our fight got so out of hand years ago, and one of the reasons I hadn't tried getting in touch with him before now. So what is this note? Some attempt at a profession of love? An apology?

Does it matter, after last night?

A memory of Rafe's face flashes within my mind, the crestfallen, disappointed defeat in those hazel eyes of his just before I shut the door on him.

A sharp tang of bitterness rises in me and it's all I

can do to finish breakfast. I scramble to clean up and leave, my earlier resolve returning with a vengeance.

I grab my stuff and haul ass out the front door, and I don't look back.

****

I'm not prepared for what I see when I re-enter my father's house. I walked into the kitchen, armed with a box of trash bags and a pair of gloves I had stashed in my car, but I'm not going to need them.

The place is *clean.*

I blink, then blink again, waiting for the mirage to disappear.

I'm standing on waxed hardwood, smelling bleach and lemon cleaner, gaping in shock at the polished table and clutter-free countertops.

And then I see the silhouette of a man, almost as tall and as broad as Rafe, pass by the doorway leading into the living room. A shriek of surprise escapes me and he freezes, his face too shadowed for me to see it.

"Who are you and what are you doing in my house?" My voice is shaky, high, alien to me. But I persist. "Whoever you are, you get the hell out right now. I'm calling the police."

I pull my phone out of my back jeans pocket, ready to make good on my threat.

"Corina. Wait."

He knows my name? My thumb hovers over my phone's keypad.

"It's me, Weylin."

The man comes closer to me, revealing a familiar, easygoing smile that shows off his perfect teeth and a dimple in his cheek.

"Channing is here, too. Rafe asked us to come over."

Rafe's younger brothers. More Ulric boys. That's

all I need. We were all friends when we were kids, but Weylin and Channing are duplicates of Rafe, though a few years younger.

I give a little wave, shifting my feet from one to the other before I jam my phone back into my pocket. "Hi Weylin," I say, forcing a smile. What am I supposed to say to him? *Hey, here I am again, the chick who dumped your brother and didn't bother to send a single word to him for three years?*

"It's nice to see you again, Corina," he says, setting aside the roll of paper towels he's holding so he can wrap his arms around my shoulders in a quick, friendly hug.

And then I realize what he's doing here, why he was holding paper towels, and why Rafe asked him to come by.

"You guys are cleaning my house?"

I know it's a dumb question, because obviously, they are, but for the life of me I can hardly imagine anyone, let alone these young, insanely attractive men, spending their Saturday cleaning up this shit-box disaster for *me*, instead of doing something, *anything* else with their time off.

He nods and shrugs, like it's no big deal to him at all.

"Thank you," I whisper, my throat suddenly gone so tight it's all I can do to speak.

"No worries," he says, shrugging again. "We're happy to help. Rafe told us you're back and asked us to come out here and see what we could do for you."

Awkward tension starts to settle in. I know he's got to be wondering what the hell is going on between his brother and me. God only knows what Rafe has told him.

"He started in on this"—he gestures to my newly made-over kitchen—"pretty early last night. He had a lot of it done before we even got here."

I take Weylin's hint. Rafe spent the entire night, while I was sleeping in his bed, cleaning up the disgusting mess my father left behind—in order, no doubt, to surprise me.

"How did you get in?" I blurt, desperate to steer the topic of conversation away from Rafe.

Weylin glances over his shoulder at the door leading down to the basement, his cheeks reddening. "The basement door outside wasn't locked. Neither was the one in here. We fixed it though, put locks on both doors. No one—else—will break in."

I nod and try not to smile at his obvious discomfort. "I'm grateful, Weylin," I admit, reaching out my hands, clasping his. "Thank you."

"What's this, now?"

I jump and let go of Weylin's hands at the sound of another voice, an all-too-familiar voice, materializing from behind me.

"You making a move on my Corina, little brother?"

Rafe.

Despite my current, constant state of confusion, of anger, guilt, regret, and resentment when I think of him, my heart does a happy little leap at the sight of his smile and the sound of his voice, saying 'my Corina.'

"It's cool," Weylin says, picking up the paper towel roll. "She was thanking me, is all." Then he winks at me and walks out of the kitchen, leaving me alone with Rafe.

I suddenly don't know what to do with myself. This is not how I thought the day would go. I'm not armed with the right words, the right feelings for all of this.

"I appreciate what you've done for me," I

manage, meeting his eyes without blinking. "And breakfast this morning was—"

The thought of breakfast abruptly reminds me of his note to me and the way he signed it. Whatever I planned to say next freezes on my tongue. Should I mention it?

"Was no problem at all," he finishes for me.

I exhale deeply, a sigh of relief.

We'll talk about it. We will. Just not yet.

"There's nothing I wouldn't do for you, Ina."

His breath hitches when he says my name. His eyes are brimming with emotion, the hazel a bright, vivid amber in the morning light. What is it? What does he mean by this?

I assume he's referring to what he's done here, staying up all night to give me a livable home. "I cannot tell you how much this means to me."

He nods, and somehow, I know, by the look in his eyes, that something is going unsaid from him. Something big. Maybe it's the note? The big 'I love you'?

I don't get the chance to find out. Channing, the middle Ulric brother, barrels into the kitchen and knocks me off my feet in a bear hug, spinning me around until I'm dizzy.

"Hey, Corina!"

No awkward silences with this brother, no way. Channing is a force of nature.

He finally releases me, but then he stares me down, his gaze raking over my body. If he were anyone but Channing, I'd punch him.

"You look amazing," he says, glancing over at Rafe to make sure, I'm certain, that Rafe is watching. "Can't believe you're not married by now, Corina."

Rafe's entire body tenses. No one but Channing is

573

foolish enough to goad Rafe like this. "Yeah, um." I hesitate, unsure of what to say. "How about you? Any wedding bells in your future?"

A darkness passes over Channing's eyes, and a hardness settles in his face. Then, as quickly as it appeared, it's gone. "No, not for me," he answers, smiling again. "Rafe's my boss now, he runs the shop since Dad and Mom retired and moved up to Alaska. Rafe runs us into the ground. These days, we don't do much of anything, except work."

Rafe's glare intensifies. "Keep it up, man. You can find yourself without a job at all, if that's what you're gunning for."

Channing laughs and delivers a solid punch to Rafe's arm while Rafe's muscles bunch visibly under his skin. The man is a coiled spring and I feel a sudden stab of concern for Channing's well-being if he doesn't back off.

"Later," Channing says to me as he turns, and then walks out the front door, the aluminum shutting with a *clang* behind him.

"What the hell was all that about?" I can't help but ask. I know I haven't lived here in years, but I don't remember witnessing any conflict between Rafe and his brothers before.

Rafe shrugs. "Channing didn't take it well when Dad retired and made me alpha—"

Alpha? "Made you what?"

"I mean." Rafe swallows visibly, like he's choking. I grab a newly washed glass from the dish-drying rack, fill it with tap water, and hand it to him. He takes a quick sip and smiles at me. "I meant to say, Dad retired and put me in charge of the shop, making me my brothers' boss."

"Oh." I guess I can see why Channing would

bristle at listening to Rafe's orders. Rafe's the eldest, sure, but unless he's changed from what I remember, Channing doesn't like to listen to anyone.

"I'm sorry, Rafe."

And I am. Regardless of what's transpired between us, and regardless of what lies ahead of us, I care about him and his family. How can I not? A pang of remorse rises within me, and I wish, with overwhelming intensity, that I could go back in time to the minute I stormed out on him years ago, and not leave. What if I would've tried harder to hear him out, tried harder to understand whatever it was he was attempting to communicate with me with his shapeshifting lie?

Three years. Gone. Wasted.

The thought makes my stomach lurch, flip, and finally settle, heavy as a stone.

I close my eyes against the onslaught of discomfort.

"Ina? Are you all right? You're pale."

His hand rests gently on my forehead, his eyes wide with concern.

I nod. "Yeah," I lie. "Fine."

His hand moves to my cheeks, my neck. He checks my pulse. "Been a rough couple of days," he says, his voice low and calming. "We're pretty much done here. The rest of the house is in decent shape. I'll get the guys out of here and you can settle in, get some rest."

He slides his hands into his pockets and I immediately miss the feel of his touch upon my skin.

"Thank you, Rafe."

"Anytime, Ina."

He disappears into another room, calling for Weylin. I stand alone, trying to regain my composure, wondering how I'm going to live with myself for breaking his heart along with my own.

Chapter Four

The house is mine now. I'm so busy painting, shopping, and redecorating, an entire week passes and by the end of the week, I realize I'm only thinking about Rafe every thirty seconds instead of every five, like I did after he returned to his cabin last Saturday. If I keep this up, my life will get better. It has to.

I buy chickens from the farm store in town. I set them up in the small coop next to the house so I can listen for trouble during the night. When I used to live here, wild animals sometimes ventured in too close after the sun went down. I remember there were a few times, when I was a kid, I'd wake up to the sound of shotgun blasts while my father killed whatever predators were hungry enough to try to eat our farm animals.

His shotgun rests next to my bed, loaded, just in case. It's the only possession of his I've decided to keep, other than this farm.

It's Sunday, eight days since I've seen Rafe, when he knocks on my door. I'm wearing an old cotton sundress, my mom's hand-embroidered apron, and streaks of flour in my hair when I greet him. He smiles, his eyes bright gold today, watching me, as he leans inside the doorframe.

You shouldn't care what you look like, I remind myself. *You ended whatever existed between you. Get over it.*

"I'm baking," I say, making an effort to keep my voice neutral, unfeeling.

"I see."

I hesitate, torn between letting him in and telling him I'm too busy for company. *Let him in. You can do this. You're neighbors, after all.*

"Come in and sit down?" I ask, putting on my best hostess face. "The first batch is out."

He enters the kitchen and slides down into one of the oak spindle chairs, stretching out his long, lean, blue jean-clad legs. "What are you baking?"

"Lemon bars." One of Mom's famous recipes.

"Hmmm," he groans, the sound sending tingles all throughout my body.

Focus, Corina.

I retrieve a porcelain dessert plate and serve him one, sitting down in the chair across from him. We'll have a nice little chat, two neighbors conversing, that's all we are.

"How was work this past week? Channing give you any trouble?"

"The usual. Though I found it hard to concentrate all week."

"You did?" I'd hoped it was possible to shift the conversation away from us, but apparently Rafe has other plans.

"Yes, Ina. I came over here today to talk about us—"

"I bought chickens," I blurt out.

He's narrowing his eyes at me, but at least he's stopped talking. I feel like a horrible person. But I can't, can't talk to him. Not now. Not about us. I need more time to build myself up, to prepare.

"That's great Ina," he says, his voice soft and tired-sounding, his gaze dropping to the lemon bar in his hand. "I know you always wanted to get things back the way they were before—"

"Before my mom died and my father became a raging alcoholic?" There's an edge to my tone, a bitter one, one Rafe doesn't deserve, and though I know this, I can't seem to contain it.

He cringes and places the lemon bar back on its dainty plate.

I don't apologize. I know he's making an effort with an attempt at meaningful conversation, but each time I think I'm in control again, each time I think my defenses are back in place, this man knocks them all to hell again and I don't like it.

"You don't have to act like this with me, Ina. I'm not going to leave you, and I'm not going to turn against you like your dad did. Please stop punishing me."

"But you did. You turned against me when you lied."

I remember, as soon as the words are out of my mouth and I can't take them back, that I had decided not to bring this up again, that I'd decided how stupid and sorry I truly am for leaving, for losing the years of the life I would've had with him if I'd stayed.

And now it's too late.

He stands up, brushes his hands against his jeans, and leaves without another word.

****

Rafe

I'm lurking outside Corina's window, trying not to feel ashamed for how desperate she's made me. The lamp in her bedroom went off a while ago, and all has gone silent, save for the crickets chirping in the woods and the chickens clucking as they settle down in their coop for the night.

I've decided to keep an eye on her, whether she likes it or not. If I do my job well, she'll never know I've kept watch over her every night since she moved back in. Because of my shifter nature, I'm semi-nocturnal and don't sleep much. I patrol, in my coyote form, around the perimeter of the farm, the house, and through the fields. Nothing should threaten her here, but I can't get through each day without doing this at night. Knowing she's safe keeps me going, and sometimes I think it may be the only thing keeping me going.

I miss her.

She's killing me. If only she'd spend some time with me, give me the opportunity to show her once again, how much I love her, I *know* I can change her mind. Especially now, since I've given up convincing her of what I am, convincing her I didn't lie to her, persuading her to give me another chance is my last and only choice.

I pace and pace, dragging my clawed feet through the dewy grass, swishing my tail through headless dandelions stems. I wish shifting would change my heart and my mind as well as my body.

I wish shifting would make me forget her.

My feet take me further away from the house. I'm lost in my thoughts.

And then I realize how far I've gone, that my prowling has taken me near the chicken coop.

They sense me, immediately. The damn chickens know I'm here. They start squawking and flapping their wings, creating an uproar so loud, I know Corina can hear it from her bedroom.

I start to move away from the coop, away from the damn birds and their screeching, which only seems to be growing in intensity.

I'm not fast enough.

Corina's walking, quickly, toward me. There's enough moonlight that I can see her face, grim and determined, her dark hair flying behind her, hear her rubber barn boots clomping with each racing step.

Shit.

She's holding a shotgun, and by the way she's swinging it toward me, she means business. I know what she sees. She sees a wild animal, a coyote, stalking around her chicken coop.

Shit. Shit. Shit.

This is it. Like it or not, I'm going to have to shift in front of her, or she's going to kill me. God, I don't want to. She *left* me for simply telling her what I am. What will she do when she *sees* what I am?

Do it. Get it over with.

I will myself to transform. I can feel my muscles starting to contract, preparing for the change, but it's taking too long. I think a part of me is holding back, reluctant after so long, resisting the urge to transform in front of her. I raise my head, turning toward her.

Now. Shift now.

I can do this. I know I can do this. Maybe this will fix everything. Maybe she'll finally believe me, finally stop hating me for a lie that wasn't ever a lie at all. I open my eyes, confidently waiting for my body to cooperate.

But then I see Corina, shotgun raised high, right in front of me, the barrel pointing directly at my chest, and I know it's already too late.

I try to dodge it, lowering myself to the ground.

Too slow.

I'm in mid-shift when it hits.

The bullet rips through me, an explosion of force and fire that knocks me flat onto my back. I can feel gravel and dirt underneath me, grating into my bare skin.

I'm human. Finally. But too late.

She shot me. I can't believe she shot me.

"*Rafe!*"

I hear her call my name, but I when I try to speak, nothing comes out. A hot, searing pain rushes through me and then—sweet, merciful numbness chases the burn.

I lurch a little onto my side so I can get up, so I can show her I'm okay.

But when I move, I realize I can't breathe. I lift

my hands to my chest. Warm stickiness oozes between my fingers. The numbness fades and my body is on fire again.

Dark-gray smoke unfurls at the edges of my vision, filling my eyes until all I see is a pinprick of color in the center—Corina's heaven-blue eyes, swimming with tears, looking down at me. I know I'm losing the fight to stay awake. I keep blinking, trying to make the darkness go away, but it's getting worse. I draw in a breath, suddenly possessed by the urge to speak to her. If this is the last chance I get, it's going to fucking count.

"D-don't." Ah, God. It hurts to talk. I swear I can hear my heartbeat, thumping out an audible, slowing rhythm. *Hurry*, it beats. *hurry, hurry.* "Don't cry, Ina," I manage, catching my breath again as I savor this small victory. "I need to tell you something. I—"

A tidal wave of agony abruptly crashes over me, stealing my breath and robbing me of the last of my sight.

"Rafe, I'm getting help. Look at me. Stay awake."

Tell her! The fading voice inside my head is desperate.

"I love you, Ina."

I did it. I *did* it.

More pressure on my chest. Her voice, distant and incoherent. A squeezing of my hand.

And then, nothing at all.

****

Corina

I'm in handcuffs, sitting on a hard, scarred, wooden bench inside a jail cell. The police arrived at the farm along with the ambulance, about fifteen minutes after I called.

I told them I shot Rafe. I told them it was an accident. My mind was so consumed with the idea that I had killed him, what may happen to me because of my confession was the furthest thing from my mind.

All I could think was, *he's not dead. He's not dead.*

What's killing me right now is sitting here, just sitting here, not knowing a single thing about what's going on with him. I keep seeing his face, turning gray as he struggled for air.

He can't—he can't die. His voice keeps playing, over and over within my mind, on a repetitive loop. "*I love you, Ina. I love you, Ina.*"

I think I'm going to vomit.

When I pulled the trigger, I thought I was shooting a coyote.

I thought I was protecting my chickens.

But then, I swear to God, I saw the coyote grow, lose its fur, and become a man.

My man. My Rafe.

It's not like I can tell the police what I actually saw.

The truth—what Rafe once tried to give me, what now seems like a lifetime ago. The truth, all along, a gift of trust I threw in his face and abandoned him for.

A surge of nausea crashes over me and I lower my head between my knees.

What have I done?

"Corina Joy?"

I raise my head, carefully, as the room spins around me. There's a uniformed policeman standing at the door of my cell, holding it open for me. "Yes?" I ask, not recognizing the hoarse, grating whisper as my own.

"Please come with me."

I stand, bracing myself against the wall. The officer leads me into another room, where I sign papers and wait, my existence becoming no more than a blurry haze.

And then, they let me go.

I'm free. All charges dropped. And there's someone waiting for me, they tell me, there's someone here to pick me up.

The handcuffs are removed. I'm ushered outside. Dawn is breaking on the horizon, dazzling me with red-gold light, the exact color of Rafe's eyes.

There's a pickup truck parked at the curb and someone standing next to the passenger door, holding it open for me. He looks like Rafe. My breath punches out of me and I stumble, catching myself before I fall. My vision clears and he approaches me, reaching out to help me.

Not Rafe. Channing.

"Is he—" The hard knot in my throat makes speaking almost impossible. I try again. "Is he dead?"

"No. He's not dead."

His grip on my arm tightens as he helps me climb inside the truck. He shuts the door and silence surrounds me. The seat is smooth, cool leather and I lean my head back against the headrest until the world stills.

No. He's not dead.

I can breathe again.

Channing slides behind the steering wheel. "You know damn well," he says, his deep voice rumbling in the cab's interior, "Rafe is way too fucking irritating to die."

I stare at him, trying to assess his tone, his attempt at humor. His lips are turned up at the corners, but his face is pale and there are purple shadows underneath his eyes.

"Tell me, honestly." I take a fortifying breath. "How is he?"

"Honestly, he's fine. Well, he's recovering, anyway."

My body sinks further into the seat as my muscles

finally release hours of rigid tension. I'm literally dizzy with relief. Dark spots dance in front of my eyes.

Channing puts the truck in gear and pulls out onto the street. "He had surgery to remove the bullet, but he's awake and talking, at least he was when I left. He told the police he was sleepwalking and you shot him because you thought he was an intruder. You'll probably have to talk to them again, but he's going to cover for you, Corina."

Now I'm crying. There's no stopping it. Big, fat tears slide down my face, dripping down my jaw. Guilt. Shame. Disbelief. It all sits heavy and ugly in the center of my chest.

"I'm sorry," I whisper.

"Me and Weylin and Rafe, we all know it was an accident. He told us everything."

His gaze narrows and slides from the road, to me, and then back again. "We're headed to see him now. You need to *talk* to him, Corina. Enough of this bullshit."

I nod, but I don't need Channing to tell me what I already know.

****

Weylin blocks the door when I try to enter Rafe's hospital room. "Please let me in," I beg. You have to let me see him."

Weylin's face is grave. Creases line his eyes. My heartbeat falters.

"What? What is it?"

He shakes his head. "The bullet passed through his rib cage and tore through muscles and tissue. The worst of it is a punctured lung. He's damn lucky."

But I *must* see for myself. "So let me through. I won't wake him. *Please*."

Weylin doesn't look happy about it, but he stands aside. "He'll be okay, Corina. But don't push him. Don't upset him."

I nod, and open the door, careful to move soundlessly.

Rafe looks wrong, all hooked up to wires and tubes and covered up to his chest in a sterile white sheet. My steps make no noise at all on the laminate tiles, but when I'm within reach of him, his eyes open. They're brown today, and sort of glassy, but they immediately fix on me.

"Ina."

I smile at him, but the muscles in my face are twitching, my lips trembling. I'm in danger of crying again, I realize, and I blink and clear my throat, trying to shake it off. Suddenly I'm shy, timid, uncomfortable. I feel like I don't belong here.

After all, this is all my fault.

"I didn't mean to wake you." I force myself to look at anything other than Rafe's ashen, tired face. A plastic cup of water with a straw sits on the table next to the machines and IV bags surrounding him. "Can I get you water or something?"

Small talk. Safe, boring, small talk.

"No, Ina." The tremor in his voice snaps my attention back to his face. His gaze has sharpened and hints of gold flare in his irises. It pierces right through me and there's no breaking it. How could I have thought him human, with eyes like that?

"Sit with me."

I pull up a chair, slowly, not wanting to make any noise. I still feel like I'm disturbing him. *You demanded to see him*, I remind myself. *Don't be such a coward.*

"Closer."

I comply.

"So you—" I scramble to arrange my thoughts. *Say something.* "You're going to be okay, right? That's what Channing said."

"Yeah." I watch in barely contained horror as he places his hands down flat on each side of his body, pushing himself higher up against the pillows. "My genetic makeup strengthens me, speeds up the healing process. Another couple days and I'm out of here."

Thank God. But then, a thought passes through my mind, sending an icy spike of terror through my chest. "What about your blood? This is a hospital. Aren't they going to find out about you? About your secret?"

He shakes his head. "My mom worked here as a nurse before she retired. She knows people here who are—who are also like me and my family. They'll take care of it."

Oh God. There are others. I'm glad I'm sitting down for this. Weylin. Channing. Mr. and Mrs. Ulric.

"So it runs in the family, then?"

He nods.

That's it, then. The love of my life, and his entire family, are magical creatures.

"Are you—" The tremor in his voice is back. "Are you—okay with me? With what I am?"

Am I? I mean, is 'okay' remotely close to the correct word for it?

"Honestly, it will take me some time to get used to the idea."

"Do you—do you still—care for me?"

Yes. "Knowing your secret, *believing* your secret, doesn't change the way I feel about you, Rafe." This I know.

His brows furrow. I want to rub those creases away. I rise from my chair and place a hand on his forehead, kneading his skin. He sighs, leaning into my touch.

"I'm so, so sorry, Rafe. I'm sorry I didn't believe

you about—" I can't bring myself to say it aloud. *I'm sorry I didn't believe you when you told me you can turn into a coyote*. Even in my head, it sounds insane.

"I know," he whispers.

"I'm sorry I left you."

"Me too." His voice is a low murmur.

"I'm sorry I shot you."

He laughs. "I forgive you."

Really? "Just like that."

"Just like that."

"Why?"

"Because I love you, Ina. I always have."

I lower my lips to his head and press a kiss to his temple. "I love you, too, Rafe. Always have, always will."

The End

12 AUTHOR ANTHOLOGY

EVERNIGHT PUBLISHING ®

www.evernightpublishing.com

Made in the USA
Middletown, DE
09 August 2019